CHAPTER 1

ALL THE MORE PERFECT

"Story older than the skies,
"It's been told ten thousand times,
"Not the first, won't be the last,
"Same old tale in different rhymes."

A s DEVIN ENTERED SARAH'S APARTMENT, he noticed she'd left her demo song playing on her digimech. *She must've left in a rush.*

"Still, there's something to be said,
"Maybe something to be heard,
"Faiths adrift in falsehoods found,
"Meanings lost within a word."

Sarah's voice shimmered in the air, rich as emeralds, glowing softly like a distant star—perfect. Devin was certain she would make it as a singer.

The door closed behind him. Outside the window, airtrains on ribbon-thin rails and flying transports swam around Kydera City's gleaming skyscrapers.

A Moray spacecraft soared across the atmosphere, its serpentine form heading toward the resplendent headquarters of the Interstellar Confederation in the heart of the Silk Sector. Gray diplomatic markings. *Probably the delegation from the Wiosper system.*

Devin pulled his black slate out of his pocket, unfolded it from its triangle shape, and snapped it flat. The silvery touchscreen glowed. He checked the time at the top, then

10/21/15 EP 21.99

realized he had no idea when Sarah would be home. He considered calling her, but he didn't want to risk disturbing her in the middle of something important. The workday hadn't ended yet.

All he could do was wait. He might be there for hours, or she might walk through the door the moment he looked up. Either way, the thought of seeing the woman he loved terrified him. He had stared down laser guns and betrayed warlords, knowing how deadly the consequences could be, and yet a mere question had him pacing and almost shaking in fear.

Sarah DeHaven, will you marry me?

Every rational instinct within him had warned him not to come, but for once, he'd allowed himself to follow the siren's song of impulse instead.

———— ➤⟡◁ ————

Less than an hour ago, that afternoon had been an ordinary, monotonous workday at Quasar Bank Corporation. Devin had waited idly at his desk for his manager's approval before moving forward with his project. Although the company was armed with more money than the entire Republic of Kydera, it was still bogged down by bureaucracy.

The weekend was only a day away. Devin thought about how he and Sarah would spend it. Then he remembered she'd scheduled back-to-back auditions, meetings, and singing gigs. Ever since her career had taken off, he'd seen less and less of her, and he was beginning to feel left behind.

It hit him.

Sarah was a rising idol, poised to become a pop culture icon. Her perfectly sculpted face and luminous black eyes were made to splash across the stars. Soon, her mesmerizing voice would reach into the souls of trillions. Every person in the galaxy who was touched by her songs would adore her, revere her. Ordinary citizens and exalted celebrities, workers and bosses, wage slaves and royalty— all would want her, and all would love her. Perhaps even as much as Devin loved her.

And there he was, just another Silk Sector drone, a "tool" like any other.

Why is she with me?

ARTIFICIAL ABSOLUTES

MARY FAN

Artificial Absolutes
A Red Adept Publishing Book

Red Adept Publishing, LLC
104 Bugenfield Court
Garner, NC 27529
http://RedAdeptPublishing.com/

Second Print Edition: June 2013
ISBN 13: 978-1-940215-03-7
ISBN 10: 1-940215-03-X
Library of Congress Control Number: 2013940243

Cover and Formatting: Streetlight Graphics

She elegantly wove her way through a perilous thicket, never living the same day twice, while he'd walked the straight and narrow path to normality for more than six years. Sarah embraced life's passions with a daring élan, whereas Devin had done his best not to care, not to think, in an attempt to simply... be.

It wasn't because he was afraid of the unknown. No, he'd been down that path, following his passions straight to hell. Although many would call his current situation dull or meaningless, he found it infinitely preferable to his turbulent teenage years and the white hole of chaos his life became after that. Those days were behind him, and he wanted nothing more than a normal, peaceful existence.

And Sarah.

Sarah, who melted his self-imposed prison bars in a haze of light, who showed him that life could have meaning beyond the frozen ideal he'd tried to become.

A second realization struck Devin:

I want to spend the rest of my life with her.

It was irrational. He had known her less than half a year. It was insane—and stupid—but he'd never been more certain of *anything*. Perhaps he would get shot down, but he had to ask, and soon. That day.

Right now.

Devin had abruptly locked his computer and left. As he passed his coworkers, ignoring their odd looks and indignant questions, he contacted his bank via slate.

After retrieving the engagement ring bequeathed to him by his mother, he'd found himself on his way to Sarah's apartment, hardly knowing what he was doing.

The holographic calendar on the wall indicated that Sarah had a meeting with a producer, but neglected to mention the time. *Not very helpful.*

Outside, the serene logo of Ocean Sky Corporation lit up as the golden Kyderan sun faded behind the twisting tower of the company's headquarters. Sarah was in that building or maybe one of its chiseled satellites. Whichever housed the music division.

Devin couldn't remember the last time he'd been scared. Whether he'd had a gun to his temple or an arsenal exploding around him, he'd always managed to keep his head straight. But waiting for Sarah to come home, he practically panicked as the lunacy of what he intended spun through his head.

Yet if everything else were cast into doubt, he would still hold on to the one absolute truth that brought him there: *I love you, Sarah DeHaven. Will you marry me?*

Their first encounter had been like a scene from one of those hackneyed holodramas for teen girls and lonely women. Devin had waited in the reception area of Ocean Sky's headquarters with the rest of his Quasar team, preparing to pitch the old tech corporation a new financial product to increase investment. Even an institution as large and established as Ocean Sky wasn't immune to the dangers of time. Although it produced headline-grabbing machines that pushed the limits of the Interstellar Confederation's restrictions on AI technology, consumers responded more to the company's rival, Blue Diamond Technology Corporation.

The double doors opened. Sarah's loose sapphire dress flowed behind her as she approached the reception screen. She glowed with an ethereal aura that was otherworldly and enticing, a radiance beyond mere beauty.

"Sarah DeHaven. I have a meeting with Ocean Sky Talent at two."

The computer responded with mechanical crispness, "Have a seat, Miss DeHaven."

Sarah glided into a seat across from Devin and crossed her shapely legs. She carried her neck long like a swan queen, betraying no emotion. She glanced around the room. Her full ruby lips became a thin line as she fiddled with a strand of long, black hair.

Knowing he shouldn't stare, Devin forced his gaze away. He wasn't alone in his fascination. All eyes in the room fixed on Sarah with longing expressions that seemed to say, "Look my way." There was something magnetic about her delicate face, slender wrists, and perfectly curved figure.

Sarah's alluring onyx gaze met his. Her face warmed into a demure, inviting smile. She lowered her eyelids.

Against his better judgment and almost against his will, Devin got up and approached. Her gaze followed him.

He didn't know what else to do, so he smiled and tried to make conversation. "I couldn't help overhearing that you're meeting with the talent division. Are you an actress?"

"Singer, actually." Sarah extended a hand. "I'm Sarah DeHaven. And you are?"

Devin took it. "Devin Colt."

Sarah glanced around the room again. "Everyone's staring at me. Is there something caught in my hair?"

"No. You're perfect." He meant it as an offhand comment, but Sarah looked down as though embarrassed. It must have come out more expressive than intended.

Silence. *Now what?*

"You could have smiled at anyone here." Too late, Devin realized he was saying aloud the question he should have kept to himself. "Why me?"

Sarah regarded him with slight confusion. "I don't know. It's like something was telling me I should get to know you."

"I'd like to know you too. Are you doing anything later?"

Her face brightened. "No. Not anymore."

Previously, Devin had preferred the company of shallow beauties he barely knew and had no intention of knowing. Sarah wasn't one of them. She avoided the hollow flirting and meaningless banter he'd grown accustomed to, navigating around his shield of artificiality, the façade he presented to the world. She even confessed the reason she'd agreed to go out with him. Her career-driven life left her craving any kind of human connection outside her industry, and so she had chosen to take a chance on him.

The night had ended with a promise for another, which ended with a promise for yet another—and by then, Devin had allowed his walls to crumble.

It hadn't taken long for his father, who insisted upon knowing every detail of his grown children's lives, to learn that Devin finally had a steady girlfriend.

Dad had pulled him into his office, closed the door, and lowered the shades. He crossed his arms and expressed his displeasure at having learned of his son's social life from a third party, then probed Devin for every detail. "It's about time you got your act together. Is she intelligent? Is she ambitious? Are you sure she's not using you, that she's not simply better than the others at hiding it?"

Devin had been sure. He'd been equally sure that nothing he did—short of, perhaps, being elected President of Kydera—would be good enough for the illustrious Victor Colt. Even then, his father would probably ask why he hadn't reached higher and aimed for Chancellor of the Interstellar Confederation. Although Devin did everything he could to become the person his parents wanted him to be, he knew he lacked the ambitious desire that had driven Victor Colt and the late Elizabeth Lin-Colt to become two of the most influential people in Kydera. He sometimes wondered if he'd inherited anything from them other than his mother's dark eyes and hair and his father's height and angular bone structure.

He also knew that, at twenty-eight, he should choose his own future, but after the hell his decisions had caused seven years ago, he had silenced any notions of "Could I?" or "Should I?" and surrendered to "I will." He *would* do as his father commanded—and remain indifferent to what it was. Yet he still wasn't good enough.

"Come on, baby," Sarah had said once. "Don't let your father bother you. He loves you, Devin. He wouldn't care so much if he didn't."

She was so perceptive, willing to listen patiently and always ready with the right kind of counsel. She was also as busy as he was. Rather than being irritated or saddened by his lack of spare time, she'd said she preferred it that way so she could advance her own career without neglecting him. At the same time, Sarah had told him many times how much she appreciated having him there to save her from isolation.

So she would be happy if he proposed, right?

———————————

What the hell am I doing?

The thought crossed Devin's mind for the hundredth time. But asking was the only way to quiet the chaos in his mind. Besides, he fit the criteria for a good husband— good family, promising future...

And stupid.

What kind of blockhead randomly decides to propose and rushes to ask immediately? Sarah deserved better.

6

She deserved something thoughtful, something that had taken effort.

Devin took the ring box out of his pocket and opened it, then looked around the apartment. How she kept everything so pristine was beyond him. Other than the digimech she'd left on, everything was where it ought to be. Sarah was like that in every aspect, flawless except for some quirk that made her all the more perfect in his eyes. Every hair in place, except for the one lock falling beside her face. Always precisely four minutes late. Her apartment decorated so crisply it might have been done by a computer but for a bizarre painting that appeared to represent some form of bird.

There was nothing out of which he could fashion a romantic scene. Sarah had professed many times that, in spite of the cynicism of modern times, she was still an idealistic dreamer who loved the sweet formulae of yesteryear. So what the hell was he doing with nothing but a ring and a question?

I should leave. Go home and plan something that spoke to how well he knew her. Write a speech about why she was the One and ask her properly. *All right, I'm leaving.*

The elevator *ding*ed outside, followed by the precise *clackity-clack* of high-heeled shoes approaching.

Shit.

Devin stood, devoid of any semblance of a clue, as the bolts of Sarah's computerized door retracted. The door slid open. Upon seeing her, he instinctively did exactly what he'd come to do. "Sarah DeHaven, will you marry me?"

Fuck!

He expected shock. He expected mockery, or horror, or even disgust, but nothing could have prepared him for what she did.

She froze.

"Sarah?"

Sarah stood halfway through the door, her hand inches from the security scanner, motionless.

"Sarah!" Devin rushed to her and put his hands on her shoulders. "C'mon, baby. I'm sorry I scared you."

Sarah didn't move. She was cold, stone cold. She didn't even blink when he looked into the voids of her eyes.

Devin probably had about as much medical knowledge as a repair bot, but even he knew people weren't supposed to seize up like that. He grabbed his slate and pressed the emergency icon.

After a second that seemed to stretch into hours, a response: "Kydera City Emergency Response Center."

A willowy arm reached around him and took the slate from his hand. "I'm sorry. There is no emergency. It was a false alarm."

Devin whirled. Sarah stood beside him, calmly folding his slate.

"Sarah! Are you all right?"

Sarah reached into his pocket and dropped the slate, standing close enough that he could feel her breath. "Of course I am. I'm ecstatic. You proposed." She picked up the ring, which had fallen out of its box when he'd dropped it in alarm. "It's beautiful, Devin."

Devin opened his mouth, but couldn't respond. The anguish of waiting followed by the horror of seeing the love of his life seize up robbed him of the ability to communicate.

Sarah knit her mildly arched eyebrows. "Baby, why do you look so scared?"

Devin tried again to speak. "I-I thought you were... you seized up. I thought—"

Sarah laughed. Something about that once-mellifluous sound chilled him. "I was shocked. That's all. The apartment was supposed to be empty. We never talked about the future. I didn't think you were the marrying kind. Baby, your proposal was the most unexpected, irrational act of randomness. Can you blame me for being surprised?"

"You were cold. That's not... I'm calling the hospital." Devin reached for his slate.

Sarah put her hand on his arm. Her grip was somehow light and firm and utterly unyielding. "No."

"Sarah, please, I—"

"I said no." Sarah's grip hardened.

Devin dropped the slate back into his pocket. He couldn't force her. "I just want to make sure you're okay. I'm sorry. I didn't mean to scare you."

Sarah's expression softened. "There's no reason for concern. A different girl might have screamed or fainted.

8

The fact that I froze should come as no great surprise. It was only for a few seconds. I understand why you panicked, but I assure you, I'm fine." She put her arms around his neck, leaned in, and kissed him. "Of course I'll marry you."

Devin's mind reeled. He couldn't forget how stiff she'd been, how empty her eyes.

Sarah put her hand on his face. "I love you, Devin. I said I would marry you. Doesn't that make you happy?"

She held up the ring. Devin automatically took it and placed it on the hand she gave him.

Sarah regarded it and looked up with a warm smile. Her eyes had regained their usual vivacity, glimmering like the twin onyxes he knew so well. The woman of his dreams, the love of his life, agreed to marry him. Everything was perfect, so why the hell was he so edgy?

Devin attempted a smile. "I'm sorry. I was worried about you."

"That's sweet." Sarah wrapped her arms around him in a close embrace and whispered, "We're going to be so happy."

Devin wanted to believe it. Moments before, he would have. Disquiet lingered within him. For reasons he couldn't explain, he felt she'd changed. The words that once would have sounded melodious seemed deliberate, the smiles calculated.

Meanwhile, her demo track looped. Sarah kissed him again as the song approached its third verse:

"Games of fate and games of choice
"Twisted, tangled, intertwined,
"Who is right, and what is real?
"All shall fade within a mind."

CHAPTER 2

DREAMS, SCREENS, AND MACHINES

*J*ANE STOOD ALONE IN A *void, unable to see anything but blackness and lines of gray symbols randomly streaking the air.*

"Oh, Pony, you're always where you're not supposed to be."

"Don't call me Pony!" Jane looked around for her brother. He was the only one who called her by that nickname. "Devin, where are you?"

Devin appeared on the other side of the lines. He looked as though he wanted to say something, but turned and walked away.

Jane tried to follow. One of the lines widened, faded, and swallowed everything in a wash of white.

A giant harp loomed over her, silhouetted against the blue-hot sun and surrounded by the stringy azure trees native to Zim'ska Re. Jane approached the harp curiously and plucked one of its platinum strings. It angrily beeped... beeped...

The freaking alarm kept beeping.

Jane reached up, feeling for the touchscreen by her bed, and banged it to stop the noise. "Shut *up!*"

She blinked away the remnants of her dream. Dreams were nothing but random crap. She knew better than to think about what they meant. Her weary head ordered her to go back to sleep. Jane flopped over and face-planted onto her pillow. The image of her brother walking away from her filled her with a sudden sadness.

"... And more now on the recent release from the Blue Diamond Technology Corporation. BD Tech has confirmed that the new starship model is called the Blue Damsel, and that the company will phase out the older Blue Tang models..."

The numerous screens on the walls of Jane's apartment flicked on to one of the news channels.

She groaned into the pillow. "Shut up, shut up, shut up! I don't wanna get up! I don't wanna go to work!"

"... In other news, BD Tech's rival, Ocean Sky Corporation, has responded to critics who argue that its virtual reality gaming technology is addictive, saying there is no solid evidence to support that claim..."

That's what they always say. They'd dispute the existence of air if it harmed their corporate interests.

Jane forced herself to get up and blearily wandered into the bathroom.

Gotta agree with the critics on this one. If you can enter a world of your own making, why would you ever leave? Besides, why pay some company to take you to your fantasy world when you can just daydream?

Jane was sure if she ever played a virtu-game, she'd end up one of those virtu-addicts who locked themselves in their mental worlds until they starved, unable to be rescued without permanent brain damage. With her tendency to get lost in her own head, she was an expert at escaping reality without technology. It was a useful skill, thanks to her soul-crushingly tedious job at Quasar.

Ugh... What is my life! How did I end up so boring?

She couldn't even tell anyone how much she hated her work, since she couldn't let it get back to the company's top executive, also known as Dad. Simply doing as he said wasn't enough. She had to *like* what he wanted for her.

Poor, poor Victor Colt, with his two disappointing kids.

Jane was supposed to have been the good one since, unlike her moody big brother, she'd never run with the wrong crowd or committed petty crimes. Up until university, she'd done everything right. Daddy's sweet little angel.

But then Daddy's angel chose to study musical

11

composition instead of bullshit.

Somehow, the more automated the world around her became, the more logic-based and statistically modeled, the more Jane craved the simple, yet inexplicable things that made humans, well, human.

That was shortly after Devin quit being such a hellraiser. The next thing Jane knew, *she* was the black sheep for wanting to spend her life writing silly songs, and Devin the golden boy for going to business school and climbing the Quasar ladder.

By the time Jane graduated from university about five months before, she'd given up on her pipe dream. The music industry was no less full of nonsense than any other, and she'd never exactly been a prodigy. She couldn't stand the thought of facing rejection after rejection only to end up another pathetic wannabe. Perhaps she could charm or fight or even bribe her way in, but what would be left once it was over?

Just another failed composer's useless endeavor, destined to be lost in the abyss of mediocrity.

Going back to the boring trade she'd spent four years avoiding had clearly been the rational choice. Daddy had been more than happy to give his little girl an entry-level position at Quasar. He often boasted about how his wise guidance and willingness to forgive steered both his prodigal offspring in the right direction, saving the legacy of the powerful Colt clan.

Jane fantasized about what she might be doing if she *did* have the talent, the ambition, the confidence. She'd played variations on that theme many times in her head, each as thrilling as the last.

"... has announced who will be performing at the inaugural ceremony for the recently elected President Nikolett Thean..."

As she continued her morning routine, Jane tuned out the irritating screens and wandered back into her dream world...

She stood center stage in the majestic auditorium of the Kyderan Presidential Palace, facing an orchestra of the galaxy's most talented instrumentalists. The audience of politicians, celebrities, and other important people settled down and waited for her to begin.

Jane raised her baton. As the orchestra played, she moved fluidly with the ebb and flow of the melody, allowing it to surge through her like a religious force. The orchestra looked to her for direction, but she wasn't the one in control. The music had a will of its own, and it was her duty to follow it and bring it down to earth for everyone else to hear. The auditorium was her temple, and the music was her god.

Jane smiled as she pictured the possibilities. The audience of big shots would be thrilled, and the billions watching across the seven Kyderan planets would be caught in the allure of her brilliance. They would demand more. They would ask her to be the music director for the Interstellar Confederation's annual ceremony, and the entire galaxy would hear her songs.

Maybe she could make it happen for real, outside the dreamscape. Any fool with a connection to the Net—which was pretty much every fool alive—could broadcast his or her talents to an audience of trillions. Maybe if she composed a masterpiece and posted it, the Networld would fall in love with it. Maybe an industry bigwig would discover it. Maybe—

Beeeeeeeeeep.

Jane looked around, annoyed.

Now what?

She found her small, company-issued videophone in its usual spot on her desk. It lit up with a list of work assignments.

You suck.

Jane grabbed a hair tie from her drawer and swept her long, dark brown waves into a ponytail. The hair must have come from her mother's side, since her father's had been a light chestnut tint before becoming dusted with a distinguished shade of gray, but why was she the only one in the family with so much of it? *Forget making it neat.* She was basically invisible at work anyway, so she might as well let it poof out into its natural, fluffy form.

"... and the infamous cybercriminal group known as the Collective has struck again, this time targeting Quasar Bank Corporation."

Jane looked at the nearest screen, interested since her company had been mentioned.

"Quasar's Netsite QuasarLive, which delivers real-time market data to millions of financial companies, was shut down for hours yesterday after a hack by the Collective caused it to deliver a long anti-greed statement to users in place of data."

Freaking yahoos.

"Change channel." Jane was in no mood to hear about the Collective's holier-than-thou statements. "Channel twenty-five."

The screens flicked to the music channel. Jane blinked in disbelief. Sarah DeHaven, her brother's perfect fiancée, filled the screen with her unearthly beauty in a wordless interlude of vocal fireworks. Seeing her up there, broadcast to that audience of trillions, flooded Jane with an intense combination of rage and sadness, both attributable to unspeakable jealousy.

Why should Sarah get to follow her passion and live out her dream? Why should she get the holodrama ending to her saga while Jane was left with the story that no one told, the story that happened ten thousand times a day, the story she knew too well?

I hate her.

Jane grimaced as her conscience pricked her. She had no right to think that. Sarah was undeniably talented, and she deserved to succeed. She certainly looked the part. Lithe limbs, stunning features, golden complexion—Jane looked down at her own pale skin, envious of Sarah's healthy hue.

She wished she hadn't hounded her brother to let her meet his girlfriend. Sarah's long list of qualities—beauty, elegance, ambition—left Jane feeling like a disaster in comparison.

Her first instinct had been that Sarah was a gold digger who wanted in on the Colt fortune. Why else would someone so perfect date her boring, toolish brother?

Despite Jane's resentments, Sarah proved too agreeable to hate. Her presence lit Devin's face with the kind of genuine smile Jane rarely saw from him. Ultimately, that was what mattered. Jane begrudgingly accepted Sarah and kept her envy-fueled, not-so-nice thoughts to herself.

Sarah's simple, haunting melody came to an end. Jane liked to think she was as good a songwriter, even though it wasn't true.

I wish I could hate her.

The video segued into Sarah's biography, which reminded Jane that everything she wanted was possible, just not for her. She couldn't stand it. "Change channel. Previous."

"... In other news, the Interstellar Confederation's Fringe Resolution LF-Three-Twenty-One has once again stalled, this time by the delegation from Wiosper."

Jane wondered what right the Wiosper system had to express its opinion on anything. It was the galaxy's nicest system, a sanctuary for the rich and the super rich. How dare they block a resolution that could help the needy Fringe systems, the ones outside the protection of the IC?

Not that Jane cared much about politics. That morning, everything seemed to make her grumpy. *It's gonna be a bad day.*

She rummaged through her cluttered closet in search of her one pair of flat-bottomed shoes. *I've gotta organize this place.*

Her apartment was chaotic and spartan at once, strewn with everyday items like clothes and cosmetics but lacking a single personal knickknack, even a family photo. She didn't need Victor Colt's sharp blue eyes and sternly lined face—proudly handsome and harder than steel when he wasn't glad-handing fellow businessmen—constantly admonishing her. Or Elizabeth Lin-Colt's powerful stare and firm mouth reminding her of her tragic loss. Jane still didn't know exactly what had happened seven years ago to rob her of her mother.

As for Devin, he always looked like a façade behind which the brother she'd known as a child disappeared. She'd never noticed how closely her brother resembled their father until after he'd donned it, for she sensed an agitated pensiveness about him she couldn't imagine ever crossing Victor Colt's perpetually confident visage. Devin seemed to be doing his best to become their father's dark-eyed clone. Although he had everyone else fooled, Jane still perceived the remnants of that uncertainty behind the corporate illusion.

Come to think of it, the resemblance paradox was true of Jane and her mother as well—same large, dark brown eyes. But whereas Elizabeth Lin-Colt's gaze had been famously piercing, Jane's made her look as if she was either dreaming or up to something. Which was often true.

Jane finally found her shoes and slipped them on. She jumped up to grab her bag from the top shelf. It tumbled to the ground, spilling its contents. Among the office access cards and forgotten lipsticks lay a circular pendant engraved with the symbol of the Via faith: two stars, one transparent in the middle with solid rays and the other its inverse.

Jane picked it up. The golden suns seemed to smile at her. She smiled back. Ironic, that an outspoken atheist such as herself owned one of those things. She wondered what caprice had made her accept it from her friend—*or is he my boyfriend now?*—Adam in the first place.

"Keep it," he'd said after she'd asked for a closer look at the symbol he always wore. "I want you to have it."

Jane had countered with every protest from "I can't. It's yours!" to "But I'm not Via," culminating with, "This is part of your proselytizing scheme, isn't it?"

"I promise I'm not trying to convert you." Since he'd seemed incapable of being anything but sincere, she knew he meant it. "It's just that you seem to like it, and I thought it could bring you comfort the next time you're feeling down."

Well, Adam, it's working. You're such a goody-goody. Why do I associate with you?

She'd met Adam at the Via temple in the Silk Sector about two months ago after wandering into the stone rotunda in search of a choir to join. Ordinarily, she would never have been caught entering a religious establishment, but she was running out of options after several secular musical groups had turned her down.

Jane accidentally arrived an hour before the open rehearsal and awkwardly waited by the pews. She heard a friendly voice.

"Hi there. Are you lost?"

A young man walked toward her. The white light of the sun streamed in from the large window at the back and almost silhouetted him, forming something of a halo. He was a bit taller than Jane, but not that tall by guy standards.

Jane noticed his Via pendant and hoped it was a passing greeting. She was terrible with people she disagreed with. "I'm waiting for the choir rehearsal."

"They'll be here in about an hour. You're not Via, are you?"

"No, but the choir's secular, right?"

"It is. I'm Adam, by the way. I'm a first-year at the seminary."

Adam stopped in front of her. Jane was finally able to make out the details of his appearance. The halo effect was gone, yet there was still something angelic about his boyish face, light brown hair, and gentle eyes, which were a bright shade of green, reminiscent of peridot.

Pretty boy. Maybe even prettier than me... Nah, I'm still prettier.

Jane accepted the hand he extended. "I'm Jane. So..." She let go of his hand and flipped through her mind for topics of conversation, but she had nothing to say to the religious do-gooder. *Nothing that won't offend him.* She leaned against a pew and examined the swirls carved into its back.

Fortunately, he continued, "I was just setting up for an event the temple's hosting this evening. It's a memorial service to raise money for the victims of the asteroid strike on Uyfi. You should come. Some of the choir members are performing."

Jane traced a finger along the swirls. "Yeah, maybe." *Sorry, but I have no interest whatsoever in attending any charity event my dad's not making me show up at.*

"I see. You think charity's pointless, because most of the donated money goes to greedy middlemen."

Jane looked up with a start. "Are the Via psychic or something?" *How'd he know what I was thinking?*

Adam smiled. "Of course not. I've just heard it a thousand times, and you had it written all over your face."

Jane crossed her arms. "Well, don't judge me for being realistic. Uyfi is one of the most lawless Fringe planets out there. You'd be lucky to get one throne of donated money past the warlords."

Adam leaned against the pew across the aisle from her. "I'm not judging you. You're probably right."

What? Jane tilted her head. "Then why do you bother?"

"Because they need our help, and even the littlest bit still counts for something, doesn't it?"

Jane disagreed vehemently. She pressed her mouth shut to keep from saying anything and turned her attention back to the swirls. The bright-eyed seminary guy was idealistic to a fault. She didn't feel like wasting her breath arguing with someone clearly delusional.

"Now you think I'm an idiot for being so idealistic." Adam sounded amused.

Jane kept her gaze on the carved pew, feeling along the smooth wooden edges. "Was that written all over my face too?"

"You do have a very expressive face."

Jane gave up on using the pew as a distraction and faced Adam. "Then I might as well say it: I don't believe in religion."

A rant bubbled inside her, churning up her chest and onto her tongue. Whenever the urge came over her, she found it almost impossible to suppress. Whenever she tried, everyone could tell she had something to say anyway. Ranting had gotten her into a lot of trouble before, and it was about to make a good-natured priest wannabe hate her. *Oh, well.*

Adam's eyes twinkled with a teasing spark. "All right, let's hear it."

Jane pushed off the pew she leaned against. "Look, I know this is your way of life and all, but I think religion is an outdated practice designed to manipulate people." She fumed about the past atrocities committed in the name of the Absolute Being and the hypocrisies of the ancient texts and the downright foolishness of the notion that people still listened to teachings written thousands of years ago. "Even the name of your deity's bogus. The only reason Via call the Absolute 'the Absolute' is because half the galaxy's reduced God to a figure of speech. People only cling to this nonsense because they're too freaking weak to acknowledge the truth: that we're all alone in a messed-up universe and have to figure it out for ourselves."

She'd been too wrapped up in her own arguments to pay attention to Adam's reactions. He hadn't tried to interject. She figured she'd offended him into silence.

But he didn't look angry or anything; he looked interested. He met her glare with a friendly smile, one without any trace of irony. "I don't entirely disagree with you. Via has been used as an excuse far too many times, and the Absolute has been called upon under all kinds of absurd circumstances. Too many people use religion as a vehicle for power."

Okay... Wasn't expecting that. Jane blinked, surprised. "So I ask again: why do you bother?"

"The Via institution may be flawed, but if it can help people live fulfilling lives and guide them to do good, is there really anything wrong with that?"

The discussion had continued well into the scheduled rehearsal. Jane found herself liking the guy despite herself. Contrary to her initial assessment, he was not an idiot. She disagreed with him about many things, but he was the first person she'd met in a while with whom she could be her real, perhaps somewhat odd, self. It helped that he was attractive.

Jane had eventually curtailed the debate and found the choir. When she'd finished, she saw Adam still there, dedicated to making the best of an event she believed was a sham. She'd found something inviting about his enthusiasm and stayed to help him, even attending the dumb shindig and wasting her money on a contribution.

After that, she'd met up with him often, since neither had any other real friends in the city. Adam was new in town, and Jane's schoolmates had all returned to their homeworlds after graduation. She discovered she liked Adam's company, despite her professed status as another Colt loner.

About a week back, she'd found out from her father that Devin proposed to Sarah about two weeks before. Jane had been furious, not only because her dear brother hadn't bothered telling her about his life-changing decision, but also because of how stupid she found the whole thing.

Adam had noticed Jane's crankiness when she'd met him at the seminary shortly after. "What's wrong?"

Jane responded with a tirade about how she probably knew more about the woman who sat near her at work than about her own brother. She waved her arms for emphasis as she marched down the campus path, too livid to care if she looked like a lunatic. "He's barely known Sarah six months! Who marries someone they've only known for six months? It's the most irrational, blockheaded thing *ever*! I'll bet he's trying to seal the deal before she gets famous and some holodrama star steals her from him."

Jane paused in a huff and was about to launch into a fresh diatribe when Adam stepped in front of her.

"Say, Jane, do you want to go out sometime?"

Huh? She stopped in her tracks and stared dumbly, wondering if she'd heard him right. "But... But you're my *friend*. Won't it be weird?"

"It doesn't have to be."

"But..." Jane's gaze fell on the seminary's temple. "Are Counselors allowed to date? Aren't they supposed to be married to the Absolute or something?"

"Jane, you're smarter than that. The Via have never had any celibacy laws. That's Origin."

"Right..."

Jane realized that she was fishing for excuses. She almost said, "Adam, you don't want to date me. I'm obnoxious, volatile, insensitive... Ask any of my exes."

Truth be told, the thought of maybe, perhaps, potentially becoming more than friends had crossed her mind. She had been quick to dismiss it because she considered Adam to be more of a best friend type than boyfriend material. Then again, that was supposed to be the best kind. Her past romantic entanglements with fascinating artists and sophisticated charmers had ended up superficial, disappointing, and brief.

So on a whim, she'd said, "Okay, let's give it a shot."

Jane stepped onto the station platform of the airtrain she took every morning to work, thoughts of Adam still whirling in her head. Other than the fact they called their meet-ups "dates," nothing had really changed between them. Which was a relief.

The steel-gray airtrain snaked around the skyscrapers. The doors opened as soon as it pulled into the station. Jane shuffled inside with the other commuters and took the nearest seat. Even though technology had long ago made it possible to never leave home—work, shopping, and anything else one might want could all be done through the Net—most companies, including her own, encouraged commuting to maintain the psychological health of their workers.

They probably had a point, but Jane, waiting for the train to move, still despised the daily ritual of sitting around with dozens of dull-eyed office workers. The journey itself only took a minute or so, but intersecting routes meant that the train sat at the station for several minutes waiting for the signal to go.

She drummed her fingers impatiently, wondering why no one had invented teleportation yet. They'd figured out how to tunnel through the space-time fabric and send communications through hyperspace. How hard could it be to dice people into molecules?

Actually, that sounds horrible. Never mind.

Bored, she eavesdropped on two businesswomen in the seats across from her.

The large woman with a pompous face sniffed. "It's *ridiculous*. They treat us like criminals, making us prove our identity with DNA and other such inconveniences. I wish they could simply round up those cybercriminals— what do they call them again? Demons?—so we can vote remotely and save precious time!"

Her companion, a thin woman with a stylish haircut, sighed. "It's such a waste that the best programmers are just overgrown children. Did you hear about what the Gag Warriors did?"

"No! What happened?"

"Well, there was that political commentator... I forget his name, but he was very influential on the Net... Glen! Paladin Glen!"

"What about him?"

The stylish woman leaned toward her companion as though telling a secret. "He's not real. He's a fictional character created by the Gag Warriors. That's why his face is always obscured in videos and his voice always sounds disguised. It's not to protect his identity; it's because they're computer-generated!"

The large woman sputtered in disbelief. Jane mentally echoed her sentiments. As someone who detested Paladin Glen, she found it funny that he and his bizarre opinions were a Gag Warriors prank. She agreed with the stylish woman that it was an awful waste of intelligence.

All hackers are freaking yahoos. Why else would they call themselves "demons"?

"The airtrain is about to depart. Destination: Quasar Bank Corporation headquarters. All aboard, please."

A handful of latecomers rushed onto the train as the scarlet warning light blinked. One last man in a black suit dashed on as the doors closed, barely making it through.

Jane recognized him immediately. Tall and square-shouldered, a picture-perfect figure who could have walked right out of one of Quasar's ads. Clean cut, clean shaven, wavy locks kept at a fashionable length. *What a tool. Yup, that's my brother.*

"Devin!" The train gave off a loud ring at the same time, drowning her out.

Jane lived in the same building as Devin and worked at the same office, but she rarely saw him unless she scheduled something. He worked much longer hours than she did, so she was surprised to see him on her usual commuter train.

As the train started moving, she approached him. "Devin?"

Devin typed furiously on his slate, engrossed in whatever he was doing.

"Hey, Devin! Hello?" He was still caught up in that freaking device, so Jane snatched it. "Devin Colt! This is your sister speaking! How are you today?"

"What?" Devin looked confused, then annoyed. "Pony, give that back."

"I think I outgrew 'Pony' about ten years ago." Jane looked at his slate. He'd been in the middle of an instant message conversation with someone with the Netname Corsair. Topic of discussion: robots. Apparently, there was one that could solve riddles. "Robots? Really?"

"It's not your concern." Devin took the slate back.

Jane raised her hands sarcastically. "Sorry. Didn't realize your robot discussions were so private."

"They're not." He folded the slate and put it in his pocket.

Jane plopped down in the seat beside him. "What're you doing here? I never run into you on the morning train."

"Just running late. How are you? How's work going? What are you doing today?"

Jane sighed. She sometimes felt as though she and her brother had run out of things to talk about. "I'm-fine-work's-fine-not-much-meeting-Adam-for-lunch." She strung her words together in a bored monotone.

Devin nodded. "Good."

"So... how's Sarah?"

"Good."

The train arrived at the Quasar platform, and the doors opened. Devin pulled his slate out again as he stepped off the train.

Jane followed him. "Hey, we haven't caught up in a while. Do you have time for dinner this week? Just you and me, no Dad or Sarah?"

Devin didn't reply, even though he was right beside her. He tapped his slate as if she were invisible.

Annoyed, Jane stopped and watched him disappear into the crowd of commuters. "Love you too, bro."

———————— ✦ ————————

Copy-paste, copy-paste, pull-data, copy-paste... Did anyone even read those stupid reports?

As Jane trudged through another mind-numbing day at Quasar, her thoughts wandered back to her run-in with her brother. Why had Devin been so distracted? Or had he really cared more about someone on the other side of a screen than the person right in front of him? The latter seemed rather sad, but he was far from the only one guilty of it; she'd often done the same to Adam.

Pull-data, copy-paste, run-app, copy-paste...

Jane gave her eyes a break from the screen and looked around. As always, the office was full of well-groomed employees arranged in tidy rows, immersed in their work. It was exactly as it looked in the Quasar ads: Vibrant. Engaged. Energetic. It was smart. It was efficient.

It was the loneliest place she'd ever known.

Still resting her eyes, Jane looked up at the internal defense guns mounted on the ceiling. Yes, the office had guns in it. Every major building in the galaxy did. *Have one deadly attack on a high-profile place, and suddenly they're standard issue. Yikes.*

The thought of going back to her copy-paste-pull-data made her brain hurt. Instead, Jane did what she, as a very bad employee, often resorted to when the monotony got the best of her: gaze at the giant fish tank across the room and daydream.

A bright green fish, translucent fins flowing behind it like a pair of scarves, swam across the aquarium. *Fuy Lae. That species is from Fuy Lae in the Zim'ska Re system.*

What a pity Zim'ska Re was such a dangerous part of the galaxy. The beauty of its planets was legendary.

Maybe one day an alien race would be discovered. Not extraterrestrial creatures from other star systems like that fish. *Intelligent* aliens, as advanced as or more advanced than humans. Maybe they would be wiser, see everything wrong with a society in which status determined success and happiness was measured in numbers. Maybe they could introduce humans to a new way of living, one that allowed them to untangle their desires and release themselves from material pressures.

Maybe those hypothetical aliens sounded a lot like Adam.

Jane set her tray down on the café table. "I don't have much time. I have so much work, I really shouldn't leave my desk today. There's data to be pulled and put into pretty charts! I seriously wonder how they haven't managed to replace me with a computer."

Adam took the seat across from hers. "I actually don't have much time either. I volunteered to help out at a shelter in the city's Outer Ring this afternoon."

"Of course you did." Jane unwrapped her utensils.

Adam smiled. "I know, I know. 'Why do you waste your

time with these things? The marginal difference they make is negligible.'"

Jane pointed at him. "Exactly!" She was desperately hungry, despite having barely moved all day. She started scarfing her dish of Eryatian meats and fruits, which had been arranged in a rosette on her plate before she wrecked it.

"Jane?"

Jane swallowed a bite. "Hm?"

"How do you feel about capital punishment?"

Seriously? Talk about an appetite-killer! She looked up. "Why do you always drop these heavy, meaning-of-life type questions on me?"

Adam backed away. "Sorry... I'm just... curious, I guess. We can talk about something else."

I'm full anyway. Jane put her utensils down. "It's okay. I think capital punishment's necessary. I mean, the prison planets are full-up as it is, and there are some truly horrible people out there. Why?"

Adam's gaze fell. "I started taking my... medical courses yesterday."

"Oh." *Shit. That sucks.*

The Interstellar Confederation had a humanitarian resolution, signed by all the member planets, declaring that criminals on death row had the right to be executed by a religious leader in a manner in accordance with his or her spiritual beliefs. Therefore, Via seminary students received schooling in the use of lethal drugs. Adam had often expressed his reluctance for that part of his future duties. At the same time, he believed that those about to die should be sent to the beyond by a trusted guide instead of a clinical stranger.

Adam fiddled with the napkin on his tray. His usually bright eyes clouded with gloom. "I wish they would do away with capital punishment altogether. Life and death shouldn't be decided by people, no matter how wise or intelligent they are. They're making us watch the execution of a drug dealer tomorrow. He was still on the run when the tribunal found him guilty and sentenced him. Didn't even have a chance to speak for himself. I know it's not uncommon for trials to go on without the suspect, but...

25

I don't like how Kydera handles its justice system. From trial to execution in a matter of days—seems heartless."

What am I supposed to say? Jane picked up her cup and took a swig of her sugary, stimulant-laced drink. "At least it's efficient. With all the fancy forensics tech out there, it's always pretty clear what happened."

Adam didn't look up. "Nothing's infallible. It doesn't seem right that the sentencing is so absolute."

Jane put her cup down. "Why? If a person does something knowing it could kill someone, he gives up *his* right to live." She leaned down to peer into his face. "That drug dealer's a murderer. What about the people who died because of his poison? They didn't get to choose who sent them to the beyond."

Adam sighed. "I know. But it won't be easy, watching a life end, no matter what he did."

He'd barely touched his food. Jane had never seen him in such a dark mood before. She scrambled to find another subject. "Hey, they invented a robot that can solve riddles." She grinned. "Pretty amazing, right? If robots can solve riddles, they'd definitely replace me if it weren't for the IC's anti-AI rules. How much intelligence does it take to copy-paste-pull-data?"

Adam returned her smile. "More than you give yourself credit for, I'm sure."

Jane rested against the back of her chair. "It's too bad the Tech Council's so paranoid, lumping AIs in with creepy shit like cloning and eugenics. It'd be pretty cool if they *could* create an artificial intelligence, don't you think? Like, a sentient computer?"

Adam shook his head. "I don't know. It seems... wrong. When does an experiment become a life? Besides, it can't be done."

"Why not? Brain science shows we're all basically machines anyway, since everything we are, everything we *think*, is directed by stuff like chemicals and neurons." She shrugged. "Wouldn't be impossible to translate all that into code."

Adam looked into the distance. "Are we the way we are because we're 'wired' that way? Or do we make choices on a higher, intangible level, and our physical beings adjust to reflect them? I believe in the latter, which is why I don't think anyone can create a true imitation of human behavior. Machine logic is no match for human irrationality."

Ah, crap. He's gone into moralizing mode again. Jane made a face. "Do you have a Via text to go with that?"

Adam placed his forearms on the table. "I know you were being sarcastic, but I actually do know one that's relevant."

Jane, interested, relaxed her expression. "Really? What is it?"

"It's one of the fables from the Book of Via." He leaned in to tell his story. "Eras ago, in ancient times, the Absolute granted a village a token with the power to create any one thing. This village was often ravaged by violent invaders, so the villagers created an obedient giant made of stone to keep them safe. They became greedy, and they ordered it to attack the neighboring lands. The Absolute was displeased at this abuse of power and punished the village with diseases. The villagers blamed the stone giant. They decided to destroy it."

Adam drew back, and his gaze turned contemplative. "But it wasn't the mechanical slave they'd thought it was. It had *chosen* to obey them out of love, and it was furious at the betrayal. It destroyed the village in its rage, but then was so miserable in its solitude and guilt that it threw itself off a mountaintop and shattered into a million pieces."

Jane raised an eyebrow. "*That's* your allegory for artificial intelligence? That has *nothing* to do with it."

Adam turned his gaze to her. "It's about creating life and the responsibility that comes with it."

"I think it's a horrible, ridiculous story concocted by a bunch of dark-age idiots. Why would a stone giant become depressed? It was never real. Ugh, religion is so *full of it*!" Jane threw up her hand for emphasis. "Hokey lessons and nonsense masquerading as morality!" She put her hands on her hips. "Adam, why the hell do you want to be a Counselor when there are so many better things you could be doing?"

Adam just gave his good-natured and infuriatingly adorable smile that was somehow amused without being condescending.

Jane pulled out her slate and checked the time. "Crap.

I've gotta get back to work." She chugged the rest of her energy drink.

"All right. I'll see you tomorrow, same time?"

Jane swallowed her last gulp. "Yup, 's long as they don't pile more work on me at the last minute."

———— ◆ ————

The afternoon passed as uneventfully as any other. As soon as Jane finished sending out her end-of-day reports, she locked her computer and zoomed out the door. She didn't take long to reach the airtrain station.

She tripped as she pushed through the crowd, crashing into a woman in a doctor's coat. "Sorry!"

The doctor reminded Jane of the distress that overcame Adam when he spoke of his "medical" training, a look she'd never seen before on his usually placid face. The expedience of the Kyderan justice system really seemed to upset him. She worried about how he'd handle watching an execution.

"The airtrain is about to depart. Destination: FFC Residential Complex. All aboard, please."

I've gotta go see him. Make sure he'll be okay, at least bring him company. Maybe apologize for insulting his religion—again.

Jane shoved her way off. She checked the screen at the station to see which train would take her to the seminary. It was about to leave, and that the next one wouldn't arrive for another half hour. She sprinted to the platform.

"The airtrain is about to depart. Destination: Via Theological Seminary of Kydera Major. All aboard, please."

Jane knocked people aside. "*Move!*"

She leaped onto the train as the doors closed. The train shot forward. She stumbled into a seat, internally grumbling about the slowpokes who had almost made her miss her ride.

Several minutes later, the seminary's colorful towers appeared in the window. The train pulled into the station. She sped out.

Jane followed the landmarks from her past visits to figure out how to get to Adam's place. She got turned around and ended up entering the brick dormitory through an obscure side door, one of those non-computerized kinds. It led to a stairwell walled off from the lower floors. Walking up seemed preferable to wandering the building's complex layout, looking for another entrance. She silently cursed the ancient building, annoyed that whoever renovated it hadn't added a few doors along with the central computer.

By the time she reached the level that let her leave the stairwell, only three flights remained. *No point in looking for an elevator now.*

She finally arrived at Adam's floor and wound through the corridors until she found his door. She grabbed the spare key he kept above his doorframe, stuck it into the old-fashioned manual lock, and burst in, hoping to startle him. "Surprise, surprise!"

She froze and dropped her smile, wondering if she was hallucinating.

Outside the dorm window hovered a triangular Barracuda spacecraft, the kind usually used by the interstellar fighter pilots. Its deep blue hull was unmarked. Through the square window on its side, Jane saw a boxy robot of the same color with multiple appendages and a rectangular head.

Inside the room, an identical robot carried a limp and unconscious Adam.

CHAPTER 3

WHAT THE HELL?

A T THE END OF THE workday, Devin remained at his desk, but not reviewing reports or double-checking numbers. The usual assortment of historical data applications and market news Netsites stretched across his monitor, which surrounded him in a semi-circle. All had been unattended for hours.

Meanwhile, he devoted his attention to the message window on his slate.

Corsair: I was finally able to trace the Seer's signal. He's out on the Fringe, somewhere in the Viatian region.

The Seer was a notoriously untraceable person who lurked around the online forums of various Netcrews. He posted as "Anonymous" and had been given the Netname by the Collective. Although Netcrews were accustomed to people browsing their conversations, the Seer had gained a kind of notoriety due to his tendency to write mysteriously well-informed posts containing explosive information and return to silence. He never once showed up in the virtual reality forums where demons, represented by avatars, gathered to speak "in person," their words transposed to the typed-out forums.

One of the Seer's recent posts had caught Devin's attention, one that seemed uncannily relevant to Sarah's strange reaction to his proposal. Devin had tried to contact the Seer ever since. Corsair claimed to have traced the most heavily veiled person on the Net, a deed many of the

Networld's most sophisticated demons—and more than a few cybersecurity teams—had failed to do. Although Devin trusted Corsair, he couldn't help his skepticism.

Archangel: How did you find him?
Corsair: I won't bore you with the details, but it was too easy. The Seer must have wanted to be found.

Before Devin could respond, a window popped up on the screen: Jane Colt calling. He pressed "accept." A video of Jane filled the slate.

"Devin! I-I didn't know who else to call." Her eyes were wide as she backed up against a mirror.

Devin had never seen her so scared before. "What's wrong?"

Jane pointed at something out of view. "It came after me and—I can't think. Devin, I don't know what to do!"

"Okay, calm—"

"*Don't tell me to calm down!*" Her expression turned from frightened to irritated.

"Just tell me what happened."

"I went to see Adam at his dorm, and there was this—this *machine*. It was *kidnapping* him!"

"What?"

"You heard me! It—It came after me! I'm stuck in the elevator, and I tried calling for help, but I couldn't get through—" Jane dug her fingers into her hair. "I—I don't know what to do!"

Whatever was going on, his kid sister was terrified, and he had to help. "Okay, Jane. Can you show me the elevator?"

Jane panned her slate.

The elevator was a Festiind model. An older one, but standard. "Take down the mirror. You should find a small glass door on the wall. The button behind it—that's the emergency door release."

The screen went blank as Jane folded her slate. Devin heard her struggling to take down the mirror. He turned to his monitor, opened a communication window, and typed a message to the local authorities.

"I'm sorry. Your message to the Via Theological Seminary's Office of Public Safety cannot be sent at this time."

That's odd.

The video of Jane reappeared. The mirror leaned against the elevator doors behind her. She looked over the camera. "I just press the button, right?"

"Yeah."

"Okay... Um..." Repeated clicking. Jane opened her mouth in panic. "It's—it's not working. Devin, it's not working! It's broken or... Shit, it's coming!"

Something whirred in the video's background. *What's that?* "Do you have your stunner?" The small weapon could fire non-lethal blasts that would knock out most would-be attackers.

Jane shrank against the wall. "No... I forgot it..."

Devin thought for a moment. There was something else about Festiind models, something that had caught his attention back when...

"Jane, lift up the carpet. There's a maintenance hatch in the center of the floor. Pull out the handle, twist clockwise, and push. It opens down."

Jane dropped the slate by the elevator door and tore up the carpet.

Open communication window, retype message, send.

"I'm sorry. Your message to the Via Theological Seminary's Office of Public Safety cannot be sent at this time."

Jane picked up the slate. "Um... Devin?" Her eyes tilted down with worry.

"What's wrong?"

"*That.*" She pointed the camera down the circular hatch, revealing the long elevator shaft below.

Shit. The maintenance workers used cable systems to navigate the shaft. *I should've remembered.*

Jane looked into the camera. "Where do I go from here?"

The whirring grew louder. Devin thought quickly. "There should be some utility conduits on the side of... Forget it. You're not going down there."

"What the hell *am* I supposed to do?"

Open window, retype, send. Error. "Hang in there. I'm trying to—"

A loud *crash* split the air as the mirror fell. The elevator doors had opened.

Jane screamed. *"Screw it!"*

"What're you doing?"

The video blurred. When the image steadied, the camera pointed vaguely in the direction of the door.

A wheeled machine with several appendages came into view.

What the hell?

Devin pressed the "record" icon on his slate. The machine raised a pointed appendage over the camera and slammed into it.

Jane had never been afraid of heights. As a child, she'd enjoyed alarming her mother by climbing the tallest Venovian evergreens on the Colt estate. Comparing her size then to her size currently, she probably wasn't much higher up. It was a little different hanging from the underside of an elevator with only a hastily slammed hatch between her and a killer robot.

Well, this sucks.

That she'd caught the bar after sliding down the hatch could only be attributed to super reflexes reserved for times of great danger or to the grace of the Absolute. If only those super reflexes or that divine grace would allow her to reach the conduit Devin had mentioned...

The faint lights along shaft's walls let her vaguely make out the conduit's square entrance. Jane saw another bar under the elevator, parallel to the conduit's top edge. She'd played on jungle gyms when she was little and remembered the motion of swinging her body to catch a bar an arm's length away, but she'd forgotten how much the friction burned her palms.

She grabbed the bar and swung forward. Her face banged into the wall. *Ow.*

After taking a moment to let the pain in her face subside, she extended her body as far as she could, barely touching the conduit's floor with her foot.

Dammit! Wish my legs were longer. Good thing I wore flats today. And pants. If I had to do this in heels and a skirt...

The inane thoughts kept her from freaking out.

Something about talking to her brother had done away with the panic she'd felt before. She wasn't about to let it take over again.

The conduit was only half her height. Even if she could stand, she would probably fall backward if she tried.

Why are utility conduits so small? Are maintenance workers all midgets or something?

A small handle below her, right by the conduit, looked within reach. She grabbed it with one hand. She had to let go of the bar under the elevator to enter the conduit, but the thought was too scary.

Above her, the machine whirred.

Jane had never been remotely religious, but in a situation as unthinkable as the one she was in, even she prayed, albeit facetiously.

Hello, Absolute One. Please let the machine be too big to fit through the hatch. And please keep me from falling. In return, I will compose a magnificent motet for You. So be it, truly.

Jane closed her eyes and let go of the bar. She bit her lip to stifle a yelp as she dropped her body weight onto one arm.

She reached up with her free hand and pressed her forearm into the conduit's cold metal floor. By pulling, bending, and twisting, she managed to fold herself into the conduit.

She collapsed against the wall in relief. *Whew! Made it!*

Jane listened for the machine, half expecting it to appear right behind her. Instead, a *beep* emitted from her pocket. Wondering what the hell it was—and why the hell she didn't know the contents of her own pocket—she reached in. She pulled out her company-issued videophone.

Oh, right. This thing.

——→◇←——

Devin sprinted down the office corridor, eyes fixed on the slate in his hand. *Dammit, Jane. Please have your videophone...*

Jane's face appeared in a window. "Devin?"

"*Jane!*" He stopped and exhaled. She hadn't fallen. "What happened?"

"Don't worry, bro. I'm all right." Even in the darkness,

Devin could tell Jane was trying to reassure him with one of her cocky smirks. "I caught the bar under the elevator and used my super jungle gym skills to get into the conduit." The smirk faded. "I don't know where the machine went, but I don't hear it anymore."

Devin rearranged his face into a calm expression. He continued down the corridor, heading for the nearby hangar where Dad kept an air transport. "I'm coming to the seminary. I'll be there as soon as I can."

"You don't expect me to *wait*, do you?"

"Of course not." Devin ran through his memories. "Look back at the conduit's entrance. There's always a manual control panel there."

"Okay, I see it." The panel creaked as it opened. Jane aimed the camera at it. "Um... There are, like, ten thousand switches here."

"Flip the green one marked seven-three-one. That'll turn on the emergency lights."

A few seconds later, a line of dim green lights flickered on along the conduit's wall, illuminating the funny look Jane gave him. "How'd you know?"

"Never mind that." Devin turned a corner. "Follow the lights. They'll lead you to the building's control room. You'll probably have to go down some ladders."

"Okay, do you have a second job as an art thief?" Keeping her videophone in her hand, Jane crawled through the conduit. "How do you know so much about the inner workings of buildings?"

I wish I didn't. "I'll tell you later."

Jane stopped and looked into the camera. "You always say that! Why do you have to keep these dumb secrets? I'm your freaking sister, Devin, and I know *nothing* about you. You never tell me anything, and whenever I ask, you act all mysterious. It's irritating as hell!"

Oh, Pony. Only Jane could lecture him while hiding from a dangerous machine in the dimly lit innards of a dormitory. Devin knew better than to defend himself. "Just follow the lights. That's what they're there for. When you reach the end, you'll see a clearly marked door."

He reached the elevator and punched "G" for *Ground* into the control panel. As he waited, he minimized the video, opened a communication window, and contacted the police.

"I'm sorry. Your message to the Kydera City Police Department cannot be sent at this time."

Something's wrong.

The elevator arrived. Devin entered. He considered trying the police again, then changed his mind and typed a message to Corsair.

Archangel: I'm sending you a video of a robot spotted at the Via Theological Seminary of Kydera Major. I've never seen anything like it.

Corsair: Is it remote-controlled or programmed to operate independently?

Archangel: I don't know.

Corsair: Who sent it?

Devin summarized what he knew. The elevator doors opened. He stepped out. As he speed-walked toward the building's exit, he began uploading the brief video he'd recorded.

"Error. File does not exist."

What?

Devin whisked through the pages on his slate, checking filenames and locations, but found nothing.

Archangel: Someone erased the file. Did you get any of it?

Corsair: A few frames. I'll upload them onto Citizen Zero's network.

Citizen Zero was an anti-establishment Netcrew often derided as being full of conspiracy theorists. Due to the combined paranoia of its members, its network was one of the safest places to secure files in danger of deletion. As soon as Corsair posted the images on the forum dedicated to that purpose—usually saving corporate documents or political memos from cybersecurity teams attempting to remove them from the public's view—they would be automatically downloaded and disseminated so widely it would be impossible to track down all the copies.

Corsair: Done, but with difficulty. No Name nearly stopped me.

Archangel: Are you sure it was them?

Corsair: Who else could it be?

Fuck! Devin tore out the door. If No Name was involved, the situation was more dangerous than he'd thought. It would take at least five more minutes to reach Dad's transport and another ten to fly to the seminary, even at top speed. *I should've left the second she called. Why the hell didn't I?*

"I'm in the control room." Jane's voice came from the slate. "Hey, Devin? Shouldn't there be watchmen here?"

Devin, still running, swiped his slate to return to the video window. "It's empty?"

"Yeah, there's no one." Jane panned her videophone to show him. Not only were the seats empty, but apart from a handful of indicator lights, all the equipment was shut down. "I feel as though there's no one else in this entire—"

The doors behind her shot open. The deep blue machine wheeled down the corridor toward her, rapidly approaching with what looked like a gun in its robotic claw, the wide barrel aimed at her.

Jane whirled and screamed. The panic surged back.

"Jane!" Devin yelled at her through the videophone, which she clutched tighter than she had the bar under the elevator. "Jane, *run!*"

Jane bolted out of the control room and down the corridor perpendicular to the one she'd seen the machine in.

"Zigzag, and make it random!"

She didn't question him. She ran left diagonally, then abruptly switched right, haphazardly making her way down the corridor. The building must have been empty, or else somebody should have heard her bang up against the walls.

An electric blast hit the wall near her head. She yelped. "What do I do?"

"Find the stairs," Devin said. "And when you do, go up."

"Up?"

"The thing's on wheels!"

Jane reached an intersection, turned, realized she was going the wrong way, and doubled back. A blast hit the wall behind her. She swung around a corner.

The door to the stairwell was right ahead. She fought the urge to run straight at it.

Left... Now right... Now left...

Jane tore open the door to the staircase and slammed it shut behind her. A blast hit it.

She ran up the stairs. After a few winding flights, her body faltered. Her heart pounded, and her breaths came in jagged gasps.

A *bang*. She spun. The machine had thrown open the door. "It can't handle stairs, right?"

Four legs extended from the machine's sides. Its wheels folded into its body, and its head shifted forward from the top to the side. It crawled toward her.

"Devin..." Jane pointed the videophone at it, battling the urge to scream.

"Listen, keep going up until it fires its next blast." Devin sounded out-of-breath. "Then, run down toward it."

"*What?*"

"It takes time to recharge, and you'll be faster down the stairs."

"But—"

"Do it. And *don't be predictable.*"

Jane swatted away the urge to ask what the hell he was thinking. She continued up the stairs. Her foot slipped. She caught herself as a blast whizzed over her head.

"*Run down!*"

Jane instinctively obeyed Devin's voice. She zoomed down the steps, riding a sudden energy as she charged toward the machine.

She jumped off the flight of stairs above it. "*Screw you!*"

She soared over the machine and tumbled to the bottom of the steps. Her body yelled at her with pain, but she shut it up with adrenaline, rocketed down the remaining few flights, and crashed through the exit out into the street.

———◆———

"*Jane!*"

All Devin could see from his kid sister's video feed was

a jerky succession of blurred images.

Beeeeeeep!

He looked up. The transport he piloted was heading into oncoming traffic. He pulled out of the lane and stopped in midair. "Jane!"

"I... I'm all right!"

The image steadied. Jane was a mess. Her ponytail was in disarray, her cheeks fiery red, and her face covered in sweat. But her terror was gone, and she grinned. "Holy *shit*, bro! I made it!"

Devin collapsed forward in relief. "Where are you?"

"The road by the dorm... what the *hell* was all that?" Jane laughed. She sounded almost maniacal.

"You're in the street?" The building had been empty. Whoever controlled the machine didn't want to be seen. It wouldn't follow her. "Are there people around?"

"Yeah, tons."

"Good. Go to the nearest police station and—"

"I know *that*. How dumb do you think I am?" The video blurred again as Jane sped down the street. "I'll call you later. And you *will* tell me how you knew all that stuff about the building."

Devin started up the transport. "I'll meet you—"

"I can handle it. Just... go back to your reports or whatever it is you do."

"Are you sure?"

"I told you, I'm *fine*." She sounded like her usual self again.

If she wants to take care of herself, I should let her be. "All right, then."

"And... um... thanks, Devin. I don't know... Just... thanks." Jane hung up.

Devin stared at the slate for a few seconds, wondering how to react. How could she be so calm?

He shook off the vestiges of tension, turned the transport, and flew back to the office.

Jane glanced at the videophone, yearning to call her brother and—and what? What could he possibly do other than coddle her? Her grip on her composure slipped, and the last thing she wanted was for him to see how scared she really was.

Dammit, I'm not a little girl. I shouldn't need my big brother holding my hand and telling me it's okay.

She felt herself shaking. She put the videophone in her pocket, ducked into the narrow alley by the dorm, and gripped her arms. *I'm fine. I just need a minute...*

A noise. She whirled, expecting to see the machine in the street. All she saw was a handful of students.

The air shook with the roar of engines. An unmarked Barracuda zipped across the sky and disappeared into the bluish-gray atmosphere.

Adam's in there...

Unable to hold back any longer, Jane put her face in her hands and cried.

Corsair: Every member of Citizen Zero has downloaded the images you sent me.

Archangel: That was fast.

Corsair: We're fast. No one knows what it is or where it came from.

Archangel: Post the pictures on the Collective's forum.

Corsair: Okay, but if we couldn't identify it, they won't be able to either.

Archangel: Maybe an ex-employee of BD Tech or Ocean Sky will recognize it. It has to have been made by one of those companies.

Corsair: BD Tech and Ocean Sky don't have ex-employees, but I'll do it just in case. By the way, I finally got the results you asked for. You're not going to like them.

Jane fidgeted in her chair, waiting for the police officer to return. He'd kept his face irritatingly deadpan as she told him about the kidnapping. The only things he'd said were "Uh-huh" or "I see" until he'd muttered, "Wait here, Miss Colt," and left her alone in the small, windowless room.

That was almost an hour ago. *What the hell is taking so long?*

The image of Adam, unconscious in the grasp of the machine's creepy appendages, played on an endless loop in her mind.

Get outta my head!

Looking for a distraction, Jane walked over to the screen on the wall. It displayed a list of apps. She pressed the news icon.

Half the screen showed a blond reporter in front of the Presidential Palace. The other half displayed footage of a clean-cut young man with amber eyes and the kind of face that exuded otherworldly charisma. Topic of discussion: a law student who was making waves in the political world. He was the first person from a Fringe system to gain a coveted internship as President Thean's assistant.

"... Jonathan King lived on Aurudise-Three before the system was evacuated due to systematic failures in its computer networks that put the population in danger..."

Jane switched the screen back to the list of apps. She couldn't stand another tale of overcoming adversity to achieve great things. Being a daughter of privilege with nothing but a disappointing career ahead made her detest those kinds of stories. She didn't need to feel any more inferior at the moment.

She had *seen* Adam—he'd been *right there*. If she'd *done something*, he might be standing beside her at that very moment, telling her why she should forgive the people behind his attack.

I just... ran.

The machine had turned toward her seconds after she'd burst into Adam's room. She stared at it, and it seemed to stare back. She fled as it fired a blast. The elevator doors opened, and she'd stupidly gone in, which was how she'd ended up trapped.

If only she'd run into the room instead. If only she'd fought it—damn the consequences. She could have grabbed a chair and smashed it. She could have kicked it until she scrambled its circuits. She could have—

"Jane Colt? Hello, I'm Counselor Mayuri. We've never met, but your father and I are old friends."

A petite woman dressed in a Counselor's uniform stood in the doorway. A serene green robe flowed down her shoulders. Its stiff hood obscured the top half of her face. She had a soft, lined chin, and she clasped her weathered hands.

What's going on?

"Do you remember how you got here?" Counselor Mayuri had a kind, motherly voice. It was downright maddening.

"Of course I do!" Jane snapped. She caught herself and lowered her voice. "Do you know where the officer went?"

"Don't worry. Everything's all right now." Counselor Mayuri pulled out a chair and sat down. "What do you think happened?"

"What do you mean? Adam was *kidnapped*. Excuse me. I don't mean to be rude, but why're you here?" Jane actually did mean to be rude. She hated people talking down to her, and the matronly woman treated her like a toddler. Besides, Counselor Mayuri claimed to be a friend of her father's. That meant she either owed him a favor or wanted him to owe her.

Colts don't have friends—only networks.

Counselor Mayuri gestured at the chair across from her. "Please, have a seat."

Jane obliged and waited for the Counselor to explain herself.

"Adam Palmer wasn't kidnapped." Counselor Mayuri spoke slowly, enunciating each word as though Jane might not understand them. "He left earlier this afternoon for a religious retreat on Dalarune. The officer told me what you thought you saw. Surely you must realize now that what you described is not possible."

Jane was too bewildered to say anything more than, "What?"

"According to our records, he left two hours before your supposed incident. He was extraordinarily distressed and asked to be added to the retreat at the last minute. Having to face his future duties as an executioner devastated him, and it caused him to question his faith. Naturally, he felt he needed the time and isolation to reflect and reconnect."

Jane bit down the desire to yell. "Listen, Counselor, your records are *wrong*. I saw Adam in his dorm a little over an hour ago."

"That dormitory was evacuated this afternoon for an automated antiseptic cleaning. No one has entered in the last three hours."

"I did! And there was no *cleaning*."

Counselor Mayuri rested her elbows on the table. "I know this must be disconcerting to hear, but you were never there either."

Jane was too stunned to speak. She bored her gaze into the Counselor's face, wishing she could look into the woman's eyes and see if that was some kind of sadistic joke.

Counselor Mayuri straightened. "The officer called my office to compare your account with our records. When I found no record of anyone entering that building, I told him I'd speak with you myself. Like I said, your father and I are old friends. I'm sure you're aware that many mental disorders, including forms of psychosis and mania, manifest in one's early twenties. It sounds alarming, but you needn't be afraid. Healthcare technology makes it possible to live a perfectly normal life as long as you receive treatment."

Jane almost wanted to laugh. "You... You think I'm having a mental breakdown."

"Either that, or you're lying."

Jane opened her mouth in consternation. "Why would I lie? I—I *was* there! I was talking to my brother the whole time—you can ask him! And it's not like there's no trace of me. I broke a mirror in the elevator!"

"Of course I checked our security cameras before I came." Counselor Mayuri seemed unperturbed by Jane's outburst. "They show nothing out of the ordinary."

"What about the Barracuda I saw leaving the building? Did I imagine that too?"

"No, there was an unmarked Barracuda in the area. It belongs to a registered bounty hunter."

Jane slammed her fists into the table. "Your records are fake. Someone's screwing with everyone's computers."

Counselor Mayuri placed her hands in her lap. "I don't understand why you're so adamant. Do you want Adam to be in danger? I assure you, our records are correct. He's at the retreat on Dalarune as we speak."

Jane wished intensely that the Counselor's words were true. If admitting she was crazy meant Adam was safe, so be it. "Can I talk to him?"

"I'm afraid not. Via retreats are about silence and

isolation. Adam will be unreachable until he chooses to return, which will likely be in a few weeks."

Jane shook her head. Until she saw Adam again, she wasn't about to give up and leave things as they were. "Call Devin. He'll tell you."

"Please—"

"Go over to that screen and *call him*."

Counselor Mayuri sighed. She approached the screen and searched a database until she found Devin's contact information. "Devin Colt?"

Devin's face appeared. He was at his desk. "This is Devin Colt. Counselor Mayuri?"

"Yes. I—"

"Devin!" Jane stood so quickly her chair fell. "Tell her what happened at the dorm. The machine... she thinks I'm crazy! She said Adam went on a retreat, and I'm crazy!"

Devin blinked as though clueless. "Jane? What's going on?"

Counselor Mayuri started to speak, but Jane cut her off, ranting about how nobody believed her and how there must be a vast conspiracy. When she finished, she looked to her brother for support.

Devin still appeared confused. "I don't know what you're talking about."

"*What?*"

"I haven't spoken to you since this morning." His voice was measured and his face calm, but Jane knew he was lying. Some instinct within her could always tell. "I think this is all a big misunderstanding."

Why, Devin? Once again, Jane was stunned to speechlessness.

He gave her an intent look. "We can talk about it later."

He's gotta have a good reason. Jane nodded, swallowing her protests.

Devin turned his attention to Counselor Mayuri. "I'm sorry, Counselor. She's been under a lot of stress, and I'm afraid I haven't looked after her as I should have. I apologize for her behavior, and I assure you, my father and I will remember your help in this matter."

Jane glared at her brother.

"That's quite all right," Counselor Mayuri said. "Your

father and I go way back, and I wanted to make sure young Jane was taken care of."

"Thank you," Devin said. "I'll be there soon to pick her up."

Jane righted her chair and slumped in it. "I'm *fine*. I'll take a taxi." She put her head down on the table. "Please, just... let me go home by myself. I need some space."

The rage drained. She resigned herself to detached silence. What happened next—Devin ending the transmission with his usual fake smile, Counselor Mayuri clearing things up with the police, someone escorting her to a waiting taxi—was a dull blur behind the image replaying in her mind: Adam in the grip of a robot, being taken away to who knew where.

Devin wondered if he should go see Jane right away. She'd be in no mood to talk to him after he'd lied and called her unstable. *At least she'll be safer this way.*

Whereas other Net vigilantes frequented the forums with indignant opinions, one entity was pure action. No Netsite, no forum posts, no mission statements. The Networld called it No Name. It was an entity as untraceable as the Seer and even more silent.

Most of the Networld assumed No Name was either an elite private security company or a devoted group of Net purists. Devin knew how dangerous they really were from what he had discovered about Sarah, what they had done to her. He wanted Jane to have nothing to do with them.

No Name had begun several years ago but only recently shown its true power: an online force that mysteriously policed the Net, fighting the efforts of all Netcrews and cybergangs indiscriminately.

While the public confused Netcrews with cybergangs—groups of online criminals who used their skills for profit rather than activism—the cyberpolice focused on the latter, dismissing Netcrews as harmless agitators and pranksters to be dealt with by private companies. Demons turned on each other often, unveiling the identities of those they disliked and blocking each others' hacks. For those reasons, the Networld had taken a while to realize one entity was behind the majority of the more sophisticated moves.

No Name had to have been behind Adam's kidnapping. Elaborately faked files, detailed planning, records in all the right places—according to Corsair, such intricate work had only been dedicated to one other person: Sarah. Not only was Adam supposed to be on a religious retreat due to distress concerning his executioner training, he'd been transferred into that class only two days before, in the middle of the term. It was too convenient. The transfer must have been orchestrated to provide an excuse for his absence. As with No Name's previous work, all the usual tells were absent.

Why would they target Adam? And why Sarah?

Devin scrolled up the message window on his slate and reread the document Corsair had sent him an hour ago. He didn't want to believe it.

A new window popped up.

Corsair: It won't change, you know.
Archangel: There must be a mistake.
Corsair: I told you. I don't make mistakes.

Devin closed his eyes. Denial would do him no good, but he couldn't bear to acknowledge the truth.

Sarah DeHaven, what happened to you?

He opened his eyes and noticed a shadow. Someone was behind him, someone who might have been there for a while. He looked back with a start.

Sarah stood there, completely still and silent as stone.

CHAPTER 4

AN IMPORTANT MAN

VICTOR COLT WAS AN IMPORTANT man. Without him, Quasar would not be Quasar, the Silk Sector would not be the Silk Sector, and the Colts would not be the Colts. Once the kings and queens of politics and business, the Colts had been reduced through generations of isolation and unfortunate occurrences to only himself and his two less than extraordinary children.

Being one of the last of a formidable clan had never bothered him. He saw it, as he saw so many things in life, as an opportunity. After the death of his parents in a tragic accident shortly after his marriage to the accomplished and beautiful Senator Elizabeth Lin, Victor had taken it upon himself to lay the foundations for a new beginning to the Colt legacy. His children did not make achieving his goal easy. Every time he sorted them out, a new problem arose.

Victor read about the latest problem. Although Counselor Mayuri had marked her communication urgent, he hadn't found time to read it until almost an entire day later. Being an important man meant time-consuming obligations filled his days.

Apparently, his daughter had suffered some kind of psychotic episode. The Counselor had taken care of everything with the police, but she was concerned about Jane's mental health. She had included in her communication a list of psychiatrists in addition to an offer to counsel Jane herself.

Victor was disappointed. No daughter of his should be mentally ill. Colts were stronger than that. But she was, after all, merely a confused young girl, and biological imbalances could not be helped. He sighed heavily.

My dear little Jane, why must you make things so difficult for me?

He would have to spend his valuable time ensuring the police, Counselor Mayuri, and any psychiatrists who might become involved kept quiet. The very thought gave him a headache. He'd had enough distractions for one day—the bothersome last-minute meeting with an exasperating client, the unexpected visit from maintenance to update the internal defense guns on his ceiling, the urgent call from a subordinate in the Eryatian system.

Victor wasn't too concerned about his daughter. Jane was a good child, if a foolish one. Thanks to advances in medicine, she would be all right once she received treatment. He was more concerned that Devin hadn't paid her enough attention to notice signs of her illness. As much as he cared about her, Victor was too busy to watch over Jane and had told Devin to look after his little sister. If Devin had done so properly, the situation with the police would have been prevented.

"Inbox," Victor barked at his computer. An abnormally large proportion of the unread communications had been sent by his son. *Odd.* "Show missed communications from Devin Colt."

The computer pulled up a long list, beginning the previous evening. The latest attempt to reach him had been twenty minutes ago. They all contained the same request for an audience. No doubt it concerned Jane's incident.

Victor leaned back in his chair and put his feet on his desk, looking blankly past the transparent walls of his office. Devin clearly knew what had happened. He should have taken care of it himself.

Very disappointing indeed.

But it was a minor misstep. Compared to the disaster Devin had once been, the current lack of responsibility was no reason for concern. On every other front, Devin was finally becoming the person he was supposed to be. He had much room for improvement, but Victor nonetheless prided himself on the work he had done with his son. His persistence had transformed a thoughtless, out-of-control youth into an elite young professional.

Devin had been disobedient as a child, and Victor and his wife had made it clear that they expected more. The boy's schoolwork had improved, but around the age of twelve, he had become the kind of nightmare adolescent every parent dreaded. It began with a few routine attitude problems. From there, it spun out exponentially, exploding into a near decade of mayhem.

There's nothing more heartbreaking than to realize the child one puts all one's energy into is nevertheless determined to stray from the road so thoughtfully planned for him.

Victor had often felt that way about his son who, despite Victor's best efforts, had persisted in wasting time, wasting resources, wasting away his life.

The Colts had always been the best at whatever they chose to do. Victor Colt and his wife were no different. Victor had ruthlessly conquered the business world while Elizabeth rose through the ranks of the Kyderan legislature. Little Jane showed promise. Perhaps she wasn't as intelligent as previous generations of Colt women, but she could charm her way into getting almost anything she wanted. Victor was well aware that in many cases, likable was the smartest thing one could be.

Devin, on the other hand, had been a thoroughly disagreeable teenager. He'd selfishly dismissed his parents' advice and willfully sought ways to upset them. That attitude led to many shouting matches.

Victor had never wanted things to go that way. No, he and his wife had always been very patient. But Devin pushed and pushed. He would make excuses and accuse his parents of not listening, then insult them by saying they didn't know anything about him and he didn't need them to make his decisions for him.

Misbehaviors had eventually become misdemeanors. By the time Devin was fifteen, he had been caught abusing substances, engaging in vandalism, and other juvenile transgressions.

But Victor Colt was an important man, and Elizabeth Lin-Colt was a powerful politician. Through their combined influence, they cleaned up after their troublesome son time and time again. The ungrateful child had never once thanked his parents for their hard work. He'd even *blamed* them for his problems, charging them with putting too much pressure on him. Of course they had to pressure him. The little fool would not have gotten *anywhere* otherwise!

"What are you planning to do with your life?" Victor had asked one afternoon. "How do you expect to accomplish anything if you're always engaging in these low-life kinds of behaviors?"

"Hey, I still bring home the grades, don't I?" Devin's young face dripped with boredom. "Thanks to your cleanup crew, I'm still a perfect student on paper, and that's all that matters, right?"

Lines formed between Elizabeth's arched black brows. "Devin, this is serious."

Devin's expression turned from indifferent to enraged. He grabbed a chair and threw it to the ground. "Dammit, I *know* it's serious! Whatever worries you think you have—I promise, *mine are much worse*! But it's *my* life we're talking about, so let me figure it out *myself*!"

Victor shook his head. "How can you be so selfish? We've seen where your 'figuring things out' has led. After all we've done for you, I don't understand how—"

"You wanna know how it started?" Devin lifted his chin as though trying to match his father's height. "I realized that my best would never be good enough, so I turned to study meds for help. You were oh-so-proud when I started excelling in school. You didn't care what I had to go through to get there. So I went further and further until all I wanted was escape. That's where *your* guidance has led!"

Victor frowned. "What are you talking about?"

"You'd know if you cared who I was instead of just what I do! I might as well be a fucking robot to you!"

"That's *enough*." The rage his idiot son always managed to provoke ignited within Victor.

Elizabeth crossed her arms. "Devin, if you don't stop this nonsense now, you won't go to the University of Kydera Major, you won't get a Silk Sector job, and you won't have a life."

"Okay, Mom," Devin scoffed. "You've got everything

planned out for me. Looks like my life is already over. Now if you'll excuse me, I've got better things to do than stand here and listen to you two repeat yourselves."

"Devin!" Elizabeth's voice was quiet, but sharp.

"That's what always happens!" Devin pointed an accusing finger at his mother. "You vent about how I'm not the son you wanted, and nothing I say matters. Then we all leave a little deafer and more fucked up than before."

Victor slammed his fist into the table. "What must I do to get through to you? Have you ever listened? Have you ever *thought*?"

"Have *you* ever listened?" Devin clenched his fists. "I'm not a machine, you know! You can't command me and expect me to do what you programmed me for! I have ideas of my own!"

Victor turned away, resisting the urge to slam the table again.

Elizabeth sighed. "Devin, what do you hope to gain out of all this? How are you planning to live?"

"Maybe I'm *not*." Devin stormed out.

That evening, Elizabeth had found him stumbling out of his room, his wrists overflowing with blood. Of all the things his son had failed at, that was the one thing Victor thanked the Absolute for. He had hoped that Devin, after a near-death experience brought on by his own misguided impulsiveness, might finally pull himself together.

But no. The number of disciplinary problems had fallen, but the boy's attitude had remained the same. Things had grown worse when he left for university. Without his parents' oversight, Devin's minor tangles with the law became full-blown criminal activities.

Seven years ago, they got his mother killed.

"Is *this* what it takes to set you straight?" Victor had stood over his son, who sat with his face in his hands. "Your mother is *dead* because of what you did!"

Devin hadn't looked up. "I know. I... I'm sorry."

"If you'd listened to me and done as I told you, *none of this would have happened*."

"I know."

"I tried so *hard*! You can't say I haven't been patient, that I haven't been tolerant beyond reason! I could have had you arrested or committed dozens of times, and if I had, *your mother would be alive.*"

"I know."

Looking back from the present, Victor saw how the situation could be interpreted differently. To honor his wife's memory, he had found it in his heart to forgive Devin, even if Devin never forgave himself.

Victor had sat down beside Devin. "Your mother loved you to a fault. If her death means you'll live the life she wanted for you, become the person she wanted you to be, then I know she would think it worth the sacrifice. Despite the hell you've put me through, I don't want to give up on you, my son."

From there, Devin finally made the changes Victor and his wife had always wanted, dutifully following the path laid out for him: graduation with honors, Kydera's top business school, a job at Quasar. Shades of Devin's former self sometimes returned, and in those moments, Victor was quick to remind him how much his past recklessness had cost. Elizabeth's death loomed over the family, but otherwise Devin's past misadventures became something of a joke Victor enjoyed complaining about.

"He was such a *mess* before I sorted him out!" he would say with a laugh. "You won't believe how much melodramatic nonsense he put me through!"

Look what I've created, he thought whenever he saw his son doing exactly what he had been intended for. *Look what my hard work has achieved.*

A *ping* from the computer woke Victor from his ruminations. Once again, Devin had requested an audience.

"Open new communication," Victor said. "Send response: affirmative. Time: immediately."

He pressed an icon on his monitor to disable the security cameras in his office and another to lower the shades on his four glass walls. Family matters did not need to be seen by outsiders. The shades, made of thin, double-sided monitors, were set on a video presentation that occurred two hours ago. Victor pressed a third icon, and the shades flicked to a view of the skyscrapers outside, making it look as though he sat in a glass box above the Silk Sector.

The comm in Victor's office beeped. "Devin Colt,

requesting entry."

"Enter."

The door opened. Devin walked in, and the door closed behind him.

Victor, still reclining in his chair, raised his eyebrows. "Well? What's so urgent?"

Devin's eyes were attentive, but otherwise his face was expressionless. "I take it you've heard about what happened to Jane yesterday?"

"Of course."

"What she described was real. There was a machine, a robot that—"

Victor cut him off with a heavy sigh. "Devin, I understand you're in denial about her mental health, but that will not help her recover. Have you been looking for a suitable mental health professional?"

"She doesn't need a doctor. Listen, she called me while she was being pursued, and I saw everything. I even recorded the conversation, but it was erased from my slate. Whoever sent the machine was careful to cover their tracks."

Victor frowned. One thing that never changed about Devin was that in his eyes, his sister could do no wrong. He'd always sided with her, no matter how imprudent her actions. It seemed she had Devin convinced her fantasy was real.

"Suppose I believe you," Victor said. "This powerful criminal who can design intelligent machines and falsify documents without detection, why would he expend all this effort on a nice seminary student whose only connection to anyone important is the fact that he is Jane's friend? If this criminal planned to ask for ransom, why not take Jane herself?"

Devin started to reply, then hesitated.

Victor gave him a severe look. No doubt he saw how ridiculous his arguments were. "Devin, I know it's difficult for you to accept, but the truth is that your sister suffered a disturbing psychotic episode. Now, I find it... touching... that you care about her enough to want to believe her."

Devin's mouth firmed into a hard line. "I can see why you don't believe me. Perhaps it would make more sense if

I begin with what I found out about Sarah. Please hear me out. It will seem... strange."

What does Sarah have to do with any of this? Victor nodded, wondering where Devin was leading.

"It began the day I proposed to her, about three weeks ago." Devin paced as he spoke, his gaze fixed straight ahead. "Her reaction was... She froze. Completely. It was only for an instant, and she recovered as though nothing had happened, but there was something different about her. She seemed... cold. It wasn't like her."

How is this relevant? "I see."

"My first thought was that something had her terrified, that she had been drugged or conditioned or otherwise mind-controlled."

Perhaps Jane isn't the only one suffering from a form of paranoia. "That's rather dramatic."

Devin stopped pacing and faced Victor. "With all due respect, sir, you didn't see her. What she did was unnatural. So I began looking into her background to see if someone was threatening her. However, our efforts were often blocked by—"

Victor held up a hand. "Stop. With whom were you working?"

"I enlisted the help of a Netcrew."

Agitation jolted Victor. He bolted upright. "You mean to tell me that after *everything* that happened, after your mother was *murdered*, you still engage in these criminal activities? Cybergangs, demons, dangerous criminals— how *dare* you fall back in with them?"

Devin's expression was unreadable. "I haven't. Please, sir, just let me finish."

———— ❦ ————

Victor Colt was an important man. Zenevieva shouldn't have been spying on him through the transparent walls of his office. But her desk was right next to it, and her view unobstructed. Was it her fault she was only human?

Several minutes had passed since Devin Colt had walked in, looking uncharacteristically distracted. Zenevieva was glad Mr. Colt hadn't lowered his shades. She wished she were capable of reading lips.

What were they talking about? Was Devin reporting a

coworker he disliked? She'd heard a rumor that he had issues with his manager. Maybe he was trying to talk his father into having the troublemaker fired.

It's not fair. I've been slaving away at this company longer than he's been out of school. Why wasn't I born into a powerful family? Then maybe I'd be on the fast track instead of always getting overlooked.

Sure, he was good at what he did, but Zenevieva was still annoyed at being outranked by the boss's son. She had more experience and was probably smarter. Plus, unlike Devin, who was known to have dabbled with the dark side, Zenevieva had a squeaky clean past.

I guess doing everything right is no match for good old-fashioned nepotism.

She rested her chin in her hand as she watched. Mr. Colt appeared relaxed in his throne-like chair. Devin stood before him, speaking furiously. It was an interesting sight, since Devin was always so collected and businesslike, the model of corporate conformity. The glimpse of what lay behind all that perfection fascinated her.

Such a good-looking young man. Maybe he's a spoiled prince, but at least he's easy on the eyes. Tall? Check. Dark? Check. Handsome? Very. It's enough to turn any woman into a cougar...

Mr. Colt slammed his desk. The office was virtually soundproof, but from the intensity of his movements—and the fact that she could hear anything at all—Zenevieva could tell he was yelling. Devin was startled into stillness for a moment, but then he shouted just as heatedly.

Zenevieva leaned forward with excitement. A Silk Sector king and his wayward prince in a duel of words—what she wouldn't give to be a fly on *that* wall!

Devin pulled a black laser gun from beneath his jacket and aimed it at Mr. Colt's face.

She gasped. She had *not* expected *that*. Frozen, she stared at the unimaginable scene. Mr. Colt held his hands up. He looked as though he was trying to tell Devin to calm down.

Zenevieva wondered why the watchmen hadn't sounded the alarm, why the internal defenses hadn't activated.

She finally found it in herself to speak. "S-Security!"

Several coworkers who had been buried in their work glanced at her. Their puzzled expressions soon changed to horror when they saw the scene in Mr. Colt's office. They scrambled to contact Quasar's security team.

Bang.

Zenevieva screamed.

Mr. Colt sprawled back in his chair. A laser burn blackened his skin and blood dripped down his face from a point on his forehead.

Devin stood over him with the gun in his hand, his dark eyes coldly blank.

The security team surged toward Mr. Colt's office. Zenevieva turned to look at them.

You're too late.

She turned back to the office, morbidly curious as to what would happen when Devin was caught—what he would say, why he had done it.

Devin was nowhere in sight.

CHAPTER 5

RUNAWAY, PLEASE STAY

COPY-PASTE... HOW THE HELL WAS Jane supposed to care about a bunch of numbers when her best friend was captive, and no one even looked for him?

Pull-data... Adam had been *kidnapped*, and everyone thought she was crazy. Daddy would cover it up. He couldn't let word get out that his own flesh and blood was losing her mind!

Agitation wouldn't begin to describe Jane's horrible desire to screech and go on a murderous rampage. It had taken every ounce of willpower she had to show up at work that morning. She didn't know how much longer she could keep it together.

Screw everything!

Jane looked away from her monitor in an attempt to quiet the screaming in her head. She tried to use her usual balm of gazing at the fish tank, but all it did was remind her of the Fringe warlords and how one of them might be torturing Adam.

Why would they want him? He was too damn *nice* to be involved in anything sinister. For freak's sake, he wouldn't even skip class! He'd be useless for ransom. He'd grown up in an Ibaran orphanage, for crying out loud! Did he fit a profile for some sick scientist's human experiments? Did a lunatic cult think he was their messiah?

They all think I'm crazy. Pretty soon, I will be!

Jane's gaze drifted toward a vent by the internal defenses. It must have led to the utility conduits—like the ones no one believed she'd crawled through less than twenty-four hours ago. Ever since, she'd fixated on every vent she saw, wondering what went on in there.

Why the hell are they so small? Is someone up there right now, fixing some piece of Quasar's mainframe? Is this whole building crawling with midget technicians?

Jane gripped the stunner in her pocket, wrapping her fingers around the small, gun-like device. If only she'd remembered to bring it the day before. Maybe she could have fried the machine's circuits. Then maybe Adam *would* be on a retreat.

She wished fiercely that she *were* just crazy. Why couldn't she just be crazy?! And why the hell wouldn't anyone believe she wasn't?

Far from giving up after getting home the previous day, Jane had acquiesced to a violent energy and called the Via facility on Dalarune, intending to prove that Adam wasn't there.

"*So where is he?*" she'd yelled.

The unfortunate receptionist was practically in tears after suffering half an hour of her verbal abuse. "I'm sorry, Miss Colt, but as I said before, our policy is very clear. Anyone who participates in the retreat is not to be contacted under any—"

"*Stop repeating yourself.*" Jane banged the table near the screen in her living room. "My request is simple: *I want to talk to Adam Palmer.* If he *is* on Dalarune, then why can't anyone find him?"

"He is most certainly here, and our records show—"

"And *why hasn't anyone spoken to him?*"

"Miss Colt, you must know by now that isolation is paramount to—"

"I don't care, and I'm not getting off the line until someone either lets me talk to him or acknowledges the fact that *he's not there!*"

She'd been in the middle of a list of threats when Devin arrived at her apartment. Furious about what he'd said at the police station, she'd ignored his request for entry. He'd disabled her lock and come in anyway, then gently told her it wasn't the receptionist's fault Adam was gone. As with Counselor Mayuri, he'd apologized for Jane's behavior, attributing it to mental instability, while Jane clenched her hands behind her back to keep from punching him.

As soon as Devin ended the communication, Jane turned her interrogative fury toward him. "Are you gonna tell me why the *hell* you lied to the Counselor? Or have you really bought into this freaking charade? Are you here to tell me I'm *actually* crazy?"

A glimmer of gold caught her eye. The Via pendant Adam had given her lay on the table. Jane picked it up, choking back the sudden urge to burst into tears.

Devin put a hand on her shoulder. Jane looked up at him. "Just tell me. What's going on? I lied because I trust you, so why don't you trust me?"

He let go and walked toward the window. "It's not that I don't trust you. I... I don't know what to tell you. Whoever took Adam is very powerful. All you're doing by insisting on your story is signing yourself into a psych ward. It's your word against the records, which the authorities view as solid evidence."

Jane slammed the pendant onto the table. "That's so *stupid!* With the Collective screwing up Netsites day in and day out, you'd think people would stop treating their freaking computers like the Absolute!"

"They left no trace, but I have people looking anyway." Devin stopped by the window and faced her. "Don't worry, Pony. I'm handling it."

Jane was too weary to tell him not to call her Pony, and she got the message: keep out, little sis.

She approached her sofa and crumpled onto its plush cushions. "All right. Fine." She'd had enough aggravation for one day. Her brother had never let her down before.

He probably saved my life today. Speaking of which... "Devin? How'd you know so much about the dorm? The conduits and whatnot?"

Devin looked out at the round form of Kydera Minor, their world's sister planet, which glowed blue-green above the city's brightly colored nightscape.

"Nothing I knew was a secret. Any of it can be found in the civil engineering section of a public library." He paused. When he continued, it was in the same artificial manner Jane had watched him use during work presentations. "I

59

used to have an interest in the construction and internal layouts of urban buildings. They may look different on the outside, but most share the same features. I assumed the dormitory was like any number of other structures built around the same time by the same company. It's practically common knowledge."

Weird. Devin had dabbled in many esoteric subjects— Fringe justice, interstellar flight, Net activism—but buildings seemed absurdly different from the rest. "C'mon, bro. What're you hiding? Dad said you used to... um... get in trouble. Were you really a thief?"

He turned away. "It's all in the past. Please, Jane. I... I don't want to talk about it."

Jane was accustomed to her brother's moodiness, but his current distress was different. There was something deeply sad about his tone—whatever he was thinking about caused him profound pain.

She nodded. "Okay."

* * *

Okay. It's okay. Devin said he'd handle it and he will. Everything's gonna be fine. I just have to get through today.

Jane brought her attention back to the office and noticed something unusual. Her coworkers twittered like schoolgirls spreading rumors. She stood but couldn't see anything out of the ordinary. "What's happening?"

A nearby woman answered, "They've locked down the upper levels. No one knows why."

A team of Quasar's gray- and violet-clad security personnel burst into the office area. The building's intercom emitted a loud *beep*, causing the chatter to desist.

"Attention: all Quasar employees. There has been a security breach. Please remain at your desks until further notice."

Jane sat down, her previous agitation displaced by an intense craving for knowledge. She wasn't *too* worried, and neither, it seemed, were the others. Such alerts were rare but no cause for alarm. The past few times had been due to sensitive documents being accessed without permission.

Maybe the Collective hacked us and is forcing us to give money to poor people.

Jane smirked. *That* would be hilarious. The company would probably have the internal defenses shoot their own central computer rather than let *that* happen.

Run-app, copy-paste...

"Jane Colt?"

A laser gun hung from a reflective black belt. Jane looked up to see a harshly buttoned black jacket. Two uniformed members of the Kydera City Police Department towered over her with stern, no-nonsense expressions.

"Yeah?" *What did I do?*

The closer one, who had steel-gray hair and even steelier gray eyes, responded, "We're here about your brother."

"Devin? Why?"

The second officer, whose rusty-iron hair framed severe features, motioned for her to stand. "I think you should come with us."

But... But why?

Jane nervously followed the two officers. She sensed her coworkers staring as the officers escorted her into an empty office.

The iron-haired officer shut the door and gestured at a chair. "Please, Miss Colt, you should sit down for this."

Jane complied. "What's going on?"

"I'm afraid we have some bad news." The officer spoke in a sharp, matter-of-fact tone. "About fifteen minutes ago, your brother shot your father in the head point-blank. He managed to elude Quasar's security, and we are currently conducting a manhunt for him."

Jane stared. The words didn't register. They were too bizarre to be real. She refused to react.

The steely-eyed officer put his hands on the armrests of her chair and leaned toward her face. "Do you know where he might have gone?"

Behind him, the iron-haired officer narrowed his eyes. "Did you know of his intentions? Has he contacted you?"

Jane shrank. The usual denials filed through her mind. That was absurd. That wasn't happening. That couldn't be true.

Instead of answering, she looked past the officers. Her gaze once again wandered toward a vent in the ceiling.

The steely-eyed officer straightened. "Miss Colt, I ask that you please cooperate."

Jane forced her eyes down. "I—I don't believe you. You—You're wrong. It *couldn't* have been Devin. You must... there must... you're *wrong*."

The officer pursed his lips. "I understand that this is difficult for you. However, the evidence is indisputable. There are several eyewitnesses. Furthermore, Quasar's security team found your brother's gun at the scene. It was recently fired. He disappeared before they could apprehend him."

Jane shook her head vigorously. "They're all wrong. Devin would never... this can't—"

The iron-haired officer held up a hand. "Please, Miss Colt. Stop denying the facts."

That's it. Jane stood and matched the officer's severe expression. She didn't care what kind of authority he or his companion had. They were idiots, and they no longer frightened her. "Listen, Devin *loves* our father. He's the perfect son, does *everything* according to Dad's wishes. Which is why you're wrong. I don't care what the evidence says."

The officer's expression hardened. "I'm afraid your brother hasn't been honest with you. We have information about his past that shows he had ample reason to resent your father."

Jane, focused again on the vent in the ceiling, didn't hear what the officer said next. Something up there had moved.

Devin?

The officers noticed her gaze and started to follow it—

"*Nooo!*" Jane deliberately collapsed forward between the officers. Both rushed to catch her.

"Miss Colt!"

She let her body hang limply against them and kept her eyes closed. She flopped like a ragdoll when they placed her in the chair, allowing her head to roll from side to side. One of them shook her and the other yelled her name. Someone slapped her across the face. She opened her eyes, startled. Steely eyes peered at her. She twisted her face into a pathetic expression.

"Tell me it's not true! It *can't* be! You *must* be lying! *Tell me it's not true!*" Jane wasn't exactly a good actress, but her being a girl meant the two manly officers wouldn't question her sobbing.

"Miss Colt—"

"He can't be dead! *Daddy can't be dead!*"

As she said it, the facts finally hit her. She choked as the realization swelled in her chest. She sobbed for real, covering her face in an attempt to block out reality. *It can't be...*

"Please, Miss Colt." The officer sounded uncomfortable. "Please don't cry."

"Your father is alive." The other sounded equally uncomfortable. "The medical team reached him seconds after the incident and placed him on life support."

Dad's alive. Jane desperately wanted to stop crying. She hated the uncontrollable way it shook her body and left her gasping for breath, the way the tears cascaded down her cheeks and fell, drop by drop, onto her chest. Most of all, she hated the damn snot. One of the officers handed her a tissue. She blew her nose rudely, certain she must be the ugliest crier they'd ever seen.

The gray-eyed officer knelt down to her level. "We apologize for upsetting you. Are you all right?"

Jane slumped in her chair and didn't answer.

"Do you know—?"

The other officer tapped him on the shoulder and shook his head. The veneer of severity remained, but to Jane, he was just another guy, his professional iciness thrown by a girl's tears.

The reddish-haired officer handed her another tissue. "How are you feeling? Do you want us to call someone for you?"

Suddenly livid, Jane bolted up. "Who're you gonna call? My dad? My brother? Adam? I'm *fine*. Just leave me alone."

The officer stiffened. "Miss Colt, we still have some questions for you."

"Look, I am not a suspect, I am not a witness, and I am not a victim." She imitated the poisonously soft tone her mother used to employ. "I talk to Devin once a month if I'm lucky, and I don't know *anything* about his life. He didn't even tell me when he got engaged to Sarah DeHaven. So unless you need a blood relative to perform some creepy ancient seeking ritual, I suggest you stop wasting your time and mine."

The gray-eyed officer stood and looked uncertainly at his companion, who gave him an I-don't-know expression. He attempted to resume his steely countenance. "Are you sure you don't know where he might have gone?"

Jane kept her toxic you're-an-idiot gaze fixed on him.

The officer cleared his throat. "That will be all for now. Thank you, Miss Colt. Again, we apologize for upsetting you. If your brother contacts you, we ask that you report it immediately."

Both officers turned and left.

Jane had completely and unapologetically lied. She knew *exactly* where her brother would be. As soon as the officers were out of sight, she went to find him.

The Colt estate, called Serena, had been in the family for generations. Jane and her brother had grown up there. They'd flown across the continent every morning for school in Kydera City and returned at night. Their parents had hired pilots to escort them, but whenever they weren't around, Devin bribed the pilot into taking the day off. He would fly Jane to school himself before running off to do no good. Some of her fondest childhood memories had taken place in those moments when it was just the two of them.

Once a thriving plantation, Serena's fertile fields had long ago been left to nature, with tall blue and purple trees rising out of the rich brown earth. Acres of untamed forests surrounded the palace-like glass and steel mansion. The only other sign of civilization was the hangar by the glittering white landing pad.

Jane loved the wilderness. It was so vast, she'd never run out of places to explore. She could live there a hundred years without knowing all the secrets of the ever-changing land or the buried riddles left behind by previous inhabitants.

Twelve years before, Devin had hijacked one of the groundskeeper's open-air hovercars and told Jane to come with him. He had something to show her.

Jane jumped into the passenger seat, excited that her big brother was hanging out with her. "Where're we going?"

"It's hard to describe." Devin strapped himself into the driver's seat beside her. "Buckle up."

Jane snapped the safety harness in place, and it tightened to accommodate her.

The hovercar soared over the fields and into the trees, speeding around the crooked branches deep into woods. Jane laughed, thrilled at the danger and eager to be let in on a secret. Devin stopped the vehicle in a clearing covered in tall waves of azure grass.

She gasped. "I didn't know this was here!" She leaped out and ran into the grass, which was almost as tall as she was. Ducking down, she teased, "You can't find me!"

"C'mon, Pony. Aren't you a little old for these games?"

Jane giggled and curled up to make herself as small as possible. She looked at the sky, which was pale red and streaked with a gold filigree of clouds. It was late. Mom and Dad would be so mad if they knew she was out.

Nah, they'd probably get mad at Devin for taking her. They were always mad at him. She didn't understand why.

Devin's face came into view, expression annoyed.

Jane grinned sheepishly. "Sorry, couldn't resist."

He smiled and held out a hand. Jane took it, and he pulled her up.

The clearing was square-ish, surrounded by trees with violet leaves woven together to form a dense canopy.

"Where are we?" Jane asked.

"A part of Serena that no one's been to in a really, *really* long time." Devin approached a jagged brown stone jutting out of the ground near the hovercar. He put a hand on it. "See this?"

Jane scampered up to the rock and inspected its dirty edges. "What about it?"

"Look closer."

Was that stupid ugly rock the big secret? It didn't look special. She pouted with disappointment. "I don't get it."

Devin gripped the stone with both hands and twisted

hard until it rotated. The ground jolted.

Jane jumped. "What was that?"

He placed his hands on her shoulders and turned her to face the clearing. An enormous rectangular section sank into the ground. It split down the middle, and the two halves parted, revealing a dark cavern.

Jane's eyes widened. "Whoa! Cool!"

Was it an underground lair? A secret passageway? She was too excited to ask as she tried to make out what lay down there.

The remaining sunlight illuminated a small, teardrop-shaped spacecraft in the cavern. Two large engines, rounded in the front and pointed at the ends, protruded symmetrically from its sides. Its dark blue finish, unmarked and banged up, looked worn and world-weary, as though the ship had been through far more than it had been meant for.

Jane stared at it. "Why's there a beat-up Blue Tang all the way out here? What's this cavern thing?"

"An underground hangar used hundreds of years ago during the civil war," Devin replied. "No one's been here since."

She grinned eagerly. "Can we go down there?"

"Sure." Devin climbed into the hovercar and motioned for her to join him. She buckled herself back into the passenger seat. He drove the hovercar down into the dingy cavern.

Several dark tunnels led from it, and bits of metal littered the rough floor. *A real civil war hangar! Cool! Wait a sec...* "Hey, Blue Tangs weren't invented until *way* after the civil war. Who put this one down there?"

"I did." Devin parked the hovercar beside the Blue Tang and got out.

Jane followed, bubbling with questions. "Where'd you get it? Did you fly it? When'd you learn to fly starships? Is it like flying air transports? How'd you find this place anyway? Why—"

"Slow down, Pony!" Devin laughed. "I found this place about a year ago. I was digging through Serena's old records and found out this area was once a rebel base. They kept a bunch of their transports here. I tried to find out more, but Mom changed the password to the records library." He rolled his eyes. "Apparently, I was wasting too much time there."

Jane smiled teasingly. "Oh, Devin, why're you always getting in trouble?"

His expression hardened.

She waited for him to say something. After about a minute of silence, she gave up. "So, where'd you get the ship?"

Devin blinked, as though waking from whatever reverie he'd been in. "Black market. It's unregistered, unmarked, and so old nobody's looking for it anymore. Even if they are, they'll never find it. They'll never find... me."

Huh? "What're you talking about?"

Devin looked up at the ship. "I'm running away, Pony. I've got it all stocked up with food and stuff. I don't even care where I'm headed."

Jane frowned. *I don't get it.* "When're you coming back?"

"I'm not. I just wanted you to know so you won't worry. Don't tell Mom and Dad until after I'm gone, okay?"

Jane still didn't understand. "But... But you have to come back. Your *life* is here."

Devin snapped his gaze toward the ground. "No, it's not. I have *nothing.*" His tone was harsh. "Every decision is made for me. Mom and Dad hate me, especially Dad. Nothing I do has ever been good enough. *I'm* not good enough. I'll *never* be good enough. I might as well be a malfunctioning robot to him—some obedient *thing* that should do what *he* wants, even when he's not ordering me around. I can't stand it. I finally found another way out, and I'm taking it."

Jane finally understood. Her big brother was leaving. Once he did, she would never see him again.

A hated tingling pricked her eyes. *No. Big girls aren't supposed to cry.* "Don't be silly. Mom and Dad don't hate you. Besides, they're not everything. What about your friends?"

Devin scowled. "Colts don't have friends—only networks."

That was a line their father had often spoken. Jane bit her lip so hard it hurt, trying to stop the forceful swelling behind her heart.

Her brother walked toward the ship, away from her. "I have no future here. You're the only thing in this whole fucking system I care about."

She ran and grabbed his arm. "So take me with you!"

"No, Pony." Devin shook her off, but didn't look at her. "You've got a shot. Where I'm going, it's gonna be dangerous. I'm probably gonna be a criminal, become a smuggler or something for the Fringe crime bosses. It's no place for kids."

Jane stomped in frustration. "*You're* a kid!"

"I'm sixteen. I can take care of myself. But not you too." Devin's back was still turned to her.

"*Then don't go!*" Unable to hold back the flood any longer, Jane hurriedly rubbed her eyes. "Tell me what's wrong, and I'll fix it! *I can fix it!*"

Her brother was leaving—forever.

Suddenly, she was a little girl again, curled up on the ground and crying so hard she shook. She felt alone, deserted, as though he was already gone. "Devin, don't go! Stay, Devin! I'll fix it, I promise! I'll fix *everything!* Just stay!"

"Pony, please..." Devin was beside her, but she couldn't hear what he said through her sobbing.

She buried her face in her knees and fought with all her might to stop the tears. "Stay, Devin. I'll fix it, I will. Please stay. Don't leave me alone here. Don't leave me behind."

Devin embraced her. "I'm not going anywhere." He spoke with a soft tension, almost like anger. "You don't need to fix anything. I'm sorry—I thought—I didn't... I'd never abandon you, Pony, I swear. I swear to you, I'll never leave you behind."

Jane slammed the air transport she'd stolen from her father's apartment beside the jagged brown stone. Afraid of being followed, she'd made several haphazard wrong turns, making for one helluva bumpy ride. Her stomach was tied in knots, but she didn't care. She opened the door, jumped into the azure field, and ran toward the parted gates.

The Blue Tang rose out of the ground.

"Devin!"

Jane realized her brother wouldn't be able to hear her and pulled out her slate. He didn't answer her call.

The Blue Tang's engines revved up.

Don't you dare. Don't you dare*!*

The Blue Tang moved away from Jane. She ran after it.

You jerk! You're not leaving without me!

"Devin!"

Devin glanced at the section of the Blue Tang's split viewscreen that showed his sister running after him.

I'm sorry, Pony.

He knew how furious she must be, how betrayed she must feel. In her eyes, he had killed their father. He hated leaving her with that belief, but it wouldn't take the police long to figure out he'd run to his childhood home. Even if he did have a few minutes to spare, he didn't know how he could convince her it wasn't true.

Jane stopped and looked up at the ship with an expression that was so lost, so hurt. Devin tried to ignore her but couldn't.

Dammit.

He lowered the Blue Tang, brought it to a hover, and pulled a lever. As the door opened, a ramp extended into the field. Devin got up and ran down it.

Jane raced toward him. "I did my best, but they might've followed me anyway! Go! *Go!*" She shoved his shoulders, trying to push him back up the ramp.

Shouldn't she be screaming accusations at me? Devin didn't move.

She stopped shoving. "What the hell are you waiting for?"

He looked her in the eye. "I didn't do it. I swear, Jane—"

"I *know*, you idiot! How *dare* you leave without me? Now, let's get outta here!"

What? "You're not—"

Jane punched him in the arm. "You *swore*, Devin! You *swore* you'd never leave me behind, and that kind of thing doesn't expire because we're not kids anymore. Now, let's *go!*"

"*Goddammit, Jane!*" Devin immediately regretted shouting when he saw Jane's startled face. He tried to speak in a more measured tone. "Listen, I have to disappear. It would be a mistake for you to—"

"*Don't* pull any of that fake crap on me!" Her eyes flashed with something between rage and despair. "If you leave me too, *I have nothing.*"

Devin desperately wanted her not to come, but he could tell by her expression he had no choice. He ran back up the ramp. Jane darted past him. He reached the cockpit in time to see her jump into the pilot's seat.

He caught her hand as she reached for the controls. "You're not piloting."

"Aw, all right." She got up.

Devin returned to the pilot's seat. He pushed the lever that folded the ramp and closed the door. Jane sat down in the copilot's seat beside him. He looked at her in disbelief.

She gave him that impish smirk of hers, and he couldn't help smiling. "You can't get rid of me that easily. Oh, and don't worry about Dad. He's on life support at the hospital, and if anyone can pull a miracle, it's him. Just watch, he'll be up and lecturing us in no time."

Dad survived. Devin closed his eyes in relief. "Good."

"How could you think I'd believe them?"

He opened his eyes. "Like you said, I'm an idiot."

He engaged the engines and pushed the steering bars forward. The Blue Tang blasted off over the violet trees, beyond the faded atmosphere, and into the stars.

CHAPTER 6

THE TARGET

COMMANDER JIHAN VEGA OF THE Megatooth warship *RKSS Granite Flame* had been disappointed at her assignment to the Lyrona zone of Kydera Major. It was the most uneventful zone in the entire system due to the extreme security of the many high-profile organizations headquartered there. But patrolling it was her duty, and she was damn good at it.

She paced before the immense viewscreen at the front of the circular bridge, regarding the darkening side of the planet. Around her, clean-cut subordinates monitored their respective stations, which lined the rounded walls with monitors. Her red uniform was so stiff she sensed every crease as she moved, and her raven hair was in a knot so tight she could feel tugging at the back of her neck. Her long sleeve started riding up. She tugged it down. The golden brown cuff almost blended into her dark skin.

That day had been another quiet one. In the distance, the *Shining Voice* and the *Invictus*, two other formidable Megas like the one she commanded, hovered above their posts, their long, triangular forms silhouetted against the atmosphere. A rounded Blue Chromis supply ship, which she'd granted permission to enter her zone, drifted across the view. A trio of flamboyantly colored Dragonets zipped out of the atmosphere in the direction of the twin planets Myretta and Keptella.

"Commander Vega!"

Commander Vega snapped her face toward the communications officer. She knew how piercing her gaze was, with her sharp black eyes and prominent cheekbones. The officer would have only dared to call her if he had something important. "Yes?"

"We are receiving a communication from the command center in Kydera City."

An unmarked junker blasted off in a restricted area. *That must be what the communication's about.* "Put it through."

A window appeared on the side of the viewscreen, revealing Admiral Landler's sternly lined face. "Commander Jihan Vega of the *RKSS Granite Flame*, you are to pursue an unmarked Blue Tang that recently left the Lyrona continent and detain its pilot."

"Yes, sir."

That was all. That was all there ever was. The communication ended.

Commander Vega ordered the weapon's officer to deploy Betta Unit J, one of the ship's swarms of small attack drones. Judging by the sorry state of her unarmed target, it was probably another hooligan on a drug run, a mere pest unworthy of the attention of fighter pilots and certainly too inconsequential for the *Granite Flame* itself. "Open a communication with the target."

"Yes, Commander."

"Attention." Commander Vega addressed the Blue Tang. "You have entered a restricted area and are being pursued by Betta attack drones. Halt immediately."

A minute passed without a response. "Set the Bettas on surround. Stop the target, but do not open fire." She turned to the pilot. "Follow it."

On the viewscreen, red fan-shaped drones flew toward Jane. Beyond them lay the immeasurable sea of scintillating stars that never failed to fill her with wonder. She should have been scared, but she was eager to see what would happen next.

Devin took one hand off the controls to pull his slate out of his pocket. "Can you give me a hand?"

Jane took the slate, unfolded it, and pressed it into a dock by the controls. "See? Aren't you glad I'm here?"

Devin said to the slate, "Activate voice controls."

The slate beeped. "Voice controls activated."

"Open Net communication. Contact name: Corsair."

Jane cocked her head. "Why don't you use the Blue Tang's communications?"

Devin turned the ship. "They're broken."

"Of course they are." She snickered. "What a piece of crap!" She looked at the slate and saw a typed-out message:

Corsair: Still working on it.

Who's this Corsair character? She was about to ask when Devin yanked the steering bars. The Blue Tang flipped over, racing in the opposite direction from the one it had been traveling in.

"*Hey!*" The artificial gravity took a few seconds to compensate. Jane felt as though liquid sloshed in her head.

"They were trying to surround us. That was the only way out." Devin reached for the control touchscreen in front of him. "I'm engaging lightspeed. Brace yourself."

He swiped a command. The ship lurched forward, flattening Jane against the back of her seat. The Bettas matched speed and attempted to block the Blue Tang. Devin twisted the steering bars. The ship spiraled.

Jane grabbed the straps of her safety belt. "You're insane."

"Drones run on pre-programmed algorithms. 'Insane' is the only way to shake them." As if to highlight his point, he zigzagged his course.

Dalarune's aquamarine surface glowed in the distance. For a moment, Jane forgot where she was as her thoughts turned to Adam. "Machine logic is no match for human irrationality." *Has he really only been gone a day?*

A drone barreled toward the viewscreen. She gasped and squeezed her eyes shut.

"Don't be afraid." Devin sounded unfazed. "The Bettas aren't firing. They're only trying to slow us down."

Jane opened her eyes. "I know. I'm not afraid." *Lies.* Her excitement had given way to anxiety five near-crashes ago. She'd stifled many girly yelps in her attempts to hide her fear.

She concentrated on her breath to keep her stomach in its place. After several minutes of spinning and staggering, she became accustomed to the crazy movements.

Lurch, spin, flip...

"How long can you keep this up?" *Oops. Didn't mean to say that out loud.*

"As long as I have to." Devin didn't seem to mind the question. "Won't be long before we pass through Ibara's orbit."

Flip, spin, lurch...

Jane took a moment to appreciate the absurdity of what she witnessed. There was her brother, still looking like a tool in his black suit, flying a junker that should belong to a Fringe smuggler when he looked as if he should be heading to a board meeting. And there she was beside him, in her inappropriately colorful office dress, feeling as though someone had copy-pasted her out of her desk and into a salvaged wreck. *What the hell.*

Devin turned from the viewscreen to face her. "It was the internal defenses."

"Huh?" A Betta flew at the ship. Jane pointed in alarm. *"Look out!"*

Devin flipped the ship in time to avoid collision. "I meant Dad. He was shot by his own internal defenses."

Jane couldn't believe the nerve of him. He wanted to tell her what had really happened—while running from attack drones sent by a giant warship and pulling the most crazy-ass maneuvers she'd ever seen. "I don't think now's the time! If—"

"Jane, please!"

Although she could only see Devin's profile, she recognized the desperation in his expression. She shouldn't fight it. She was also just as anxious to know what he wanted to tell her, so she bit back her protests.

Devin glared at the viewscreen. "I tried to tell Dad that everything you'd said about the machines was true. He started going off at me. I didn't want to hear it, so I turned away from him. I noticed the internal defenses were online. I tried to warn him, but—"

A drone barreled toward the ship, and he yanked the controls much harder than necessary. "One of the guns fell out of the defense system. It was mine. I don't know how it got there, but I realized what it looked like, and I ran. Someone must've hacked the monitors on the walls and projected a fake video of me. I listened in the conduits when they interviewed witnesses. They were so certain, like they'd expected something like that to happen. They said they always knew there was something wrong with me."

Jane clenched her fists. "They're liars. *I* didn't believe it. I saw you in the conduits. The officers were about to see you too, but I distracted them. Pretended to faint like a ninny and forced them to take care of me." She smirked. "You're welcome."

Devin shot her a rather impressed look. He snapped back to the viewscreen as a drone collided into the Blue Tang from above. "*Shit.*"

A jarring alarm buzzed. The cockpit door slammed shut as the Blue Tang's emergency protocols engaged. Jane heard the ominous *whoosh* of air leaving the ship and prayed the door would remain sealed. Devin scrambled to engage this-or-that control. The viewscreen filled with red as Bettas surrounded the Blue Tang.

The whooshing ceased, and the alarm stopped. Jane exhaled when she saw the message indicating the hull breach had been sealed off.

The Bettas blocked the Blue Tang in every direction as Devin tried to break their perimeter. "Dammit, Jane! What the hell am I supposed to say when they ask why you're here?"

Jane watched the drones in nervous silence. An idea struck her. "Hold me hostage. Use me to make them back off."

Devin looked horrified. "*Hell* no."

"I'm serious! Tell them you'll shoot me if they don't let you go. They'll have no choice! Here, use my stunner. It'll look the same from a distance." She reached into her pocket.

Devin grabbed her arm. "Hell no."

Before she could ask why the hell not, a new message appeared on the slate from Corsair.

Corsair: We've hacked the *Granite Flame.*

"How long?" The slate transposed Devin's question.

Corsair: Very soon.

Jane reread the previous messages to see if she'd missed something. "What're you talking about? What's the *Granite Flame*?"

"The warship controlling these Bettas." Devin released the steering bars. "Citizen Zero's been working on getting into the Mega's central computer."

"Citizen Zero? Is that like Earth Zero?" The long lost and virtually mythological planet from which humans had originated seemed like an odd name to reference, even for a demon.

Jane realized Devin was allowing the ship to idle in the sphere of Bettas. "Why're we sitting here?"

He watched the viewscreen. "Just wait."

<hr>

The fugitive's daring antics impressed Commander Vega. The Blue Tang had made it past the orbit of the Kyderan system's outermost planet. Pity the hooligan was a good-for-nothing criminal. In another life, he or she could have been a decent fighter pilot. *What a waste.*

"Broadcast a message to the target."

"Yes, Commander."

Commander Vega addressed the Blue Tang. "You are under arrest. You are to—"

The Bettas broke their formation. A gap opened in the perimeter, and the Blue Tang zipped through it.

"*Follow it!*" Commander Vega glared at the weapons officer. "Why did you break the perimeter?"

The officer looked flustered. "It's not me, Commander. I didn't—"

"Commander Vega!" the cybernetics officer called. "The *Granite Flame's* central computer has been hacked, and the command code for the Bettas has been changed. Someone else has control of them now."

"Get them back!" Commander Vega barked.

"We're locked out of the system, and it's going to take several minutes for—"

"Do not waste my time with excuses for your ineptitude." Commander Vega turned crossly back to the communications officer. "Open a communication with the

Shark Team."

"Yes, Commander!"

"Shark-Three and Shark-Seven," she said, calling for two of her Barracuda fighter pilots. "Man your ships. Pursue and disable the target."

Two quick voices responded over the comm, "Yes, Commander!"

Commander Vega pursed her lips in vexation. Why had the command center not informed her that she pursued a demon? She had assumed her target was a lone hooligan. Judging from the cyber attack, he or she was more likely a member of that bothersome Netcrew, the Collective. A similar incident had occurred a few months ago in the Lithran system. The command center should have warned her that hacking was a possibility.

Irritating, but not a serious threat. And still not worthy of direct confrontation with the *Granite Flame*, which would surely result in the junker's destruction. Commander Vega abhorred waste. No matter what the hooligan had done, it most likely wasn't worth wasting ammunition and certainly not lives.

"Commander Vega, Shark-Three and Shark-Seven have taken off."

"Good. Open a communication with them." In accordance with protocol, Commander Vega gave the two pilots an overview of what they were permitted to do along with a strict warning not to harm any bystanders.

When she was finished, the customary "Yes, Commander!" was missing.

"Shark-Three and Shark-Seven! Did you hear me?"

"I... not... to... you... hear..." Static obscured the voice.

"Commander?" The cybernetics officer sounded nervous. "The hackers tampered with the communications."

"*What*?" Commander Vega strode over to him. "How are those hooligans still in our system?"

Before the cybernetics officer could reply, the communications officer said, "Commander Vega, we are receiving an anonymous written transmission."

Must be the hooligans. Commander Vega spun toward the viewscreen. "Put it through!" The damage had been done. Little risk remained in allowing an anonymous communication.

A message typed out in real time:

We are Citizen Zero. We are the strangers here. We believe in neither nation nor religion, neither good nor evil. We believe in freedom, not authority. There is no system that cannot be corrupted, no truth that cannot be questioned. If you think we are fake, remember ideals are never fake. If this is a mistake, we will make one more mistake. Beliefs cannot break. We will do whatever it takes.

Commander Vega scowled, piqued at the arrogance and sanctimony the self-righteous delinquents displayed in their trite so-called mission statement. "Who sent this?"

"We're trying to trace them, but they are very heavily veiled."

"Keep trying. And open a communication with the command center."

"Yes, Commander."

Admiral Landler's displeased face appeared on the viewscreen. "Yes, Commander Vega?"

"I want to know whom I am pursuing." Commander Vega restrained her frustration and kept her tone firm. "Because I was not informed of the nature of the target, I was unprepared to deal with the cybernetic attacks that are now preventing me from controlling my drones or communicating with my fighter pilots. Had I known of this possibility, I would have taken extra precautions to prevent these occurrences."

The admiral knit his bushy eyebrows. "The target has no known current affiliations with cybercrimes. We were not aware of this possibility. Recent intelligence indicates that the target was once involved in a cybergang, but we were not informed until now."

Commander Vega understood. When she had received her order to pursue, nobody had known *who* was in the junker, only that he or she had entered a restricted area.

Admiral Landler looked down at something out of Vega's view. "It is now confirmed that the target is a twenty-eight-year-old male named Devin Colt. The details are being transmitted to your ship."

Devin Colt's case file appeared in a new window on the viewscreen. The more Commander Vega read, the more furious she became. He was not some punk hacker. He was a cold-blooded murderer who'd shot his own father out of uncontrolled rage. The thought of a child executing his parent disgusted her. *Monster.*

She narrowed her eyes. "Sir, I request permission to use deadly force to prevent the target's escape if necessary."

Admiral Landler nodded. "Granted."

* * *

A long line of interstellar tunnels that served as bridges between star systems stretched across the forward view. The sight reminded Jane of a cosmic string of black pearls. Warped images of the stars and ships shimmered at the center of each moon-sized sphere. The tunnels' edges glistened with distorted visions of vehicles passing through, which quickly resumed their proper forms as they sped toward the Kyderan system or curved into other tunnels.

Ever since the Bettas had gone offline, the Blue Tang had been playing a kind of ring-around-the-rosie with two Barracudas. Since the Blue Tang couldn't outrun its pursuers, the only choice was to stagger toward the tunnels. The Barracudas had only fired a few light blasts aimed at the Blue Tang's engines, which Devin had avoided. Clearly, they'd been ordered not to use any *real* force.

The communication window on the slate shifted. Jane looked over at it, wondering what Corsair, whoever he was, had to say.

Corsair: I tried powering down their lightspeed engines, but now that they are aware of us, they have taken precautions and are making things more difficult.

"Can you blind them?" Devin asked.

Corsair: Let me see.

He's good. Jane didn't know much about computers, but it had to take some fancy digital footwork to mess with a Megatooth warship.

The Barracudas changed course, heading away from

the Blue Tang.

What's happening? "Devin, the Barracudas... They're leaving."

Confusion crossed Devin's expression. "Corsair, did you call off the Barracudas?"

Corsair: No.

Jane glanced briefly at the image of the warship behind them. She doubled back with alarm. "That's not good."

The enormous red Mega seemed to expand as two long rows of cannons extended from its sides.

Holy shit. "They can't— They wouldn't—"

The warship fired a bright red blast. Jane screamed. The Blue Tang pitched violently as Devin veered to avoid getting hit. More blasts came. He twisted the ship to dodge them.

Jane turned to prayer once again, reverting to facetiousness to deny the danger.

Dear Absolute One, You can't let me die yet. I still owe You that motet, remember? So be it, truly. This would make Adam so mad...

An abrupt lurch. Jane crashed forward. The straps of her safety belt cut into her torso. "This is *absurd*! Why would you send a huge freaking *warship* after a stupid little junker like us?"

Something was hit. Alarms blared.

"*Fuck this.*" Devin directed the Blue Tang straight at the tunnels, weaving slightly, but otherwise making a line toward his target. Blasts hit the ship from behind. More alarms. Bits of the damaged hull formed a dusty trail.

Jane watched in horror. "What are you doing?"

No response. Devin's gaze fixed on the viewscreen. As the Blue Tang drew closer to the distant swarm of civilian transports and supply ships by the tunnels, she understood.

We're gonna make it. She clenched her safety straps. *We're gonna* make it.

The blasts stopped. Puzzled, Jane looked at the rear view. The warship no longer fired.

Corsair had left another message:

Corsair: I have successfully disabled their targeting systems and their viewscreen. They won't be able to track you or fire without risking civilian casualties.

Jane's muscles seemed to melt from relief. She released the straps. "He's a *genius*! Tell Corsair I send him a hug!"
Devin smiled. "My sister sends you a hug."

Corsair: Uh... Thanks?

"How long before they get their systems back?"

Corsair: Not long.

A few minutes later, the Blue Tang reached the edges of one of the interstellar tunnels. Devin steered the damaged junker into the spherical vortex. It instantaneously sent the ship out of the Kyderan system and across the galaxy.

CHAPTER 7

FALSEHOODS FOUND

THE TUNNEL SPEWED THE SCARRED Blue Tang out at the edges of Iothe, one of the most peaceful systems in the Interstellar Confederation. Devin, tired of the alarms' ringing and buzzing, flipped a switch to disable them. His first thought was to leave Jane at one of the nearby floats—self-sufficient space habitats about the size of a city—and insist that she return to Kydera before he put her in any more danger.

Jane seemed to figure out his intent when the ship turned toward the IC system. Devin tried to tell her that *he* was the target, and that it wasn't her fight.

"Not my fight?!" Jane bolted upright in her seat. "Some sonuvabitch *shot my father* and *framed my brother*, so you bet your toolish ass it's my damn fight! You can be a jerk and knock me out or something, but if you do, I'll get my own black market starship and continue looking for the deranged asshole, anyway!"

You're not winning this time, Pony. Devin tried to ignore her as he veered the ship.

Jane unbuckled her safety belt and stood. "Hey!" She shoved his shoulder. "Do you really expect me to go back to my stupid boring life as if nothing happened? Turn this freaking ship around!"

He continued toward Iothe. "Dammit, Jane, you could've been *killed*! I won't let—"

"You have *no say* in what I can and can't do!" She pointed at the viewscreen. "Like I said, you can dump me on some float if you want, but if you do, it's not the freaking Mega you should be afraid of!"

"Listen—"

"*Try me*! Leave me there and see what happens!" She put her hands on the armrests of his seat, leaned down, and looked him in the eye. "You know what? *Do it*! I'll find the bastard *myself*!" She pushed off the armrests and crossed her arms.

Damn, she actually would. The thought of his kid sister running around some shady sector alone looking for black market ship dealers made Devin more than edgy. It would be better to keep her near.

Besides, he realized suddenly, No Name had already targeted everyone around her. *She could be next.* The thought filled him with dread. At the very least, having Jane along meant he could protect her.

With a sigh of surrender, Devin maneuvered the Blue Tang back toward the interstellar tunnels. Jane smirked in triumph.

He gave her a stern look. "Just promise me one thing. Promise you'll do as I say, no matter what."

She raised an eyebrow. "What is this, your version of pulling rank?"

"Jane—"

"All right, all right!" Jane rolled her eyes. "As long as it doesn't involve me getting abandoned, then fine. I get it. We're fugitives. Big Brother knows best." She plopped down in the copilot's seat. "Where're we going anyway?"

"The Viatian system."

Devin steered the Blue Tang through one of the interstellar tunnels, curved it around, and brought it toward a different tunnel. He wove the ship in and out of the shortening lines of spheres as he went further and further from the IC systems.

As the minutes stretched into hours, his thoughts turned to Sarah. He wondered what she would think of all this, if she would believe him—and if he would get the chance to see her again and ask.

About three months before, Devin had taken Sarah to the Colt estate to meet his father. He'd planned to introduce them for some time, but something had always come up that prevented Dad from joining them. This time was no different.

Devin ended the communication with his father and turned to Sarah. "Once again, Quasar needs his immediate and undivided attention. I'm sorry to have dragged you all the way out here for nothing."

Sarah smiled good-naturedly. "It's all right. I've wanted to see Serena since you first mentioned it. Show me around?"

"Sure." He considered giving Sarah the general tour of the historic mansion, then decided to show her something more personal.

He took her out in a hovercar to his favorite childhood haunt: a waterfall deep in the forest, which poured into a wide, clear creek. Large gray stones and tall trees with red and violet leaves surrounded it.

Devin stepped out of the vehicle. "I used to spend hours here." He approached the rushing water and felt the cool mist carried in the wind. "If I was still enough, the wildlife would come out of hiding. I watched them go about their placid lives, wishing I could be like them—living in simple, unthinking bliss. It was one of the few places I could go to escape the pressures of being a Colt—the expectations, the orders, the perpetual disappointment."

Sarah, who walked beside him, put a hand on his arm. "That must've been hard."

"I ended up where I was supposed to." He stopped near the edge of the creek.

"Do you like what you do at Quasar? You never talk about work."

Devin kept his gaze on the waterfall. "There's not much to talk about. And it doesn't matter whether I like it. It's my life."

They all think I'm perfect. He thought about the many times his father and those he called friends had commented on how he seemed to have it all. *The ruse must be working.*

Sarah said slowly, "I know you're not as detached as you pretend to be. You keep your face expressionless whenever you're not conforming to a corporate ideal, and it's as if you're hiding yourself. Why is that?"

Devin looked at her. "I'm not like that with you, am I?"

She smiled. "Of course not, baby, that's why I asked. You're different with me than with everyone else. Why do you always shield yourself?"

"I'm not shielding myself." Devin turned away and walked along the water. "I'm protecting the rest of the world from who I really am." He focused on the rough stones lining the creek. "I was a disaster until about six years ago, wreaking so much havoc it was absurd. By the time I realized the hell I found myself in was my own damn fault, I'd already devastated my family, all because I was trying to find myself, to find *purpose*, like every other stupid kid with grand delusions. All I could do was stop caring about the things that drove me to that insanity, and I've kept it up to this day. If there were a drug that could remove emotion, I'd take it in a heartbeat. Forget meanings, forget beliefs. I just want to live."

He stopped. Those were thoughts he'd long ago decided should remain unspoken. Why had he confessed them? No one could know that he projected the mask of a well-adjusted professional while hollowing out what lay behind it, cutting away every passion, every hope until he wondered what remained.

He turned to face Sarah. She gazed at him lovingly, sympathetically. That she could love him made him believe there must be something good left within. He often felt as though she'd been sent by a supernatural force to save him from his capacity for madness.

He smiled wryly. "You probably think I'm insane."

She approached him. "I'm glad you told me. I want to understand you."

"You won't like me much once you do."

She hooked her arm around his. "Why would you say that?"

Devin turned his gaze back to the waterfall. *Might as well finish.* "Because I'm still a disaster. I've fixed the outside as best I can, but there's something deeply wrong with me. The only chance I have to overcome it is to simply do what's expected."

Sarah was quiet for a moment. "I think I understand. Life's passions cause more pain than anything else. They leave us wanting, but not knowing what for, reaching

85

for an ideal of living beyond mere existence, but no idea as to how to attain it. But you don't have to give up on happiness. In fact, look at all the good things you have— stability, security... someone who loves you. Remember that, and you'll realize you're already in the haven you seek. *This* is paradise."

She put a willowy arm around him and kissed him softly. "I love you."

"I love you, too." *More than I could ever say.*

Sarah leaned her head against Devin's shoulder, and he put his arm around her. For a while, he simply stood there with her, watching the never-ending flow of the waterfall and listening to the whispers of the wind against Serena's untamed beauty.

You're right, Sarah. Now that you're here, this is paradise.

———————

The Blue Tang exited the interstellar tunnel closest to Viate. It was the only tunnel in the region and several light-hours from the star system. A message appeared on the slate:

Corsair: The Seer is on Viate-5. He's a junk dealer there, and he said he'd contact you when you get closer to the planet.

Devin entered the planet's coordinates into the Blue Tang's navigation system and set the ship on autopilot. Considering what it had been through, the ship's ability to function normally seemed miraculous. BD Tech hadn't been exaggerating when they said they made the best.

His pursuers wouldn't figure out which of Kydera's hundred or so tunnels he'd gone into, let alone which of the vast number of possible combinations he could have taken. *We'll be all right for now.*

Jane had been silent since they'd left Iothe. She sat curled up in the copilot's seat, lost in a melancholy reverie.

"Hey," Devin said. "You okay?"

Her eyes glistened. "He's gonna make it. Victor Colt is all about being the exception."

Devin didn't know how to respond. The anguish he'd felt when his father had been shot had nearly overwhelmed him, and he could only attribute his quick escape to survival instincts he hadn't known he still possessed. The only thing he could do to hold himself together was to accept that father might as well be dead and deal with it.

But that didn't mean his sister had to. If blissful denial would help her handle her grief, then he wasn't about to shatter her hope.

Jane released her knees and sat up straight. "I'm not just being optimistic. He *will* recover."

Devin tried to smile. "Of course."

She clenched her fists. "Do you think it was the same bastards who assassinated Mom? Dad said it was a gang controlled by a Fringe warlord. Do you think that warlord went after him too? Is that why we're out here?"

Devin looked away. He owed Jane the truth, and he swore to himself he'd tell her someday—but not that day. She'd never speak to him again, once she knew.

"Devin?" Jane peered into his face. "What aren't you telling me?"

He ignored the question in her eyes. "Viate is one of the few Fringe systems that isn't run by warlords. I'm hoping to trade the Blue Tang for a lesser model. Anything made by BD Tech is worth a lot out here."

He paused, trying to find another topic. "You wanted to know what Citizen Zero is, right? They're an anti-establishment Netcrew, and Corsair's one of their most influential members. Most people dismiss them as paranoid conspiracy theorists, but they're probably some of the best demons out there. You saw what they did to that warship."

Jane took the bait, and the question in her eyes brightened into curiosity. "How *did* they do that?"

"They hack into corporate or government computers to steal documents, looking for proof of corruption. I asked Corsair to see if they could get the command codes to the ship patrolling Lyrona. I knew I'd have no chance of escaping otherwise."

"Who's Corsair anyway? How do you know him?"

Should I lie? After a moment of hesitation, Devin said, "We were both members of a cybergang called Legion. It was years ago, back when... back when I was younger."

"You were in a cybergang?" Jane leaned over her

armrest. "Is that what Dad meant when he said you used to get in trouble?"

"Yeah." It wasn't the whole truth, but it wasn't a lie either.

Jane must have sensed his unease, for she didn't ask for details. She rested her head against the back of her chair. "So Citizen Zero's like a smaller version of the Collective."

"They started out as an offshoot of the Collective, but now they're suspicious of it. Several of their members were unveiled and killed after getting involved with one of the Collective's leaders, Mastermind."

"Hacking can get you *killed*?" Jane stared in wide-eyed disbelief.

Devin smiled, amused by her doll-like expression. "You don't know much about cybergangs, do you? They work for Fringe warlords, drug kingpins, interstellar mafias— the most dangerous people in the galaxy. There's a lot of overlap between the two, but unlike Netcrews, who operate entirely online, cybergang demons often get physically involved with their jobs. Being unveiled and having their identities revealed is the worst thing that can happen to them."

"So who's Mastermind?"

"No one really knows. He first showed up about twenty years back and made a hobby out of messing with the Fringe systems. The things he did determined the outcomes of their turf wars. The Collective revered him for it. He disappeared about ten years ago, after several of the demons he worked with turned up dead."

Jane grabbed her armrest and pulled herself forward. "What were they doing? What happened to Mastermind? How was he was so powerful? What—?"

"Slow down, Pony! I don't have the answers. I don't think anyone does."

Devin had more to tell her, but he couldn't bring himself to say it—not yet. In a matter of days, his world had flipped inside out, until it had splintered entirely, leaving him a wanted fugitive with no idea as to how he could begin piecing it back together.

He might have to run for the rest of his life, because of what he'd discovered about Sarah. And hell, after everything, he still might not be able to save her.

Jane seemed to notice the change in his mood. She grinned sheepishly. "I know I ask too many questions but... just one more?"

"All right."

"Got anything to eat in this joint? I'm starving!"

Devin turned toward the storage compartment behind his seat. He opened it, pulled out a package of food, and tossed it to her.

Jane ripped it open and regarded the nutrition bar inside with distaste. "This has been here for twelve years, hasn't it?"

"Yup."

"Nutritionally-optimized, chemically-preserved, imperishable space food?" She wrinkled her nose. "Lovely."

Devin gave her a joking glance. "It's not too late to return to civilization."

Jane looked as though she was considering going on a rant. She raised an eyebrow with a distinct expression of not-impressed. "Really, bro? You really want to go down this path again?" Her expression turned serious. "Look, I know I shouldn't be here. I know I'll probably... slow you down or get in the way or something. But I also know there's a chance you'll have to disappear forever and..." She attempted a smirk. "I think you remember what happened the last time you tried to ditch me like that."

Devin nodded, recalling the intense guilt he'd felt that day, when he'd carelessly betrayed the one person who had always been there for him, never asking for anything.

He checked the time on the control screen. It wasn't late according to the time zone they had come from, but it would be the middle of the day local time when they arrived at the Seer's location.

"You should go back to the living quarters and get some rest. We won't have much time once we get to Viate-5, and I know how grumpy you are when you're sleep-deprived."

Jane popped the last bite of her nutrition bar into her mouth. "What about you?"

Devin shrugged. "I don't sleep much."

"All right, then." She balled up the emptied food wrapper. "Don't wanna wander around some sketchy desert planet in a daze."

She got up and pressed the button to open the cockpit door. She started to leave, then poked her head back in. "You won't try to ditch me while I'm out, right?"

"Of course not."

"Okay, g'night!" Jane left the cockpit, and the door closed behind her.

Devin gazed at the growing yellow star that was Viate, wondering how he would tell her the rest. It wasn't fair keeping her in the dark, with her friend involved. *Damn, why'd they have to involve Jane?*

He should have told her as soon as he'd found out, but he hadn't been able to face it himself—the truth he'd sought since Sarah froze like a marble statue.

Despite his attempts to tell himself everything was fine, Devin had soon given in to his internal disquiet and searched for answers. He had known he'd need help and contacted Corsair.

Corsair had apparently been using voice commands when he responded:

Corsair: Yeah, sure, no problem. But you're gonna need another Netname so the bad guys won't know what you're up to.

Anonymous: I'm already anonymous.

Corsair: Yeah, right. Any nov could trace you, and if you level up to someone like me, you're completely exposed. For example, your name is Devin Victor Colt, you work at Quasar Bank Corporation, and you live in the FFC Residential Complex in Kydera City.

Anonymous: You already knew who I was.

Corsair: You've got a 22-year-old sister named Jane Winterreise Colt who... Is that her? She got kinda hot at university...

Anonymous: Knock it off.

Corsair: Uh... Sorry. Anyhow, I sent you an attachment.

Devin opened the file and found a list of the Netsites he'd visited along with specific details about his most recent activities and movements, as well as similarly extensive facts about his father, sister, fiancée, and even some of his colleagues at Quasar.

Anonymous: Point taken.

Not long after that stunt, Corsair had sent Devin a special communications program, one that would scramble his signal, and created a veiled online identity for him.

Archangel: I told you to use "Anonymous."
Corsair: Everyone and their pet alien calls themselves "Anonymous." You need something with flair.
Archangel: Why "Archangel"?
Corsair: Because you're the great avengin' angel who took down all the demons in Legion.

Devin had been annoyed, but there was nothing he could do about it other than shake his head at Corsair's peculiar sense of humor.

Their first move had been to look through Sarah's records and learn all they could about her. Devin considered following her to see if she was secretly meeting someone nefarious. He abandoned the idea when he realized it could put her in danger. An online investigation would keep her physically out of it, for the time being.

No matter how careful he and Corsair were, they were always caught. The amorphous entity known as No Name seemed to target their efforts specifically. Corsair had used that information to recruit Citizen Zero, whose members were eager to find out who No Name was and why they would care so much about Sarah DeHaven.

Corsair: I'm telling you, it's because she isn't "Sarah DeHaven." She's got background info in all the right places, but every time we try to check them out, No Name blocks us. The few bits we've managed to get our hands on are elaborate fakes. School records, performance creds— nothing's older than a year. No Name must've created them. Why else would they be so keen on keeping them hidden?
Archangel: We can't be sure.
Corsair: Come on. Okay, so they're amazing fakes that

could only have been exposed by us geniuses, but they're still fakes.

Devin hadn't wanted to believe it, that the love of his life had been lying to him since the day they'd met. No Name prevented Citizen Zero from *proving* that "Sarah DeHaven" was a false identity. Yet, he couldn't ignore the possibility.

I love you, Sarah DeHaven. But who are you?

In the meantime, he hid his apprehensions from Sarah. He couldn't help sensing something different about her, as though her warmth had been replaced by a precise imitation.

Once, Devin had entered Sarah's apartment unannounced and found her staring at the wall, frozen in a cold, emotionless state. A split second later, her face brightened into a demure smile. The moment had been so quick he hadn't been sure it had happened.

Sarah walked up to him. "Baby, what are you doing here?"

"Just wanted to see you," Devin said. "What were you doing?"

"Thinking about us." She put her arms around his neck and kissed him. "I'm going to marry you, Devin. Doesn't that make you happy?"

Contrived, as though someone had trained her to act out the motions of the person he knew as Sarah DeHaven. Nevertheless, Devin was certain that the Sarah he'd fallen for, the one who was so full of passion and understanding, was still there behind that mechanical mask, and that once he found the bastards controlling her, things would go back to the way they were.

But with no way to know who she even was, the only thing Devin could do was at least find out whether Sarah was under the influence of mind-altering drugs. When her producer called a few minutes later and she turned her attention to her slate, he quietly went into her bathroom, pulled a few black strands from her hairbrush, and placed them in his pocket.

This is absurd.

He wondered if all that time he'd spent in Citizen Zero's virtual forums turned him into one of those paranoid conspiracy theorists.

"What are you doing?" Sarah stood behind him, reflected in the mirror.

"It was windy outside," Devin said sheepishly. "I wanted to make sure I didn't look messy or anything."

Sarah blinked, expressionless. A moment later, she laughed. "You've spent far too much time in the corporate world. Trust me, I don't care if you're a little disheveled."

The laugh had been unnerving, almost unnatural.

In spite of his doubts—and questions as to his own sanity—Devin had asked Corsair to locate someone with a background in drugs affecting the human mind. Corsair pointed him to a round-faced graduate student at one of Kydera City's small colleges. Finding her and bribing her into testing the hair sample was easy enough.

"Seems clean." The grad student handed Devin the results of a preliminary test. "No signs of the usual drugs."

Devin scanned the document on her slate. "Run some extra tests. It could be hard to detect."

The grad student took the slate back. "Whatever you say. This could take a while, so make yourself comfortable."

Devin leaned against one of the empty lab benches and pulled out his own slate to see if Corsair had made any progress in discovering Sarah's true identity.

Corsair: Still nothing. Check out the Collective's forum. There's something you've got to see.

He followed the link Corsair had sent him. The Collective had released several confidential documents stolen from a secretive government science program, one that developed technologies potentially in violation of the IC Tech Council's regulations—and basic ethics. One of the technologies was a brain implant that could control a person's thoughts and movements.

Corsair: The implant was completed years ago. She could have had one this entire time. They say they were only experimenting with it as a potential educational enhancement. You know, so people can download info instead of learning it. I think that's bullshit.

Devin should have been surprised. Instead, he found himself numb. It made sense, more than any explanation involving drugs or behavioral conditioning. The only way to find out if Sarah had an implant was to scan her. Considering her refusal to go to the hospital previously, he knew she would never agree to one.

The grad student returned. "All right, mister, where'd you get that sample?"

Devin continued reading the leaked documents. "Why?"

"It's got to be the best fake I've ever seen."

He looked up with a start. *Fake?*

The grad student held up a vial containing Sarah's hair. "Can't even tell it's synthetic. Not until you get down to the molecular level. Whoever created it must be a *genius*. Wish it'd been me. But fake is fake, even if it is brilliant."

Devin suppressed a shudder. Corsair had said the same thing about Sarah's identity.

The grad student chuckled. "Some frizzy-haired princess must've paid the moon for this. Shame to see all that brainpower go into a beauty product, don't you think?"

"Yeah." Devin wondered if the fact was relevant. Women were always doing strange things to their hair. He handed the grad student his slate. "Have you seen this?"

"Seen what?" The grad student flipped through the pages of leaked government documents. Her eyes became round. "Holy *shit*, that's creepy! How's *that* okay when the Tech Council's banned so much other stuff? The mind-control program I worked in was drug-based, and it was to get criminals to cooperate. Wait a sec, do you know someone who's being mind-controlled?"

"I'm not paying you to ask questions."

"Right." She handed the slate back. "Well, I'm a chemist, so I don't know anything about brain chips, but I can tell you this: if someone has one, it won't be easy to find. If the government has people wandering around with microcomputers in their heads, they won't want them finding out when they go for a checkup. It's the same with the truth serum implants I worked with. Let me tell you, the only way to find one is to use one of those hardcore body scanners, like the kind they use when they capture terrorists to make sure they're not bugged or something."

Devin paid the grad student for her help and her silence. As he left the lab, he contacted Corsair to ask how he might obtain such a scanner, legally or otherwise.

Corsair: Thought you'd gone straight.
Archangel: Not anymore. I understand if you don't want to get any more involved.
Corsair: Back out when I'm so close to exposing a government conspiracy? No way! But the kind of tech you're talking about is only used by the most secretive agencies. Even *I* can't get into their systems.
Archangel: What if I went directly to the people who designed the scanners? Ocean Sky or BD Tech?

Ocean Sky and BD Tech proved impenetrable. Instead, Corsair had used his special skill set to direct Devin to an independent inventor working on something similar—and who had an assistant drowning in student loans. It hadn't taken Devin long to track him down and bribe him into letting him borrow a prototype of the new scanner.

The rotund young man handed Devin a sleek metal device. "It won't give you the results directly. You can download the data onto a slate and get someone else to interpret it for you. It's kind of complicated, and... Um, I'd do it myself, but then my boss would see that I'd accessed his computer... I don't want to get in trouble, okay? Please get this back, or I'm so dead..."

Devin tucked the device into the inside pocket of his jacket. "Like we agreed, I'll be back in an hour. Who could interpret the results for me?"

"Um, so you need this program... I can tell you where you can download it, if you can get into the boss's computer..."

Devin pulled out his slate.

Archangel: I got the scanner, but I need a program on the inventor's computer to interpret the data. Cover your tracks.
Corsair: Don't I always?

Sarah had been working on her album at Ocean Sky Studios that day. Devin had often talked about dropping by for one of her recording sessions but had always been too busy. The visit provided him the excuse he needed.

He arrived in the middle of a take and watched from behind a soundproof window as Sarah sang, her voice captured by the dozens of slender microphones. A screen behind her displayed detailed analyses of each note in colorful graphs.

Devin knew the song by heart and could almost hear her words through the silence:

"Now they fall, and now they rise.
"Sense breaks down, and silence fails.
"Language dies in rage untold.
"Words may end, but song prevails."

Then the wordless run. From the way Sarah's body flowed with the notes, the way her eyes reflected every rise and fall, he sensed her pouring her soul into the song, just as she had before he proposed.

Perhaps nothing had changed with her. Perhaps *he* was the one being mind-controlled by his paranoia.

His slate beeped.

Corsair: The Collective's forum. *Now.*

He saw the Seer's post.

It concerned artificial intelligence. Not only the programming, but the physical aspects of creating a mechanical being that could look, act, and communicate like a human. The post was shockingly well-informed, detailing potential scientific methods for creating synthetic skin and specific pre-existing computer codes that, if combined, could theoretically mimic human behavior.

Furthermore, the Collective's pooled knowledge of No Name indicated that the entity seemed particularly concerned with hiding the kind of information the Seer described. And No Name had been quick to remove it.

Corsair: So much for the Tech Council's restrictions.
Archangel: This is ridiculous. She is *not* an AI.

Devin thought it an insult to Sarah that he would even consider such a thing. She was *real*—he was certain of it.

Corsair: What if she was replaced by a mechanical lookalike? What if the real Sarah is captive somewhere?

He couldn't fight that one. At the same time, the idea was too unbelievable. False identities and mind control were one thing, but artificial intelligence? Despite the shift in Sarah's behavior, she'd done nothing *robotic*.

His certainties fell away, leaving a sinking feeling that the fantastical had come true. His fiancée had been replaced by an artificial doppelganger. A part of him desperately wanted to forget the whole thing and trust the woman he loved. However, if something had happened to her, he couldn't stand aside and leave things as they were.

Archangel: I need to talk to the Seer. Can you help me find him?
Corsair: I'll try.

Meanwhile, he still had a borrowed—stolen—scanner in his jacket, and Sarah was still on the other side of the soundproof glass, finishing her song.

Strange. Devin hoped that he *would* find an implant. At least that would mean that she was still there. It hadn't fully hit him yet, that she could be gone, that she might have been taken weeks ago.

Sarah glanced in his direction once during the take. When she finished, she opened the door and approached him. "Baby, what are you doing here?"

Devin forced a smile. "Came to hear you sing. I've been promising to visit for ages."

"Don't you have work?"

"Quasar won't collapse without me. Can I join you inside?"

Sarah looked at him blankly. She seemed to do that

a lot—freeze in an expressionless state, save for the occasional blink, then come to life a moment later. Was her AI program calculating? Determining the correct reaction?

Stop it.

As it had so many times before, Sarah's face warmed into a demure smile. "Of course, but you have to be quiet, okay?" She returned to the soundproof room and motioned for him to follow. "Computer, visitors present."

The computer beeped in acknowledgement, and a row of chairs fell out of the wall. Devin took his place in one of them as Sarah walked to the center of the room.

She smiled shyly. "Last time someone sat in those chairs, I was auditioning, and my whole career depended on my being perfect."

"It's only me this time." *She's nervous. Can an AI get nervous?*

"All right, here goes..." Sarah squared her shoulders. "Computer, commence take seven."

"Command acknowledged. Commencing take seven."

Three tangerine lights lit up in front of Sarah, then went dark one by one as they counted down the tempo. Sarah closed her eyes in concentration as the instrumental introduction began.

Devin slipped his hand into his jacket pocket and pulled out the scanner.

Just drop it.

But he couldn't.

"Story older than the skies..."

The scanner whirred softly. For a moment, he thought Sarah must have heard, but she didn't react.

"Maybe something to be heard..."

Devin had no idea how long the prototype scanner would take. Hopefully, it was comparable to the hospital scanners, which took less than a minute to complete their tasks. But it was designed to be compact and more extensive, and it was experimental at best.

"Who is right, and what is real?"

On the tiny screen, the progress bar filled so slowly. He soon forgot his impatience as Sarah's rich emerald voice mesmerized him.

"Words may end, but song prevails..."

The song came to its ruminative conclusion. The scan was barely seventy percent complete.

Fuck.

Devin shut the scanner off and swiftly placed it in his jacket pocket. The last lingering notes of the instrumental coda faded.

Sarah turned to him expectantly. "What did you think?"

"It was perfect."

Devin wasn't sure when he'd nodded off, but he awoke with a start when a waterlogged towel was flung onto his face. He tore it off. *"What the hell?"*

Jane doubled over laughing. "You didn't budge when I poked you, and... I couldn't resist!"

Devin shot her an annoyed look.

She grinned. "I know, I know. 'Oh, Pony, aren't you a little old for these games?'"

"Will you ever grow up?"

"Ah, c'mon, you know you don't want me to."

Devin marveled at her cheeriness. *You're right, Pony. I hope you never change.*

"I didn't just wake you to be annoying." She jerked her head at the viewscreen. "It's time to get off autopilot."

A message blinked across the top: "The ship is approaching the Viatian system. Please switch to manual piloting."

After double-checking the coordinates, Devin disengaged autopilot and steered the ship toward Viate-5.

Jane jumped into the copilot's seat. "Just wondering,

what's your Netname?"

"Archangel. It was Corsair's idea of a joke."

She snorted. "You're so full of it, bro. You *love* it. 'Fess up!"

Devin smiled in response.

"Speaking of Corsair, isn't it a bad idea to use that thing?" Jane nodded at his slate. "Can't it be traced?"

"Not with the program I'm using. Corsair wrote it himself. Each communication bounces off so many random signal towers, it's impossible to find the origin. It'd be difficult to find a relevant message to trace in the first place with all the information flying through hyperspace. The program also forms a wrapper around any Netsites browsed."

Jane opened her mouth, then shut it and pulled her lips in, as if holding back a tidal wave of questions she wasn't sure were okay to ask.

Best to get to the point. "I think a criminal entity called No Name was behind both the attack on Dad and your friend's kidnapping. I should've told you yesterday, but... I guess I just needed the time." Devin explained what he knew about No Name, how they'd faked the seminary documents and how they were the only entity able to stage a crime so elaborately. "Even Citizen Zero wouldn't have been able to hack Quasar's central computer like that. Not to mention the police reports in the ensuing investigation."

Jane's brow creased. "So... So this 'No Name' took Adam?"

"Yeah... and Sarah."

"Sarah? What does she have to do with this?"

"She's... not human."

Jane laughed. "Of course she's not. She's one of those perfect superhumans who make us mere mortals look like failures."

Devin shook his head. "No, Jane. I mean it literally."

Her smile fell. "What're you talking about?"

"Someone took Sarah and replaced her with an android lookalike more than three weeks ago."

Jane simply blinked with a mixture of bewilderment and inquisitiveness.

"I realized something was wrong the day I proposed." He described as objectively and concisely as he could what had happened that day and what he had done next: the background check, the lab, the scanner. "It took Corsair several days because the scan was incomplete, but he got the results: Sarah was completely synthetic. The Seer was right. Someone created a lifelike AI, one that could deceive a person. I should've figured it out sooner."

Jane's look of curiosity became one of sympathy. She hugged one knee to her chest and rested her head on it. "How long have you known?"

"The results came in shortly after Adam was taken. Speaking of which, there's one more thing I've been meaning to tell you."

Jane lifted her chin. "Yeah?"

"Corsair intercepted a transmission to the Barracuda you saw. It was so scrambled he could only make out a few words: 'Adam Palmer is a special case and is slated for replacement.'" Devin fixed his gaze on the viewscreen. "I don't know when they took Sarah. Her replacement was so... perfect. She even sang like her. If she hadn't frozen, I would never even have known the woman I love was replaced by a goddamn robot."

"I'm sorry."

"I think I was set up because what I know could blow apart whatever twisted plan is in motion." He kept his tone matter-of-fact. "Well, I plan to blow it apart anyway. Sarah's been gone for weeks, and it would be nearly impossible to find her now. Adam was only taken the day before yesterday. I'll find him, and then I'll find her."

"Do you think she's—" Jane broke off and pressed her mouth shut.

Devin knew what she wanted to ask. "I don't know if she's even alive. But when shit happens, you just have to deal with it. I intend to find the bastards behind all this and... deal with them." He noticed the alarm in his sister's eyes and said as reassuringly as he could, "By calling the authorities, of course. We'll find Adam. He'll be all right."

"That's my line," Jane mumbled. She let go of her knee and leaned toward him. "Devin, I know you'll always see me as a little girl, but I can handle myself. You don't have to coddle me."

Unsure how he should respond, Devin turned his attention to the controls as the ship approached Viate-5.

He didn't know what he hoped to find there or what the Seer could possibly tell him.

Sarah's voice echoed through his mind with a line from her song: *Faiths adrift in falsehoods found.* There was one thing no discovery, no matter how extraordinary, could change. Whatever he would learn, whatever he would have to do, he would still hold on to one absolute truth: *I love you, Sarah DeHaven. And I swear, I will find you.*

CHAPTER 8

VIATE-5

"THE SEER" WAS A MISNOMER. He did not know why the Collective called him by that name. He had never been associated with any religious establishments or mystical organizations, and he was certainly not capable of seeing the future. Nevertheless, he did not care what he was called as long as he knew he was being referred to. He had abandoned his given name sixteen years and five months before, and he had accepted twenty-eight different monikers since then, "the Seer" being the most recent.

The Seer looked down at his modified slate and regarded a digital image speculating as to his appearance. It depicted him as tall and gaunt. That was accurate, as he was six foot three and a hundred and forty pounds. However, his skin was dark, not pale, and his hair was black, not blond. His broad face and wide nose bore little resemblance to the image's sharp features. He did not understand why the artist made those assumptions.

The Seer sat cross-legged outside his hut, a dusty structure built from salvaged spacecraft parts, on the cracked brown earth. The day was hot, and the air was better outside. A strong wind rustled his loose brown clothing. Tall, jagged mountains, created by millennia of unstable tectonic activity, surrounded an area of about a square mile around his hut. Pale weeds protruded from fissures in the ground. Because he lived in a remote, unnamed desert sector, the Seer only saw other people when he made supply runs to the settlements.

He preferred it that way.

A large warehouse behind the Seer's hut contained spare parts, old machines, and used vehicles. Many people referred to it as a junkyard. That word, like his own moniker, was a misnomer. *Junkyard* implied that the items the warehouse contained were junk. *Junk* implied that the items had no value. The Seer's goods, on the contrary, were very valuable to those who sought them.

The Seer waited for his next customer: a man who went by the Netname "Archangel" and who had sought him since he had revealed a portion of his knowledge concerning artificial intelligence. The Seer had allowed Archangel's affiliate, who went by the Netname "Corsair," to trace him after determining Archangel's true identity. The time had come for someone else to know what he knew. Devin Victor Colt would probably not abuse the knowledge.

The Seer had recently finished communicating with the customer online and had agreed upon an exchange: the information the customer sought and an old, but functional ship of an inferior model in exchange for a damaged Blue Tang. Blue Tangs were scarce in the Fringe systems. They were highly desired for their maneuverability and durability. Once the Seer repaired and armed the ship, he could sell it for a good price.

The Seer swept his left hand across his slate's touchscreen, looking through the Collective's forum posts in search of information concerning No Name. The entity had not impeded the efforts of the Netcrews recently. Members of the Collective speculated that the people behind No Name had retired. That theory was incorrect. The entity had a purpose, and it was dangerous. It had been able to defeat the Seer on several occasions, and the Seer had once been considered the best programmer in the galaxy.

A rumble from above disturbed the air. The Seer looked through the binoculars he wore on a cord around his neck. A dark blue spacecraft entered the atmosphere. Its unmarked hull was heavily damaged. It was almost certainly the Blue Tang he waited for.

The Blue Tang landed on the dry ground about three hundred yards in front of the Seer's hut. The Seer stood and walked toward his dusty brown hovercar. He climbed in, set it to hover two feet above the ground, and drove toward the Blue Tang. He stopped about twenty yards from the ship, got out, and waited for his customer.

The Blue Tang's rectangular door slid open, and a metal ramp extended to the ground. Two people walked out—a man and a girl, both dark-haired.

The man appeared to be in his late twenties, about six feet and two inches tall and a hundred and ninety pounds. His well-proportioned face would be considered attractive by the standards of most societies. Black pants, black office shirt, a rectangular black bag commonly used by urban dwellers on the left shoulder.

The girl was about five feet and six inches tall and a hundred and twenty pounds. She spoke animatedly as she walked, waving her arms to emphasize her words. Her copious wavy hair extended to approximately five inches below her shoulders. She, too, would be considered attractive. Her white dress with a pattern of abstract purple flora flared at her hips and ended about one inch above her knees.

The girl's dark eyes were larger than the young man's, but she had similar bone structure. The Seer determined that the two people shared genetic material. Their outfits were typical of office workers, although the girl's dress was more colorful than ordinarily accepted.

The girl laughed as the young man listed the advantages of working at a place called "Quasar." She smacked him on the arm and called him a liar and a "tool." She placed her hands on her hips—likely indignant. The young man smiled and told her she was right, that he did find the finance industry to be dull. The girl made her hands into fists and quickly raised her arms—triumph.

The familiarity indicated that they were most likely brother and sister.

They were not the desperate refugees or hardened criminals the Seer was accustomed to. Too clean, their gaits too proper, their accents too close to the Interstellar Confederation's ideal standard for the Set Language. The Interstellar Confederation's mainstream society would call them "well-bred."

As the two visitors approached, the Seer's assessments

were confirmed: Devin Victor Colt and his younger sister, Jane Winterreise Colt.

Devin walked briskly toward the Seer and looked directly at his face. "You must be the Seer."

Unsettled by the eye contact, the Seer averted his gaze. "I am. You must be the one who goes by 'Archangel.' Who is your companion?"

Jane shrugged. "Don't have a Netname, so I guess I'm 'Anonymous.'" Her pace was as brisk as her brother's, which was impressive, as she had significantly shorter legs than he did, and the heels of her short black boots were approximately three inches high. "You're different from what I expected, Seer. Some secretive smart guy lurking around, completely untraceable... I thought you'd be a super-spy or something."

The Seer did not understand. He had never interacted with Jane Winterreise Colt. She had no basis around which to form expectations about him.

She stopped about one yard from the Seer, apparently unperturbed by the wind blowing her long hair across her face. "It's *scary* how much you knew. How the hell did you find all that? Why were you even looking? Did you know there was an actual AI out there this entire time? Are there more?"

"Oh, Pony," Devin said. "How many times do I have to tell you to slow down?"

Jane faced him and put her hands on her hips. "And how many times do *I* have to tell *you*? Don't call me Pony!"

"I'll always call you Pony."

"Jerk." She rolled her eyes.

The Seer had seen that movement many times but was uncertain as to its particular meaning. He determined that there was no utility in responding to Jane's questions at present.

"First, I will take you to the ship of which we spoke." He returned to his hovercar, climbed in, and waited for the Colts to follow.

Jane rushed toward the passenger seat beside the Seer and jumped in. "Beatchya!"

Her brother smiled as he got in back.

The Seer tried to understand why Jane would find it

important to sit in the front. If it were to prevent motion sickness, she would not be so gleeful.

People were strange. She was stranger than most people.

The Seer chose to speak of something relevant. "The ship is an Ocean Sky model called a Stargazer. If you wish to elude the authorities of the Interstellar Confederation, I suggest that you avoid all technology manufactured by the Blue Diamond Technology Corporation. The company places tracking devices in everything they manufacture, but it does not inform its customers of this fact. It has probably activated the device in the Blue Tang."

"Freaking *bastards*!" Jane's choice of words indicated that the information angered her. "I don't think there's one in ours, though. Devin bought that black market junker over a decade ago!"

The Seer chose not to correct her misuse of a form of the word *junk*. "The tracking devices are built into the machines' hardware. It is impossible to remove or deactivate them."

He stopped the hovercar next to the warehouse. "Wait here."

He climbed out, walked to the wide door, and put his hand on the security scanner. The door slid upward. He returned to the hovercar and drove it into the warehouse. "The Stargazer does not have any tracking devices. I have modified it to include veiling technologies that prevent it or any devices on it from being traced. In addition, it includes the basic supplies necessary for survival, such as food and water."

Jane looked around. "You're well-prepared."

"Approximately ninety-four percent of my customers seek fast getaways."

"Why would they want a Blue Tang, then? Couldn't they be traced, too?"

"Very few people are aware of the tracking devices. Furthermore, the Blue Diamond Technology Corporation is the only entity capable of tracking their technologies. They are not interested in the activities of petty criminals."

The Seer stopped the hovercar beside a gray spacecraft that stood on a thick landing tripod. The ship tapered in the front. Two cylindrical engines protruded from the back.

The dirty hull was a patchwork of metals from many past repairs. He left the hovercar and approached the ship.

"Is *that* it?" The fluctuations in Jane's voice indicated that she did not mean the question literally. She knew the ship she stood before was the aforementioned Stargazer.

The Seer was uncertain as to what other emotion she implied.

She continued with similar fluctuations, "And I thought our Blue Tang was a piece of crap. This has gotta be the *ugliest* ship I've ever seen!"

"Its appearance does not affect its functionality," the Seer said. "This ship was customized by numerous individuals before I came to possess it."

Devin walked around, examining the Stargazer. Jane gazed at the ship and tilted her mouth into an unusual smile.

The Seer tried to analyze what that expression meant but was unable to draw a conclusion. "I assure you, it is fully operational."

He approached one of the landing tripod's legs and pulled a lever. The ship's door creaked open, and a ladder extended to the ground. Jane climbed in. Devin followed.

After approximately four minutes, they climbed out again.

"Is the ship satisfactory?" the Seer asked.

Devin approached. "Good enough. As soon as you tell me what I want to know, the Blue Tang's yours."

"What do you want to know?"

"Start with who you really are."

The Seer looked at the ground as he considered what he wanted to reveal and how much would satisfy the customer. "First, you tell me whom you really are."

"You know exactly who I am. You wouldn't have let Corsair find you if you didn't."

That was true. "Your real name is Devin Victor Colt, and you were known as 'Hellion' seven years ago. This young woman is your sister, and her name is Jane Winterreise Colt."

Jane turned to her brother. "Hellion?"

"Legion," Devin said. "I didn't choose that name either."

She snickered. "You've got the worst luck!"

The Seer did not understand why she found Devin's

answer amusing.

"So who're you, Seer?" Jane's eyes were round—curiosity. "What's *your* real name?"

"The answer is irrelevant, as that identity no longer exists," the Seer said. "I was once an employee of the Blue Diamond Technology Corporation. They recruited me when I was a student at the University of Kydera Major, because I was the best programmer in the Interstellar Confederation."

"Well, you're modest." Jane's tone carried unusual pitch changes.

"How is that modesty?"

"No, I meant... never mind."

Jane Winterreise Colt was an odd girl. He had stated the facts. Modesty was irrelevant.

She extended her right arm in a sweeping motion. "Please, continue."

The Seer could not comprehend her gesture. He ignored it and returned to the subject. "I worked for the Blue Diamond Technology Corporation for ten years and four months. I had a good life until the company hired a programmer named Revelin Elroy Kron twenty years and six months ago. He had a doctorate degree. They made him my superior. Dr. Kron was an unusual man. He enjoyed engaging in illicit activities. I never understood why. He had access to any information he wanted. He enjoyed manipulating transmissions between powerful criminals. He called himself 'Mastermind.'"

"*Kron* was Mastermind?" The emphasis on *Kron* suggested that Jane did not believe the information.

"Yes." Proof of Mastermind's identity was not part of the deal, so the Seer had no need to offer any. "I worked with Dr. Kron for three years and seven months. He was very cruel to me, and I decided I did not want to work with him. The company would not let me transfer to another division, and therefore, I left."

Jane angled her head. "So what're you doing out here? If you're so brilliant, why didn't you switch jobs or start your own company or something?"

"The Networld says that there are no ex-employees of the Blue Diamond Technology Corporation. That is a good approximation. I am the first employee to leave the company in fifty-seven years. The company gives employees many incentives to remain. They were concerned that I would use my talent and knowledge to aid a competitor. They had no legal means to compel me to stay, but some of their methods were not legal. I was concerned for my safety, and I chose to disappear."

The Seer paused and looked at the ground. "I believe that is enough information about me. I will show you the rest. You will need to take the Stargazer, as the destination is on the other side of the mountains. I will program the ship's computer to only accept control from the two of you. Since No Name is targeting you, this is a necessary precaution."

The Seer climbed into the Stargazer. The Colts followed. He entered the cockpit and pointed to a circular scanner beside the control screen. "Place your hand there."

Jane placed her hand on the scanner first, and then Devin did the same. The Seer gave the computer the commands necessary to lock the system.

"I will take my personal aircraft," he said. "Once I retract the warehouse roof, wait until you see my vehicle, and then follow me."

He returned to his hovercar and pressed a button. The warehouse roof retracted. He drove the hovercar to his small brown aircraft, which only held one person, entered the vehicle, and took off.

The flight took approximately thirty-four minutes. The Seer landed his aircraft in front of a wide, rectangular building in the middle of an open area by the mountains. Dust covered the building's concrete walls, making it appear light brown in color. No one inhabited the sector. Only the Seer had visited it in the last five years.

The Stargazer landed. The door opened, and the ladder extended. The Colts exited the vehicle.

The Seer pointed at the building. "This is an abandoned laboratory and workshop. It was built approximately eight years ago and abandoned approximately five years ago. I discovered it approximately six months ago. This area is a wasteland. No one comes here."

Devin regarded the building. "What does this have to do with what you wrote on the Net?"

"Follow me." It would be easier to show him.

The door to the building was broken and permanently open. It led to a long corridor. The two elevators no longer operated, and so the Seer entered the first door on his left and walked up three flights of stairs. He exited the staircase on the top floor and approached the second door on the right.

The Colts followed the Seer into a rectangular room. A cracked window at the back served as the source of light. Four black tables stood in the center. Another four lined the unpainted walls, which had broken wires protruding from them. The building had once contained a complex central computer.

Jane walked across the room. "What the hell?"

Numerous android body parts lay scattered on the tables and on the floor. They appeared very realistic. The items no longer served any purpose and therefore could accurately be described as *junk*.

A severed android arm lay on the table in front of the Seer. Slashes in its synthetic skin revealed clean machinery underneath. Four artificial eyeballs rolled on the floor beneath one table, disturbed by the wind from the cracked window. The scleras were too clear to pass for human, and the blue irises too bright. A spool of synthetic blond hair sat on the table along the wall to the Seer's left with a piece of synthetic skin next to it. The skin had been cut to resemble a female human face with closed eyelids.

Jane stared at it. Her eyebrows pushed together, and her mouth opened—disgust. The Seer did not understand her disgust. Disgust was a normal human reaction to objects that could potentially carry diseases. The area's desert conditions meant that disease-carrying microbes did not survive.

Devin extended his hand toward the synthetic face, paused, and then touched it. He had no discernible expression. "It's different. Hers was more... real."

His statement piqued the Seer's interest. "Have you encountered an artificial being?"

"Yeah."

The Seer was not surprised to find that his theories had been correct. He needed more information to determine what the presence of artificial beings implied. He chose to let the Colts explore the laboratory further before asking his questions. They would be more likely to answer when they were less distracted by the novelty.

———————◆◇◆———————

Jane approached a table along the back of the room. *This has gotta be the creepiest thing I've ever seen.*

On the table lay a torn human face. Well, an artificial one. Its lone eyelid was folded inside-out, and the black surface of the table filled the place that should have held an eye. Full lips were parted in a lifelike manner. The nose had been ripped in half. Most of the right cheek was missing.

Jane couldn't resist touching it to see how real it was. It felt as though it could have been her own face.

Yikes.

The Seer stood in the doorway, expression blank. Devin looked as though he was trying to remain as straight-faced, but Jane could tell the sight disturbed him as much as it did her. As far as she was concerned, he had every right to be creeped out. Once, his fiancée's body parts had been strewn across a workshop, with strands of her hair rolled up like thread at a cloth factory. Jane pictured Sarah's delicate face lying on some table being perfected by a mad scientist with obsessive precision as he voyeuristically watched a hologram of the real Sarah.

Creepy. That was the only word she could think of. The rest of her vocabulary had fled in revulsion.

Devin approached a table containing several metal rods. "So you knew there were lifelike AIs out there after you found this place."

"I could not ascertain if the artificial beings existed," the Seer replied in a clipped monotone.

He sounds a bit like a robot himself.

"This laboratory only indicates the possibility of an artificial being that appears human. There is nothing here about the programming. All the computers have been taken or destroyed. I do not know who built this building or who stripped it."

Devin picked up a rod and angled it in the sunlight. "Where'd you get the info about the behavioral programs?"

The Seer remained still, his face barely moving. "As I mentioned before, I worked at the Blue Diamond Technology Corporation under Dr. Kron. That is where I obtained some of the information."

Does he always have to say its full name? He's gotta be the weirdest person I've ever met.

"Dr. Kron was obsessed with artificial intelligence. My project under him was to aid in the creation of a computer program that could convincingly mimic human behavior. He did not care that this project violated the Interstellar Confederation Technology Council's regulations. We were not successful. After I discovered this laboratory, I determined that the primary purpose of creating lifelike androids was to impersonate human beings. This would require corresponding artificial intelligence. I found the rest of the information by illegally obtaining material from various companies and academic institutions."

Jane saw an open door to the side and, curious, walked through it into the next room. Android body parts littered that place as well. She approached a round metal object on one of the tables, reached out, and turned it around.

What the hell—what the hell—what the hell.

The android skull had a pale synthetic face plastered on to the front, complete with eyeballs and teeth, meant to be a young man with soft, boyish features. Its mouth hung open in a freakish yawn.

Holy shit.

Jane stared at its fake green eyes. Something about their peridot color reminded her of Adam. She shuddered as she thought about a mechanical copy of him lying in pieces somewhere. *Why Adam?*

She could rationalize replacing Sarah. Sarah was destined to be the next queen of pop culture. Whoever controlled her—or a version of her—stood to make a shit-ton of money. But Adam was just a seminary student, and an idealistic one at that.

"I think I get why you want to be a priest," she'd said during a lunchtime meet-up at the seminary's cafeteria. "Tons of malleable idiots want a leader to cling to, and religious leaders have power over people's *souls*. If you get those dumbasses to believe in you, they'll do whatever you want in the name of the Absolute."

Adam took the chair across from her. "Is that why you don't believe in religion? Do you really think I'm that shallow?"

"Of course not. I'm just saying it'd be a clever thing to do. Imagine all the power you could have."

"I didn't come here to gain power. I came because I believe in the Absolute and in living by the morals taught by the Via."

Here we go. Jane rested her chin on her hand and let her face go slack to emphasize her boredom. "Why don't you become a monk, then? Why bother with all this Counselor nonsense?"

Adam's eyes lit up as they always did when he spoke of what he hoped to do. "There are so many lost people looking for someone to guide them to a life of purposefulness and fulfillment, and I want to be that someone."

Freaking idealist. She wished she could slacken her expression further.

"If I can help even one person..." He smiled good-naturedly. "You're already making fun of me, aren't you?"

"Ah, you're such a goody-goody," Jane grumbled, as she had on many similar occasions. "Why do I associate with you?" *Seriously, why do I?*

"Charity, I guess." Adam bowed his head. "Thank you kindly, Miss Colt, for deigning to fraternize with a 'dumb religious freak' like me."

From conversations like that one, Jane knew that even if Adam were presented with opportunities to brainwash people, he'd rather spend his life building schools for Fringe settlements or something similarly bleeding-heart.

Then again, people listen to those bleeding-heart types.

Maybe his replacement was meant to be part of some kind of money-laundering scheme? Get people to donate to his causes and funnel the cash to the bad guys? What kind of bad guys could build freaking *AIs*?

Devin peered over Jane's shoulder at the android head.

Jane looked up at him. "I guess it all began here."

"Perhaps."

She examined a thin, transparent tray full of synthetic skin. It was the same shade of beige as the head but rougher and older-looking, a version of what its skin might look like if it were capable of aging. Beside the tray, a male-looking forearm stuck out of a box-like machine. Jane pressed one of the machine's unmarked buttons. The android hand clenched and unclenched in movements that were fluid but not too smooth.

It's so real.

Unnerved, she backed away. "This can't be the work of some mafia. You know what? I'll bet it's BD Tech. It wouldn't be the first creepy thing they came up with, and corporations are good at hiding their shit." *I'm starting to sympathize with the conspiracy theorists.*

"The Blue Diamond Technology Corporation is not advanced enough." The Seer had joined them in the room when she wasn't looking. "I am unaware of any entity that is. How lifelike was the artificial being you encountered?"

Devin walked toward the window. "No one could've guessed she wasn't real."

"How did you determine that the being was artificial?"

Devin gazed out at the distant mountains. "I... surprised her one day, and she froze."

"The being did not know how to react. Your action did not compute. You must have behaved highly irrationally."

"Yeah, I did."

"I would like to know more details concerning this encounter." The Seer must not have noticed the distress in Devin's expression. "When—"

"Shut up!" Jane wanted to smack him. "It's none of your damn business!"

"It's okay, Pony." Devin faced the Seer. "Does anyone else know about this place?"

"No," the Seer said. "You and your sister are the only ones to whom I have shown this building. I have determined that I can trust you."

"Oh, that's wonderful," Jane scoffed.

"I am glad that you think so," the Seer said.

I guess sarcasm doesn't "compute."

The Seer continued, "This facility appears to have been used to create ten different models. The ones on this level are the most complete. That is why I brought you here. I have concluded that none of these models were successful.

They would have been easily identified as synthetic by the average human being."

Devin looked as if he was trying, unsuccessfully, to hide his discomfort. "They were experimenting."

"That appears likely. What was the identity assumed by the artificial being you came into contact with?"

Jane seethed at the Seer's lack of sensitivity. "Why the hell should we tell you?"

Devin put a hand on her shoulder and looked directly at the Seer's face. "You said you could trust us. Look me in the eye and tell me I can trust you."

The Seer looked blankly at nothing in particular for several seconds. His gaze slowly shifted toward Devin's. For the first time, he appeared uneasy. "You can trust me." He immediately averted his gaze again. "I ask again: what was the identity assumed by the artificial being you came into contact with? By studying it, I may be able to discover its origins. I believe you desire this knowledge as well."

"Sarah DeHaven," Devin said, tone controlled.

The Seer asked more questions about Sarah. Jane, hating to see her brother so uncomfortable, went into the next room.

It was different than the previous two. It looked more like a chemistry lab than a psychopath's basement. Jane approached a row of test tubes sealed with deep blue stoppers and leaned in for a closer look at the clear liquids inside. Fake tears, maybe? Fake spit?

Ew...

She wondered what other fake bodily fluids an AI would need.

Gross! Why did I go there? Talk about too much information!

She tried to think of something else, and the question that came to mind was: *what happens to the stuff they eat?*

Jane recalled a dinner she'd had with her father, Devin, and Sarah about two weeks before. Dad had wanted to get to know the soon-to-be newest family member.

But I guess the only thing any of us got to know was how convincing an AI can be.

Dad had nodded approvingly at Sarah. "Music is indeed a great profession. You are a very brave young lady."

Sarah lowered her eyelids. "Thank you. My music comes from my heart, and I only hope I can truly move the people who listen to it."

Jane rolled her eyes. *That's what they all say.*

"Jane!" Dad snapped.

Jane realized she'd been caught being rude. "Sorry." *Don't rant.*

Sarah smiled. "I know I sound like a cliché. Every artist says the same thing, that they have a real connection with their creations and seek only the purest form of expression. But that doesn't mean it's not true."

Oh, I know it's true. Trust me, I know better than most.

Dad beamed at Sarah. "I think what you're doing is admirable. Music is a noble and sublime form of art, and I would be proud to have someone so deeply engaged in it as a member of the Colt family."

Jane clenched her fists under the table. *Don't say it.*

Dad frowned. "Jane, if you have something to say, then please, go ahead."

"Okay, why is it all right for *her* to be a singer after all the grief you gave me about composing?" The words tumbled out before Jane could stop herself. *Dammit!*

Dad sighed, as though already weary from explaining something so clear to him. "Sarah is a budding *success*. She is gifted in ways you've never been, and she has secured a contract with a top music studio, proving it was a smart path to take. You, on the other hand, never did more than pen a few odd-sounding tunes."

Jane clenched her fists harder. The only response her father would accept was an apology, something she always ended up doing despite her desire to stand firm.

"You're wrong," Devin said before she could reply. "Jane's music may be harder to understand, but only because it's original and most people are too stuck in their ways to consider anything new. I think she's more talented than you can comprehend."

Jane smiled appreciatively. "Thanks, bro."

Dad had given Devin a hard look. He'd turned to Jane and sighed again. She'd known what he must've thought: "My dear Jane, why must you make things so difficult?"

I'm trying, Dad. I'm at Quasar like you wanted, right?

Jane brought her attention back to the chemistry lab, annoyed that the recollection had turned her thoughts to her father and how unless she followed his will, she was inadequate.

Then again, I had it easy. I was his sweet little angel, more his pet than his heir, and he let me get away with things because at the very least, I could be pleasant and decorative. Can't imagine what Devin must've put up with.

Looking for a distraction from her angst-ridden thoughts, Jane regarded a complex glass apparatus full of deep blue liquid. It seemed to sparkle in the sunlight, and she reached toward it.

"You should avoid contact with the liquid substances. They are most likely unsafe for human exposure."

Jane looked back. The Seer stood in the doorway. She retracted her hand. "Any idea what this stuff is?"

"I am not a chemist." The Seer turned to Devin, who passed him as he entered the room. "I have told you everything I know that is of use to you. There is no more reason for me to stay."

Jane waved. "See you later."

"It is unlikely that I will see either of you again." The Seer left the room.

The Seer exited the building. He did not know why, but he liked the Colts. The girl was very strange, and he found her fascinating. The young man had trusted him with confidential information. The Seer was unsure how he could help.

The presence of artificial beings had been confirmed, which meant he could move forward with testing certain theories. Some of the knowledge on which his theories were based dated back to Earth Zero and had been lost to most over the centuries. Because he was one of the few people who retained that knowledge, the Seer knew why the Interstellar Confederation Technology Council restricted the development of artificial intelligence and encouraged the belief that it was not possible. The council claimed the restrictions were part of an ethical resolution to prevent the creation of artificial life. The Seer had predicted that the preventative measures would not be successful, and that artificial intelligence would come into being a lot sooner than anticipated. In that sense, his moniker was not a misnomer after all.

He had not been as forthcoming as he had professed. He had knowledge about artificial intelligence that he had not told Devin. He also had information about Devin that he had not told Jane. Revealing that information would have served no purpose. However, he was not a good judge of relevance when it came to subjective matters, and he had left information in the Stargazer for the Colts to find.

A small red machine entered the atmosphere. The Seer regarded it through his binoculars. It had an elongated shape that tapered to a point. Gold markings on its cone-shaped engine indicated that it was from the Republic of Kydera. The machine was a Guppy drone, used by larger spacecrafts to probe planets. It did not have a long range. The larger spacecraft would already be in the Viatian system.

The Seer climbed into his aircraft and flew away.

CHAPTER 9

THE HOSTILES

"COMMANDER, GUPPY SEVEN-ZERO-THREE HAS LOCATED the target. He's on the other side of the mountains, in a building that appears to be abandoned."

Commander Vega nodded with satisfaction. "Good. Recall the other probes to these coordinates. We will pick them up later." She turned to the pilot. "Take us to the target's location."

Jane examined a row of android heads, identical but for slight variations, displayed on a metal rack. She recognized the head of an amber-eyed young man as the one she'd seen on the news while waiting at the police station: Jonathan King, the political wunderkind who had obtained a coveted internship in the office of the President Thean, a position whose past alums had become powerful leaders.

Maybe she was wrong. She'd only seen the portrait briefly, and the faces before her looked too much like impeccably symmetrical wax figures to pass for human.

It'd make sense to replace him.

Jonathan King could be President of Kydera someday. Conspiracy theories ran amok in Jane's mind. If No Name sought power and influence...

Then why Adam? Religious domination's the last thing he's good for.

Once, Jane had met up with Adam after his meeting with Counselor Santillian, one of his advisors. She waited on an ancient wooden bench in a hallway lined with portraits of the seminary's most famous graduates.

Adam looked exhausted when he emerged from the Counselor's office. "Hi, Jane. Thanks for waiting."

Jane folded the slate she'd been reading. "Was she actually there this time?"

"No. We spoke via video transmission."

"How'd it go?"

Adam collapsed on the bench. "Not well. According to her, I'm lazy. She told me off for not participating in the so-called leadership groups and missing networking events."

"*Networking*?" Jane laughed. "The seminary's starting to sound like business school."

"Some people treat it that way." He shook his head. "There's always that one person who would do anything to climb to the top, even at the expense of others. I think Counselor Santillian wants me to be like that. She keeps saying that if I applied myself properly, I could go far. And then she harangued me for wasting my time on volunteer work when I have more important things to do."

"Sounds like she's grooming you to run the next mega-temple." Jane stood and approached the portrait of a well-known Via Superior who had scores of diehard adherents. "I don't get why you wouldn't want to be like this guy. It'd be nice to have everyone listen to you, wouldn't it?"

Adam joined her. "I can't say I haven't thought about it. They say the higher you climb, the more people you can help. But I'd rather be out there with them than managing from afar. I told Counselor Santillian, and she called me 'unwise' and my decisions 'unintelligent.'"

"What a bitch."

"That's not fair. She's just pushing me to be my best, and I appreciate that she cares so much. I only wish I knew why she's so determined to turn me into something I'm not. I'd be a terrible Superior."

Jane agreed. Adam was too freaking nice to be one of those religious leaders who aired their loudmouthed opinions and swayed people's views.

So why the hell replace him?

She stared at the row of fake faces. She imagined Adam's face lined up on a lab bench like that. A shudder chilled her. "Hey, Devin? This is really freaking me out. I'm gonna get some air."

Devin didn't look up from the vial he examined. "Don't wander far."

Jane left the room and ran down the staircase. She burst out the building's open door, catching the heat of the Viatian sun with her face. The building had been stuffy, and she was grateful for the wind.

A splotch of red colored the rocky yellow ground near the Stargazer. Wondering what it could be, she approached it.

Why's there a Guppy drone out here? She examined its gold markings. *That symbol looks like the one on that warship—*

"Oh *shit*!" Jane ran back into the building. "*Devin*!" She zoomed up the stairs. "Devin, they found us! We've gotta go!"

Devin ran toward her. "What is it?"

Jane pointed back. "There's a freaking Guppy out there!"

She sprinted down, out, and toward the Stargazer, no easy feat in her stupid heeled boots. *Why the hell didn't I wear flats?*

Devin grabbed her and yanked her back.

The ground in front of her shattered into an explosion of rock and dirt. Jane screamed. A red Barracuda soared across the sky.

Devin spun her toward the building. "Back inside!"

Another Barracuda fired, splattering yellow earth. Jane felt Devin's hand on her back, pushing her along as she ran. Luckily, the building wasn't far. She made it inside as a Barracuda swooped down and blew holes in the concrete walls.

Gripping her wrist so tightly it hurt, Devin dragged her into one of the rooms.

She shook her arm in protest. "Let go of me!"

Devin released her and looked out the window. "*Fuck*."

Barracudas landed outside. Jane rushed into the room across the hall. Devin followed. Barracudas landed on that side too.

She gasped and instinctively grabbed her brother's arm as two cannons emerged from the top of each of fighter ship, aimed straight at the building.

Commander Vega clasped her hands behind her back

and extended her neck proudly. Her Barracuda team surrounded the target. He had no choice but to surrender.

She was unhappy with the method by which she had located the target. A few hours after his escape from Kydera, a representative from BD Tech had contacted her, claiming the command center had asked for the company's assistance. The company had internal methods by which to track the target's Blue Tang, and they'd located the vehicle in a Viatian junkyard. Although Commander Vega was suspicious of the company's motives, it was not her job to pursue the matter.

An unexpected second person accompanied the target: a woman. According to the case file, Devin Colt had no accomplice. The woman was doubtless a Fringe criminal he'd bribed or intimidated into helping him trade his Blue Tang for that pathetic-looking Stargazer. Commander Vega would be more than happy to clear the galaxy of one more outlaw.

The *Granite Flame* hovered above the area before the building, high in the atmosphere but well within the target's visual range. Commander Vega ordered the communications officer to activate the external screen, which was used to broadcast ubiquitous messages. The warship's underside appeared in a rectangular area of the viewscreen. Two red gates retracted, revealing a wide screen that projected an enormous video of her face. Massive speakers extended on either side. Her voice would be heard for miles.

"Attention, Devin Colt. This is Commander Jihan Vega of the *RKSS Granite Flame.* You are surrounded by Barracuda fighters. If you do not surrender, I will have no choice but to fire on you. You will probably not survive. Come out with your hands behind your head. You have one minute."

Jane punched her brother in the arm. *"Do it,* you idiot!"

"Like hell!" Devin strode toward the exit.

She rushed to block his path. "You are *not* going out there."

"She's not giving me much of a choice!"

Jane shoved him back as he tried to go around her. He

might've been willing to surrender, but she sure as hell wasn't. "What about Adam? What about Sarah? How am I supposed to find them and clear your name on my own? Don't you *dare* ditch me, you jerk!"

"Listen—"

"I'll tell them I'm your accomplice. They'll believe me. Goddammit, Devin! If you don't do it, *I swear I'll go down with you.*"

———————

Commander Vega waited. Forty seconds had passed.

Forty-five.

Fifty.

"Devin Colt, this is your last warning."

"Commander! We're receiving a video transmission from the planet."

"Put it through." Perhaps the woman wished to surrender even if Devin Colt was too foolish to. "Shark Team, hold your fire."

A skewed image appeared in a section of the viewscreen. The target stood behind the woman—or rather, the girl. She couldn't have been much older than twenty. Devin Colt gripped her arm tightly with one hand and held his other arm against her throat. The girl looked pleadingly into the camera and mouthed, "Please help me."

Bastard.

Colt's face was cold, expressionless. "Hello, Commander. This is my sister, Jane. If you fire on me, she dies as well."

The transmission ended.

"Sonuvabitch!" Commander Vega didn't know whether Jane Colt had been kidnapped or manipulated by her older brother into joining him. Having looked through the girl's file the previous day, Commander Vega knew Jane was innocent. *What kind of monster uses his own sister as a shield?*

"Shark Team, disengage!" She would rather risk the target escaping than endanger the girl's life. Admiral Landler would probably reprimand her, but her abhorrence of collateral damage was well known. He would excuse the matter once she had apprehended the target. And Jane Colt would live.

It was time to send in the ground troops. "Open a

communication with the Flame Team."

"Yes, Commander!"

"Attention, Flame Team." Commander Vega made no effort to hide her disgust. "We have a human shield situation on the ground. Man your Remoras and use caution when entering the building. Acquire the target, but do not allow any harm to come to the hostage."

"Yes, Commander!"

Commander Vega narrowed her eyes. When she eventually caught Devin Colt, she was determined to see him face the ultimate justice.

———— ➤✦◆✦◆◄ ————

The triangular Barracudas retracted their cannons. Jane elbowed her brother. "I *told* you it'd work!"

"Yeah, good plan." Devin looked stormy.

"You didn't have a choice, bro. I didn't give you one." A low rumble. Two wide crimson shuttles with long wings emerged from the Mega. "Ground troops?"

Devin nodded. "Let's move."

Jane followed him out of the room and into the stairwell. "Hey, this could be a good thing, right? Now someone official will know about the AIs. That'll make them investigate the things you were investigating, No Name and stuff. They'll figure out you were framed."

"I wouldn't count on it."

"What's the plan?"

"No idea."

She smirked. "Any conduits we can climb into?"

Devin looked over his shoulder, expression amused. He entered the chemistry lab on the top floor. Jane ran in after him and carefully maneuvered around the glass apparatuses. Outside, the Barracudas left as the Remoras landed. Red-clad soldiers in black boots, round helmets, and protective vests exited the shuttles.

Devin pulled a black laser gun out of his bag.

Jane glanced at it uncomfortably. "Where'd you get that?"

"Had it in the Blue Tang." He pressed the edges of his bag shut. "Don't worry. I won't shoot anyone."

Jane reached for the stunner in her pocket, only to find it missing.

125

Dammit! Must've left it in the Blue Tang.

Devin raised the gun. "Go under the table."

What's he up to? Jane crawled under the table beneath the window.

Devin hesitated, suddenly looking nervous. His expression firmed, and he fired repeatedly at the window. Shattered glass pounded the table above Jane's head and tumbled to the floor.

She looked up questioningly. "What was that for?"

Devin watched the window. "Hopefully, they'll come up here while we go down another way."

Jane crawled out and ran toward the door. Devin pulled her down. A burst of white light wiped out her vision. Apparatuses shattered. She screamed.

"It's only a stun blast." Devin sounded calm.

Broken glass and spilled liquids surrounded her. "What do they have, a freaking stun *cannon*?" She started to get up.

Devin grabbed her shoulders. "Wait."

A second blast flew through the window. A nearby apparatus exploded. Jane held up her arm to protect her face, and her skin burned as a liquid splashed onto it. Pieces of glass scraped her wrist. "*Ow!*"

"Jane!" Devin reached into his bag, grabbed a bottle, and poured the water onto her scratches.

"Knock it off!" Jane pulled away. "I got *scratched*, for crying out loud!"

"The Seer said those liquids could be toxic." Devin ripped off his office shirt, revealing the black T-shirt underneath, and used it to hurriedly wipe her arm.

Jane yanked the shirt from him. "This is no time to be paranoid!" She sprang up. "Soldiers with guns coming at us, remember? Now let's *go!*"

She dropped the shirt and sprinted out of the room. Devin passed her in the corridor. He leaned against the wall by the stairwell, looked down, and then gestured for her to follow.

As Jane rushed down the stairs, she held her arms out for balance and fixed her eyes on the steps to keep from tripping.

One flight down... Two...

She crashed into Devin, smashing her nose against his T-shirted back. A blast hit the wall in front of them. *Shit, that was close!*

Jane ran up the stairs and turned into the nearest corridor. She couldn't hear her brother behind her, so she looked back.

Devin backed up against the wall beside the doorframe on the level below. He held his gun by his shoulder. White blasts flew past him. He looked out into the corridor, undaunted by the chaos. The moment the blasting stopped, he stepped into the doorframe.

Bang.

Jane jumped.

Devin rushed toward her. "I took out his weapon."

She didn't move. "When'd you learn to shoot like that?"

Instead of replying, Devin pushed her out of the stairwell. He stood against the doorframe, firing down the stairs as blasts from below hit the walls, aiming high, as if aiming to miss.

Jolted by an abrupt sense of unease, Jane turned. A soldier entered the corridor from the staircase at the other end. "*Look out!*"

Devin ducked. A blast hit the wall above him. He quickly straightened and fired several times. The soldier darted back into the stairwell.

Boots pounded up the stairs. Jane ran. Two soldiers emerged from a stairwell in front of her. Devin shoved her into one of the rooms.

Except it wasn't a room. It was a freaking elevator.

"*Shit.*" Devin pushed her behind him.

Several blasts whizzed past. Jane nervously backed up against the wall as he exchanged fire with the soldiers. She looked around. *This isn't my first time trapped in an elevator...*

The vent in the high ceiling was clearly unreachable. *A lotta good that'll do us.*

Devin followed her gaze. He fired up at the vent.

Jane gasped. *What the—*

Snap!

The ground dropped as the elevator fell.

She bit her lip. *No more screaming.*

———————— →◇← ————————

"Commander Vega!"

She turned to the officer, concerned by the alarm in his voice. "Yes?"

"Three unidentified Barracudas are approaching the target site from the South-West. They are unmarked and heavily armed. I believe they are hostile. They are not responding to attempts to communicate."

Who would attack us in such a remote area? "Deploy Betta Unit E. Attack mode."

———————— →◇← ————————

The elevator tipped. Through the open door, Jane saw the wall, then the crooked corridor, and then the wall again. Something clanged.

Devin grabbed her from behind and twisted her around as the elevator hit the ground, slamming her body into his.

It took a moment for Jane to regain her sense of up and down.

Devin looked dazed. He'd apparently taken the full impact against the corner of the elevator, cushioning her. "Sorry, should've warned you. You okay?"

Jane got off him. "Are *you* okay?"

"Yeah."

As soon as she found her balance on the tilted floor, she held out her hand and helped her brother up.

She peeked into the dim corridor. All the doorways were dark except those of the stairwells on either end. *Must be a basement level.* She didn't see anyone, so she climbed out of the elevator. Devin picked up his gun and stepped out behind her.

A soldier emerged from a stairwell. He held up a gun. Devin hit the weapon before he could fire. It flew out of the soldier's hand and smashed against a wall.

Jane darted into the nearest room. Metal and machinery scattered across its floor. She ran to the door that would lead away from the soldier. It was locked. "Dammit!"

A series of knocks, as if something fell to the ground. *What's that?*

Devin grabbed a table and threw it sideways. He pushed Jane behind it and pulled her down as he crouched. A high-pitched mechanical shriek and an explosion of light filled the room.

Jane felt as though someone had stuffed her ears with cotton. She gave Devin a questioning glance.

"Flash grenade." Devin looked around. He must have dropped his gun.

A weapon's black form lay just beyond the shelter of the table. Jane scrambled to snatch it. Devin pulled her back, and it fell from her hand.

A slow *scrape* and a soft *thud*—boots impacting the ground.

"Did you get it?" Devin mouthed.

Jane nodded and grabbed the gun. She froze as she realized what she held in her hand. "*Shit!*"

"What?"

"It's... I have a..."

The footsteps were practically next to them.

"*What is it?*"

"A *blow dryer!*" Jane looked at Devin helplessly as she held up the cosmetic device that had looked so weapon-like in the dark. He pressed his lips together as though suppressing a laugh.

The soldier peered over the table. Devin sprang up and threw a quick jab at the man's throat. The man choked and stumbled. "Go!"

Jane dashed out. A cry—the soldier's. Devin shoved him back while kicking his leg out from under him. The man fell backward.

The blow dryer was still in her hand. She acquiesced to the urge to hurl it. The device landed near the soldier's head and turned on, blasting his face with a stream of air.

Jane couldn't help laughing as she and Devin, who stopped briefly to pick up his real gun, ran out of the room. She rushed toward the front stairwell, heard soldiers' voices, and spun toward the back.

———————◆———————

Commander Vega looked over the weapons officer's shoulder. According to his chart, one Betta remained. It flashed on the screen and disappeared.

The weapons officer spun toward her. "Hostiles have destroyed the Bettas, Commander! They avoided all attempted strikes and hit each drone with no misses. It was as if they knew the algorithms. Contact Shark Team?"

Commander Vega watched the three triangles representing the hostiles. "No. Activate the cannons."

———◆———

Please let there be no one outside.

Jane tore up the back stairwell after her brother. Her muscles ached, and she breathed so hard she felt lightheaded.

She reached ground level and saw light from the open doorway—

Boom.

She couldn't stop the scream that time. A cacophony of rumbles and cracks followed the explosion, accompanied by distant cries of shock and pain. Shadows of debris splotched the light.

Before she could register what happened, another *boom.*

———◆———

"Hostiles are bombarding the—"

"Flame Team! Pull back *immediately*! I repeat, pull back *now*!" Commander Vega clenched her jaw to contain her rage and horror. Her troops didn't stand a chance.

The *Granite Flame*'s cannons fired at the deep blue Barracudas. As with the Bettas, the hostiles avoided the targeting system.

"Switch to manual targeting!" The officer had probably been correct about the hostiles knowing the *Granite Flame*'s algorithms. They could predict the system's moves.

The back of the building collapsed. The comm overflowed with the alarmed voices of the Flame Team as the hostiles continued their assault.

———◆———

The explosion forced Jane and Devin back down the stairs as the ceiling caved on the ground level. Jane exited the stairwell on the floor below. She sprinted toward the front.

Who the hell *is bombing us? Can't be the Mega, not when there're soldiers in the building.*

The building crumbled behind her. Jane felt as if she, too, would collapse and prayed the adrenaline would kick in before she did. The light from the front stairwell was too bright, and she wondered if the wall had fallen. Devin turned into it. Jane followed a few steps behind. A wave of relief washed over her. The stairwell was exposed.

Three deep blue Barracudas soared over her as she climbed over the broken concrete. What sounded like cannon fire thundered behind her. She cleared the rubble and ran with all the speed she could muster, cursing her body for causing her so much grief. *Where the hell's the adrenaline?*

Boom.

A roaring explosion knocked her to the ground in a searing blast of heat. Her back burned as though someone had set it on fire. Looking back took far more effort than it should have. Through her hazy vision, Jane saw pieces of a dark Barracuda mixed with the demolished building. Only a few soldiers stood by the Remoras. She wondered with a heavy feeling where the rest were.

Devin pulled her up. "C'mon!"

Something exploded, and a rainstorm of dark powder fell. The Mega must have destroyed a Barracuda.

Jane fixed her eyes on the Stargazer and ran. She was so close...

There it is.

Her feet flew beneath her. She zoomed toward the ship, scarcely aware of the scorching heat or her bursting heart. The image of the Seer at the landing tripod flashed through her mind. She found the panel he'd used and pulled the lever. The door opened, and the ladder extended.

She barely felt the rungs as she sped into the vehicle. She jumped into the pilot's seat and slammed her hand against the scanner as her muscles, breath, and heartbeat broke down.

Devin entered behind her—when had she passed him?—and took the copilot's seat. The viewscreen activated. Jane ignited the engines. Unable to hear her brother's words over the rushing in her head, she gripped the steering bars with a mad kind of glee. She pushed them forward. The Stargazer launched into the atmosphere.

In the viewscreen's rear view, the last Barracuda hurtled into the remnants of the building.

⟶⬦⬦⟵

Commander Vega listened with growing fury as the Flame Team leader listed the unaccounted for members. Almost three quarters were missing. She kept her face proudly calm, belying her internal rage as she ordered a rescue team to the planet. Only a rubble-filled pit remained where the building had been. Two of the hostiles, upon sustaining damage, had crashed into it. Judging from its shattered state, no one had survived.

"Commander, the target is leaving the planet."

Commander Vega recalled seeing Devin Colt and his sister enter the Stargazer. She wondered how the target escaped when so many of her people had been buried. "Shark Team! Man—"

"Commander!" The pilot switched the viewscreen to a forward view. The Stargazer flew straight at the warship.

"Move to avoid!" The *Granite Flame* lurched as the pilot maneuvered it. None of the warship's many views showed the Stargazer. Commander Vega snapped her face toward the navigation officer. "Where is it?"

"The target engaged lightspeed. It's out of visual range."

"Track it!" *Incompetent.*

"The sensors can't find them."

Commander Vega strode to the officer's station. The screen before him displayed a chart of the Viatian system with color-coded points identifying half a dozen other vehicles.

The target was nowhere to be found.

Chapter 10

RECOVERY, DISCOVERY

SEVERAL HOURS—DEVIN LOST TRACK OF just how many—had passed since Jane so recklessly flew at the Mega. He watched the tracker from the pilot's seat. The *Granite Flame*'s probes returned to their mothership. So the Stargazer really was untraceable. He leaned back in relief.

Several minutes later, the *Granite Flame* left the Viatian system and flew toward the interstellar tunnel at lightspeed.

Finally.

Devin steered the Stargazer, which he'd maneuvered at random to stay out of visual range, toward the tunnel, approaching it from a different direction. The Mega was several light-hours ahead; they'd be back in Kydera before he left the region.

He got up and checked on Jane in the living quarters. She was still asleep in the hammock. She'd been so tired from the chase, poor kid. He still couldn't believe what she'd done after taking the Stargazer's controls.

"What are you doing?" Devin had asked. "You can't fly this thing!"

Jane had ignored him and placed her hand on the scanner.

"Knock it off, Jane!" He'd strapped himself into the copilot's seat. "This is different from your practice sessions. Stop messing around before you get yourself killed!"

Jane took off, a wild look in her eyes.

Taking the controls from her would have been dangerous, so Devin put his own hand on the scanner. Although he gained some control over the ship's system, he didn't have the authority to override her actions. "*Jane!*"

"Hey, bro!" Jane appeared exhausted and energized at the same time. Her face lit up like that of a child with a new toy. "Watch this!" She flipped the Stargazer toward the warship.

"*What are you doing?*"

"They'll move, and then they won't be able to find us!" She twisted the steering bars forward, accelerating the ship to its maximum sub-lightspeed.

The warship grew larger on the viewscreen. "Stop!" Devin yelled. "This isn't a game!"

"They'll *move!*"

The Mega veered to avoid collision. Devin swiped the control touchscreen, engaging lightspeed.

Jane pushed her hair off her sweaty face. "Yes! They'll never find us now!"

He was still reeling. "*What were you thinking?*"

"What do you mean?" She grinned. "I got us outta their sight!"

"There are other ways!"

Jane lifted her chin. "Like what? We could've engaged lightspeed right away, but they'd've followed, and we'd have to do that stupid ring-around-the-rosie thing you did last time! Besides, who are *you* to tell me off? You dropped us in an elevator for crying out loud!"

She had a point. A part of him wanted to upbraid her, but he couldn't help feeling a little proud of his kid sister's boldness. "All right. Good job."

Jane collapsed back in her chair. "Thank you!"

"But that's enough. I'm piloting."

"Okay." She stumbled as she got up. Her face looked feverishly red and sickly pale at the same time, and she seemed to have difficulty focusing her eyes.

Devin moved into the pilot's seat. "I've got this. You go get some rest."

"Aren't you tired too?"

"I'm fine."

"Okay, then. I'm gonna pass out now." Jane had held the wall for support as she left the cockpit.

There had been no dream. Jane had slept more soundly than she'd thought possible. Although her eyes refused to shut again, her limbs felt as though they sank into the creaky hammock. Her body wanted desperately to stay put, but her mind was wide awake.

Whoa.

Her head spun as though the Stargazer flipped again. She rested her back against the wall, waiting for the feeling to subside.

The world came back into focus. Jane kicked off her high-heeled boots and returned to the cockpit.

Devin sat in the pilot's seat, concentrating on his slate. Dust covered his black clothing. His wavy hair fell all over the place, some of it stuck to dried blood from a cut near his cheekbone. Jane hadn't seen her brother, the perpetually groomed corporate tool, looking that messy in years.

He noticed her. "Hey, you're up. Feeling better?"

"Yup. Good as new." *Lies.* Her muscles ached with every move, and her head throbbed as though her brain banged around her skull. The small cuts on her forearm stung with disproportionate pain, as if that chemical still burned her skin.

Devin's gaze fell to her wrist. "How's the arm?"

Hurts like hell. "It's fine. Just needed to wash it off."

"Let me see—"

"Stop being paranoid! I've gotten worse from playing with Klistosian gold-cats." Jane plopped down in the copilot's seat. "So, what's going on?"

"The Mega left the system a while ago. The Stargazer's on autopilot, heading for the tunnel. Not sure where we're going after that."

"What're you doing?" Jane peered at his slate. A number of windows were open, containing news stories with dramatic titles like "Financial Prince Shoots Father in Cold Blood" and "Tribunal Weighs Evidence in Attempted Patricide."

"Catching up on the news," Devin said dryly.

Jane huffed. "They're all idiots."

"There's one about you."

"Really? Can I see?"

He swiped the slate and handed it to her. An article, titled "Victor Colt's Daughter Missing," splashed across the screen. It speculated that Devin's crime had traumatized her, augmenting her budding psychosis and causing her to run away.

Jane was somewhat amused. "Clearly, they haven't alerted the media about what happened on Viate-5, or the title would be 'Dangerous Fugitive Uses Helpless Sister as Human Shield.' Speaking of which, what the hell was that? The bombing, I mean?"

Devin took his slate back. "Someone covering their tracks, probably the people behind No Name. They must've sent the Barracudas as soon as they saw a military ship approach the system."

"Do you think they crashed into the building on purpose?"

"They didn't seem too keen on surviving. I'm guessing they were unmanned."

A message window appeared on the slate.

Corsair: I'm freakin' amazing.

Jane angled herself for a better view. "Seems chattier than usual."

"He's probably using voice commands."

Archangel: What is it?
Corsair: I found your crazy kidnapper machines.

Jane gasped. "He found Adam?!"

"Just the machines."

"Still, he's awesome!"

Archangel: Are you sure?
Corsair: Uh... I don't make mistakes, remember? Here's your proof, you doubtin' nonbeliever. They're on Travan Float.

Devin opened the attachment.

Several very blurry but, for Jane, unmistakable images

of two dark, boxy machines appeared. "That's them!"

Archangel: You're good.

Corsair: I'm a freakin' genius. Do you know how much shit I had to pull to find those things? No one else would've even recognized them!

Archangel: Okay. You're a genius.

Corsair: Thank you. So... Uh... I don't know where on the float they are. Background's too fuzzy. Hey, if there were a way to be more precise, I would've found it. A float's better than the entire galaxy, right? Considering the size of the universe, that's *very* specific!

Archangel: When were the pictures taken?

Corsair: Less than an hour ago. Going there?

Archangel: Yes.

Corsair: Heh. Home sweet home, right?

Jane leaned against the copilot's seat. "Does he live there?"

"No, he hasn't been there in ages." Corsair logged off, and Devin closed the communication window. "Travan Float's a hellhole, but at least we're one step closer to finding your friend."

"And we *will* find him." It was only one clue, but it made Jane feel as though everything would be all right. "What's Travan Float anyway?"

"Travan's a Fringe system." Devin rested his head against the back of his chair. "Its planet was rendered uninhabitable by a nuclear war about two hundred years ago, and all that's left is the space habitat they built when the time came to evacuate. It's one of the most lawless places in the galaxy. As far as I know, a crime boss called Madam Wrath runs it. She and her predecessors never cared what happened as long as people kept paying. It's a haven for outlaws."

"Sounds wonderful." And like the kind of place for a mad scientist who wanted to replace a seminary student with a robot to hide. Maybe Sarah was there too.

Devin yawned, slouching uncharacteristically. He looked beat.

Jane nudged him. "Hey, bro, your turn to get some rest."

"I'm fine."

"Liar. I don't even remember the last time you slept."

"I got some shut-eye while we were autopiloting to Viate-5."

"Well, we're autopiloting now. Don't worry. I'll wake you if anything weird happens."

"All right." Devin folded his slate and got up. "No stunts, okay?"

Jane held up her right hand as though testifying in court. "I swear by the Absolute, no stunts." She moved into the pilot's seat. "G'night!"

"Night, Pony."

Jane hugged her knees and looked out into the immeasurable darkness, awed by the glittering abyss. No matter how many times she went to space, the stars always burned with infinite possibilities.

I flew a freaking starship today.

She grinned, recalling the exhilaration. She wasn't sure what instinct had told her to take the controls when she'd never really flown before. She'd taken some piloting lessons at university, but only to prove she could do anything her brother could.

Now, I've gotta figure out how to think fast when people— or things—are chasing me.

Never again would she be the damsel in distress, freezing in helplessness or running in panic when someone she cared about was in trouble. She remembered how her brother had led her during the chase and shielded her as though she were a little girl.

No more of that. Once we get to Travan, I'm gonna act instead of just following my big brother around.

Excitement coursed through her as she imagined finding the machines and confronting the bastards who'd sent them. She pictured herself kicking them in the face until they told her where Adam and Sarah were, then victoriously dragging their sorry asses back to Kydera Major, where her father would be awake and waiting for her.

But if Dad knew what she'd done—abandoned everything and ended up on the wrong side of the law—he would be enraged, no matter what her intentions had been.

He would've wanted me to stay out of it. Hell, he would've wanted me to tell those officers about Devin's Blue Tang and let him get caught, then count on the system to sort it out.

That would have been a lot smarter, would have spared her the trouble she'd faced since. Jane wondered where the rational side of herself had gone. Then again, the "system" had already failed her once. Perhaps not trusting it, especially with No Name lurking, wasn't such a foolish thing to do.

If Dad could see me now, out on the Fringe in a black market junker, he'd probably disown me.

Nah, he'd sigh loudly and ask why I make things so difficult. As he had after she'd timidly told him about switching her university major to music.

"You too, Jane?" Dad had pulled his mouth down into the sternest frown she'd ever seen from him. "I thought that kind of misbehavior had been confined to your brother, but it looks like you were cursed with the same flaw. Very well, have your fun. You'll get your head on straight eventually."

At the time, Jane had been grateful for his patience, for receiving disappointed sighs instead of roars of fury. He'd acted as though allowing her to chase her dream was another indulgence for his little girl. She wondered whether he'd ever seen her as an individual with a will of her own.

Rather than one of those AIs—some obedient thing that should do what he *wants even when he's not ordering me around... Why am I so moody? Think about something else!*

A shiver shook her body. Jane realized how chilly she was. She glimpsed Devin's rectangular office bag by the pilot's seat. Remembering that he had a jacket in there, she grabbed it and opened it.

Curious, and always up for going through her brother's stuff, she rummaged to see what its other contents were. A weird spherical device lay beside the laser gun. She picked it up. Unable to recognize it, she figured it was some kind of grenade and put it back carefully.

Where'd he get something like that anyway? Why doesn't he tell me anything? Jerk.

Jane put on her brother's black suit jacket and rolled up the sleeves, mentally grumbling about how unfair it was that he'd received all the strong genes while she'd inherited her mother's slender frame.

She placed her hands in the pockets. Her knuckles touched something hard and smooth in one of them. She pulled the object out. It was a rectangular case about the size of a playing card. Beneath its sapphire lid, a portrait of Sarah stared back at her.

We'll find her, Devin.

Was Sarah even alive? Was Adam? Jane thought about the terrible things that could have happened to them and any number of people on the target list of a perverse, nameless enemy. Her heart pounded, and cold gripped her from within. She curled up and buried her face in her knees. *What if Adam's dying somewhere?*

She pictured how Adam would respond if he saw her freaking out: "Stop scaring yourself, Jane. It'll all work out in the end. You'll see."

"That's not rational," she'd replied once. "There's no 'end' to look forward to, just more of the same. Nothing ever changes, and you know it. If I get through today, I'll still have to deal with tomorrow. What's the point?"

"Not everything is rational. Sometimes you have to trust that everything that's happening is somehow for the best."

Jane usually hated when people talked like that. For some reason, it was okay when Adam did. Strangely enough, she'd even listened. There were so many things only he could get her to do...

About two weeks before, the seminary had selected Adam to give a student sermon at the campus temple. Jane had begrudgingly gone to the sparsely attended service for his sake.

Adam pushed back the hood of his forest-green Via robes. The illuminated golden Via symbol formed an unearthly aura around him, making his peridot eyes seem to glow with an otherworldly brightness. In those moments, surrounded by the temple's colorful trappings and mesmerized by Adam's almost ethereal appearance, Jane forgot briefly that she was an atheist.

He'd looked right at her. "In this world of ever-advancing technology, we must never let go of what it is that makes us human."

Jane had thought she would zone out at some point. Instead, she'd been surprised to find herself absorbing every word as he spoke of the importance of compassion, weaving in allegories from various Via texts and framing them in intricate yet down-to-earth language. Something about him was magnetic, hypnotic even. She understood why his advisor pushed him so hard.

After he finished speaking, Jane sat awkwardly still while the rest of the congregation recited prayers and carried out rituals. The whole thing reminded her why she found religion so freaking creepy, and she told Adam as much when she met up with him after the service. "Don't get me wrong." Her voice had reverberated against the walls of the emptied temple. "*You* were great."

"Thanks." Adam was back in his normal clothes and looking like his ordinary, nice-boy self again. "I wrote it for you."

Jane leaned against a pew. "Indeed."

"It's true! I thought: How can I make this appeal to someone who thinks everything I believe in is a joke?"

"Sorry," Jane said sheepishly, but she could tell he didn't resent her for it. "I guess I don't get the point of all that, the chanting and arm-waving and stuff."

"The ritual may seem strange to you, but it brings comfort to those who believe, serves as a way to make them feel more connected with the Absolute. It's a physical reminder of the Absolute's presence and the idea that they're part of something greater."

"But I don't understand how talking to... um... no one... helps with anything."

A teasing spark lit Adam's eyes. "Let's try it, then."

Jane raised an eyebrow. "Excuse me?"

"Just start by addressing the Absolute One, end with 'so be it, truly,' and the rest is up to you."

Jane pushed off the pew and stood erect. "Hell no." She didn't care that she was in a place of worship. "No way you're getting me into that shit. No offense."

Adam smiled. "What's the harm? By taking part once,

141

you can learn what it is you're opposed to, instead of fighting something you've never understood."

Jane gasped indignantly. "That's not true! I'm not atheist because I don't know any better. It's because I *do*! I know all about the history, the hypocrisies, the manipulations, and all that nonsense!"

"How can you really understand something you've never been a part of? You were raised to believe that there is no higher power, and that's why you find everything we do so alien. What if you'd grown up Via, believing in the Absolute? Or Origin, believing in God? Or otherwise religious, calling your divine being something else entirely? You keep telling me that people should try to see things from various perspectives. Why shouldn't that apply to religion?"

Jane groaned. "I hate it when you're right."

Adam put his hands on her shoulders. "Try it. Even though you don't want to participate in the institution, you can still take comfort in the spirituality."

She grimaced. "Fine. But I'm not kneeling."

"Fair enough." Adam let go.

Jane faced the altar and folded her hands like she'd seen Adam do when he prayed. She closed her eyes. "Hello, Absolute One. I don't know if You can hear me. Hello? Hello? Are You there?"

"Jane!"

She opened her eyes. "What do I say? I don't know where to start, other than to ask for... I dunno... a raise or something dumb like that."

Adam shrugged. "Say whatever's on your mind, and be honest about it."

"Ugh, you're useless. Okay..." She closed her eyes again. "I know, Absolute One, I have no right to speak to You. But I'm here now, so here goes. Please help me do well in... everything, protect me from evil, and all that. Please help me find a way to be happy, even though I'm caught between the life I can't have and the life I can't stand."

She paused, and sudden anger ignited within her. "Hey, listen, I'm sorry I'm not wiser, stronger, smarter, nicer, whatever. Forgive me. I can't be everything I should be. And forgive me for being so extraordinarily arrogant. It's the only thing that gets me past my debilitating insecurity.

If You can hear me, please help me be something more than me. And I'm sorry if I've wasted Your time by praying here today. So be it, truly."

"Jane..."

Jane's eyes stung. Somewhere in her mockery, she'd struck something real inside. She blinked furiously, annoyed at herself. "I'm fine."

"Are you?" Adam's voice was gentle. "I know how hard it must be for you, being caught between what you want and what your father wants you be. But it's your life, and—"

"And I gave up my dumb pipe dream because that's all it ever was," Jane said sharply. "I've told you before: There's no sense in wasting my life chasing something I can never be. Everyone loves to parade around with stories about the people who made it, like Sarah freaking DeHaven, but what about the ones who give it their all and end up with nothing?"

"That's your father talking."

"Well, he's right." Jane turned to the altar. "Hey, Absolute One, back me up here. You've got a limit on the number of people You can bless, haven't You? We can't all be special, or it doesn't mean anything. I guess I'm not one of Your chosen ones, and if that's the case, so be it. Truly."

"You don't have to be a 'chosen one' to—"

"Can we get out of here?" She was in no mood for another of Adam's be-true-to-yourself speeches.

Adam seemed to get the message, for he said, "Of course," and let the matter drop. He put an arm around her. It was strangely comforting.

As they left the temple, Jane's mood lifted with an unexpected sense of relief from having vented. She thought she might—*kind of, maybe*—understand why people clung so tightly to their irrational beliefs. It was nice to have someone, even someone invisible and unresponsive, to depend on, to hold on to, to credit for one's fortunes and blame for one's troubles. She almost wished she were one of those illogical worshippers.

As she and Adam made their way across the campus, Kydera Minor's blue-green form lit the seminary so brightly that the streetlights hardly seemed necessary.

"Funny," she said. "I've been to systems across the

galaxy, but I've never visited our world's sister world."

"Me neither, although it almost became my new home." Adam looked up at the planet. "I didn't ask for it. They just told me one day that I'd been transferred to the seminary on Kydera Minor. Counselor Santillian applied on my behalf because a last-minute spot opened, and she said I should take it because there are more opportunities over there."

Jane stopped in her tracks. "Wait, you're leaving?"

Adam faced her. "No, I turned it down. It wasn't easy convincing them to let me stay here. You won't believe the amount of bureaucracy I had to deal with—the arguing, the legal nonsense, the bribes, the threats. But I said I'd drop out before I'd let them transfer me against my will."

That doesn't make sense. "You fought the system to stay somewhere with *less*?"

Adam nodded. "Counselor Santillian kept saying anyone else would jump at the opportunity. I told her to make that 'anyone else' happy and leave me be."

"Why didn't you go?"

"I wanted to stay with you." He must have been kidding, because he'd smiled and added, "I couldn't bear the thought of leaving you alone with those Quasar tools."

Jane reclined in the pilot's seat for over an hour, daydreaming and otherwise allowing her mind to wander, even composing part of that promised motet in her head. Her previous wooziness had dissipated, and the pain in her arm had dulled.

She pulled her slate out of her pocket, marveling at the fact that it hadn't gotten lost or broken during the whole Viate-5 fiasco. She half-heartedly surfed the Net.

Nothing held her interest. *I give up.* She folded the slate and dropped it in her pocket.

Maybe I can practice flying.

She put her hand on the scanner, indicated that she was the only pilot—to disengage copilot capabilities—and switched off the autopilot. She placed her hands on the steering bars and moved them to the right.

The ship didn't turn. Jane checked the navigation chart. The Stargazer continued on its straight trajectory toward the tunnel.

Did I miss something?

The stars in front of her abruptly disappeared, replaced by a video. She gasped in confusion. *What the hell?*

It was a close-up of Devin. The timestamp indicated that it had been taken about seven years ago, around the same time their mother had been assassinated. He looked so much younger. His hair was longer and his complexion slightly darker, but what really gave away his youth was the boyishly offhand attitude he gave off with his defiant smirk, a look bizarrely incongruent with his situation. Two guns pointed at his head.

Jane couldn't see who was threatening her brother, only the menacing black barrels.

Someone hissed, "*Get on with it.*"

Devin kept smirking, but Jane recognized the anger in his eyes. "Hi, Mom. Hi, Dad. These assholes want me to plead for my life and tell you to give them a shit-ton of money. Well, fuck that. I know no one's coming to save me."

The view of the stars returned. Jane blinked in disbelief. Questions rioted in her head, each screaming louder than the next for attention: Who put that video there? When had Devin been held hostage? Why had no one told her? Who were those bastards? What the hell happened?

Seven years ago... Jane recalled how unspeakably furious she'd been after her mother's death when she couldn't reach her brother, whom she'd desperately needed. He hadn't even attended the funeral. Jane had demanded that her father track him down and *make* him come back.

Dad had acted oddly distant, saying "Devin won't be back for some time. He signed up last-minute for a study abroad program at Iothe Central University."

Jane had been unable to contact her brother for almost a year after. When he finally returned, he seemed different. He'd listened to her long, tearful tirade in silence.

When she'd run out of ways to say, "You jerk! How could you leave me?" she'd thrown her arms around him.

Devin had returned her embrace. "I'm sorry, Pony." His voice was barely more than a whisper. "I... I don't know what to tell you. I know I should've been here for you, but I couldn't come back until now. I didn't mean to be gone so long. Please... Forgive me."

Jane had thought the grief and injustice of losing their mother had caused him to shut himself away. She wondered just how much she didn't know.

The last time she'd seen her brother before his supposed trip to Iothe had been after coming home early from school. To her surprise, she'd found Devin's black one-person air transport on the landing pad by the Colt mansion.

Excited, she rushed toward the front door, which was open. Her brother and her parents stood in the foyer.

She stopped. Something felt wrong, and the first words her mother spoke, in her poisonous quiet tone, confirmed it. "How could you betray us like this? How could you commit these—these *crimes*?"

Devin's expression turned furious. "I've *had it* with the questions! I know you don't really want an answer!"

Dad slammed a table. "*Enough!*"

Jane jumped. She pressed herself against the wall outside to stay out of sight.

Dad continued, "You're a *criminal,* and I won't have any more of this! I *won't!*"

"You've done so much over the years." Mom's voice was almost a whisper. "But this is beyond *anything* we've seen before. How many times have we cleaned up your messes? I don't understand why you have to keep pushing."

Devin remained still for several seconds, as though willing himself to remain calm. "I was only—"

Slam.

Dad strode up to Devin. "*No more of your excuses!* I've had *enough.* You're *dead to me!*"

Jane backed away.

Her mother stepped between the two. "Victor, please. Let's not—"

"No, Elizabeth. No more." Dad pointed at Devin. "I'm *through* with you. Understand? We're *finished. I have no son.*"

"Victor—"

Slam. Something shattered.

Jane flattened herself against the wall, too afraid to peek inside. After several moments of silence, Devin stormed out without seeing her.

Oh, Devin, why are you always getting in trouble?

Her dumb brother had always flouted the rules, and she'd often heard conversations like those. Her father's dramatic rhetoric was legendary. Even though it was scary as hell, she was sure he never *meant* the things he said. He was probably just pissed-off at Devin for getting arrested at a protest or something.

Jane was fifteen at the time, and like all fifteen-year-olds, she'd thought herself cleverer than her parents. While playing the perfect daughter by day, she'd become a covert composer by night. Doodling silly songs instead of studying—that was her rebellion, her alternative to sneaking out to parties or hiding unapproved boyfriends.

About a week after the latest flare-up between her parents and her brother, Jane stayed up late working on her latest masterpiece. Her stomach rumbled. Dinner had been almost eight hours before.

Her parents would be terribly upset if they found out what she'd been up to, so she crept out of her room as silently as possible in search of a snack.

"You're *heartless*, Victor!" Her mother's voice was shrill behind the door of the master bedroom.

Her mother *never* shouted.

Dad roared, "How can you *consider* paying? You *know* he's in on the scheme! Devin got *himself* into this mess, and he can get himself out!"

Jane ducked back into her room but kept the door open, too curious to leave.

Mom yelled back, "What if he can't? You'd really abandon your *son* as if he's expendable?"

"*Don't*. Don't act like this is my fault. I've been more than patient with the boy. I've done *everything* for him, and he continues to betray me. *He's* the heartless one."

Jane wanted to cry out in protest.

"I don't care *what* you think." Mom's voice was firm. "I'm doing it."

"You'll be playing into their hands!" Dad shouted.

"He's my *child*, Victor! I can't—"

"They're *bluffing*! Those are the people he walked away from *us* for!"

"And if they're not?"

"I told you, he's *dead to me*."

Mom's response had been low and inaudible. After straining her ears in vain for several minutes, Jane had quietly closed her door.

At the time, she had thought someone blackmailed her parents over something Devin had done. The apparent severity had led her to believe he'd either committed a felony or knocked up some girl. Despite her usual tendency to side with her brother over her parents, she'd seen the reason behind her father's refusal.

Not anymore.

She recalled the reddish-haired officer's words: "We have information about his past that shows he had ample reason to resent your father."

This must've been what he was talking about. She resented her father too. No, more than resented. She didn't understand how he could be willing to let her brother die like that.

And then there was the timing of the whole thing. The video had been recorded just days before her mother's death.

Could the hostage thing have something to do with that?

No one had told her who *actually* assassinated Senator Elizabeth Lin-Colt, only that the case was related to a Fringe warlord, and that the details were classified due to an undercover operation. Had the warlord taken Devin hostage to get to her mother? Where had he been all those months after?

Jane got up, aiming to wake him and ask. She reached for the button to open the cockpit door, then froze.

"It's all in the past," he'd said, eclipsed by deep sadness. If being cut off by their father and held hostage was the "past" he referred to, the one that hurt him so much to think about, she should leave him alone.

Jane sat back down and looked at the navigation chart. Travan Float was less than a day away. *Better focus on today's mysteries than get caught up in the past. Where'd the video come from anyway?*

Must have been the Seer. He'd seemed to know a lot about Devin. Had he really found the video and programmed the Stargazer to show it to her once she was alone? Why would he do that?

So weird.

Shivering, Jane pulled Devin's jacket tighter around herself and gazed into the endless night.

———————✦◇◇✦————————

Travan Float reminded Jane of an enormous black bug with a round backside, a tiny head, and a pointed cone sticking out of the underside.

She had no trouble docking in one of the float's many seedy hangars. A few swipes of the control screen was all it took to extend an airtight tunnel from the Stargazer and lock it onto one of float's hatches. The hatch itself baffled her, since it was ancient and non-computerized.

Jane examined the confusing array of levers and large wheels on the rectangular metal door. "What the hell is all this? Devin, you deal with it."

Devin's apparent familiarity with the setup surprised her. After he pushed the hatch open and emerged from the ship, nobody asked questions, only for money, which he silently handed to the mean-looking old woman.

The first thing Jane saw upon leaving the docking corridor was an open area designed to look like a city square. All the buildings stood at the same height, and a ceiling sat on top of them. The place was dim. Most of the light radiated from a giant hologram of a middle-aged woman with slanted black eyes, short black hair, and a piercing expression. Flame-yellow words circled her: Madam Gloria Wrath, Proprietor of Travan Float.

Characters from all walks of life passed through the square. A drug dealer sold his poison out in the open as if it were candy. A man in a gaudy outfit, surrounded by armed thugs, entered one of the stores. An air transport, emblazoned with the glowing image of a woman in a lewd position, emerged from a large window and maneuvered around Madam Wrath's hologram.

Jane was taken aback by the sight of a Via Counselor leading a row of raggedy children out of a wheeled transport. It reminded her that the float wasn't just a shady harbor, but rather a city of sorts. "Lovely place."

"Stay close." Devin kept one hand on his bag, probably to reach his gun faster in case of trouble.

The thought of another gunfight, one that used actual

ammunition instead of stun blasts, terrified Jane. She tried not to let her anxiety show as she followed her brother across the square. *Nothing's gonna happen.*

A group of tough-looking men and women carrying large, distinctive red guns surveyed the populace.

"Are they the police or something?" she asked.

Devin glanced at them. "Madam Wrath's thugs. They're called Wrath Guards. So yeah, they're supposed to police the area."

Jane heard a cry. A skinny man held up his hands as a muscular woman waved a gun in his face. She yelled at him until he handed her something, then knocked him out with the handle of her gun.

The "police" barely acknowledged the situation.

Jane inched closer to her brother. "Heh. Like I said, lovely."

A Wrath Guard grabbed him by the shoulder. "You! Don't I know you?"

"You have me confused with someone else," Devin said coolly.

The thug eyed him suspiciously, then let go. Devin continued on his way, his mouth pressed in a hard line.

Jane looked around. "Where do we start?"

"Not sure." Devin turned into one of the doorways. It led to a long corridor lined with sketchy-looking shops. "Let's try the tech dealers. They'd be better at recognizing the machines."

He looked up at one of the signs above a boarded-up store, which had "Later Bitchez!" scrawled in brown graffiti across its sign. "Damn."

Jane tried to make out the words under the graffiti. "What were you looking for?"

"Hello again," said a husky female voice. A woman with blond dreadlocks, heavy black makeup ringing bloodshot eyes, and a bronze ring between her flared nostrils clung to Devin's shoulder. She pressed her face against his. "Is it possible you've got even more handsome, Black Knight?"

Devin pushed the woman off. "I don't know what you're talking about."

Jane ran to keep up as he walked away.

The woman chased him. "Don't pretend ya don't know

me! I was the one who helped ya find that kid, remember? You wouldn'ta got the job done if it weren't for me! Hey!" She stopped and put her hands on her hips. "Asshole!"

Jane kept her gaze on the woman, too fascinated by her peculiar appearance not to stare. "What the hell is her problem?"

"The majority of people here are drug abusers," Devin muttered.

Still looking back, Jane forgot to watch where she was going. She crashed into someone. "Sorry!"

The dirty-looking man grabbed her arm and leered at her. "No need to be sorry," he said, words slurred. He grinned at Devin. "You her pimp?"

Devin pulled Jane away before she had a chance to react. "Get away from her."

Jane was too incensed from the man's assumption to come up with a suitable retort.

The man blocked her as she tried to leave. "Gotta special client waitin', eh? You're *niiiice.* Lemme guess. He stole you from the IC?"

Devin pulled out his gun and aimed it at the man's face. "*Get away from her.*"

The man held up his hands with a sneer. "Oh, okay, I get it. Gotta keep the best goods untouched, eh? Yeah, I'll bet the bosses'll pay a *fortune* for fresh meat like that."

Jane was enraged. "Why—why you—you *fat-faced, shit-brained slimeball!*"

"Aw, c'mon, baby. Don't be mad! Let me make it up to you." He licked his lips and reached toward her face.

Jane twisted and kicked her heel into the man's stomach. The man doubled over. Devin caught her as she stumbled. She spun, shocked at her own action.

The man growled. "Fuckin' whore!"

He reached behind him and started toward her—

Bang.

The man bellowed as he fell to the ground, clutching his thigh. Blood seeped from his wound, darkening his pant leg around a burnt-edged hole from the laser blast.

The gun he'd apparently been reaching for slid toward Jane. She hastily kicked it away. *Holy shit!*

Devin glowered at the man. "Get up and leave. Keep

your mouth shut."

The man cursed as he staggered to his feet. He snarled, but his eyes betrayed his fear. His gaze fell toward the black barrel still aimed at him. He limped away.

Jane couldn't believe what had just happened. She watched until the man disappeared around the corner. *What the hell? My brother freaking* shot *a guy! But that bastard deserved it.*

A squat robot about half her height rolled over to the man's gun, opened its square body, and swept the weapon inside with its flat arm. *Damn. I should've taken the gun. Could be handy in a place like this.*

Devin put a hand on Jane's shoulder and pushed her along as he walked back toward the square. He kept his gun in the other hand. "You're going back to the ship."

"Like hell!" Jane twisted out of his grip. "I'm not going *anywhere* until—"

"*Dammit, Jane!* You saw how dangerous this place is!" He didn't look angry—he looked fearful. Jane couldn't remember the last time he'd seemed scared like that.

She could tell she wasn't going to win. "Fine."

She allowed her brother to take her back to the Stargazer and nodded innocently when he told her to stay.

But she wasn't about to sit still, not when she was so close to finding Adam. A few minutes after Devin left, Jane returned to the villainous city of sin.

CHAPTER 11

HELLUVA PLACE

AGLEWING GULPED HIS BEER. It was the cheapest stuff at Hellfire 13, and it tasted like piss. But booze was booze, so he drained the rest of his glass. His face burned. Maybe he shouldn't have chugged that. He'd need a clear head if a prospective employer approached.

Hellfire 13 was one of those super exclusive nightclubs where if you wanted to get in, you had to know someone. Or pay off a lot of someones. It wasn't one of those swanky establishments with crystal chandeliers and silk on the walls, although there were plenty of those around Travan Float for rich crime bosses. Nah, Hellfire 13 was a shithole with cheap decorations and litter all over the place.

It was so hard to get in because the people who frequented it were the types who didn't want to be found. They weren't your average drug dealers and pimps and shit. They were the *really* paranoid types: demons who only went by their Netnames and mercs who went by no names at all, people who made a living by being hard to find. They were creatures of the night, and it was always night on Travan Float. Hellfire 13 was the place to find those people if you wanted to hire one, which was why every so often, you'd see a boss in a fancy outfit go into one of the VIP rooms. Those were sorta nice on the inside.

Eaglewing, along with his pal Fedora, had gained access to the club almost eight years before by hacking the giant killer robot that guarded the door and either let you in because you were on the List or shot you in the foot because you weren't. It'd been pretty epic when they succeeded, since they were little kids at the time. The other demons had been so amused they put the two on the List just for kicks. After Eaglewing and Fedora had been hired for a few jobs, no one questioned their right to be there.

Eaglewing pushed the edge of the bar, and his barstool swiveled. He scanned the dark place for girls. His gaze wandered past the dirty dance floor, which had several metal stripper poles in the middle, and over to the virtu-game center by the wall. A couple of people with VR visors that looked like big metal blindfolds were wired in. They sat motionless in their chairs even though they were probably having epic adventures in their heads.

"See anything?" Eaglewing could barely hear Fedora's low, dumb-sounding voice over the club's pounding music. As much as he loved his buddy, Eaglewing had always thought Fedora looked like a dope with his round face, big lips, and shaggy hair sticking out from his signature brimmed hat. Good thing he was a helluva lot smarter than he looked.

A spike of black hair flopped onto Eaglewing's face. He pushed it back. "Just the usual assortment of creepy demon chicks, drugged-out junkies, and hookers, and only a few of 'em at that."

He'd seen a few good-looking ladies, but they'd come on the arms of the bosses and were therefore off-limits. That was the problem with living on a float best known for its crime rate: no decent girls around.

It was still a million times better than the ghetto he and Fedora had grown up in. They'd met back when they went by their real names as fellow thieves on a good-for-nothing Fringe planet. Their combined knacks for messing with computers got them their ticket out. They'd hacked a smuggler ship into thinking they were members of its crew. When the actual crew found out, they dumped the two on Travan Float. But it was okay, since there they could get work as hackers for hire instead of scraping by on what they could steal.

Fedora glanced at the small stage at the back. "I wish the show'd start already."

"Yeah, me too." Bored, Eaglewing looked up at the

muted screen over the bar.

Ah, Sarah DeHaven. My new favorite.

He was more than happy to watch the music video again. Sarah looked like a goddess in her colorful getup, with its high collar and ripped-up skirt. Anyone else would have looked ridiculous wearing that. Eaglewing rested his chin on his hand. He wasn't the type to believe in love, but the effect Sarah DeHaven had on him seemed pretty damn close.

The club's music switched to a crazy electronic fanfare as an overenthusiastic announcer voice blared over the speakers: "Welcome to Hellfire Thirteen!"

Eaglewing snapped out of his Sarah DeHaven-induced trance. Swirling, flame-colored lights flashed around the club.

The club's round-bellied entertainment manager, Van Dinh, strode onto the stage. "Gentlemen of the underworld, for your pleasure and entertainment, I present the *Hellfire Furis!*"

A string of fiery holographic numbers, one through thirteen, splashed across the black backdrop. Each number morphed into a letter, spelling "HELLFIRE FURIS."

Van Dinh spread his arms. "Let's hear it for our thirteen lovely ladies!"

Here we go again.

The letters exploded.

"Destini!"

A new set of flaming letters appeared, spelling "DESTINI." A hot blonde in a skintight red dress strutted across the stage. Eaglewing hooted and catcalled with the rest of the crowd as she stopped in the back corner and struck a sexy pose.

"Rubi!"

The letters spelled "RUBI" as an equally hot redhead in a skimpy yellow outfit sauntered across the stage and struck a pose in the opposite corner.

Eaglewing had seen the routine enough times to have it memorized. Next came curly-haired Triniti, Fedora's favorite. Fedora stood and cheered extra loud for her. Then platinum blonde Stefani, then big-boobed Candi, then Eaglewing's favorite, pouty-lipped Harmoni. But instead of spiky-haired Mandi, a new girl followed.

Eaglewing leaned forward. The new girl had big eyes and long dark hair that was kinda poofy. She wore Mandi's usual getup: tight purple shorts and a see-through lace top over a black bra. But despite her slutty clothes, she was... *cute*. Not that fake baby-doll type of cute. Actually cute.

The holographic letters spelled "KITTI." She looked confused as she walked across the stage and took her place. She put a hand on her hip and popped it out, then ran the other through her hair, craning her neck back in an exaggerated version of what the other girls did. A little half-smile played in the corner of her mouth, as if she thought the whole thing were a big joke she might as well have fun with. She seemed shorter than the others—she wore normal-looking black boots instead of tall, spiky shoes.

The rest of the introductions went on as expected: blue-haired Roxi, babyish Chastiti, super-curvy Kerri. The girls formed a V with Van Dinh as the point. Two ropes dropped from the ceiling. A pair of black-haired girls in gold catsuits entered. They climbed the ropes and twisted themselves into them as the holographic letters spelled, "VALERI & NIKKI."

"And now, saving the best for last—the pride, the glory of all Travan, that goddess of heat, our very own Hellfire Queen—*Juli!*"

Van Dinh left. The crowd hollered enthusiastically. A long-legged girl with a sheet of golden hair pranced up the center of the stage, shining in her flame-colored light-up dress. She took her place at the center of the V, her name spelled out behind her in glittering fireworks.

The intro to a popular club song boomed over the speakers. Juli opened her mouth seductively and belted it out. The other girls sang backup and improvised sexy dances while the two girls on the ropes performed fancy flippy tricks.

Eaglewing hooted with everyone else, but he felt a little tired of the whole shindig. He knew why the girls' stage names were emblazoned so brightly. Guys had to know their names to request... private shows afterward. Yeah, the Furis were hot, but Eaglewing had been a regular at

Hellfire 13 long enough to tell that they were drugged out and dead-eyed, going through the same motions every night in limp, half-hearted movements.

Except the new girl. Her eyes were bright and alive, and she seemed to be having a blast as she oohed and ahhed in the background. Her movements weren't exactly sexy, but they were damn cute. Eaglewing could hear her above the others when she came in at the chorus:

"Let me burn.
"If it's with you, I embrace the fell.
"Even the gods above can't save me now.
"Doom awaits, and I don't give a damn.
"I'll let you drag me straight to hell."

Her voice was pretty, not cracked from trying too hard. Her enthusiasm seemed genuine—and innocent.

Eaglewing fixated on her as the Furis continued their performance. He wondered how a nice girl like that had ended up on Travan Float and fantasized about rescuing her. He glimpsed Fedora staring at her with a stupefied expression. For some reason, that made Eaglewing unhappy.

After the Furis finished their last song, a staircase extended from the edge of the stage. Juli flounced down and into one of the VIP rooms. The other girls scattered, some twisting themselves around the stripper poles and others suggestively approaching select club patrons.

Fedora gawked at Kitti. "Didja notice the new girl?"

"Yeah." Eaglewing followed the girl with his eyes. She looked lost as she crossed the dance floor.

Van Dinh strode toward her. "You! New girl! VIPs requested you. Get your ass in there with Juli."

Kitti crossed her arms. "I don't think so."

"Whadaya mean?" Van Dinh grabbed her wrist and yanked her toward him. "Listen, you little bitch—"

"No, *you* listen!" Kitti twisted out of his grip. "I'm only here because your girl Mandi overdosed and you were hollering in the alley about needing an extra body on stage. I don't work for you! You should thank me for covering your ass!"

"You said—"

"I said I'd fill in for the show, and that's *all*."

"I'm calling—"

"Who? The boss? I'm sure he'd be thrilled to know how you screwed up and let one of your girls get wasted. So I'm walking away, and you're not gonna stop me. Got it?"

Van Dinh scowled. "If you don't come with me *right now*, you'll be sorry."

Kitti grabbed a gun from a tall woman's holster and aimed it at Van Dinh's face. "*Now* will you leave me alone?" She sounded more exasperated than threatening.

She turned to the tall woman, whom Eaglewing recognized as a merc identified only by her distinctive silver armbands. "Sorry, ma'am. I just need to borrow this for a minute. Some guys can't take a hint!"

Oh, shit. What's she thinking?

The lady merc regarded Kitti for a moment, then glowered at Van Dinh. "I'd listen to the girl, if I were you."

Van Dinh opened his mouth, then closed it, then opened it again, mouthing wordlessly like a dumb fish.

Eaglewing snickered. The girl had him cornered. She had a mercenary on her side. *And you don't mess with the mercs.* Most were really assassins who did other stuff in their spare time, like transport dangerous shit. Piss one off, and your head could end up backward on your shoulders.

Van Dinh sputtered, "You—you're—you're not getting paid!" He stormed off.

Kitti smirked. "Oh, no. Whatever will I do." She handed the gun to the lady merc with a grateful smile. "Thank you, ma'am."

"Watch yourself, kid." The lady merc put her gun in its holster and walked away.

Fedora ogled. "Whoa, she's awesome."

"Yeah, that was pretty epic." Eaglewing ran through some pickup lines in his head, trying to find a way to approach Kitti without creeping her out. He was suddenly very aware of the heat in his face and *really* wished he hadn't chugged that beer. His usually pale complexion probably looked redder than the Deroon sun.

Fedora hopped off his barstool. "Yo, Kitti!"

Kitti turned around. "Yeah?"

"You were awesome on stage and even awesomer when

you chewed out Van Dinh. Can I buy you a drink?"

She pushed her eyebrows together. "Who're you?"

Fedora took off his hat and bowed with a dopey grin. "Fedora, at your service."

Eaglewing joined his buddy. "And I'm his pal, Eaglewing. Y'know, you were by far the best one up there. I could hear your pretty little voice above the others. You a pro or somethin'?"

Kitti looked past him. "I'm just a wandering musician, taking random gigs like the rest of my kind."

Eaglewing knew what that look meant. She was trying to escape.

Fedora seemed to notice as well. "How about that drink?"

"No, thanks." She walked toward the tables.

Eaglewing followed. "What're you lookin' for? We practically live here, so we know everything worth knowin'."

Kitti stopped. "I'm looking for a demon. I heard this is where a lot of them hang out. Know any good ones?"

"You're in luck!" Eaglewing jerked both thumbs at himself. "We happen to be two of the best demons on Travan Float."

"Really?"

Fedora butted in, "We're members of the Gag Warriors. Remember that whole Paladin Glen thing?" He patted his chest with pride. "Yeah, that was us."

Eaglewing was annoyed at his pal for taking the spotlight. "It was *my* idea. I was like, what does anyone know about the talking heads they listen to? Let's mess with *their* heads by makin' a fake one!"

Kitti cocked her head. "You're not a *real* hacker, then. You're just a prankster."

Eaglewing pointed at the club's entrance. "We hacked the guard bot back when we were kids! Y'know, the big scary thing that keeps unwanted people outta the club? Yeah, we messed with the codes and made it bow to us when we entered. We're legit."

Fedora lifted his chin boastfully. "We've done stuff for Madam Wrath herself. We were the ones she hired for the Gaipoi job."

Kitti blinked, apparently clueless. "What's that?"

"You've never heard of the Gaipoi job?" Eaglewing spoke

before Fedora could answer. "Madam Wrath got pissed-off at the warlord in charge of the Gaipoi Quadrant on Djuvai, so she put together a Travan crew to steal some of his favorite shit. She *personally* came down here and hired *us* to hack the security cams! They woulda failed if it weren't for the killer virus we wrote."

Kitti laughed.

"Hey, I'm not makin' this up. Ask anyone here!" Eaglewing waved at a nearby demon. "Yo, Wine! Who was the reason the Gaipoi job went down so smoothly?"

Wine grimaced. "If I say, 'You two,' will you shut up about it?"

Eaglewing took that as the testimony he needed. "See? We're good!"

Kitti arched her eyebrows. "Nice."

Fedora grinned. "Now will you get a drink with us?"

Kitti batted her eyes. "Okay, one drink."

Man, she's cute. Eaglewing flagged down the multi-limbed robot hovering behind the bar. "Bartender! Three beers!"

The bartender bot acknowledged their orders with a *ding-ding* and floated off.

Eaglewing sat down beside Kitti as she climbed onto a barstool. "So, your name's not really Kitti, right?"

Fedora took the seat on her other side. "Of course not. No one goes by their real names here. So's it Katherine?"

Kitti tucked a strand of long, wavy hair behind her ear. "Now why would I tell you? You didn't tell me *your* real name."

Fedora jerked his thumb at Eaglewing. "He's Dave Adlersflugel, and I'm Saul Sharda."

You dumbass! Eaglewing looked around hastily. Everyone seemed too wrapped up in their own business to have been listening. He decided to roll with it. "Y'know, Adlersflugel means 'Eaglewing' in one of the ancient languages."

Fedora tipped his hat. "I just like fedoras."

"Fedora..." Kitti drew out the word. "Doesn't that sound a little effeminate?"

Eaglewing burst out laughing and slapped the bar. "She thinks you're effeminate!"

Fedora shot him a pissed-off look. "At least I'm not a

dork like you! Who remembers the stupid dead languages?"

Kitti smiled sweetly. "Don't get me wrong. I think fedoras are great. More people should wear hats."

Fedora looked as if he might melt.

The bartender bot returned with their beers. Eaglewing pulled his glass toward himself. "Hey, we told you ours. What's yours?"

Fedora guzzled half his drink. "Lemme guess. Scarlet?"

Kitti giggled and shook her head.

Eaglewing threw Fedora a disgusted look. "That's a stripper name, you moron. She's a nice girl. So, is it... Alice?"

"Adrianna?" Fedora said.

"Amber?"

Kitti raised an eyebrow. "Are you gonna go through every name alphabetically?"

Fedora grinned. "Yeah, till we get it right!"

She smiled coyly. "Fine. It's Jane."

Fedora threw his hand up. "Oh come on! I told you our *real* names!"

"That *is* my real name. I'm just plain Jane. Sorry to disappoint you guys."

Eaglewing inched closer to her. "Hey, I like it. Sounds classy."

Jane pulled away. Eaglewing, not wanting to be a creeper, backed off.

A green-haired demon known as Gambler waved in his direction. "Fedora! Eaglewing! You heard? Word's going around the float that Black Knight's back in town."

Eaglewing swiveled his barstool to face him. "C'mon, Gambler, how many Black Knight sightings have there been over the years? And how many turned out to be legit?"

Gambler approached the bar. "I overheard it from a Wrath Guard, and he seemed pretty sure."

Eaglewing scoffed, "You're also the one who believes the scammers who say they've captured an intelligent alien."

Gambler jutted his chin. "Hey, you never know. Space is big."

Fedora twisted around to face Gambler. "Dude, we've settled hundreds of worlds over hundreds of years. If there were intelligent aliens to be found, *someone* woulda run into them by now. Stop being so fucking gullible!"

Gambler scowled. "When Black Knight shows up and starts shooting up the place, don't say you weren't warned." He made his way over to the tables and joined Wine.

Eaglewing spun his stool back to the bar. "That guy'll believe anything."

Jane watched Gambler and Wine curiously, as though eavesdropping on their conversation.

Eaglewing tried to regain her attention. "There've been tons of rumors about Black Knight, but I'm tellin' ya, he's *gone*. He slipped up last time he was here. Lost his signature helmet and let everyone see his face. Fedora and I were there when it happened, and, man, it was *epic*. There was this huge firefight, and then he blew up half the storage sector going after one little demon. Talk about overkill!"

Jane kept her gaze on Gambler and Wine. "Who was he?"

Eaglewing leaned back so she'd see him. "One of the most notorious mercs Travan's ever known. I got here after his heyday, but pretty much everyone who lives here has something to say about him. I mean, this guy wasn't just scary, he was *sick*."

Fedora piped up, "Even the bosses were afraid of him. He was in and outta here for a decade before he disappeared six or seven years ago. Everyone's been wondering what happened to him."

Jane had a funny look in her eyes. "I see."

Eaglewing took a swig of his beer. "So, what's a nice girl like you doing in this shithole? Why're you lookin' for a demon?"

Jane lowered her eyelids and closed her mouth into a little pout.

Fedora leaned toward her with concern. "What's wrong?"

She looked up with her big dark eyes. "Can I be straight with you guys? It's just... weird... I don't know how to tell you..."

"With words!"

Eaglewing smacked Fedora.

Fedora winced. "*Ow!*"

"You deserved that!" Eaglewing turned back to Jane, ignoring Fedora's grumbles. "Hey, you can trust us. You've got our real names. That's the ultimate trump card around here."

Jane hesitated. "I'm looking for two... machines. Big, boxy robots capable of extending multiple appendages. No one's seen them before, and I have no idea who owns or controls them. I know it sounds insane, but..." She sighed. "I *have* to find them."

Eaglewing recalled something he'd seen on the Net a few days ago. He patted the bar in excitement. "I've hearda that! Corsair posted it all over the Collective's forum! Before No Name deleted it, that is."

Jane's eyes brightened. "You know Corsair?"

"Yeah! He's in the Gag Warriors with me 'n' my buddy here." Eaglewing stroked his chin. "The machines you're talkin' about, they're these weird-ass blue things on wheels, right?"

"Exactly! Corsair said they were somewhere on Travan Float but couldn't get more than that." Jane's face fell. "I don't know if anyone can help me, though. If Corsair couldn't find them, who can?"

Fedora perked up. "Uh, *we* can? Corsair's good and all, but we're *pros*! I've hacked this float so many times I've lost count! I'll find your machines in fifteen minutes, tops!"

Jane looked at Fedora admiringly. "Could you?"

Eaglewing was bummed he hadn't volunteered first. "I'll bet it'll take less than ten! And the number's a hundred and seven."

Jane turned that admiring look toward him. "Whoa, that's impressive."

Eaglewing grinned, lost for a moment in those eyes.

Fedora whipped his slate out of his pocket.

Eaglewing craned his neck. "What're you doin' over there?"

"Finding those machines, duh!" Fedora typed furiously.

Eaglewing got up and went over to him. "They still usin' that password algorithm?"

"Yup, dumbasses. Okay, I've remoted into the Wrath Guards' drive. What'd we call the wares we left there last week?"

"G-R-A-Five-S-Zero and F-Three-R-N-A-N-Zero-Zero." Eaglewing looked over Fedora's shoulder. "Whadaya know? They're still there! Make that five minutes."

Fedora opened a program. "Ugh, their coding's a mess! It gets worse every time!"

Eaglewing glanced at Jane. "It's 'cause we keep messin' with it, and they never figure out how to put it back." He pictured Madam Wrath's people puzzling over the code and sneered. "I've left some real doozies in the comments. So why do you wanna find those machines?"

Jane put a finger to her lips. "It's a secret."

Fedora elbowed Eaglewing. "Dude! You gonna help or what?"

Eaglewing and Fedora did their thing while Jane watched. They'd hacked the float so many times before that, even though Madam Wrath's security people kept changing stuff around, the basics were the same.

Eaglewing was right. It took a little more than five minutes to access the security footage.

Fedora pumped his fist. "That's gotta be a record! Uh... So there are a lotta cams. Tell me if you see something."

He pressed an icon, and the feeds from the float's numerous cameras flashed across the screen one by one. A few minutes passed. Eaglewing didn't look for the machines, though. He stared at Jane's pretty little face.

Jane's eyes widened. "*Stop!*"

Fedora, who had also been staring, jabbed his finger onto the touchscreen. The footage displayed the two weird-ass boxy things Eaglewing had seen on the Net, except the pictures were a lot clearer. The view fizzled out, replaced by a plain blue screen.

Fedora swiped his figure across the frozen slate. "*Fuck*! Those *bastards*! Anyone got something sharp?"

Jane pulled a pin from her hair. "What happened?"

Fedora accepted the pin. "No Name got me."

"Are you sure it was them?"

Fedora stuck one of the hairpin's prongs in a tiny hole on the slate's edge, forcing the device to reboot. "Yeah. Madam Wrath's guys woulda left a scary message, and they're the only ones who police the systems here. Plus, they wouldn't've caught us so fast."

Jane bit her lip. "Did you see where those machines were?"

Eaglewing returned to his barstool. "The cam was in one of the big warehouses on the float's lowest level, in the storage sector."

Jane pulled her own slate out of her pocket. Eaglewing wondered how it fit in those tight purple shorts of hers.

He heard a cry and looked back. A bunch of people tried to get the attention of a man sprawled at one of the virtu-game consoles. The man stared up with empty eyes.

"Freaking addicts. I don't get how anyone can get stuck in there. It's just a game." Eaglewing turned to Jane. "So, how'd you know about No Name? You don't seem like the type to hang around Netcrew forums."

Jane tapped her slate. "I read. I heard they're like independent cyberpolice, except they've also been doing strange things like faking documents and hiding information. Any idea what's going on there?"

Eaglewing peered at her slate. She was messaging someone. "The Collective thinks they're into some kinda AI shit. Fedora and I tried trackin' 'em, but they keep dodgin' our wares. It's like they never stay on the same drive for more than a minute."

Fedora gave up on his slate and threw it on the ground. "Fuckers. They've been kinda quiet lately. Until they fried me. Still, were we fast or what?"

"Yeah, thanks, guys, you were great." Jane smiled, but she looked worried. "Well, it's been fun, but I've gotta find those things before they disappear again." She got up and walked across the dance floor toward the exit.

Eaglewing jumped off his barstool and followed. "Hey, wait a sec. They're not goin' anywhere! Someone left 'em in storage! You've got some time."

Fedora rushed to catch up. "You know, in one of the ancient languages, 'Jane' means 'God is gracious.' I think God has been most gracious by bringing you here. Won't you grace us more with your presence?"

Eaglewing smacked his own face, cringing at his buddy's lameness. "What the *fuck* was that? You *tryin'* to scare her away?"

Jane stopped. "Listen, guys, I'm grateful for your help, I really am. But I have to go now."

Eaglewing realized what her game had been. "You played us!"

"I'm really sorry... I just... I had to find them."

Eaglewing wanted to be mad at her, but she looked so guilty with that pout of hers, and her big eyes were so full of worry, more like fear. He was mad at himself for being mad at her. "Hey, no worries, I get it. You're in some kinda trouble, aren't you? Don't be scared. We've all gotten in over our heads at some point. Tell me what's goin' on."

Fedora nodded. "Yeah, we can help."

"I don't think you can, but I appreciate the offer." Jane checked something on her slate, then folded it and stuck it in her pocket. "Maybe I can stay a bit longer, since it'll take him a while to get here..."

One of the galaxy's hottest club songs boomed through the speakers. Colorful lights swept across the dance floor, some of them spotlighting the Furis on the stripper poles.

An eager smile spread across Jane's face. "I freaking love this song!"

She rocked out as though possessed by the music. Eaglewing cheered her on, pumping his fists to the beat. Fedora bobbed his head in an attempt to dance. Jane seemed to shake away whatever had made her so anxious, escaping into the haze of swirling lights and pounding music.

A purple spotlight landed on her. She laughed. She grabbed a pole, hooked her knee against it, and spun to the ground. "Wheeeee!"

"*Jane*?" A tall man in a black T-shirt approached with a look of horror. Eaglewing thought he looked familiar but couldn't figure out why.

Jane got up. "Devin! That was fast. How'd you get in here?"

Devin pulled her away from the pole. "What the hell are you doing? Where the hell are your clothes?" He opened the bag he carried on his shoulder, pulled out a black jacket, and tried to wrap it around her.

Jane pushed him away. "Oh you're one to talk. You're the one who tore your shirt off like a freaking meathead!"

Devin gave her a stern look. "Put the jacket on. You look like a child prostitute!"

She placed her hands on her hips. "I can dress as I please, and there's nothing you can do about it!"

Eaglewing boldly stepped up to Devin. "Who the fuck

are you?" *Probably a jealous ex.*

Devin looked down at him. "Who are *you*?"

He suddenly seemed very tall. Eaglewing backed away nervously.

Jane rubbed her forearm. "It's okay, Devin. This is Dave. He and Saul here were helping me out."

Fedora huffed. "Uh, that's *Eaglewing* and *Fedora* to you."

Jane gave him an apologetic smile. "Right, sorry."

Fedora slumped his shoulders. "He your boyfriend?"

"Yes," Jane said in a breathy voice. She clung to Devin's arm and made a kissy face.

Devin pried her off, and she giggled. "Knock it off, Pony. I'm her brother."

Eaglewing regarded Jane, then Devin. *I see the resemblance.* Same straight nose, same wavy hair, except Jane had much more of it.

Devin wrapped his jacket around Jane again, and she accepted it with a sigh. "What're you doing in this hellhole? I told you to stay in the ship!"

Jane pulled the jacket on. "Good thing I didn't, because Eaglewing and Fedora here found the machines we're looking for."

"That's right!" Eaglewing said. "They're in a warehouse in the storage sector. The big kind, like the ones used by the arms dealers."

Devin looked impressed with Jane, and she gloated.

Fedora rounded his mouth into a surprised O. "Whoa! I know you! You're Bl—"

"You have me confused with someone else," Devin interrupted.

Black Knight? No way! No wonder he looks so familiar.

Gambler was right for once. The rumors of Black Knight's return *were* true. Maybe hitting on his sister wasn't such a good idea.

And shit, he hasn't told her *who he is. Smart.*

Devin pressed the edges of his bag together to close it. "How'd you two find the machines?"

Fedora looked awed. "Hacked into the security cams, but my slate got fried before I could get a closer look. I'm pretty sure it was No Name."

Devin grabbed Jane's arm. "We have to go. *Now*." He walked quickly toward the exit, pulling her along.

"Thanks, guys!" Jane called over her shoulder.

Fedora started to follow. "Hey, wait up!"

Eaglewing grabbed his arm. "Let 'em go."

Fedora stopped and stared after Jane. "We coulda helped or something!"

"Maybe, but we oughta stay outta it. You don't mess with the mercs."

Fedora frowned. After a moment, he muttered, "Yeah, you're right."

Eaglewing returned to his spot at the bar. *Guess that's the last time I'll see her. Damn. She was really cute.*

Fedora sat down beside him and looked sullenly at Jane's untouched drink.

Eaglewing shrugged. "Meh, plenty of stars in the night."

"True that." Fedora picked up his beer.

Eaglewing picked up his own and clinked glasses with his pal.

Jane walked down a grimy corridor lined with bars, whorehouses, and other hives of debauchery. Her brother kept her close, glaring at any drunk who glanced at her the wrong way. One particularly rude man got a threatening gun in the face.

Devin kept the gun in his hand after the man stumbled off. "Now will you tell me why you're dressed like this?"

"It's my Hellfire Furis costume. That's how I got past the bouncer bot: I went into the club as a performer." Jane described how she'd looked for a back way into the club and seen Van Dinh slapping an unconscious girl while yelling at his assistant to find him another. "I went to tell him to stop hitting her, and he asked if I wanted a job. I saw my way in, so I said 'sure' and nicked Mandi's outfit. We sang all my favorites." She smiled as she recalled the joy of being able to, just for a moment, forget the craziness of the past few days.

Devin's expression relaxed. "Had fun?"

"It was awesome. Okay, your turn. How'd *you* get in?"

"They mistook me for someone else and let me through."

Jane narrowed her eyes. "Do you really expect me to

believe that?" *I don't get what's so secret about conning your way into a club.*

Devin stopped at one of the doors that led to the float's public transportation system. He opened his bag and dropped the gun inside, then grabbed a card and swiped it against a square scanner. The doors parted, revealing a box-like transport.

Devin stepped inside. "C'mon." He punched a code into the control panel. "Hold onto something."

Jane entered and grabbed a handrail. The doors closed. She was about to ask how he knew his way around so well when the transport zoomed forward. She forgot her question as she clung to the bar, struggling to remain upright.

A few dizzying turns and a terrifyingly long drop later, the transport stopped.

Jane kept her grip on the handrail as the doors opened. The ground seemed to sway beneath her. Her head ached as if someone had jammed a pole through her forehead, and her face tingled with cold. *Ugh. This is no time to be motion sick.*

She stepped out of the transport. A group of Wrath Guards stood at the end of the corridor.

One of them pointed at Devin. "Hey, there he is!"

Devin pushed Jane back into the transport as the Wrath Guards fired, along with the float's internal defense guns. He reached into his bag and grabbed the odd spherical device she'd seen previously.

She covered her ears as a high-pitched electric squeal ripped through the air. An invisible force knocked her into the back wall of the transport. The lights cut out.

A few seconds later, a neon green luminance broke the blackness. Devin had a glow-torch, a cylindrical light powered by phosphorescent chemicals. He pulled Jane into the corner behind him. She pressed her back against the wall, unable to see anything but the vague green light.

A series of unusually loud and sharp *bangs* rang out. Each shot seemed to jam a new pole into her head. She squeezed her eyes shut. She couldn't tell which shots were fired by the thugs and which by her brother. A minute later, she heard shouts from the corridor, followed by the sound of running.

"Jane, let's go."

Jane opened her eyes. "What was that?"

Devin stepped out of the transport. "I could see them, they couldn't see me, and they were smart enough to run."

She stood. "That's not what I meant! What was that blast?"

"Portable electromagnetic pulse bomb. Knocked out power to the whole sector, and probably some of the neighboring ones." He walked briskly down the corridor.

Jane rushed to catch up. "Where the hell did you get something like that?"

"Had it on me."

"You expect me to believe you happened to be carrying it around in your freaking *office bag*? Liar! Why can't you just tell me?"

Devin stopped at an intersection, swept his glow-torch, and proceeded down the corridor to the right. "Let me know if you hear anyone coming. Looks like Madam Wrath put a hit out on me. Either she has a hell of a grudge over the trouble I caused last time, or No Name's pretending to be her. Do you remember anything specific about the warehouse?"

"Only that there were a bunch of machine bits around. Wait, you've been here before?" Jane was more annoyed than frustrated when Devin didn't respond. *Guess I should be used to it. Jerk!*

Under ordinary circumstances, she would have harangued him about keeping secrets from her when she told him everything. Walking down a dark corridor while keeping an eye out for armed thugs hardly counted as ordinary circumstances, so she kept her rant to herself.

She jogged to keep up with Devin's hurried pace. Each step took more effort than the one before. Her aching head felt strangely heavy. *What's with me? It's just a little speed-walking! I'm probably sleep-deprived and dehydrated.*

A pair of wide metal doors stood at the end of the corridor. They looked eerie and supernatural in green light, reminding Jane of gateways to the underworld she'd seen in fantasy holodramas.

Devin stopped and opened his bag. He pulled out a small handgun, the kind that used bullets. His bomb must have disabled all machines, including laser guns.

No wonder those shots were so piercing.

He handed her the glow-torch. "I picked up some supplies while you were partying. Aim the light at the door."

"Okay." Jane held the light steady as Devin regarded the crack between the two doors. He fired first at the bottom, then at three points in the middle, then at the top.

After flicking the gun's safety switch, he dropped the weapon in his bag. "All right, we should be able to pry it open. This warehouse is the only one not controlled by the arms dealers, so I figured the machines would be here. I hope I'm right."

He pulled at one of the doors. His unsolicited explanation had raised more questions for Jane than it had answered. *How does he know that? Aren't arms dealers super-secretive?* The thought of finding the machines and maybe Adam kept her from asking.

Jane put the glow-torch under her chin so she could have both hands free to help Devin with the door. Straining her arms sharpened the pain on her forearm from where the chemical had splashed.

Something snapped. The door slid open. Jane stumbled backward. She dropped the glow-torch as she grabbed her brother for support. *Adam's gotta be in there.*

She snatched the light and slipped through the opening. All she could see in the mostly empty warehouse were a few boxes and a bunch of robots, most of which lay in pieces. In the center, isolated from the rest, sat two familiar machines, deactivated, with their appendages and wheels folded. Jane wanted to grab Devin's gun and blast them to hell.

Then she noticed what they guarded: a box about the size of a coffin attached to a complex-looking cylindrical-shaped machine. Her heart jumped, and she ran to it.

The box's control panels were dark. A set of thick cords wound around its center. Jane grabbed one and tugged with all her strength.

Devin pulled out the handgun. "Back up."

He crouched by the box and fired at the cords. The bullet tore through them, chopping them in half. Jane shoved the glow-torch at him. Cold air blasted her face as she ripped off the lid.

Inside, Adam lay with his eyes closed. Several round pads adhered to his face, connected to wires radiating from his head. Needles protruded from his neck and arms, attached to opaque tubes snaking into the box's walls.

CHAPTER 12

TIME TO GO

JANE WANTED TO YANK THOSE creepy needles away from Adam, but for all she knew, doing so could make his comatose state permanent. She had no idea how a stasis box worked. Did blowing the power mess with whatever kept him suspended? Clueless, she examined the box's machinery. *How the hell am I supposed to wake him?*

"Jane!"

Jane looked over at Devin, who opened one of the other boxes in the warehouse.

Devin went through the box's contents. "Jam the door with something."

"But—"

"Your friend's drugged." He moved to the next box. "The power could return any second and trap us here."

Jane tore herself from Adam's side. She searched the darkness for something she could use. Her gaze fell on a headless, cube-shaped robot body. She heard a *bang* and whirled. Devin aimed the handgun at one of the warehouse's internal defense guns and fired again.

Good idea.

Jane pushed back the sleeves of her too-big jacket, shoved the machine body toward the warehouse's double doors, and rammed it into the gap.

The lights came back on, making everything insanely bright. A deafening alarm shrieked.

A quick series of blasts. Jane spun frantically. Devin aimed his laser gun at a pile of deep blue machinery.

He reached into the pile and grabbed something.

"They reactivated."

Jane wished she'd had her chance at revenge even though the machines were only instruments. "Should've been me."

Devin shot something beside her. "Fucking machines!"

He blasted the other robots, taking them out with a deadly precision that reminded Jane of all her questions. After he finished, he approached and gave her the handgun. "In case things get ugly. There are only ten shots left, so don't use it unless you must."

Jane took the weapon, cold and small, yet frightening in its power.

"Jane?" Adam sat in the box, blinking. He held his head with one hand.

"*Adam!*" Jane rushed over and threw her arms around him, relieved that he was able to wake up after all.

"Good to see you too, but why are you armed?"

"Yikes, forgot I had this." She stuffed the gun into her pocket. "Holy *shit*, Adam, *are you okay*?"

"Yes, just... confused." Adam brushed his light brown hair to the side, peeled one of the pads off his forehead, and examined it with bewilderment.

"You won't believe what—"

The sound of blasts interrupted her.

Devin shot out the door, aiming high. "Hey! I'm glad you lovebirds are reunited, but it's time to *go*."

Jane's mouth fell open. "We are *not* lovebirds!"

Crack.

The force of the doors crushed the machine body holding them open.

Jane hurriedly helped Adam remove the rest of the pads and tubes. Adam winced as she tugged the needles out of his arms. When she finished, she stood so quickly that black dots splattered across her vision. She started toward her brother, then noticed Adam still in the box. He clutched his forearms with his hands.

"What's wrong?" she asked.

"I don't know." Adam took her outreached hand and pulled himself up. "I'm... hallucinating or something. What happened to me?"

Jane didn't get a chance to answer. A blinding light

and a high-pitched squeal inundated her senses. Her head seemed to split in half, and she had the bizarre desire to chop it off and be done with the pain.

———————— ➤◄◇►◄ ————————

Devin regretted using the flash grenade as soon as he'd thrown it. He'd only had the one, and seventeen levels separated him from the Stargazer. About a dozen Wrath Guards had run straight at him. Despite his instinct to rush in firing, he couldn't have taken them all. They currently lay unconscious on the floor, but they wouldn't stay out for long. He'd destroyed the internal defenses in the corridor. The coast was clear.

He turned around. "Jane! Adam!"

Jane held her head with both hands, her mouth open as though screaming in silence.

Devin took a step toward her. "Jane, what—"

"*Warn me next time!*" Jane yelled.

Crack. The machine body between the doors crumpled.

"Let's *go!*" Devin watched the corridor, weapon raised in case more Wrath Guards showed up.

Jane climbed onto the machine body and slipped out, giving him a furious glare. She looked back. "Adam!"

Devin turned. Adam stood still, clutching his arms. "*Adam!*"

Adam snapped to attention. "Sorry." He ran to the doors and started to climb onto the machine body, then froze.

"*Move!*" Devin yelled.

Adam blinked rapidly. "Sorry." He climbed out.

Crack.

Devin jumped onto the machine body and into the corridor. The doors slammed shut behind him.

He glared at Adam. "What the *hell* was that?"

Adam gave him a helpless, apologetic look. "I'm sorry... I—I didn't mean to..."

Devin put his hand in his pocket to make sure the computer chip he'd taken from one of the machines was still there. It was.

Adam leaned against the wall and closed his eyes.

Jane approached him worriedly. "How long were you out?"

"No idea." Adam opened his eyes. "The last thing I

remember was entering my dorm room. I feel like... I'm losing control of my limbs or something..."

Definitely drugged.

The float's internal defenses fired around the corner. *Too many—can't destroy them without getting hit.* Devin looked up and found the vent leading to the utility conduits.

Jane followed his gaze. "Not more conduits."

"Get back." He blasted around the vent's edges until it fell, leaving a square hole in the ceiling. The gun clanged as he tossed it up. He jumped, grabbed the opening's edge, and pulled himself in. His head brushed against the metal ceiling. Cold air breezed past him.

Crouching, he surveyed the dark conduit. *Nothing unusual.* He reached down, grabbed Jane's wrists, and hauled her up.

"Give Adam a hand. I have to figure this place out." Devin approached the control panel a few yards away. Dozens of switches greeted him, labeled with letters and numbers. He ran through his memories, trying to recall the float's layout—and which switch would turn on the lights.

Adam looked up the hole where the vent had been. "Say, Jane? I know it's a bad time to ask, seeing as we're running for our lives and all, but... what's going on? It's not every day I wake up in a box to the sound of guns going off."

Jane lay on her stomach. "You were kidnapped. I went to your dorm and saw this deep blue robot carrying you out the window. That was... about three days ago." She reached down, grabbed Adam's wrists, and bit her lip as she pulled.

Adam grabbed the edge of the conduit. "Wait... what?"

Jane let go of him, sat up, and held out a hand. Adam took it, and she grabbed his wrist with her other hand.

"No one would believe me." She sounded strained as she leaned back, hauling him up by one arm. "They said you'd gone on a retreat and couldn't be reached because of religious isolation."

Adam pressed his elbows into the conduit floor and pushed himself up. "That was... clever."

AN-50N—that's it. Devin flipped the switch with that label. A line of green lights flickered on above him. "C'mon."

Jane crawled behind him. "Adam, can I just say those stupid Via retreats are full of shit! Who the hell goes and cuts themselves off from the world so no one even knows when they've been *kidnapped*? It's the most *idiotic* thing I've ever heard of!"

Adam followed her. "That's not very nice. Isolation is paramount to—"

"*Don't*! Do you have *any idea* how many times I got that freaking line? Your cultish Via programs are downright *stupid*!"

"Again, not very nice."

Jane stopped and faced him. "*I don't care*! Dammit, Adam! You were *gone*, and no one was even looking for you because they thought you'd gone off to commune with the Absolute or some bullshit!"

"You're right," Adam said gently. "I guess they are pretty dumb."

Good answer. Devin had only met Adam once before, when he'd run into him and Jane at Quasar's café four weeks back. Dad had charged Devin with finding out just what kind of boy Jane spent so much time with. Devin could barely remember anything about the kid other than that he was nice. There was nothing anyone could say against him, and while that was an admirable trait, Devin found it puzzling that his vivacious sister would enjoy the company of someone so... boring.

He approached an intersection. Spidery mechanical arms waved in his face. He instinctively blasted. After destroying the repair bot, he noticed the gun it had been carrying and was glad he'd shot first.

Jane peered over his shoulder. "Oh, so that's why these things are so small. Damn machines." She looked back at Adam. "Just so you know, we're on Travan Float. Heard of it?"

Adam nodded. "People at school often joke about Counselors being sent to work there if they get in trouble. It's supposed to be a crime-ridden cesspool."

"It is. And whoever took you left you here, boxed up in a warehouse like you were a piece of cargo."

"Who were they? What did they want with me?"

Seeing a shadow before him, Devin held up his gun.

The shadow didn't move. He looked closer. *Only a broken ceiling panel.*

He relaxed and moved forward. "The Networld calls them No Name. They wanted to replace you with an AI lookalike."

"Is he kidding?" Adam sounded perplexed.

"Afraid not," Jane replied.

"So lifelike androids... they exist?"

"Yes." Devin tried not to think about the lie he'd lived with or his disappointment that nothing in the warehouse told him where Sarah might be. "On the outside, they're completely indistinguishable from humans. Before you ask where they're coming from—I don't know. I've already run into one of them."

Devin expected Adam to ask where or when, but something in his voice must have discouraged questions.

"Thanks. For finding me, I mean." Adam sounded almost fearful, like he was intimidated.

Devin hadn't meant to scare the kid, and he felt a little bad for having yelled at him earlier. He jerked his head toward Jane. "It's her fault we're here. I had to do *something* to stop the ranting."

"*Hey!*" Jane cried.

"You also get the credit!"

"Yes, I do." She gloated. "Oh, and Adam, in case you were wondering, that's why I'm dressed like a... hey, bro, how'd you put it?"

"A child prostitute," Devin said dryly.

"Heh, yeah. I got into one of those underground criminals-only clubs as a performer and sweet-talked some demons into hacking the float's security cameras for me."

"I was wondering about that," Adam said. "Didn't seem like your usual style."

"I actually like it. What do you think?"

"That's entrapment! Either you'll get mad at me, or your big brother will beat me up! I'm not answering."

Devin smiled. "Smart choice."

A wide shaft lay ahead. He hoped it was the one he sought. Travan was an old float, and so its transports still used cables. The thick black cords moved lightning fast as box-like cars zipped up and down at dizzying speeds.

At the end of the conduit, Devin looked out and was

relieved to see crude rungs on the shaft's wall above him. The rungs had been put in place over the years for innumerable heists and criminal missions, forming a ladder from where he was on the lowest level to the top of the float.

He shoved his gun into his bag, grabbed the first rung—which was right above the conduit's opening—and climbed up. Less than a yard behind him, a cable moved continuously upward. Across the shaft, another cable—the other half of the revolving cable system—moved downward. A transport above him latched onto it and the other downward-moving cables, went down a few levels, and then latched onto a horizontal cable set. It disappeared into a tunnel.

"We're *climbing*?" Jane groaned. "Are you serious?"

"It's safer than the stairwells," Devin replied.

"And we'll get trapped if we used the transports. I hate being a fugitive." She sounded drained, which was strange since it usually took a lot to wear her out. They hadn't exactly been running around—yet.

Devin looked back. "You okay?"

Jane sighed. "I'm fine." She climbed the ladder behind him.

Adam emerged from the conduit. "I know I'm approaching my question quota for the day, but... who's after us?"

"The float proprietor's goons," Jane replied. "She put a hit out on Devin, and they don't seem too concerned with collateral damage."

"What? Why's there a hit on Devin?"

"I got too close to their evil plans," Devin said.

He was between the third and fourth levels when Jane yelled, "Devin! Above you!"

He looked up. A robotic arm with a gun reached out of a conduit a couple levels above him. He flattened himself against the rungs. A laser blast flew past his head.

Devin whipped out his gun. As he destroyed that repair bot, another emerged. And then another from a different conduit. And then another. Every time he hit one, it seemed two took its place, all sticking out of different conduits above him and firing relentlessly. Fortunately for him, the robots used small caliber lasers that did little more than pierce the shaft's metal walls. They had terrible aim.

Devin shifted his position and fired back. *Why would anyone send them? They're not exactly attack drones.* Repair bots had visual sensors designed for myopic close-up work, making them useless for targeting anything more than a yard away. *Must be because nothing else would fit in the conduits.* Their presence seemed to confirm that No Name had infiltrated the float's central computer, and that Madam Wrath had nothing to do with what was going on.

It wouldn't be long before his luck ran out—or a missed shot hit one of the kids. He looked behind him at the fast-moving cable.

Jane must have had the same idea as he did. Before he could say anything, she jumped off the ladder and grabbed the black cord.

"*Jane!*" Devin watched in alarm as she zoomed up the shaft. For several tense seconds, there was no reply.

"I'm up here!" Jane's voice sounded small and faraway, barely audible over the blasting and the whooshing of the transports.

Adam stared up the shaft. "Please tell me you're kidding."

Devin shot another robot. "Go!"

"You go first—you're the one they're after!"

Devin would've told the kid to *move it* but was forced to jump when a blast broke the rung he held. He caught the cable with one hand, which burned from the friction as he flew upward. He couldn't hear anything over the roaring of air.

The top of the shaft rapidly approached. He pushed off the cable and caught one of the rungs.

"Devin!" Jane's head stuck out of a conduit two levels above him. "Where's Adam?"

"He's coming." Devin pressed himself against the ladder as a transport nearly clipped him, then climbed into a conduit. He looked back.

Adam flew up on the cable, expression terrified. He passed Devin and was almost at the top of the shaft when he let go and grabbed the ladder. Adam's grip on the rung slipped, and he fell.

Fuck! Devin heard Jane scream as he reached out and caught Adam's arm. *That was too close.*

Adam grabbed the nearest rung. "Thanks." He

sounded shaky.

Jane exhaled and closed her eyes. When she opened them again, they were still filled with horror.

Adam looked up at her. "I'm all right, Jane. That was... fun."

Whoever controlled the machines must have decided it wasn't worth firing upward, for the shooting had stopped.

On the conduit's ceiling, the number twenty-six gleamed in painted white numbers. *Nine levels above the Stargazer.*

"Jane," Devin said. "We overshot. Come down to this level."

Jane climbed into the conduit behind him, then turned back. "Adam, c'mon."

Adam reluctantly released his grip on the rung. He started climbing in, then abruptly stopped and grabbed his wrist. "Sorry... Those drugs... I keep feeling like..."

"Like what?" Jane asked.

"Like I should attack your brother," he finished apologetically.

Devin wondered what the hell kind of drug No Name used on the kid. He knew firsthand how powerful mind-altering drugs could be, and he had to give Adam credit for his willpower.

But if he succumbs and attacks me, it'd be easy enough to knock him out.

As Devin approached an intersection, a robotic arm fired at him. The blast missed and punctured the ceiling. He shot back, pulling the trigger repeatedly to destroy the machine.

Jane reached around him and picked up a piece of burnt metal. "Safer than the stairs, you said."

A mechanical hum. Devin whipped to the side and shot another armed bot. "We should get out of here."

Jane flicked the metal at him. "You *think*?"

He approached a vent in the conduit's floor. Below him lay a richly decorated lounge covered in luxurious tapestries embroidered with flame-like patterns. The place appeared deserted. He aimed his gun at the vent's corner and fired around its edges until it fell onto the black carpet. Hearing nothing from below, he stuffed his gun into his bag and jumped down.

The fall was further than he'd expected. The impact rippled up his body like a shockwave. He straightened.

The lavishly adorned room glowed red from the light of scarlet chandeliers. Sculptures of vicious creatures stood in the corners. Large black chairs ringed a circular table. A tall black shelf displayed holographic heads, each with a name and date emblazoned underneath—portraits of memorable adversaries Madam Wrath had eliminated. The room must have been her private lounge in some club.

Damn. I should've known.

At least that meant no security cameras would give away his position.

Jane looked down with a doubtful expression, as though asking if she was really expected to jump the distance.

Devin glanced at the shelf. "Wait there."

He approached it, aiming to grab it so she could use it as a ladder. Someone sat in a chair whose back had faced him. He pulled out his gun with a start.

"What is it?" Jane asked.

Devin kept his weapon raised as he walked toward the occupied chair. To his surprise, he found Madam Wrath lying there, limp but breathing. Two barely discernible injection sites dotted her neck.

"It's Madam Wrath." Devin prodded her with his weapon. She didn't react, so he prodded her harder. *Still nothing.* "She's out cold."

"*The* Madam Wrath?" Jane sounded surprised. "Then who the hell is ordering everyone to hunt you?"

"Must be No Name." Devin shoved the shelf toward the hole in the ceiling.

"Those guys keep getting scarier and scarier." Jane climbed down.

Meanwhile, he kept a watchful eye on Madam Wrath.

"*Jane!*" Adam cried.

Devin turned in time to see his sister land on her back. He rushed over and knelt beside her.

Jane sat up. "I'm fine." She drooped forward.

Devin dropped his gun and caught her by the shoulders. "Hey, Pony, look at me." He was alarmed when she didn't immediately retort.

Adam climbed down. "Jane, are you hurt?"

"I'm fine." Jane looked up at Devin. "And don't call me Pony." Her smile was a weary imitation of her usual cocky smirk.

Devin let go of her. "What happened?"

"Ah, it was stupid... lost my grip." She closed her eyes and put a hand on her head. "Just got the wind knocked outta me... Gimme a sec... Okay, I'm good."

She opened her eyes and slowly got up. Devin picked up his gun as he stood. Jane swayed, and both he and Adam rushed to support her.

She shook them off. "I told you I'm *fine*. C'mon. Let's go before the queen bitch wakes up." She marched toward the lounge door.

Had they been anywhere else, Devin would have insisted she stop and rest, but they didn't have much time before No Name figured out where they were.

She reached for the door's controls.

"Wait," Devin said. Jane drew her hand back. "We can't go out into the club. Madam Wrath's known for being private. There should be a second exit."

He lifted one of the tapestries and felt along the wall in case he missed something with his eyes.

"Over here!" Adam called. He held up a tapestry, revealing a rectangular door.

Devin approached. Knowing the door would be locked, he blasted around its edges. He kicked the center, and it fell back.

The dark, deserted corridor ahead didn't look familiar. The alarms sounded distant, as though coming from a different level.

Jane stepped out of Madam Wrath's room. Devin held out a hand to stop her. He approached the perpendicular corridor, which was illuminated by dim yellowish lights, and checked the ceiling for internal defense guns.

Nothing. And no one. "C'mon."

Most of the float's levels had the same layout. Devin tried to recall where the stairs would be.

The club was right by the transport shaft, directly above the storage sector... Shit. Shouldn't have made that turn.

He pivoted and went back. "We're going the wrong way."

Jane walked beside him. "How do you know this place

so well, anyway?"

"You're not going to tell me off?"

"Of course I am. You're slipping up, bro! Whatever happened to those super mercenary skills of yours?"

Jane had no way of knowing how close her joke was to the truth, but the mention nevertheless made Devin uneasy.

"Mercenary?" Adam asked.

Devin turned into the dark corridor. "She's kidding. The staircase should be just up ahead. Once we—"

He stopped. Someone was approaching.

No, not someone.

Devin spun and fired a rapid succession of shots before the giant guard bot could raise its weapon. Although damaged, it continued trundling toward him on its short, thick legs. It clumsily expelled blasts as he repeatedly hit its weapon. That model must have been built to withstand lasers.

"*Run!*" he shouted.

Jane grabbed Adam's wrist and sprinted down the corridor. Devin pulled the trigger again and again. After what must have been a thousand shots, he wore down the robot's weapon. It kept moving forward, but having rendered it harmless, he left it and ran into the staircase.

He couldn't see Jane or Adam—they were probably a few levels below him. He raced down the steps and leaped down half-flights of stairs, hoping any Wrath Guards who may have been alerted to his whereabouts would take time to catch up.

No such luck.

———————— ◆◇◆ ————————

Jane whirled when she heard the gunfire, which was muffled by the thick dullness that had filled her ears since she'd fallen in Madam Wrath's room. Devin was a level above her, firing up the stairs at someone she couldn't see.

Each blast seemed to pierce her skull. The pain was so intense it was all she could do to keep from screaming. Her vision faded in and out as thick black dots filled in from the edges and then retreated. She felt as though she might pass out with every move she made. *Ugh. Why am I so damn weak?*

"*Go!*" Devin called as he exchanged fire with the

unseen someone.

More blasts rang out as another someone joined the firefight. Jane pulled out the handgun in her pocket. She switched off the safety and ran toward him.

"I said *go*!" Devin yelled.

"I can help!" Jane continued up the stairs. Someone grabbed her shoulder. Startled, she stopped. She saw it was Adam and relaxed.

"Jane, don't," he said. "He'll be better off if he's not worrying about you."

Jane wanted to object, but he was right. She reluctantly went back down the stairs. She'd barely made it down one more level when an explosion boomed above her. She looked back with a start.

Devin ran toward her. "What part of *go* didn't you get?"

"What the hell was that?" Jane demanded.

"Bastards tossed a grenade at me. I threw it back before it went off."

It's like he's done this before.

A blast came from above. She ducked. "Don't these assholes have anything better to do?"

Devin fired back. "*Go*! I mean it!"

Jane stood too quickly. Black brimmed her eyesight. Her legs melted beneath her. She tried to move forward, and her heel caught the edge of the step. She tumbled down the stairs. The handgun flew from her grip.

"*Jane!*"

Adam called her name, but she couldn't answer. She crashed into the wall on one of the landings.

She opened her eyes as wide as she could. All she saw were pale blurs between black splotches. Her head whirled. She struggled to figure out which limb should go where. Confusion overwhelmed her as wordless shouting and meaningless commotion droned through the buzzing in her ears.

Her vision cleared. The barrel of a laser gun pointed right at her, held by a skinhead thug with a nasty grin. Somewhere behind the terror and the fog of noises, she knew she should run or something, but she couldn't even figure out how to scream.

Bang.

She shut her eyes. Hot liquid splashed onto her face and chest. For a moment, she wondered why she felt no pain. She opened her eyes. It was the thug who'd been shot. He fell sideways. Blood poured from a hole above his lifeless eyes.

Behind him, Adam stood with the gun in his hands, his expression unexpectedly calm and merciless as heat.

His face filled with concern as he rushed to her side. Jane couldn't make out his words as he knelt beside her.

"I'm..." She didn't get a chance to finish, for the thick black dots returned at a vengeful pace. The warmth drained from her body.

Devin shot the nearest Wrath Guard through the chest. He ducked back into the stairwell, resisting the impulse to run into the corridor and blast away the other three. Good thing he did—seconds later, the internal defenses unleashed a volley of shots that finished off the thugs even though they'd probably been aiming for him.

He repeated the axiom he'd learned seven years back: *No faces, no pasts—just targets.*

Unable to cross the doorway without getting hit, he waited for the guns to overheat. They wouldn't be able to sustain that kind of firepower for long. The blasts tore the wall beside him and grazed his shoulder. A searing pain shot through him. He quickly assessed his injury.

Surface bleeding, laser burn—hurts like hell, but I'll be okay.

The shots stopped. Devin rushed down the stairs, praying that Jane hadn't run into trouble while he'd been cut off.

He rounded a corner. Jane lay unconscious near a dead thug. Adam knelt beside her, aiming the handgun straight up at him. "Adam! It's me!"

Adam lowered the gun and collapsed against the wall. Red stained his hands and clothing. Jane had traces of blood smeared across her face and shoulders, but she appeared uninjured.

Devin rushed down the rest of the stairs.

"You're bleeding." Adam sounded concerned.

"I'm fine." Devin knelt beside Jane. "What happened?"

"She dropped the gun when she fell. He went straight for her, didn't even look at me. She fainted after I..." Adam looked at the dead thug and didn't finish.

Didn't think he'd have it in him. Devin silently thanked whatever gods might be listening that the kid wasn't as maddeningly nice as he seemed. "You had no choice." He gave the old line even though that kind of reasoning seldom did any good.

Adam glanced at Jane. "I'm sorry... I've been trying to wake her, but she won't... She's..."

Devin put a hand on Jane's shoulder and shook her. "Jane!"

She remained limp. *Shit.*

She'd seemed off since Viate-5. He should've disregarded her protests that she was fine. He should've... but there was no time for that. More Wrath Guards—or hacked robots—could attack at any moment.

"I'm sorry," Adam said. "I don't know what happened. She fell and... I'm sorry."

The repetition sparked Devin's impatience. "What the hell are you apologizing for?" He handed Adam the laser gun. "Shoot anything with a weapon."

Adam took the gun. He stood and looked down at the body of the man he'd killed. He seemed shaken by the sight, but there was no sorrow or regret in his eyes, only a stony darkness Devin hadn't thought possible on the kid's gentle face.

Devin placed one arm under Jane's back, the other under her knees, and scooped her up. He glimpsed a number on the wall. *Nineteen—two more levels.*

Adam, with the laser gun in one hand and the handgun in the other, passed him on the way down the stairs. Aiming into the corridor on the level below, he fired upward several times. He destroyed the internal defenses even though they hadn't activated. His shots were clumsy, and it was clear that he'd never held a weapon before that day. Devin was sure he'd get them all on blast volume alone.

"Clear!" Adam backed up against the doorframe and watched the corridor. He held the laser gun, which looked far too big for him, up at his shoulder. He kept the handgun ready at his side. The sight of the pretty-boy priest-in-training armed like a hit man was rather amusing.

Fast learner.

"One more level," Devin said. "Then it's straight across the square."

Adam kept his eyes on the corridor. "Okay. By the way, this laser gun has unlimited ammunition, right?"

"Basically."

"Good, because my aim's *terrible.*"

"You're doing great."

Devin crossed the doorway. Adam passed him again, stopped at the next landing, and took out the internal defenses on that level. *He's pretty calm for a first-timer.*

They didn't run into any trouble as they entered the deserted square. The shrieking alarms must have discouraged everyone but the Wrath Guards from being out in the open. Even they seemed to have quit, probably because their comrades had been gunned down by the very float they protected.

Madam Wrath's glowering hologram shone in the center. It reminded Devin of how far No Name's reach had to be if they'd been able to get past her guards and knock her out, then take control of her float. He'd never been more grateful to be on an old float whose many breakdowns and repairs had disconnected most of the doors from the central computer.

He crossed the square. "We're docked at V-Two-Eight-Eight."

Adam ran into the hatch-lined corridor ahead and fired at the internal defenses. Devin wondered why, if No Name was so determined to get rid of him, they hadn't fired at Adam. Collateral damage clearly wasn't an issue. They probably needed him alive. *They must need Sarah alive too.* That conclusion was something of a leap, but Devin didn't care. He needed to think it: *I can still save her.*

"Devin?" Jane blinked up at him.

"Hey, Pony, it's okay." He entered the docking corridor. "I've got you."

Her gaze turned to his shoulder. "You're hurt..."

"It's nothing. Just looks bad. We'll be out of here soon."

"Put me down!" Jane's protest sounded small and weak. "I mean it!"

"You passed out. I—"

"Stop treating me like a freaking princess and put me down already!"

"*Look out!*" Adam yelled.

Devin ducked and shielded his sister as blasts pierced the air above him. The shooting stopped. He looked back. A destroyed robot lay on the ground.

Jane took the opportunity to twist her way out of his grasp, giving him an annoyed look. She darted toward Adam. "Nice shooting."

Adam looked surprised. "You're awake!"

"Yup, and recharged. C'mon, slowpokes!" She raced down the corridor, then stopped and steadied herself against the wall.

Is she okay?

Footsteps approached from the square.

"Adam!" Devin called.

Adam hastily tossed him the laser gun.

Devin fired in the direction of the footsteps. Returned shots flew at him, but they all missed. Thugs shouted at each other. One of them yelled, "*Fuck this!*" The footsteps reversed and faded away.

Jane ran to V-288. She turned a large wheel at the hatch's center, pulled a lever, and yanked the hatch open. As she and Adam entered the airtight tunnel, Devin blasted a few repair bots that stuck out from the vents. The Stargazer's door creaked. Two giant guard bots rounded the corner. They were probably blast-resistant. He rushed into the tunnel as the bots opened fire.

By the time he reached the ship, Jane had already started up the engines.

"I'm in! Go!" He thrust the lever that shut the door and retracted the tunnel.

Devin entered the cockpit as Jane drove the ship toward the hangar's exit. He didn't have to tell her to move over; she got up and slid into the copilot's seat. According to the tracking chart, several armed ships outside the hangar headed in their direction. He engaged lightspeed, a dangerous thing to do in such a crowded area. But without shields or a way to fire back, his only option was to run.

The Stargazer zoomed out of the float. It trembled as

it scraped against another ship. The attackers matched speed. A few were in visual range. Devin wrenched the controls to avoid their fire. The Stargazer wasn't nearly as maneuverable as the Blue Tang had been. Hit after hit impacted against the hull.

The ship came to an abrupt halt. An alarm buzzed as "unauthorized pilot" printed across the viewscreen.

"*What the hell*?" Devin put his hand on the scanner again. Nothing changed.

Jane sprang up. "My turn!"

Devin switched seats with her. They were doomed if they sat there. She pressed her hand against the scanner and hurriedly engaged lightspeed. The attackers, which had streaked past when the Stargazer stopped, doubled back.

Erratic. That was the only word to describe what Jane did next as she flipped and swerved the Stargazer in no particular direction. She moved away from the interstellar tunnel she should have headed for to escape or toward the hostile ships she should have avoided. But it seemed to work. Whoever piloted or controlled the other ships couldn't keep up with her antics. Several hit each other in the crossfire.

Devin was impressed. "Good job."

"Thanks." Jane's head drooped. He realized that her seemingly brilliant flying wasn't entirely due to her reflexes. She smiled tiredly. "I'm a better pilot when I'm woozy."

Adam gripped the back of her seat for support. He remained silent, as if not wanting to get in the way. A look of pain crossed his face. He doubled over, clasping both forearms. The ship lurched, and he stumbled.

Devin rushed to catch him as he fell. "Still?"

Adam grabbed the back of Jane's chair again. "It never quite stopped."

Jane twisted the ship to avoid a torpedo. "What the *hell* did they do to you?" She wasn't fast enough, and the missile hit the Stargazer's roof. A sizable piece flew off the hull and crashed into an oncoming attacker.

She gasped. "What was that?"

Devin returned to the copilot's seat. "Solar panel."

"*What*?" Jane yanked the controls. "Are we gonna lose power and die?"

Devin checked the ship's status on the control screen. "No, the other one's all right."

"Okay, so as long as we don't lose that one too or get hit by a missile and explode, we're good, right?"

"Yeah."

Jane flipped the ship again, narrowly avoiding collision with a Barracuda, which crashed into another ship that careened from the opposite direction. Both ships burst into an eruption of flaming debris.

Devin glanced at the tracking chart. The remaining pursuers were out of visual range, heading for the interstellar tunnel.

Don't be predictable. "Jane, fly back toward the float."

"Huh?" Jane's face lit up. "Oh. Good idea."

She veered the ship. Her hands shook, causing the Stargazer to zigzag.

Her apparent weakness troubled Devin. "Engage autopilot."

"Okay." After pressing the necessary controls, Jane collapsed into the back of her chair. She tugged at one of her sleeves, then looked up at Adam. "Sorry about all the craziness. You okay back there?"

"I'm all right." Adam appeared shell-shocked, his eyes wide and his voice quivery. "Nice flying."

"Thanks."

Devin's slate beeped. He pulled it out of his pocket and unfolded it.

Corsair: Real ghosts? I believe in them, funny things.
Archangel: What?
Corsair: Like that unnamed murderer. Either dark blue or computerized. Yeah. What a scary bunch that guy was involved in. I think. Nastiest, really. Kind of ghost, that is. Like, he could be anywhere or anything. Eh, that's my opinion. Please understand. Living with the opposite of my first swim's teacher is hard—you know, the famous one.
Archangel: You're not making any sense.
Corsair: Eh. Coming clean here. Kind of hard to admit the truth about ghosts.
Archangel: What are you talking about?
Corsair: Stop. First. I want you to help me as you did

back when you were your own opposite. Figure it out. Don't talk to me until you have.

Was Corsair trying to send a message? Or was he simply babbling under the influence of alcohol or something? Devin had planned to tell Corsair about the computer chip he'd taken from the deep blue machine. *Doesn't seem like a good idea right now.*

Jane peered at the slate. "What'd he say?"

"No clue." Devin folded the slate. "Tell the ship to keep going like this for about three hours, then have it turn around and head toward the tunnel. That should give them enough time to give up on us."

"Okay." Jane programmed the autopilot. When she finished, she slumped onto the control panel and buried her face in the crook of her elbow.

"Hey, Pony—"

"I'm tired, that's all." She turned to him, resting her head on her arm as though too tired to lift it. "I know this is our third big getaway and all, but I'm still not used to having to run for my life like I'm in a freaking holodrama."

"I'm taking you to an IC hospital as soon as we're out of here."

Jane bolted up. *"Like hell*! You know we can't go anywhere near the IC! What about Dad? What about Sarah? What about *justice*, Devin? You know the *system's* not gonna sort it out for us! I'm telling you, I'm *fine*. Sorry I'm not a tough guy like you, but that's no reason to act like I'm some fragile ninny."

"You fainted."

"I got knocked out, you idiot. In case you didn't notice, I fell down the stairs."

Adam reached forward and felt her forehead.

Jane raised an eyebrow. "Really?"

"Temperature's normal," Adam said. "Still, you really should get some rest. You've been through a lot."

She groaned. "Not you too!"

"I'm just worried about you. You really scared me back there."

Jane looked up at Adam and smiled sweetly. *Too sweetly.* Devin turned away with a mental grumble.

"Adam, I... um... wanted to say thanks. For saving my life. I was surprised when you shot that thug. I mean... I never thought you could... you know?"

"I did what I had to." Adam's voice was almost a whisper. He paused, and then continued in what sounded like an attempt at offhandedness, "I'm just glad I hit him, because unlike your brother, I have the shooting skills of a repair bot."

"Hey, it worked, didn't it? We can't all have super mercenary skills. Speaking of which, Devin? Where'd you learn to do all that?"

Devin turned. His sister brimmed with unasked questions. *Might as well come clean about some things.*

"I got mixed up in a... gang... back at university. I didn't know what I was getting myself into. They taught me some of their tricks, and I helped them with some of their jobs. After I found out who they really were, I tried to leave, but they have their ways of keeping a person around."

Jane leaned toward him. "Is that where you were after Mom was assassinated? When you disappeared for all those months?"

Devin nodded and told her he'd become an informant for ISARK, the Intelligence and Security Agency of the Republic of Kydera. "That's how I got out. They gave me immunity in exchange for my help in taking down the bad guys."

"Whoa." Jane looked surprised, but mostly impressed. "Why didn't you tell me before?"

"Didn't seem relevant." The agonizing guilt Devin always felt when he thought about what he'd done seeped into his mind.

Jane looked as though she had more to ask, but she didn't pursue her questions. "That's pretty awesome. So my brother's a super-spy."

"If you say so." Devin noticed the color had drained from her face. "The autopilot's set, so you can—"

"I'm *fine*."

"Please, Jane," Adam said. "I think—"

"Will you guys stop being paranoid?" Jane looked at Adam, then at Devin. "I can't fight you both. I guess you can't take me anywhere I don't want you to anyway, now that the computer's befuddled."

She got up slowly and walked toward the door, holding the wall for support. Adam tried to help her.

Jane shook her head. "I'm fine. Really. You two behave." She left the cockpit.

Adam stared after her, his eyes betraying a kind of longing Devin recognized and knew too well. *So another one's fallen for Jane. I wonder how long he'll last.* He put his focus on his slate.

Why the hell was Corsair talking about ghosts? Was he even trying to say anything? Devin had no idea what Corsair's life was like outside the Net. For all he knew, the alcohol theory was correct.

"Devin?" Adam sounded timid. "I was... I mean..."

Devin knew what the kid wanted to ask. "I'm a fugitive." He didn't look up as he answered. "Someone framed me for my father's murder after I found out Sarah was replaced by an AI. It was that entity called No Name, the same bastards who took you and were chasing us just now. I had to run, and Jane caught up and insisted on coming. You know how hard it is to say no to her."

"I... I see. I'm sorry."

Devin waited for a follow-up question. None came. He found the kid's quietness exasperating. "If you have anything else on your mind, go ahead and say it."

Adam hesitated. "Poltergeist."

Devin spun toward him. "What?"

"Your friend on the Net—he said ghosts are funny things."

Damn, I should've seen that. No wonder Jane's always calling me an idiot.

Devin reread the messages.

Poltergeist... Your own opposite... Hellion.

In his communication, Corsair referenced the past, a past only Devin would remember. *"Unnamed" must refer to No Name.* Corsair said he was "coming clean." Perhaps he was answering the question Devin had never asked, but had always wondered: What's your name? Corsair wasn't exactly a riddle master. The code had to be relatively simple.

First swim... hard... The Hard Planet. Fragan, in the Anven system.

A minute later, the meaning became clear, hidden in

the words and the first letters of the sentences: *My real name is Riley Winklepleck. No Name has made the Net too dangerous. I'm at the BD Tech programming facility on Fragan. Come find me.*

CHAPTER 13

A FREAKIN' GENIUS

AN AUTOMATED MESSAGE, REMINDING RILEY to renew his access card, popped up on his company-issued videophone. He wrinkled his nose at the sight of his real name. *Riley Winklepleck*. Heh, with a name like that, it was no wonder he refused to share it with anyone he didn't have to, even the one actual friend he had, about whom he knew almost everything, but to whom he'd told pretty much nothing.

Devin had never asked, and Riley had no reason to share. Besides, who wanted another tale of a Fringe kid shuffled into a rundown Via shelter after his drug dealer parents got themselves killed? Who cared how, despite the Via's best intentions, he'd grown up neglected in a worn-out system? How his intelligence was dismissed as arrogance and his talent ignored?

Riley flicked the videophone across his desk. It slid into a pile of candy wrappers. He turned his attention back to the slate in his hand and continued coding his latest project for Citizen Zero: a worm that would capture info from Ocean Sky's network and slow down their system. With all his reasons to be anti-establishment, who could blame him for being so involved? However, he often found their highfalutin' mission statements and grandiose conspiracy theories too heavy to be a full-time thing. "We are the strangers here." What failed holodrama writer came up with *that*?

Which was why he enjoyed messing around with the Gag Warriors. Riley opened a new window and browsed the Gag Warriors' forum. Someone had posted a video of a woman expressing shock at the Paladin Glen hoax. Riley snorted. Paladin Glen—*hah*! So many losers clung to the words of a fake fanatic generated by a clever program Riley helped develop. Insert *rights* or *freedom* or other bullshit buzzwords with plenty of references to the Absolute, and people ate it up!

Break's over. Riley returned to the worm-coding window. *I've got a job to do.*

Oh, he had a *real* job with a paycheck, but it was only so he could have money to buy equipment and food and stuff. The videophone beeped again. He ignored it. How important could a message to a maintenance worker be? He'd only taken the job at BD Tech's programming center on Fragan—nicknamed the "Hard Planet" by Citizen Zero because its institutions were so difficult to hack—so he'd have an easier time spying on the company's systems. Funny how he, the guy who directed repair bots to fix lighting units, was a million times smarter than those smarmy tools who sold their talents to the Man.

Riley could've been one of those tools if he'd wanted, could've gone to a top-notch university and graduated with tons of honors instead of barely passing at a vocational school. But it was more fun using his amazing abilities for *his* purposes, not some company's.

Better yet, for *messing* with companies. Riley put the finishing touches on the Ocean Sky worm and posted it on Citizen Zero's forum. *Your turn, guys.* He yawned. *All righty, work's done. Time for some fun.*

He found the file for his latest Gag Warriors prank and double-checked the code, which had taken weeks to perfect. The idea was to bombard Quasar's security system with oceans of requests, all randomly generated and stupid. Quasar was the epitome of everything wrong with the galaxy: greed, corruption, other evil corporation things. The Networld had been quick to applaud the Collective's hack a few days ago. *Riley's* move would make that stunt look like amateur play!

Yup, everything's ready. He could pull it off whenever he wanted. Just for kicks, he spent a few minutes adding more stupid requests to the program. When he finished, he chucked his slate onto his desk and stretched in his chair.

The star-filled view outside his window caught his attention. He got up, folded his body into the narrow window seat, and gazed into the night. *Devin's out there somewhere. Hope he figures out my messages before No Name does. Maybe I should've made them more weird. Or less weird. I dunno. Word codes are hard.*

Riley hadn't seen Devin in almost seven years. They'd kept in touch, but Riley had always been vague. He was too used to being alone, and he didn't want to depend on anyone. Still, it was nice knowing he had someone who'd help him out if he got in trouble.

Will Devin recognize me? Probably. Riley hadn't changed much since he was thirteen. Same pale face, same slanted black eyes, same skinny neck. Which sucked. Who wanted to look like a little kid at twenty? *At least I've got normal-looking hair now, instead of a stupid black helmet cut.*

Maybe revealing his name and asking to meet in person wasn't such a good idea. Riley's entire life was on the Net, including the majority of his boring day job, where he was ordered around by disembodied transmissions and pretty much never talked to anyone. He wasn't sure he knew how to interact with actual people anymore.

Nah, I was right.

No Name was getting *scary*. What started as a super-secret Net purist group had exploded into full-on supervillain stuff. Riley had heard about what happened on Travan Float from his fellow Gag Warrior Eaglewing. It had him *freaking out*. Faking docs was one thing, but hacking a whole float, including its bots and the ships docked there? Even Citizen Zero didn't have the know-how to do that. Hell, maybe even the Collective couldn't pull *that* one off.

Riley wondered what had gone down on the float that had been his entire life for thirteen years. Not that he cared what happened to it. Last time he'd seen the place, he'd been in the copilot's seat of a Barracuda, running away with no intention of going back.

Back then, he was just another punk-ass Fringe demon. He'd been around eleven when he started going around the Net as a prankster called Poltergeist, screwing with the computers of people who pissed him off. Mostly mean

Travan thugs and gooey Via volunteers.

One day, a cybergang called Legion had asked him to join their cause: doling out Net justice to the rich and corrupt. Riley, always up for messing with authority figures, had gladly signed up.

He'd been more than happy to help them hack into government systems to expose the hypocrisies of loudmouthed politicians and windbag bureaucrats. He'd been even happier when they asked him to get security codes and blueprints so they could steal money from rich people and big companies. They'd told him the money was to help the unfortunate Fringe planet Djuvai, but Riley couldn't have cared less about that.

That guy Hellion, on the other hand, had cared, and cared a lot. He seemed... weirdly naïve. Riley had figured out early on that the justice nonsense Legion espoused was a sappy way to lure people in and disguise their real activities.

But Hellion seemed to truly believe, and what was more, he wasn't much of a hacker. Seemed as though Legion was a way for Faceless, a nasty gang of scary types who called the shots, to get him involved in their so-called missions. It hadn't taken Riley long to figure out that Hellion was in fact Devin Colt, son of a Kyderan power couple. The knowledge shot him full of resentful irritation.

Poltergeist: Stop it with your bullshit. You talk all day about fighting the system, but you *are* the system! This is your rich boy way of getting your kicks, isn't it?

Hellion: What are you talking about?

Poltergeist: I unveiled you, you poser. Why'd you get involved in all this, huh? Trying to get Daddy's attention? I'll bet you don't give a shit about anything but yourself!

Hellion: You've got the wrong idea about me. I won't deny that I used to pull all kinds of rich boy shit, but that's over. I didn't join Legion to prove any kind of point. I did it because I've seen how the system can fail and because it's the only way I can make a dent in the injustice. So yeah, I do actually care.

That attempt to sound all noble only ticked Riley

off further.

Poltergeist: Why? You have a nice, fancy life on your stupid IC planet, so why don't you leave us Fringe types alone? I've had more than my fair share of shit, and I don't need any more coming from some spoiled prince!

Hellion: What happened to you?

Poltergeist: What do you care? Do you really wanna hear about another Fringe kid who was left to rot in one of those stupid shelters? Wanna hear how my parents were blasted away? How nobody even cared who did it? How my first hack was to modify my record so the shelter people would stop treating me like shit?

Hellion: I didn't know.

Poltergeist: I'm smarter than *everyone* in this stupid place, but I'm stuck here! I've got no life and no future, and I don't need some trust fund brat hanging around!

To his surprise, Devin hadn't been defensive. He'd sent Riley several messages asking how he was and offering to help. Riley had ignored them at first. After a few weeks, he'd caved and responded after realizing that shit, the guy was as much a do-gooder as he claimed. Eventually, he'd even videophoned Devin and revealed his face—something he'd never done before. It was weird, having a friend...

Devin had tried to convince Riley to leave Legion, saying that even though their cause, which for some reason he still believed in, was admirable, their methods were too dangerous for a little kid like him. Riley had rolled his eyes at the suggestion, dismissing it as more high-minded idealist talk.

Maybe he should have listened.

Someone requested entry. Riley hopped out of the window seat and checked his homemade security system. He recognized the nice-faced guy in the hall as Adam Palmer, the dude who'd been kidnapped by machines and "slated for replacement."

Guess they made it, after all.

Riley pressed a button by the door, which slid open. "Yo, Adam. Come on in."

Adam seemed a little thrown by the fact that Riley knew his name. As he entered, he reached into the black bag he carried on one shoulder and rummaged around. Reddish splotches stained his shirt. *Must've been a scary getaway from Travan Float.*

Riley pressed the button again. The door slid shut. He twisted a bunch of physical bolts into place. As far as he could tell, the veiling devices he'd put in place to make sure BD Tech couldn't track his Net moves still did their jobs. His puny room was the one spot on Fragan the evil corporation didn't own.

Satisfied, he sat in his chair and reclined. "So, how'd you guys get into an IC system without getting caught? Or did Devin send you and is still, you know, hidin' out on some Fringe planet?"

"No, he's here," Adam replied. "He's with the ship, a few miles north. We got in the old-fashioned way: by being very, very quiet. Apparently the Stargazer's untraceable because of modifications made by someone called the Seer."

"Oh, cool."

"Devin wanted to come himself, but Jane wouldn't let him." Adam smiled. "They argued for ages, with Jane telling Devin it's too dangerous because he's a fugitive, and Devin telling Jane she's not strong enough to go. I volunteered, but they both turned to me and said 'no'—the one thing they could agree on."

"So... Uh... Why're you here, then?"

"I took Devin's bag and left while they were still arguing. I'm not the only one No Name's after, and at least I'm not feeling weak or being hunted. They weren't happy when I messaged them and told them where I was, but it was too late by then."

Riley noticed a computer chip in Adam's hand. "Whatcha got there?"

Adam gave it to him. "Devin found this on one of the machines that took me. Can you get anything off it?"

"Uh... Duh?" Riley held the chip up and examined it. Something about its deep blue color and silvery squiggly lines seemed weirdly familiar. "I'd better go back to the ship with you. The freakin' corporation has eyes everywhere. I blinded them a while ago, but you never know, you know?

How'd you get here, anyhow?"

"Walked out of eyeshot of the ship and then called a taxi. *I'm* not a fugitive, and there were no internal defenses or robots around for No Name to misuse."

Riley threw Adam a you're-dumb look. "Uh... You know taxis are monitored by a central computer, right? Like the kind No Name likes to mess with?"

"They are?" Adam looked out the window in alarm.

Riley tucked the chip into his pocket. "Hey, chill. They don't know you're here. I would've seen some sign of 'em if they were snoopin' around the Fragan systems. Lucky for you, space is big. They probably didn't think to look for you guys in the IC. Either that or the Fragan computers were too hard for them. Not too hard for me, though."

Adam's expression fell into dismay. "I never realized how extensive computer networks are. I'm new to all this."

"Yeah, we're taking my hovercar back." Riley grabbed his orange backpack and packed some equipment. So far, interacting with another human being hadn't been so bad. He couldn't help feeling a little antsy about meeting someone he'd last seen in person seven years ago, someone who...

It was kind of funny, and it was something Riley would never admit. If anyone ever asked, he'd tell them to go to hell. But since that thing seven years ago, Devin had been Riley's... man, he hated the word. His hero.

———◆———

Everything with Legion had gone to hell after the botched Quasar job. Riley had known for a while that Faceless was the real boss, but he hadn't realized that they in turn worked for the notorious Voh Nyay Twins, identical twin warlords who ran a large chunk of Djuvai and shamelessly funded terrorist attacks against IC systems, especially Kydera.

Riley had lost track of Devin after the job went down in flames. One day, he read on the Net that an undercover ISARK mission unveiled the several members of Legion. Wouldn't be long before he, too, was discovered. No honor among demons.

It wasn't the authorities he feared. He would've been relieved if the cyberpolice got to him first. What freaked him out was that ISARK made several well-publicized raids on Faceless' hideouts, and Faceless covered their asses with the warlords by blaming Legion. They planned to use the ISARK info to wipe out the Legion demons.

As long as he was on Travan Float, he didn't stand a chance. He snuck out of the Via shelter and hacked a pirate ship into thinking he was a crewmember. It would've worked, except he'd never before seen the inside of a starship and got lost.

"Gotcha!" A muscle-bound woman with blond dreadlocks grabbed him. She held him by the arms so he couldn't move. "Whatchya doin' here?"

Riley squirmed. "I just wanted off the float! I'll work for free! I can hack *anything*!"

The woman snarled. "Ain't no place for you here." She turned to the other pirates. "What should we do with this little shit?"

A man with yellow teeth growled. "I say lock 'im in the storage unit we cleaned out. That'll give ole Blaze a fun surprise when he go lookin' for them valuables!"

The woman stomped her strangely shaped boots as she laughed. "I love it! Fuckin' hilarious!"

Riley tried to twist out of her grip. "If you leave me here, I'm dead!"

"Yeah, kinda the point." She dragged Riley down to the storage sector. Although he struggled the entire way, he was too small to break free. She shoved him into the empty storage unit and slammed the double doors shut before he could run out.

Riley banged against the metal. "They're gonna *kill* me! *If you leave me here, I'm dead!*"

The woman walked away, laughing. After several useless attempts to break open the door, he curled up in a corner and cried.

An entire day passed. Riley heard several people walk by, but they ignored his pleas. His terror dulled into depressed resignation. His short, sorry life would end soon, and there was nothing he could do to save himself. Thirteen freakin' years of misery—that was all the universe could spare for his sad existence.

The dreadlocked blonde's distinctive footsteps approached. "Hey, little shit. Looks like you were right. Someone's comin' for ya. Didn't think you'd be worth the trouble, but I guess ya must've been a real pain-in-the-ass for someone so small."

Riley whimpered, "Please let me out."

"Nah, already told him you're here, and I wouldn't wanna piss him off. You should be honored. They sent Black Knight. He arrived yesterday askin' 'bout a scrawny little demon with black hair, and I was like, 'Hey, I know where you can find one.' Now this is the guy even the *bosses* are scared of 'cause he won't just kill ya, he'll get creative. Dunno whatchya coulda done to deserve to be killed by him."

"Please..."

"Y'know he got in trouble soon's he stepped on the float? Yeah, some boss he pissed off put a hit on him, and there was this big fat firefight in the square. I saw the whole thing. He lost his helmet, and I'm tellin' ya, he was *handsome*! I think *everyone* got a good look while they could. Ten yearsa scarin' the fuck outta people, and we finally get to see his face! What a show!"

She laughed nastily. "Wellp, won't be long 'fore he'll be comin', I guess, soon's he decides the funnest way to off ya. I best get goin'. Would hate to have him thinkin' I was helpin' ya or nothin'."

Riley trembled. Black Knight was Faceless's most feared member, known for toying with his victims. *What'll he do to me?*

Hours passed.

Then, he heard them: metal-heeled boots clanging against the metal floor.

They stopped.

A sharp pole jammed through the bottom of the crack between the two doors, then retracted. It pierced the crack at three places in the center, then at the top.

Shaking but otherwise paralyzed, Riley watched as gloved hands pried open the doors. The tall, infamous form of Black Knight, clad head to toe in black combat gear, entered. In his signature black helmet, pointed at the front with a red slit over the eyes, he looked more like a monster than a man.

Riley buried his face into his knees, praying the merc would shoot him in the head and get it over with. More clanging—the footsteps approached. He shook so hard, hugged his knees so tight...

A gentle hand on his shoulder. "Hey, kid."

Riley looked up with a start. Devin knelt beside him, holding Black Knight's helmet under one arm. "*Devin?*"

Riley jumped up and threw his arms around his friend's neck, not caring if it was a girly thing to do.

Devin put a hand on Riley's shoulder and looked him in the eye. "I'm getting you out. It's gonna be okay."

"I thought... how did you... why would you...?"

"I wasn't about to let them kill you." Devin stood and pulled Riley up. "C'mon."

He unclipped a small bomb from his utility belt and set it down against the back wall. "Get ready to run like hell."

He pressed some buttons on the bomb, grabbed Riley by the arm, and ran out the door.

Boom.

Riley froze in terror. Devin scooped him up and kept running. A chain of explosions thundered, getting bigger each time.

Devin put Riley down, grabbed his gun, and shot around the edges of a vent in the ceiling. He helped Riley up and then jumped and pulled himself into the conduit. Riley followed him through the float's system of conduits and transport shafts until they reached the docking area.

Devin shoved Riley into a Barracuda and took off like lightning. "They won't even look for a body. That storage unit you were locked in is right next to an arms dealer's warehouse. There won't be much left of the storage sector by the time it's over."

Riley, still shaking, watched Travan Float shrink in the rear view.

"Hey," Devin said. "Everything's gonna be okay. I'm taking you to Ibara, in the Kyderan system. They call it the Orphan Planet because it's pretty much dedicated to making sure kids like you have a future. I wish I could do more, but I've gotta get back to Faceless before they figure out I'm not Black Knight."

"I can't believe you came," Riley said, finally able to speak.

Devin smiled. "Told you I cared."

"I'm freakin' amazing!" Riley sat on the cockpit floor with his slate hooked up to some equipment, which was in turn hooked up to the Stargazer's central computer. It had taken longer than he'd hoped, but he'd managed to decipher the info from the kidnapper machine's chip.

Jane rushed in. "What is it?"

Devin entered behind her. "Did you find something?"

He'd wanted to stay while Riley did his thing, but Riley had insisted he couldn't work with someone looking over his shoulder.

Adam walked in after Devin, and all three looked at Riley expectantly.

Trying to look chill, Riley rested his back against the wall. "Duh. Wouldn't be gloatin' if I hadn't."

He typed some commands into his slate. The Stargazer's computer displayed the info on the viewscreen. Several names appeared under the heading "Complete List of Actives." Next to each, a square displayed a close-up picture of the subject against a deep blue background. One of them Riley recognized: Sarah DeHaven.

Jane's eyes were round with amazement. "Are those the AIs?"

No, they're Nem monkeys. "Uh... Duh?"

Jane's expression turned to annoyance. Riley reminded himself to be more polite in the real world.

He scrolled down the list. "Most of the files are messed up because the chip was damaged and all. Dude, there are *tons* of them!"

Adam took a step closer to the viewscreen. "Am I on there?"

"Nope. Probably because your... uh... counterpart isn't, you know, active yet. Or maybe because you're a 'special case.'"

Riley typed some more commands. One of the AI files popped up: a guy with amber eyes named Jonathan King. The file occupied a quarter of the screen and detailed, in computer-speak, the moves he'd made, what its purpose had been, and whether the action had been "successful."

"Looks like this one's been around awhile," Riley said. "It's basically a list of commands that were sent to him, like 'apply for this internship' or 'cancel that interview.' It goes back about two years."

Jane looked as if she was trying to read the code. "So someone's controlling them. They're not... sentient?"

"I dunno. I guess not *every* move is detailed. Seems like the programming lets them do a lotta stuff on their own, like, the everyday stuff, but someone tells them when to make the bigger moves. Man, there's a lotta info here! You guys got lucky!"

"Riley."

Riley heard Devin's voice and, not accustomed to being referred to by his real name, looked up. He wasn't sure what to make of Devin's lack of expression. *Did I do something wrong?* "Yeah?"

"Show me Sarah's file."

Riley scrambled to bring it up. Sarah's face appeared next to Jonathan King's portrait. Her file was heavily damaged and only contained a partial log of her recent actions. "So, it explains why she froze. There's an error from when you... uh... surprised her."

"And?"

"It says she was sent a command to... uh... say yes. So you'd be distracted and forget everything, you know, so you wouldn't figure out she's... she's..."

"She's a machine," Devin said flatly. "When was she replaced? Does it have any information as to where she is now?"

Riley wished he had the answers Devin wanted. He hurriedly nitpicked the commands to see if he'd missed something, mentally bashing himself for not being better.

Devin knelt down to Riley's level. "Relax, you're doing a good job." He smiled. "You're a freakin' genius."

Riley gave him an apologetic look. "I can't find anything else about her. It's not on the chip or was wiped out from the damage."

"Is there anything on there other than the AI files?"

Riley poked around a bit more. Everyone watched him. He jittered nervously. He considered asking them to leave again, then reminded himself that he was the *best* and should enjoy the opportunity to show off.

Several minutes later, he realized why the chip looked so familiar. His jaw dropped. "Ooooh shit."

Jane sat in the pilot's seat and looked down at Riley. "What is it?"

"So, this thing, and the thing it came from, since it was custom-made for that thing..."

"Yeah?"

Riley entered a few more commands. An image of a dark blue gemstone with the words "BLUE DIAMOND TECHNOLOGY CORPORATION" emblazoned across it in white letters appeared beneath Sarah's file.

Jane opened her mouth in surprise. "Holy crap. I *knew* it! I *knew* it was BD Tech!"

"I dunno about that," Riley said skeptically. "Someone probably stole the machines from one of their labs. Or maybe one of the engineer guys went rogue and is helping No Name. I mean, the company's got a lotta fancy shit, but nothing *close* to these AIs. Besides, they may be an evil corporation, but they're not *criminal*. They wouldn't go around the Tech Council like that. Trust me, I've been through their secret files."

Devin stood. "Whoever it is, what do they want?"

"Maybe they're trying to take over the galaxy." *Okay, that sounds pretty dumb when said aloud.* Riley jerked his head at the portrait of Jonathan King. "I mean, look at this guy. Every move he's been commanded to make puts him on the path to being the perfect politician. The people getting replaced, they all stand to make it big."

"Like Sarah. The perfect singer."

"Uh... Yeah. I guess they're all perfect somethings."

Adam tilted his head, expression confused. "Except me. Why me? I'm so... boring."

Jane looked up at him. "I've been trying to figure that one out for ages. I guess they could program your replacement to act like one of those power-grabber types, but isn't the whole point to make the switch unnoticeable?"

Devin's face hardened. "Seems that way. Nothing on the chip indicates when Sarah was taken?"

Riley fidgeted. "Uh... No. The earliest thing in the log is the... error. If there's anything else, it's not there anymore."

"I see."

"So... Uh... That's everything." Riley tapped his fingers on the back of his slate. "I mean, I can show you more about the other AIs..."

"No, I've seen enough. I appreciate your help."

"Anything for an old pal."

Riley suddenly remembered why he'd wanted to talk to Devin in person, before he'd been distracted by the chip and stuff.

He put the slate down. "So I've been doing some diggin' on my own, and what I found, it's kinda scary. Remember Mastermind? The big bad demon from ten-ish years ago? Remember how a bunch of demons who got involved with him ended up dead? Turns out, they were all working on the same thing."

Jane leaned forward. "Let me guess: artificial intelligence."

"Yup. I think Mastermind's behind No Name. I know he disappeared and all, but I think this is him being more discreet. The Seer showed me some things, and I figured out that all the guys who got killed had written some unique part of the code. I'm guessing Mastermind wanted to hog all the good stuff."

"Then it *is* BD Tech. Mastermind works there."

"Nah," Riley scoffed. "I'd know if he did."

Devin kept his gaze on Sarah's file. "His name is Dr. Revelin Kron. The Seer told us, and I think it's been proven we can trust him."

Riley's jaw dropped again. "*What*? No, it's *not possible* that No Name's working in the same building as me, and I didn't catch on. Dude, Kron runs the entire Fragan facility! There's no way in *hell* he's involved in all this criminal shit. Besides, I've checked him out several times. If Kron was behind all this, *I would've known*."

This is beyond crazy. No Name's online footprints had been too scattered to trace, but—

Riley recalled something else the Seer had told him. He snatched up his slate and buzzed through the Stargazer's central computer, concentrating so intensely he forgot he had people watching him.

He found them: the files the Seer had put in the ship. One was an old video, but that wasn't relevant. Riley brought up his findings on the viewscreen, and several orange lines of code replaced the AI files.

Hoooly shit.

The Seer had done the impossible: He'd traced one of No Name's actions.

Riley couldn't wipe the dumbfounded expression off his face. "I guess it takes one to know one."

Devin knit his eyebrows. "What did you find?"

Right, not everyone reads computer-speak. "You know how No Name's been around for ages but was really quiet back in the day? Their first known hack was about ten years ago, when they stopped one of the Collective's attempts to release a bunch of confidential BD Tech info."

"What about it?"

"The Seer traced that hack. It originated right here on Fragan. Dude, you're right. Kron's gotta be with No Name."

Riley collapsed against the wall behind him, wondering how he could have missed something so epic. He felt stupid.

Maybe he should aim that awesome security hack planned for Quasar at his own company instead. *Man, I always knew Kron was evil, but not actually... evil.* "I work for the freakin' devil. I've gotta quit. I've gotta get outta here."

Devin's expression darkened. "Not yet. First thing tomorrow, we're going to see him."

CHAPTER 14

SO OBVIOUS

D R. REVELIN KRON MASTERMINDED ALL things programmed at BD Tech: the new-fangled robots, the advanced programs, and then some. With his pale face, cropped gray hair, and weak chin, he didn't *look* as important as the sleek businessmen at the corporate headquarters on Kydera Major, but without his brains, they wouldn't have anything to sell. All the *key* work happened under his watch. Virtu-games were written, the ships were programmed— everything *important* happened on Fragan. That was why corporate let him get away with just about anything and gave him pretty much everything he asked for.

Like his office. He'd wanted it circular, so they'd built it special. He stretched, leaning away from his crescent-shaped desk. He almost never left his large chair because his awkward, round-shouldered build made him look as if he perpetually slouched when standing.

Kron swiped his monitor, which surrounded him in a semicircle, and opened a file on the entity known as No Name. When he wasn't driving his underlings, he spent most of his time keeping an eye on that thing. He'd tracked its activities over the years, gleefully watching it grow into the monstrosity it had become.

Upon realizing what it was capable of, Kron had attempted to stop it before changing his mind. Shame to end something so brilliant. However, it remained a danger to him, so to keep it in check, he'd alerted the IC's cyberpolice to its presence.

That had been a risky move. If the cyberpolice dug in the wrong direction, they could discover Kron's involvement with the "unidentified cybercriminal." Kron pulled up the most recent reports they'd sent him. Their incompetence seemed to keep them from figuring out what No Name really was, let alone what had gone down ten years before.

"Unidentified cybercriminal may have attacked a float near Travan."

"Unidentified cybercriminal is believed to have been involved with the bombings on Viate-5."

"Unidentified cybercriminal appears to be destroying information concerning artificial intelligence."

Of course it is! If anyone else found out...

Kron wished he could anonymously data transfer information from his brain and upload it into the heads of the cyberpolice. He couldn't tell the cretins what he knew *directly*. No, that would only get *him* in trouble!

He skimmed some more reports. They all told him the same thing: *We have no idea what's going on.*

How? It's so obvious!

Kron checked a security monitor on one of the side screens. People called him paranoid because of all his cyber shields, but if they knew...

An error, scarcely perceptible, easy to miss for the average person. Before he had a chance to take a closer look, the door flew open.

A dark-haired young man stormed in, carrying a laser gun. "Game's up, Kron. Time to come clean."

"Devin!" A geeky little maintenance worker ran in after him. "This was *not* the plan! I said we'd get answers from the *computers*, not—"

"Sorry, Riley. This seemed more direct."

I've seen that maniac somewhere... More annoyed than afraid, Kron held up his hands with a sneer. "You want the company's secrets? Take them. Take the whole damn computer if you think it'll do you any good."

Devin aimed the gun at Kron's face. "I don't care about the company, *Mastermind*."

How the devil does he know about that? No one *knows about that!* Kron feigned confusion. "Mastermind?"

"Don't give me that bullshit." Devin's gaze bored into

Kron's. "Where's Sarah? What have you done with her?"

Kron frowned, confused for real. "I don't know what you're talking about."

Devin reached into his pocket, pulled out a slate, and tossed it to Kron. "Open it."

Kron tentatively unfolded the slate.

Oooooh shit.

The screen displayed a list of names and photos. Kron recognized it. *How did this deranged* whacko *get that?* He couldn't know. Inconceivable. Kron was the *only* one who could *possibly* know. He snickered. "You're out of your damn mind! Do you hear me? You're completely *nuts*. I have no idea who these people are!"

Devin's expression didn't change. "Riley, I think you should go now."

"Uh... Okay." Riley sounded nervous. "But don't forget—"

"I know."

Riley left and shut the door behind him. Kron looked up at the internal defense guns. *Where the devil is my security team?*

Devin followed his gaze. "Don't bother. Your entire security system's been shut down. No one's coming to rescue you, so if you want to live, I suggest you tell me what I want to know."

"Then *obviously*, you *won't* kill me. There's stuff in *here*," —Kron pointed at his head— "that you'll never find if you use *that*." He pointed at the gun.

"Is it really worth dying for?"

Kron shook his head. "No, no. No, it's not. I like to think I'm an accommodating guy. So, what is it that you want?"

"Tell me where Sarah is."

"Who?"

"And while you're at it, tell me why the *hell* you're doing all this!"

"Doing what?"

Devin glowered.

Yikes. Better play nice. Kron nodded rapidly. "Okay, okay. So you know I'm Mastermind. I admit it: I was the guy messing around with all those crime bosses twenty years back. But I *quit*! It wasn't worth all that trouble for a hobby anymore!"

"Stop." Devin's voice was dangerously soft. "No Name originated *right here* and I want to know what you've done with Sarah."

Kron gestured impatiently. "For the last time, who's Sarah?"

"*Sarah DeHaven.*"

"The singer?" Kron realized where he'd seen Devin before. "Hey, you're the guy from the news! The one who shot his bigwig father! Ooooo... I remember now. You're Sarah's fiancé! Damn, you are one *lucky* sonuvabitch! Every guy in the galaxy wants *her*."

"I won't ask again."

Kron nodded. "Okay, okay. So you think I'm No Name. Ease up! I'll tell you everything! I will!" Obviously, he wasn't going to tell the lunatic *everything*, but when a madman on the rampage had a gun pointed at your face, you did what you could to please him.

Even if Devin did find, well, everything, he couldn't do anything about it. No one would believe a fugitive.

With a flick of his hand, Kron beckoned. "Come on down. I have something to show you."

Devin kept his gun aimed at Kron as he walked around the monitors.

Kron jerked his thumb at the cyberpolice reports. "Look! No Name's been scaring *me* too! Why do you think I quit being Mastermind? I was the one who sent the cyberpolice after it, so obviously, *I'm not No Name.*"

He swiped the monitor, flipping through the reports to prove how long he'd tracked the entity. He slipped his other hand under the table, pressed a hidden security button, and glanced at the security monitor. Strange. The alarm had already been tripped—about ten thousand times. So had all other alarms in the building.

Kron realized what that glitch had been.

The most inane cries for help inundated the system. Emergencies from every corner of the facility bombarded the system with messages like "Oh, no! I'm wearing colors!" and "Oh, help! I have an opinion!" Kron recognized the Gag Warriors' handiwork.

He tensed. *Shit. I thought they were targeting Quasar...*

"Don't try that again." Devin's gaze was fixed on him.

He must have seen the attempt to call security.

Kron nervously put his hands up. "Sorry. But as you can see—" he pointed to himself— "*not* No Name."

"Then who is?"

"How am *I* supposed to know?"

Devin pressed the gun into Kron's temple.

"Okay, okay!" Kron said quickly. "Believe me, if I knew where this No Name was, I would've found it and gotten rid of it by now! But I've been tracking it, much better than the cyberpolice! And hey, you want Sarah DeHaven? I can *give* you Sarah DeHaven!" *The sooner I give him what he wants, the sooner he'll leave.*

Devin lowered the gun. Kron turned to his monitor and typed at top speed. *Why does he need me to find her? It's not as if she's missing.*

He glanced at the security monitor again. The shields he'd put in place... but the Gag Warriors couldn't have been *that* thorough. Even if they took out the whole *company,* his *custom* ones couldn't be breached by...

Kron brought up a real-time video from a security camera in a Kydera City apartment building, which Sarah had just entered. He pointed. "She's right here!"

Devin raised the gun. "I want the *real* Sarah."

"What do you mean? This is Sarah DeHaven!"

"She's an AI, and you know it."

"How did you know that?" Kron realized what Devin meant by "real" and laughed. "Ooh, so you think she's a person who got *replaced* by an AI! Sorry to burst your bubble, but this is the only Sarah DeHaven there is!"

Devin's face was still. "You're lying."

"I'm not! Why the devil would anyone replace people with robot copies? I mean, come *on!*"

Devin's expression remained unreadable, but something about him scared Kron into solemnity. "Okay, okay. Like I said, I've tracked this No Name business for years. I don't know how you found out about the AIs, but I've known about them for a while now, and *they're not replacing people.* Hey, look, I can prove it!"

Kron typed a few commands. A folder, in which he'd stored everything he knew about the AIs, occupied the monitor. He opened the file for Sarah DeHaven. Several documents appeared side by side.

He waved at them. "*Everything* about her life before a year ago is fake! It's *so obvious* once you look into it! That No Name's put documentation in all the right places so people wouldn't suspect anything, but"—he couldn't help snickering—"you're engaged to a one-year-old!"

Saying it aloud made it funnier. Kron threw his head back and guffawed.

———— ◆◇◆ ————

It can't be true. Sarah, his Sarah, the one he'd fallen for— she must have been real.

Devin shoved the gun into the back of Kron's head. "*The truth. Now.*"

"I just gave it to you!" Nasty mirth spread across Kron's odd-looking face. "She's not the only one! They've *all* been... How do I put it? *Inserted* into strategic places. But good for you, getting to date *that*! She's a real beauty, isn't she? Wish *I* had a toy like her!"

Devin shook his head. "People *are* being replaced. They kidnapped a student a few days ago. An intercepted transmission said he was 'slated for replacement.'"

Kron's grin faded. "That's new. Hey, I don't know about everything No Name does. I'm a little behind with the tracking, so maybe it's started something I haven't seen before. But I'm telling you, with all *these* AIs," he jerked a thumb at the list of actives, "what you see is what you get. There's only one Sarah DeHaven, and she's right there." He nodded at the security footage from Kydera City. "So now you know. You can stop worrying about some other version of her needing rescuing and go marry your robot love doll!"

Kron guffawed again.

It was the ugliest sound Devin knew, and it took all his self-control not to pull the trigger and be done with the horrible man. "I don't believe you."

Kron's round blue eyes glinted with malicious amusement. "You want more proof? Look what I've got *here*!"

He scrolled down the folder on the monitor and pressed a deep blue icon. A hologram of Sarah from the neck up appeared before him. Voyeuristic stills of various women printed across the monitor.

Kron selected one of the pictures, which filled the screen with a video of a curly-haired young woman speaking. The camera was placed behind the shoulder of the man she flirted with, who asked why she'd approached him.

"I don't know," the young woman said. "It's like something was telling me that I should get to know you."

Kron tapped the monitor, and the video stopped.

Devin suppressed a shudder. He found something eerily familiar about not only the woman's words, but her expressions—the nuances in her voice, the subtleties in her eyes.

The hologram of Sarah came to life.

"I don't know." She spoke with the same lilt. "It's like something was telling me that I should get to know you."

The image froze again.

It's not possible.

Kron looked up at Devin. "See? It's *so obvious*! Want more?"

He swiped at the video to fast-forward and played another section. The same young woman confessed the reason she'd agreed to go out with the man. Her career-driven life left her craving any kind of human connection outside her industry, and so she had chosen to take a chance on him.

Kron stopped the video again. The hologram of Sarah repeated the woman's words, words Devin recalled all too well. He held every muscle still to keep from betraying the chaos in his head.

Kron seemed to take his silence for an invitation for even more. He played a second video.

A young woman with an auburn braid placed her hand on the cheek of a narrow-faced man. "Come on, baby. Don't let your father bother you. He loves you, Arthur. He wouldn't care so much if he didn't."

The hologram of Sarah repeated her words, "Come on, baby. Don't let your father bother you. He loves you, Arthur. He wouldn't care if he didn't."

The same dynamics in her words. The same shades of motion in her face.

It's... not possible.

Kron seemed downright eager to show him the next one: the auburn-haired woman with a hand on the man's arm as she described life's wondrous blessings. "Remember that, and you'll realize that you're already in the haven you seek. *This* is paradise."

The same optimistic expression lit Sarah's face. "Remember that, and you'll realize that you're already in the haven you seek. *This* is paradise."

It looked so natural.

Kron's face twitched with delight as he scrambled to show yet another video. Each move he made chipped at Devin's self-control.

On the monitor, a young woman with long, dark hair approached a reception screen. "Anya Nejem." Her voice was rich and beautiful—and familiar. "I have a meeting with Pulsar-9 Models at ten."

"Sarah DeHaven," the hologram echoed. "I have a meeting with Pulsar-9 Models at ten."

That was the first time Devin had heard her voice. The words differed, but the tone, the musical cadence it carried—he could never forget the way it had captivated him.

"It's not possible." Devin whispered the words repeating in his head. "She... she's a singer. Music... It's all about..."

Kron huffed with impatience. "About *what*? *Soul*? What we perceive as *soul* is a bunch of teeny-tiny physical movements! Facial tics! Voice quivers! I'll admit, these things are really, *really* hard to fake. What do you think this program is? A *test*. So Pa— so No Name could make sure Sarah's movements and voice were believable before sticking them in the android body, which, I'm sure, took long enough to make.

"Hey, hey, check *this* one out! This one's my *favorite*!"

Devin didn't react. He didn't know how to react in a way that wouldn't involve Kron's brains splattering across the monitor.

Kron selected a video of the same dark-haired woman. Anya stood by a lake with a dewy expression and held hands with a man whose back was to the camera.

She smiled demurely. "I love you."

Devin's face went cold. He knew that smile.

The hologram of Sarah warmed into the same demure

smile, the one he loved so much. "I love you."

She spoke with the same dewy expression, one that had once brought him joy, wonder, hope. Not anymore. Just—pain.

Kron placed his hands behind his head. "What we have here are select files No Name calculated would be most useful. Most of her programmed actions are a mishmash of various expected human responses. What she does is draw upon these responses after weighing competing variables. She adapts them to customize her reaction, creating the *illusion* of emotion. People anthropomorphize anything that *looks* convincing. But she's a philosophical zombie—all smiles and pretty words on the outside but nothing on the inside!"

Devin stared at the image of Sarah on the monitor.

Kron bolted up with a mad kind of glee. "Holy *shit*! You actually *loved* her, didn't you? You fell in love with a fantasy, with a... a..." He snorted. "With a machine!" He guffawed again.

Devin clenched his fist around the handle of his gun, his hand shaking with rage.

Don't kill him.

⎯⎯⎯⎯⎯◈⎯⎯⎯⎯⎯

Kron was actually glad the maniac had burst in. It'd been a boring day, and that was the most entertainment he'd had in ages. The poor bastard probably devoted his heart and soul—his entire being—to an empty shell created to be a perfect imitation. It was too funny. Just because he could, Kron played another video: a musician passionately explaining why she loved her art.

He clucked with mock sympathy. "Aw, don't be mad. You should be glad she's *not* sentient. Isn't that what every guy wants? A babe that picks up on what you respond to and evolves to suit you? Best of all, *she's not real!* You can do whatever you want to her, and it doesn't matter! She's the *ultimate whore.* If it weren't for those damn regulations, I'd make love bots like her BD Tech's next big product, and every guy in the galaxy would sell his mother to buy one!"

Devin remained motionless. Kron found his tough-guy act pathetically amusing. He knew he shouldn't poke the sore spots on a madman with a gun, but he had one more statement to crown the entire uproarious situation.

"I know why she dated you," he said mockingly. "No Name was testing a series of new algorithms, and you must've fit the criteria the AI was to adapt to. See, most of the others were programmed to enter strategic relationships, but notice that these videos are about"—he snickered—"*romance*. She was *engineered* to make guys like you fall in love with her. All the better to advance her singing career! It's *so obvious!*"

The hologram of Sarah repeated the musician's words. Devin appeared to lose his expressionless mask as he watched.

Kron sneered. "Hey, you should be flattered. She's on the way to super-stardom, and you'd make..." He snorted. "You'd make excellent arm candy for her galas. Too bad she'll dump you now that you're a jailbird!"

"*That's enough.*" Devin pressed the gun into Kron's temple, finger against the trigger.

Shit, he means business this time. Kron's mirth melted into nervousness. "Okay, okay, I'm sorry! I did what you asked, right? You wanted the truth, *there it is*! It's not *my* fault! *I* didn't make her!"

Devin leaned in threateningly. "You're holding back. You've been trying to distract me with... You know who No Name is, and I want you to tell me. *Now.*"

Gun to the head's a pretty good reason to spill your guts. "Okay, okay! There was this thing ten years ago called the Pandora Project—"

Kron glimpsed a slight movement on the wall. An internal defense gun pointed straight at him. Fear engulfed him in that split second as he realized what was happening.

It was so obvious.

CHAPTER 15

FLY, JUST FLY

JANE HELD HER HEAD DETERMINEDLY high as she steered the Stargazer toward the BD Tech building. The Gag Warriors' security hack could only last so long before the corporation's people sorted it out. Her body felt heavy, as though someone had filled her with molten lead and let the metal harden into her limbs. At least she wasn't shaking.

I've been through worse.

She recalled the time she'd conducted a symphony with a raging fever, the time she'd campaigned for her mother on no sleep, the time she'd smiled through a charity ball with a twisted ankle—in four-inch heels. Fatigue and headaches were nothing, especially compared to the real problems she had to deal with. She wasn't about to let a little wooziness stop her. Besides, her brother fretted about her enough as it was. She didn't need another reason for him to see her as a delicate little girl.

She brought the Stargazer to a hover. The ship was in terrible shape. The landing gear had jammed the previous day, forcing her to practically crash-land on Fragan. The engines had stalled during takeoff. The needle on the temperature gauge, a semicircle with blue on the left and red on the right, slid out of the "normal" zone and into "caution." As if that weren't enough, the status report displayed warnings about the generators' capacity and the steering's stability. It seemed only blind fortune kept the ship in one piece.

Don't you dare fall apart on me, you piece of crap. I'm using every bit of strength I've got here, and you'd better, too.

Adam sat beside her in the copilot's seat, gazing at the bright clouds filling the viewscreen. Jane had suggested that he go with Devin and Riley into the city and return to Kydera.

He'd looked at her as though that were the most ridiculous thing she could've asked. "I'm not going anywhere."

"You should get out of this mess while you can," Jane had insisted. "You saw how dangerous it can get. And remember, we're also being hunted by the *good* guys." *I'm starting to sound like my big brother.*

"I'm not going anywhere," Adam had repeated.

Jane had sighed resignedly while Devin smiled at the sight of her being in the same situation she'd put him in.

Her head drooped involuntarily. She hurriedly lifted it. Adam's brow creased with concern. She tried to act as energetic as usual. "How many times must I tell you I'm fine? I'm just tired."

"Are you sure?" Adam had an unusual, drawn look about him, as though he hadn't slept in ages.

Jane had a feeling she knew what troubled him. "Worry about yourself. You look like hell. When was the last time you got any rest?"

"Define 'rest.'"

She hesitated. "Nightmares? It's because you shot that thug, isn't it?"

Adam lowered his gaze and nodded. "I'll get over it. I'd be more disturbed if I *weren't* haunted. I did kill someone, after all, and of course I feel guilty about it. But I try not to dwell. I keep reminding myself how much worse it would've been if I hadn't acted. I'm not sorry." He spoke more to himself than to Jane.

Jane wanted to reply, wanted to ask him how he was holding up or at least thank him again for saving her life, but her energy was focused on not giving in to that leaden feeling and face-planting onto the control panel.

"Jane? Are you all right?"

Jane shot Adam a cross look. "Of course I am."

In reality, she wanted nothing more than to sink into the floor. Each time she stood up, thick black dots crowded her vision. Her skin tingled as though someone had poured ice over every inch. She suspected it was because of that

222

chemical on Viate-5—maybe she'd been poisoned...

It didn't matter. Despite Riley's best efforts, the Stargazer refused to accept command from anyone but Jane due to some technical problem she didn't understand. She couldn't afford to be weak, not when her brother needed her.

I don't care if I'm sick or dying or what. I'll be fine—I have to be.

She checked the sleeve of her jacket to make sure it covered the painful, strange-looking reddish marks on her arm.

Adam glanced at the clock on the control screen. "Devin's seven minutes late. I hope nothing's wrong."

Worry crept into Jane's mind. She refused to yield to it. "I'm sure everything's fine. Things like breaking into a top-secret computer take a while."

Her hands stung with cold. She thrust them into her pockets. Her fingers brushed against the smooth metal case containing Sarah's portrait.

I hope you find her, Devin.

"I still can't believe someone made AIs so lifelike," she muttered. "But I guess they're really nothing more than a bunch of convincing puppets."

"Are they?" Adam's gaze turned pensive. "Riley said they perform most of their everyday activities on their own, meaning they have some kind of control, maybe even awareness. Sarah... She might think she's real, and that she's the only one. She could truly love your brother."

"Don't be ridiculous," Jane scoffed. "That's irrational. You can't program a computer to feel. Or give metal and synthetic skin a—a heart. She's a machine, and that's all she'll ever be. If she were anything more, she wouldn't have obeyed to that command to give Devin false hope just to distract him from a computing error." Her voice quivered. She looked away, wishing she hadn't said anything.

Adam was quiet for a moment. "I guess the only consciousness you can be certain of is your own."

A beep. Jane grabbed her slate and unfolded it.

Corsair: Roof. Now.

She tossed the slate to Adam and shoved the steering bars forward. The Stargazer swooped toward the building's roof.

Devin ran across it. Jane was about to tell Adam to open the door but found he'd already left the cockpit. She brought the Stargazer to a hover. The ladder extended before Devin. He grabbed it. Several armed security officers came into view, firing in his direction.

"He's in!" Adam called. "Go!"

Jane steered the Stargazer into the atmosphere. Someone entered the cockpit—*Must be Devin.* "What happened?"

No reply came. Instead, Adam returned to the copilot's seat.

"Where's Devin?" Jane asked. "Is he hurt?"

Adam buckled his safety belt. "Looked like a blast grazed him, but it's not bad. Something's troubling him, though. He went into the back and didn't say a word."

"Tell him to get his butt over here! This is no time to mope!"

"Jane," Adam said. "He's not coming."

"What?" A sudden panic rushed through her, overriding all movement and all thought, even the weariness. According to the tracker, several Anven cruisers were on their way. She had no idea where she was supposed to go.

"Engage lightspeed," Adam suggested.

Jane automatically swiped the icon on the control screen. The Stargazer zoomed. Her hands froze on the steering bars. Despite her cockiness about piloting, she'd taken comfort in her big brother's presence. He'd take charge if she forgot what she was doing. *Where am I supposed to go?*

Adam leaned toward her. "Relax. The authorities are well out of eyeshot, and they can't trace us, remember? As soon as we're out of the IC's reach, you can berate Devin for leaving you on your own, but for now, just fly."

Just fly. They'll never find us. "How far are we from the tunnels?"

Adam checked the navigation chart. "About sixteen light-minutes."

"Are the authorities after us?" Jane didn't dare look at the tracker herself.

"We're invisible. They won't even see us. Just stay out of sight."

Just fly...

The panicked tension subsided, replaced by determined calm. She steered the ship into an arbitrary tunnel. Never mind where it or the other tunnels she wove through led, as long as they took her as far from the IC as possible.

The heavy weariness returned. Jane resisted it, telling herself to keep her head up and focus.

The engines' temperature gauge appeared on the control screen. The needle flashed at the red zone, as though saying, "Look! Your engines are overheating!"

Sorry, ship. I can't exactly stop now.

Something rattled. Jane hoped it was stuff jangling in the storage compartment, not the engines breaking down. Her chest tightened with trepidation, and her shoulders tensed. She fixed her attention on the navigation chart to keep from looking at the gauge.

The chains of tunnels became shorter and shorter. The Stargazer exited one that stood alone against a sea of stars. According to the navigation chart, the ship was a few light-minutes from an asteroid field labeled "Xaxone 12587—Retired."

Xaxone was an industrial company with several interstellar mining operations. The field must have been one of their abandoned sites, containing nothing but stripped space rocks. Jane pulled the steering bars to flip the Stargazer and return to the tunnel.

The ship didn't react.

She wrenched the controls, but the ship continued toward the field. She tried veering instead. Alarms pealed. A warning appeared on the control screen, saying the generators couldn't take it anymore. The ship rapidly lost power.

Panicked, Jane cut power to the engines. The ship continued moving toward the asteroid field at lightspeed. *Right—things keep going in space...*

The indicator lights by the brakes went dark. *Shit. I can't even stop.*

Anxiety gripped her chest like a pair of hands digging into her heart. She felt every nervous breath in her lungs.

"What's happening?" Adam asked.

"The generators are dying." Jane tried to keep her voice steady. "Ship's breaking apart and all that. No big deal."

She revved up the engines. Without power, she couldn't steer. Asteroids covered the viewscreen. She scrambled to maneuver the slow-reacting Stargazer. The needle on the temperature gauge kept flashing. The ship screamed with alarms, begging her to turn off the engines before they caught fire.

Hold together, you ugly little bucket of bolts!

The tension made her nauseous. She kept her face calm and her eyes fixed on the viewscreen. If she so much as blinked, she could crash. Her vision faded in and out, as it had on Travan Float. Black dots filled in from the edges. In some moments, all she could see were pale blurs amid darkness.

She forced her eyes open as wide as she could to make sure it wasn't her eyelids drooping. *What the hell is wrong with me?*

Jane didn't have much time to think about it between dodging space rocks and ducking abandoned mining equipment. The steering bars resisted her movements, and she felt her control over the vehicle slipping. In spite of her best efforts, the Stargazer bumped up against asteroid after asteroid. It shook as sparks spewed from the distressed control panel. The rattling grew louder.

With no way to stop, her only choice was to keep going and wonder how long she could ignore her vehicle falling to pieces. The needle on the temperature gauge fell past the red zone. It stopped flashing, as though the ship had given up on its warnings and accepted its eventual destruction.

Please, ship. Please don't explode...

"We're almost there." Adam's voice was calm. "Only thirty light-seconds until we pass through the field."

Jane nodded quickly in acknowledgement. Empty space lay ahead. She focused on weaving through the asteroids, tuning out the rattling, the alarms, the terrified cries in her head. *Just fly...*

The Stargazer banged against one last asteroid and hurtled out of the field.

All the tension released her at once, and her shoulders

caved. "We made it."

"Well done." Adam sounded both relieved and impressed.

Jane cut power to the engines again and switched off the alarms. The ship continued tearing through space. With nothing for it to crash into, she figured they were all right. *For now, at least.* She collapsed back into the chair, worn out.

"Jane?"

"I'm *fine.*" Jane sat up and looked at the status report. "But the Stargazer's not."

No way to brake, hardly any power, busted engines— she recalled all the hits the Stargazer had taken under her piloting, and her confidence drained. "I broke it. I broke the damn ship. We're stuck here."

Adam gave her a bright, reassuring look. "It's not your fault. You were given a junker that hardly functioned, and you still managed to get us out of impossible situations. You saved our lives."

His encouragement did little for her grumpiness. "You don't have to be nice."

"I mean it. We'd have been blasted away at Travan if it weren't for you."

Jane couldn't help smirking. "I did outfly a fleet of merc ships. It was so weird. There must've been about twenty ships launched at the same time, and the way they flew... It's like they were drones. Maybe they were unmanned, but—"

Adam grasped his forearms as he had on Travan Float.

Alarmed, Jane asked, "What's wrong?"

He relaxed as though freed from whatever gripped him. "I'm all right. It's... I don't know how to put it. You know how you go through life with these inaudible nudges within you saying, 'I should do this,' and then you do it? I feel like someone's putting those thoughts in my mind, except I really don't want to do what they're telling me to. They're in my head, but... they aren't mine."

That's weird. "I thought the drugs had worn off."

Adam shook his head. "I'm just better at ignoring them. Right now, something within me wants to take the slate and tell the galaxy where we are. I have no idea why."

"What the hell could they have done to you?" Jane

thought for a moment. "The government developed a mind-control implant. Maybe the bad guys put one in you while you were out."

Adam looked as though he found the explanation ridiculous and apparent at the same time. "That would explain some of the stranger ones. Although, to be honest, I don't think this is the first time this has happened."

Huh? "What do you mean?"

"I mean... remember when I was transferred to Kydera Minor? A part of me, a very loud part, told me I should take the opportunity and go. I guess we all have our inner battles, but this was different. It felt... unnatural, like a part of myself I didn't recognize. If I'd listened to that instinct, I would've left without saying good-bye. But there were things about staying that meant much more to me."

Jane tried not to read into the tender turn his voice had taken and replied flippantly, "You're so cheesy. Besides, that was your everyday mind-versus-soul dilemma, the kind you're always philosophizing at me about."

"It was more than that." Adam looked past her. "It was foreign, like another voice in my head trying to... for lack of a better term, possess me." He brought his gaze back to Jane. "With all that's been going on, I guess No Name must've implanted me or something. At the time, though, I thought I was succumbing to the pressures of my advisors."

Jane slouched in her chair. "I know that feeling. Sometimes I feel like I'm being mind-controlled by my dad. It's like he's in my head giving me orders even when he's not around, and my thoughts are actually his." *Knock it off. I'm not turning this into another Dad conversation.* "But anyway, what's happening to you now is different. It seems to be telling you to... betray us."

"I would never do that," Adam said firmly. "I swear, Jane, I'd never do anything to hurt you."

What am I supposed to say? She wished Adam wouldn't talk like that. "Yeah, I know." She kept her tone casual in an attempt to steer things back toward normality. "Hey, the first thing we're doing once we get outta here is finding one of those super-advanced body scanners and checking you for a brain chip."

How're we supposed to leave with no power? Where can we go that'd be safe?

Jane got up. The familiar black dots surged across her vision. She grabbed the back of the seat to steady herself. Her knees buckled, and she felt herself sinking...

Her focus returned. Adam supported her, his arms around her. Jane vaguely remembered him calling her name.

She quickly left his embrace. "Just a head rush. Stood up too quickly, that's all. Devin's been back there long enough. I'm gonna go tell him off now."

Jane left the cockpit and walked into the living quarters. Her brother sat on the ground against a wall, staring at a hologram projected from his slate.

"What're you doing?" she asked.

"Catching up on the news again." Devin dully tossed the slate away.

Jane picked it up, wondering why he was so upset. The hologram displayed a reporter standing outside a courthouse. She tentatively pressed "Play."

"Although the defendant is still at large, the tribunal has reached a verdict concerning the attempted murder of Victor Colt. Due to the heinous nature of his crime, Devin Colt has been sentenced to death."

Stunned, Jane sank to the floor beside her brother.

"The execution has been scheduled for two weeks from today. The authorities have been granted permission to perform the execution upon arrest if Devin Colt is not apprehended by that time."

They were going to *kill* him. She knew his life had been in danger from the moment he ran from Quasar, but hearing it passed off as justice made it worse—and real.

She stopped the hologram and whispered, "They can't."

Devin leaned his head against the wall. "I'm not surprised. They have evidence, witnesses... Hell, they could've dredged up motive. Everyone knows I never got along with him. Play the previous one."

Jane peered into her brother's face, trying to figure out what his expression meant. It was somehow rage and resignation, loss and utter defeat. She'd never seen him like that. She didn't know what else to do, so she played the previous video.

A hologram of Sarah appeared. "Devin Colt always scared me. He was so charming, and I was foolish enough to believe him when he said he'd changed. By the time I realized what a monster he really was, it was too late. I tried to work up the courage to leave him, but I was too frightened." She looked down, as though suppressing tears. "I wish I'd said something to someone. Maybe they would've noticed there was something wrong with him, and none of this would have happened. Please understand, I only agreed to marry him because I was afraid of what he'd do to me if I refused. I want nothing to do with him, and I hope they catch him soon."

Jane smoldered with fury. "*Bitch*. She's not real anyway. Your Sarah would kick her ass if she saw this."

"She *is* my Sarah." Devin's voice was low. "She's the only Sarah there ever was. I fell for an illusion."

What? Jane's body shook. She wasn't sure whether it was from the weakness fast enveloping her body or the intense sorrow bruising her heart. To keep still, she hugged her knees, unable to find it in herself to ask her questions.

Devin seemed to read them in her expression. "I found Kron. He's not involved with No Name. He was tracking their activities, and he showed me some of their files. I knew something was wrong when I found out that Sarah's identity was faked. I shouldn't have tried to deny it, should've believed the obvious and spared us all a lot of grief. I saw her test program, saw how her expressions, her voice—even some of her words—were taken from watching the way other women behaved, combined to create a perfect lie."

The madness behind his eyes made Jane shudder. She didn't dare speak as her own eyes welled up at the sight of her brother's pain. He sounded as though he'd given up on everything, as though... he wanted to die.

"Don't look at me like that." Devin sounded disgusted. "I didn't lose anyone. Sarah never existed, so how could I lose her? It's kind of funny if you think about it. I'm engaged to a one-year-old. That's what Kron said. And he laughed. He laughed away as he watched my world shatter."

There were no tears in his eyes and no quiver in his

voice, only a flat statement of fact. Jane nevertheless sensed his agony. A rush of fury engulfed her. *"I'll kill him."*

Devin looked away. "He's already dead. Shot through the head, his brilliant brains splattered across the images of the women who became Sarah."

Normally, Jane would've known her brother couldn't kill anyone in cold blood, but the unfamiliar iciness in his voice, the stillness in his face, the madness—she was at a loss as to how to answer.

"I didn't do it." Devin smiled wryly. "But I might as well have. They'll pin it on me, and I don't blame them. I did run into his office waving a gun. No Name's all about perfection, right? The perfect singer. The perfect love. And now, I'm their perfect murderer."

Jane's question burst from her lips: "What happened?"

"He was about to tell me everything. He mentioned something called the 'Pandora Project' and then..." Devin pointed his finger like a gun. *"Bang."* He flicked his wrist.

"Was it the internal defenses again?"

"Yeah. No Name's favorite modus operandi. I guess Kron was a liability, and they were waiting for someone like me to come along so they could off him without drawing attention to themselves."

"Wait, how could they have known you were there? The Gag Warriors shut down the cameras. Riley said you'd be invisible!"

"Unlike Sarah, they're not perfect."

"Forget Sarah!" Jane's fury returned even as she felt herself fading. "She was never real anyway, so forget all about her! What we have to do now is *clear your name.* Show those idiots who call themselves 'justice' you didn't do it!"

"Maybe I did." Devin's voice was almost a whisper. "Dad's good as dead because of me. Hell, even Kron's dead because of me. All because I tried to save a girl who never existed."

"Devin..."

"I don't care anymore." His tone turned harsh. "Sarah was my one shot at happiness, my one way out of this numb misery I call life. She never existed. That chance never existed, and I was *stupid* to believe anything could change. I have no future, no hope... nothing."

"You've got me!" The darkness invaded into Jane's vision again. "I... I'll always..."

———◆◇◆———

"*Jane!*" Devin reached toward his sister as she slumped to the floor. He was too late to catch her. Her eyes were closed and her breath shallow. One arm lay across her stomach. He noticed a reddish scar on her wrist and pushed her sleeve back. Burns covered her forearm, some sickeningly discolored.

Shit. The chemical—it was *toxic.*

Adam scrambled into the room. He knelt beside Jane, put a hand on her shoulder, and shook her. "Jane, wake up! Jane!"

How long had she been sick? How much pain had she hidden behind those cocky smirks? If Devin had paid attention to her instead of obsessing over Sarah, he would've noticed her weakness was more than fatigue. "I should've taken her to a hospital the moment we landed on Fragan."

"Don't blame yourself." Adam put a hand on Jane's forehead and brushed her hair out of her face. "She's ice cold."

Jane's eyelids fluttered. "Adam?" They fell shut, as though she didn't have the strength to keep them open. "Where's Devin?"

Devin took her hand in his. "I'm right here, Pony."

The corner of her mouth flickered, as if she was trying to smile. "Devin, don't be sad. You'll always have me."

"I know." He picked her up. Her body hung limply in his arms, and he felt no warmth in her skin.

"I'm fine." Her voice was faint. "I need some sleep, that's all."

Devin placed her in the hammock. "I'm getting you help."

Jane's eyes popped open. "Don't you dare!" She barely lifted her head before sinking back. "You know we can't... What about justice, Devin? What about..."

Her eyes closed, and her head lolled to the side. She looked like her own ghost, and she suddenly seemed so fragile.

I should never have listened to her protests. I only did because it meant I could keep looking for Sarah.

Devin backed away, feeling as though his very presence endangered her. "This is my fault."

Adam approached the hammock. "I didn't know she was sick either."

Devin started to leave the room. He knew what he had to do. "Take care of her. I'll figure something out."

Concern crossed Adam's face. "She wouldn't want you doing anything that would put you in harm's way. She loves you too much for that. You have no reason to blame yourself. You haven't done anything wrong."

Devin stopped. "How could you know that? You barely know me. In fact, why did you believe me in the first place, when I said I was framed?"

"Why wouldn't I?"

Devin recognized the idealistic nonsense filling the kid's head and wanted to shake the blind faith out of him. He left in silence.

He entered the cockpit and looked down at the useless control screen. The ship was dead in space, floating aimlessly through the void. Even if he could pilot it, less than a day's worth of power remained. Where would he go? No Name had infiltrated two of the IC's most powerful companies and attacked their big shots, the ones with the best security. They'd hacked an entire float and destroyed a building full of soldiers under the nose of a Megatooth warship.

And Jane had been poisoned.

Fuck.

A thought entered his mind as he recalled something Kron had said, the possibility that... *I'm probably wrong.* Even if Devin were right, there was nothing he could do about it—nothing that wouldn't make things worse. When it came to the Pandora Project, knowledge was lethal. Perhaps it was best to dismiss the notion.

He returned to the living quarters and stood in the doorway. Adam wrapped a blanket around Jane and kissed her softly on the forehead. *Damn, he really loves her. Poor kid.*

The look in Adam's eyes said he would be there for her,

no matter what, looking out for her even if she didn't think she needed him. Devin hoped the kid truly was who he appeared to be. As long as he was, Jane would be all right. If he wasn't... Well, she'd still be better off with him than on the run with her fugitive brother.

The brother whose carelessness nearly killed her.

That's it. Time to end this.

CHAPTER 16

THE INTERROGATION

AN ABRUPT LURCH WOKE JANE. Her hammock swayed. The ship must have bumped into something. She pushed through the crushing weariness and sat up.

Adam leaned against the wall, asleep on the floor beside her.

Must've been out a while. "Adam? Adam!"

Adam blinked. "Sorry, didn't mean to fall asleep."

"What's happening?"

"I don't know."

Devin entered and looked at Jane with a strange sadness. *What's wrong?*

"Hey, Pony." His voice was quiet. "I'm glad you're awake. Everything's going to be fine."

Rhythmic marching boots pounded the decking. Jane bolted from the hammock and stumbled out of the living quarters. Her vision blacked out, and she fell.

Devin caught her. When her eyesight returned, she saw the open door of the Stargazer and the airtight tunnel attached to a larger ship. The boots belonged to four crimson-clad soldiers, led by a regal-looking woman in a red commander's uniform: Commander Vega of the *Granite Flame.*

"Devin, what did you do? *What did you do?*" She tried to run, but Devin held her back. "Let me go! I'll get us outta here! I'll make us disappear!"

"Jane, stop! It's no use!"

"They'll *kill* you! We've gotta go! We've gotta..." Jane felt herself sink. Darkness covered her vision.

When she came to, she found that Adam held her. Devin waited by the ship's door.

Jane tried to escape. *"Let me go!* I've gotta get to the cockpit! I've gotta get us outta here!"

The soldiers entered, and one of them handcuffed Devin.

Commander Vega clasped her hands behind her back and lifted her chin. "Devin Colt, you are under arrest for the attempted murder of your father and for the murder of Dr. Revelin Kron. You have been sentenced to death, and you are to be taken back to Kydera Major for processing."

Jane couldn't find the strength to say aloud the cries in her head: *You can't! He's innocent! No Name's still out there! You've gotta to let him go!*

Devin looked at Commander Vega. "My sister's very ill. Please see that she receives medical attention."

Commander Vega nodded and waved a hand at the soldiers.

Jane wanted to cry out, to fight, but her body sank again. She could barely see through the black veil before her vision.

Devin glanced over his shoulder as they led him away. "It's fine, Pony. They'll take care of you."

A heavy cold consumed Jane, and the darkness returned.

Commander Vega usually left interrogations to her subordinates, but she wanted to handle Devin Colt's interrogation herself. After ensuring that her cybernetics team rigorously monitored the *Granite Flame's* central computer for potential hacks, she left the bridge in the hands of her second-in-command and went down to the brig.

She entered the small interrogation room and sat down at the steel-gray table across from her prisoner, whose hands were chained before him. High-tech heart rate monitors and movement-scanning machines surrounded him. Behind him, a large screen displayed the results. Commander Vega had only ordered them to be employed due to protocol; her intuition was the only lie detector she'd ever needed.

Colt stared blankly at the wall. "Is Jane all right?"

"She's unconscious but stable." Commander Vega

sensed an unusual melancholy about him, and he suddenly looked very young—too young to die. Something about the situation felt off, but she wouldn't let that keep her from objectivity. *He's a murderer.* "Your sister was poisoned by a toxic chemical. If my medical team hadn't reached her when they did, she would have died within a day, and you would have been responsible for her death, as well."

"I didn't even know she was sick. She was so strong..." Colt shook his head. "And so stubborn."

Commander Vega clasped her hands and placed them on the table. "Why was she with you?"

"I kidnapped her. Needed a human shield, remember?" He was clearly lying, sarcastic even.

"I want the truth."

"That's the only truth there is." His stare seemed to challenge her, daring her to elicit a different answer.

I shouldn't waste my time on the matter. "What about Adam Palmer? Why was he with you?"

Colt broke his stare. "Found him on Travan Float. Jane wasn't having a mental breakdown when she said he'd been kidnapped."

Travan Float... Commander Vega mentally ran through the facts. "A recent report from one of the Fringe patrols stated that Travan Float lost control of its internal defenses and robotic units. A space battle followed, between various unrelated mercenary and pirate ships that appeared to have no motive. Were you involved with that?"

Colt nodded. "They were after us. It started after we broke into a storage unit and found Adam drugged in there."

"Adam Palmer has been on Dalarune since the day before you shot your father." From the records, Commander Vega knew he had to be lying again. The lie detectors told her he was not. People had been known to overcome the machines before. Given his past as an ISARK informant, he might have training in that area.

Nevertheless, she pursued her questions. "Your father was a great man. He gave you everything—life, opportunities, even cleaned up after your indiscretions. Why did you want to kill him?"

Colt looked her in the eye. "I didn't."

Commander Vega felt her jaw tighten. "You have already

been convicted, and there is no use in lying. But I am the one who has been pursuing you, and I want to know what would drive you commit such an atrocity."

"I didn't. I swear. I went to talk to him, and he lowered the shades in his office. Anything that was seen from the outside was a computer-generated video." Colt lifted the corner of his mouth into a humorless smile. "They can make fakes very convincing these days."

How far will you go? "Your gun was found at the scene."

"Someone installed it in the internal defense system."

"The forensics report said the blast's trajectory was consistent with being fired point-blank at Victor Colt's forehead."

"It was forged."

You have an answer for everything, don't you? Irate frustration chipped Commander Vega's composure. The lies were as insulting as they were blatant. Yet that off feeling prevented her from being sure they *were* lies. For the first time since she'd been given command of the *Granite Flame,* she felt uncertain.

She looked past Devin Colt at the screen showing the lie detectors' results. According to his heart rate and eye movements, he told the truth, but again, the machines had been outwitted in the past.

Stubborn bastard. Next topic, then. Commander Vega unclasped her hands and rested her back against her chair. "What about Dr. Kron? Why did you murder him?"

Colt leaned toward her. "I haven't murdered anyone. I've only killed when I had to."

Commander Vega stiffened. "I read your ISARK file. You hunted that man like an animal, and you killed him in cold blood."

"That's not what I did."

She realized she digressed and returned to her intended subject. "You were seen in BD Tech's Fragan facility carrying a weapon, the same weapon we confiscated upon your arrest. The security team was alerted to your presence by an anonymous tip and found you fleeing the scene of Dr. Kron's murder. What were you doing there?"

"I went to get answers. I wanted to know—" Colt broke off and examined her face, as though trying to read her.

"Have you heard of an entity called No Name?"

"*I* will be asking the questions," Commander Vega snapped. "To what are you referring?"

"The IC cyberpolice have been tracking them for years. Kron was tracking them too. They're like phantoms in the Net. No one knows who they are or how much they've done, but they're powerful.'"

"How is this relevant?"

"I thought Kron was behind No Name. I tried to make him tell me what he knew. He was about to tell me, and they shot him. Just like they shot my father."

Commander Vega bristled. "How dare you. Isn't it bad enough your sister almost died because of what you've done? Why can't you take responsibility instead of blaming a fantasy?"

Colt didn't blink. "It's no fantasy. This is their way of getting rid of me because I found out what they're doing. I know you won't believe me, but you asked for the truth, and I'm giving it to you."

Commander Vega had much more to say, but she'd come with a purpose and couldn't allow her personal irritation to get in the way. "Dr. Kron had ties to several amateur programmers ten years ago." She kept her words objective. "They were talented hackers who had previously refused BD Tech's attempts to recruit them, and they all died or vanished under mysterious circumstances. Do you know anything about that?"

Colt nodded. "Some think they were working on artificial intelligence. The Collective believes No Name is involved in something similar."

"The murdered programmers were members of the Collective. They were also involved with a well-known cybercriminal with the alias 'Mastermind.'"

"That was Kron. That's why I thought he was No Name." Colt looked down and knit his dark eyebrows in thought. "He was using them for the Pandora Project... He was mining the Collective for talent."

"What are you talking about?"

Colt met Commander Vega's gaze. "Right before he died, Kron mentioned something called the 'Pandora Project.' Someone tracked No Name's origins to the BD Tech facility on Fragan. Kron may not have been No Name, but he must've been involved in its origins, and they killed him and those programmers to cover it up."

Commander Vega's frustration grew to a dangerous level. "Your conspiracy theories will do you no good."

"I have no reason to lie."

"You have no reason to tell the truth either."

"Yes, I do." Colt spoke intensely. "Whatever happens to me, I want No Name stopped. You should too. They're the ones who sent those Barracudas to Viate-5."

"That's enough!" Commander Vega stood. "Seventeen good men and women died that day because of you!"

"How could I have been behind it? I was in that building too. My *kid sister* was in there!"

Commander Vega scowled. "You didn't care when you used her as a human shield and let her slowly die right in front of you."

Colt looked as though he'd been punched. He opened his mouth, then closed it, as though he had something he wanted to tell her, but couldn't. "I didn't send those Barracudas."

Commander Vega slammed her hands on the table. "You must have been involved. How else could *you* have escaped when my people were *massacred*?"

"We barely made it. It was No Name, the same ones who have been behind *everything*. They were covering their tracks. Why else would they have attacked right when your troops went in? That building stood abandoned for five years!"

Commander Vega glared at him. It made sense. *A little too much sense.*

"And what about Travan Float?" he pressed. "Do you really think Madam Wrath would care enough about one person to kill her own thugs in an attempt to gun me down?"

Commander Vega strode for the exit. "This is a waste of time. I *will* find the truth, with or without your cooperation."

The door closed behind her. Her mind filled with doubts that, try as she might, she couldn't dismiss. Records and evidence told her that Devin Colt was a mentally unstable liar. The lie detectors' results meant nothing. He had once spent almost a year living a deception, as part of an undercover operation.

The intuition that had never failed her before told Commander Vega he'd been honest and that she was missing something. All the same, facts were facts. Disputing them was irrational.

She made her way into the medical sector. Jane Colt lay unconscious on a hospital bed. The girl had been so desperate for her brother to escape. She must have gone with him willingly, volunteered to be his human shield on Viate-5. *Foolish girl. Loyalty can be a fault.*

She could have had Jane Colt arrested for aiding and abetting a fugitive, but as far as she was concerned, the girl's only crime was loving her brother. Commander Vega was prepared to argue vehemently against anyone who suggested she be considered an accomplice.

Adam Palmer sat in a chair beside the hospital bed. He held the girl's hand and watched over her as she slept. He seemed to glow with sweet innocence. Commander Vega approached. Even if her prisoner had thrown her intuition, the boy would be an easy read. "Palmer."

Palmer stood quickly. "Yes, Commander?"

"What were you doing on that Stargazer with Jane Colt and her brother? When did you leave Dalarune?"

"Commander, I was never on Dalarune. The last thing I remember before waking up on Travan Float is entering my dorm room at the seminary. That was almost a week ago. Jane and her brother found me, and I went with them because I wanted to know who took me and why."

He was telling the truth—she was certain of it. There was no more to say. Commander Vega started to leave.

Palmer caught up to her. "Commander?"

Commander Vega stopped. "Yes?"

"Devin's innocent." Palmer's gaze pleaded. "I know the evidence is against him, but... He didn't murder anyone. He's only here because he wants Jane to be safe. He's a good man, and he doesn't deserve to die."

Ordinarily, Commander Vega would have responded by sharply telling him that he was a fool. Something felt different that time. She continued on her way without a word.

An alarm blared. Her second-in-command shouted over the comm, "Commander! There is an unidentified spacecraft approaching the ship. It is armed, and I believe it is hostile. It has not responded to attempts to communicate. I have deployed Betta Unit S."

"Very good." Commander Vega entered the elevator. A hostile in such a remote area was likely a lone mercenary or another lost fugitive.

She pressed an icon on the elevator's touchscreen. An external view appeared. The hostile was a small, triangular ship. It easily evaded the Bettas, heading straight toward the *Granite Flame*.

The hostile crashed into the Stargazer docked at the warship's side. A disproportionately large explosion ensued. By the end of it, nothing remained of either vehicle.

Commander Vega entered the bridge and listened to the second-in-command's brief report. Apparently, the sole purpose of the hostile had been to destroy the junker.

The evidence was still indisputable. It was the word of a convicted murderer and a love-struck boy against solid facts and hard proof. Everything had once been so clear, but no longer. Commander Vega's confidence was nothing more than a façade she presented to herself. She tried to stand by her certainty, to line up the proof of Devin Colt's guilt with the strange circumstances that seemed to follow him.

But the cracks began to show.

CHAPTER 17

GLARES AND NIGHTMARES

"PONY, AREN'T YOU FORGETTING SOMETHING?"

Jane noticed a small open door that led to a room full of wires.

That door was her chest; those wires, her insides.

She closed her chest. Metal rods replaced her fingers, but she could still feel with them, still sense the smoothness of her mechanical body beneath the cold fingertips.

Devin, whose body was also made of metal, stood before her. A pair of deep blue claws slowly tore him apart.

"Stop!" Jane lunged toward him. A large window trapped her. She frantically tried to crash through it, but it seemed unbreakable.

Sarah appeared beside Devin. She laughed as she watched his destruction. "Devin won't go to heaven!"

The claws ripped Devin's body in half. "I'm just a machine, Pony. We're all machines."

A wall of flames devoured what remained of him.

"Devin!" Jane screamed and fought as hard as she could, but she couldn't get to him… couldn't save him…

His face disappeared into the fire. "Why do you care? I'm not even real."

"You're real! I don't care if we're made of metal and wires! We're real! Devin! Devin!"

"Jane, it's all right. It's just a dream."

Jane opened her eyes with a start. Adam hovered over her, looking down with concern.

"Where's Devin?" Several needles attached to opaque

tubes stuck out of her hands and arms. She wanted to rip them out.

Adam caught her hand. "Calm down. It's okay. You're safe."

"Where am I?" Jane looked around. She lay in a white bed with a metal rail, situated in a small room and surrounded by medical equipment.

A memory and cold realization hit her.

She bolted up. "*Where's Devin?*"

Adam hesitated. "We're at the Central Hospital of Kydera City. You're in one of the private rooms in the Colt Wing. Your father's across the hall."

"*Adam!*"

Adam drew back, his brow creased in an apologetic expression. "I couldn't stop him, Jane. I had a feeling he was going to turn himself in, but it wasn't my place to tell him what to do. And you were dying."

Dying?! "I was fine!"

Adam shook his head. "You barely made it. You've been unconscious for more than three days."

"What?" It felt like a few hours, at most. Jane even had the kind of dull headache she always got when sleep-deprived.

A cold line trickled down her back, as though someone threaded her spine with a string of ice. *The execution has been scheduled for two weeks from today...*

The Republic of Kydera had no appeals court. There was no need. Thanks to the computers, their system was flawless, infallible, efficient. The science behind forensics methodologies, which had taken generations to develop, had proved indisputable time and time again. DNA didn't lie, including the DNA of computers. Sophisticated scanning programs tracked all movements in the codes. If a dozen people saw Devin Colt shoot his father, and the computers showed no signs of having been tampered with, he must have done it. Or so the thinking of the almighty "they" must have went.

Jane lay back in her bed and stared at the white ceiling panels. *Due to the heinous nature of his crime, Devin Colt has been sentenced to death...*

"I've petitioned President Thean to commute your brother's sentence." Adam seemed to read her thoughts.

"Riley and I are working on an online movement to gain support. I won't let them execute him, Jane."

Jane's lip quivered. "Where is he?"

"The Kydera City Penitentiary. I tried to see him, but he's not allowed visitors—not even you, I'm afraid. They said prisoners on death row are only allowed visitors the day before their scheduled executions."

Jane firmed her mouth. "It's not going to happen."

"No, it's not. Riley and I stirred up quite a storm over the whole case. We've pointed out all the problems they overlooked. For example, your father was known to lower his shades whenever he had a visitor unless it was something he wanted made public. He wouldn't have allowed a private quarrel with his son to be seen. The justice system won't overlook the facts."

Jane nodded. It would work. She'd find the evidence to prove her brother's innocence. She'd bang on President Thean's door demanding clemency, if she had to.

Adam glanced at the digital clock on the wall. "I have to go soon. I have a meeting with some people helping with the petition."

Jane sat up. "I'm coming with you." Her head felt light, and she drooped forward.

Adam caught her shoulders. "Not today. You're not strong enough yet."

"Yes, I am!" *He's right—I'm really not.* She wanted to sink back into the bed after barely a few seconds of sitting up. But Devin was *her* brother, and *she* was the one who should be looking out for him.

"Adam, I really appreciate everything you've done, but let me take it from here. You should go back to your life." Jane smiled jokingly. "I'm sure you've got a lotta homework piled up. Better catch up before they stick you in a remedial class."

Adam sat down in the chair by her bed. "That's not important. I'll drop out if I have to."

"Please, you don't have to do all this." Jane paused. *How do I say this?* "I know you're only doing it because... because of me. But this whole thing with Devin... It's not your problem."

Adam took her hand. "Of course it is. You love him so

much you hid your pain for days while your life drained away. I won't let them take him from you. You know I... I would do anything for you."

"Damn, you're such a sap." Jane pulled her hand away with an inexplicable frustration. A hurt look crossed Adam's face. She softened her expression. "You don't have to do anything for me. I'm not... I'm not the one you should pin your hopes on. I know we... heh... went out a few times, but... I'm the wrong kind of girl, Adam. I'm not..."

"I don't expect you to be anything. I care about you, that's all."

Despite her efforts not to read into it, Jane recognized the tenderness in Adam's voice. Her awkward frustration hung in the air. She looked away, wondering what she could say.

"I'm sorry if I've made you uncomfortable." Adam sounded calm. "I know this comes at an odd time for our... for lack of a better word, relationship. We were friends before, and I'm still your friend now. Friends don't abandon each other, especially at a time like this. I just want you to know that I'm here for you, and, like I said, I don't expect anything."

Jane looked at him and saw only honesty.

Adam leaned back with a slight shrug. "Besides, I don't want to see anything happen to Devin, either. Even if he were a complete stranger, I still wouldn't want to see an innocent man executed. You know how I feel about capital punishment." He smiled that infuriatingly adorable smile of his and extended a hand. "Friends?"

Jane took it and smiled with relief, grateful for his understanding. "Friends."

Adam checked the time again. "I really should be going. I'll visit again in a few hours. They told me you'd be able to go home soon after you regained consciousness, but you have to keep the needles in, okay? They're giving you what you need to get better."

Jane sighed. "Yes, Doctor."

Adam left. Jane obeyed her body's command to lie back down. She considered sleeping, but as soon as she shut her eyes, the image of Sarah from her nightmare swam across her vision. *Devin won't go to heaven!*

"Bitch." Jane opened her eyes and glared at the ceiling. *Dreams are nothing but random crap.* She tried to forget her latest one.

Her thoughts turned to her father across the hall. She pressed an icon on the touchscreen by her bed to call for assistance.

An elderly nurse appeared at the door. "Yes, Miss Colt?"

Jane pushed herself up with her elbows. "I want to see my father."

"Advanced as medical technology is these days, you still need your rest, at least for a few more hours while the medicines restore you to full health."

"Please, I haven't seen him since—since it happened. I just want to see his face again."

The nurse opened her mouth to speak, then smiled resignedly. "All right, dear. I guess it can't hurt."

The nurse approached the touchscreen and pressed an icon. The bed rose, hovering a few inches above the ground. She detached the touchscreen from the wall and used it to guide the bed out of Jane's room and into the one across the hall.

The nurse stopped Jane's bed beside the one where Victor Colt lay unconscious, attached to so much medical equipment that, for a moment, Jane's mind flashed to the AI workshop and the human-looking android parts wired into various machines.

"Hi, Dad." Jane had so much she wanted to tell him, but she didn't want the nurse to hear. She said it silently in her head.

I love you, Dad. I know you'd hate that I let myself get pulled into this mess, but I'm doing it for you, and I'm doing it for Devin. If I don't act, they'll kill him, and the bastards who did this to you will get away. I still hope the justice system will realize they're wrong, but if they don't... I don't care what I have to do. I won't let him die. If you want to stop me from being a fool, wake up and yell at me. Please, Dad. Please wake up...

Tears streamed down Jane's face. She felt the nurse's comforting hand on her shoulder.

Wait a sec... The best evidence of Devin's innocence lay right in front of her. Her father had been shot from the ceiling, not point-blank. Surely the doctors had noticed—unless No Name hacked their systems and altered the records. "Whom do I talk to about a second opinion?"

The nurse frowned. "Excuse me?"

"I want my father's scans redone. The originals must've been wrong. There's no way he could've survived being shot point-blank. It must've been from a distance, from the internal defense guns on the ceiling."

"I'm sure the records are correct."

"Please..." Jane widened her eyes into a pitiable expression. "My father and my brother are all I've got, and if there's the slightest chance my brother's not guilty..."

She covered her face, and it wasn't long before the tears returned. The nurse first tried reassuring her that the Kyderan justice system was infallible. After a minute of Jane's sobbing, the nurse agreed to have a doctor come in for a second opinion as soon as possible.

Jane wiped her eyes. "Thank you." Exhausted, she reclined in her bed.

I love you, Dad. You'll always be in my heart, but I've gotta get you out of my head.

———◆———

According to the night nurse, Adam had visited, but Jane had been asleep, and he hadn't wanted to disturb her. She wished he had. He'd put himself down as her contact, and she'd been told she needed him to check her out of the hospital. The medicines had restored her completely. Even the scars on her arm had vanished. She felt energized and ready to go. She'd tried simply walking out, only to be escorted back by a pair of orderlies.

Jane wasn't in the mood for holovision, but she needed something to keep her mind from replaying her disturbing nightmare.

You're real! I don't care if we're made of metal and wires! We're real!

"Shut *up!*" She pressed the button to activate the holovision projector, which flipped through arbitrary channels. A hologram of Adam appeared.

What's he doing there? "View channel!"

Adam stood before a crowd of reporters. "If the police were to examine the facts more closely, they would see the inconsistencies. Devin Colt is innocent, and I think it's clear that evidence was planted and records tampered with. I pray President Thean will give us more time to prove what is, for me, an indisputable truth."

Thanks, Adam.

A reporter started detailing the case. Jane had no interest in listening to people tell untruths about her brother. "Change channel."

Every news channel obsessed with Devin Colt's crime, and every entertainment channel fawned over the music sensation Sarah DeHaven. Jane shut off the holovision with a huff. She lay against the tilted back of her hospital bed and daydreamed about pouring Lithran stinger ants on the bastards behind No Name.

Someone requested entry. Jane eagerly swiped the icon to open the door. "I saw your bit on the news!"

It wasn't Adam who walked in. Riley grinned, waving his scrawny arm too quickly. "Hi, Janie!"

Jane blinked in surprise. "Riley! What're you doing here? Where's Adam?"

"I'm right here." Adam, carrying a canvas sack on his shoulder, entered behind Riley.

Riley shoved his hands in the pockets of his baggy orange pants. "So, I quit BD Tech and came looking for you guys, but not before I did a little diggin'."

Jane sat up and hugged her knees. "How'd you get here without No Name catching you?"

Riley spread his arms, shoulders raised. "Uh... Bought a Moray ticket? Riley Winklepleck's a boring maintenance worker with a clean record. No one's interested in him. *Corsair* has been gettin' in plenty of trouble, but he's just a name on the Net, and not a unique one at that. Online me can kinda fade into the crowd until the time comes to do some major demonizin', like I did on the Hard Planet. *Man*, have I got some *stuff* to tell you!"

Jane hugged her knees tighter in excitement. "What is it?"

"First of all, you can chill. I... uh... rescheduled the security cams' maintenance shutdown for right now, so we're invisible." Riley seated himself in the chair by the bed. "I doubt No Name'll try anything anyhow. They've been quiet. Their little stunt on Travan Float kicked up a lotta commotion, and I guess they don't wanna attract any more attention. And the news has been all over Uh-Dame here because of the whole amnesty thing, so they're not gonna snatch him again with everyone watching."

Jane felt her shoulders relax. "Thanks, Riley."

Riley grinned awkwardly, as though unaccustomed to gratitude. "Anyhow, here's what we know: Kron, paradin' around as Mastermind, was working on something with several members of the Collective. Most of those demons were killed or disappeared, and a little while later, *bam!*" He slammed the chair's armrest. "No Name was born. Now, Adam told me that Devin told you that Kron told him that there was this thing called the Pandora Project. Uh... Did I get that right?"

Riley turned to Adam for confirmation. Adam nodded.

How would he know? Jane looked up at Adam. "Were you eavesdropping?"

Adam tilted his chin down in a sheepish expression. "I didn't mean to, but that Stargazer didn't exactly have soundproof walls."

Riley waved impatiently. "*Anyhow,* I found out the Pandora Project was an aborted... uh... project at BD Tech about ten years ago, around the same time the No Name people first reared their ugly mugs. I had to dig *really hard* to find out about its existence, and I think it wasn't aborted at all. I think the Pandora Project *is* No Name!"

Jane raised an eyebrow. "You also thought Kron was No Name."

"Hey! I had good reason to! All the evidence pointed to old Kuh-Ronie, but now I think it's bigger than one megalomaniacal dude. Uh... What do Kron, Fragan, and the Pandora Project all have in common? *BD Tech!*"

Jane kept her eyebrow raised. "You think the galaxy's most successful tech corporation is secretly policing the Networld, kidnapping seminary students, and hacking Fringe floats?"

Riley pointed confidently. "Yup!"

She was skeptical, but then it started to make sense— more sense than when she'd thought it was Kron and maybe a handful of his cronies. The people behind No

Name clearly had money, manpower, and influence. BD Tech certainly had plenty of those—more than some star systems. With all the power they wielded, it wouldn't be hard to skirt the IC's tech regulations.

Jane's other eyebrow lifted as she widened her eyes. "Holy *shit*. The Pandora Project is code for this business with the AIs, isn't it? It's BD Tech's attempt to... to basically take over!"

Adam rested his arms on the bedrail. "Could be. If they control the people who influence the galaxy—politicians, academics, even cultural icons—they could really... have power over everything."

I'm kind of impressed. "It makes so much sense. I mean, people buy influence all the time, but why pay a superstar or bribe a politician when you can create them? Why risk your superstar being a flop or your politician not winning when you can engineer them to give the people what they want?"

The IC's strict voting laws made hacking elections impossible, but if the Gag Warriors could fake a talking head who swayed the opinions of multitudes, then a company as powerful as BD Tech could undoubtedly guarantee wins for their AI politician.

Riley put his hands back in his pockets. "Uh... I don't think it's the *entire* company. I think it's a cabal *within* BD Tech. You know, an inner circle of their biggest players. I couldn't find anything about the Pandora Project other than that it existed and then it didn't. I'm guessing Kron and his amateur pals developed the AI codes, and the bad guys didn't want them knowing what they were *really* up to. I mean, this is clearly a long-term plan. Actives like Sarah can create almost immediate rewards, but actives like Jonathan King? It's gonna be a while before they're seasoned enough to be useful."

Adam looked over at Riley. "How did they develop the technology so fast? And without getting caught by the Tech Council? As far as I know, people are still arguing over Ocean Sky's riddle-solver."

Details, details. Jane dismissed the questions. "They're an evil corporation. What *can't* they get away with? I think Riley's right. It's probably a select few who abuse the rest of the company and hire crooks to do their dirty work. Hey, why don't we show the authorities what we found? I mean, we're not exactly ISARK agents, and if *we* could figure it out... What about showing them the chip from the machine? Or the info the Seer gave us?"

Riley shrugged. "It's gone. No Name, or I guess... uh... the Pandora people, blew up your Stargazer right after Devin was arrested. Some little ship came out of nowhere and *boom*." He flicked his hands to indicate an explosion.

Damn you, No Name. "What about all your research? The stuff you dug up?"

"We don't have any proof," Adam said patiently. "I'm having a hard enough time convincing people of Devin's innocence, and there *is* evidence of that."

Shit. He was right. Clear as it seemed to Jane, most people would think she was having another psychotic episode. "Screw the Pandora Project. First, we've gotta show those idiots that Devin's not a murderer. Adam, can you please help me check out?"

"Sure." Adam took the sack off his shoulder and handed it to Jane. "By the way, I brought you some proper clothes."

"Thanks." Jane opened the sack curiously. A thought struck her. "Riley! Who greenlit the Pandora Project? If there's a record of its existence, then *someone* must have signed off on it, right? One of the bosses?"

Riley started to answer, then shut his mouth and thought for a moment. "Uh... Must've missed that." He held up his forefinger. "I'll find out."

The moment Jane stepped out of the hospital, she found herself facing a horde of reporters who blockaded the hospital.

"My brother's innocent," was the only thing she could say that didn't involve a long string of insults. Realizing she had a platform by which to be heard, she said as matter-of-factly as she could, "The forensics must've been either faked or tampered with. If online pranksters can shut down BD Tech's security, surely someone can hack the police department's computers."

The crowd shouted loud protests and prying questions. Jane had no patience for any of their bullshit. She rudely pushed through them.

"Miss Colt! Can you give us details as to what happened while you were missing?"

"How did your brother coerce you into going on the run with him?"

"Had he shown previous signs of his murderous intentions?"

Jane shot back at the last one, "What the hell? What kind of question is that? If you won't report the truth, why do you bother at all?"

She felt Adam's hand on her shoulder. For some reason, his presence made her calm down.

"Come with me." Adam guided her through the crowd. He blocked any reporters who approached and politely told them she had no comments. Normally, Jane would have insisted on taking care of herself, but she was too agitated to deal with the situation and was glad for his help.

She saw an empty air taxi ahead and rushed toward it. The door opened, and she hurriedly climbed in. She motioned for Adam to join her.

Adam looked back at the reporters. "I'll meet up with you later."

"Okay." Jane closed the door and turned to the pilot. "FFC Residential Complex, please."

The pilot dropped Jane off on the landing pad next to the courtyard of her apartment complex. Weird, returning to the normal world after being a fugitive. Her mind was at a loss, but her legs automatically steered her toward her apartment.

A familiar figure exited the neighboring building. Jane ran up to her. "Sarah!"

Sarah stopped. "Hello, Jane. I'm glad to see you're all right. I heard you were in the hospital."

"I know what you are, but I don't know what it's like to be you." Jane couldn't help herself. "Please tell me it's not all an illusion, that there's something... real... in there."

Sarah didn't react. A chill flooded Jane's body. *Is she... calculating a response?*

Sarah's eyebrows pushed together. "I don't understand. I'll admit, some of my stage persona is for show, but—"

"That's not what I'm talking about, and you know it."

Jane took a breath. "He loves you, Sarah! He really, truly *loves* you! Do you even know what that means?"

Sarah's face relaxed, arranging into a regretful, melancholy expression. "Of course I do. I loved him too."

"Then why did you say you were afraid of him, make it sound like he was... threatening you or something?"

"It's complicated. Sometimes the people you love are the people you fear. I should've left him earlier, before I let things go too far."

Jane gritted her teeth. "You're *lying*. Sarah, I *know* the truth, that you're... mechanical."

Sarah regarded her blankly, then laughed. "Jane, I don't know what kinds of drugs they gave you at the hospital, but I think you should take it easy. It was nice seeing you."

She started walking away, the precise *clackity-clack* of her heels ringing against the pavement.

Sorrow struck Jane as she inexplicably clung to the notion that the mechanical being before her was still somehow a person. "Sarah, wait."

"Yes?"

"He's going to die. Because of you. Because he wanted to save you. Come with me to see him. You're his fiancée— they'll let you in."

"No. I never want to see him again." Sarah reached into her purse and removed something. Jane recognized the ring Devin had given her, the one that had once belonged to their mother.

Sarah approached Jane and handed her the ring. "I'm not his fiancée anymore."

Jane clenched her fist around it. "Look me in the eye and tell me you at least loved him once."

Sarah met her gaze. "Of course I did, but it's over. I'm sorry you'll be losing him, but I won't be sorry when he's gone. He's a murderer who frightened me, and I want nothing more than to forget him. Good-bye, Jane."

Jane watched, frozen by fury, as Sarah entered the air transport waiting for her. *She's just a machine. A metal robot covered in synthetic skin. There's no reason to be angry with her. She can't even think.*

Sarah's eyes had seemed empty when Jane looked up

close, as if her eyelids adjusted to create expressions in a manner that was deliberate, engineered. *Or is it because I know what she is?*

Jane recalled what Adam said about how the only consciousness she could be certain of was her own. The persistent images from her nightmare started filling her head again. She shook them away with frivolous brainstorms about the deliciously horrible things she would do to the Pandora cabal.

You bastards. Why did you have to go and ruin my life? Hey, Absolute One, is this Your idea of a joke? I complain about being bored, and You throw me into this mess? I wish I could go back to boring.

Three days had passed since Jane's release from the hospital, and she'd spent them scrambling to convince the world of Devin's innocence. In the process, the distraught heaviness she'd initially felt was replaced by an indomitable denial. There was no way in hell she would let anything happen to her brother, and therefore she had no reason to be anxious.

"You know what?" she'd said to Adam after he talked her out of her last panic attack. "To hell with this freaking out! Devin's *not* gonna die. That *jerk*! I'm gonna save him, and then I'm gonna kill him!"

Riley called and informed Jane that he'd found something. She rushed to Adam's dorm, where Riley was staying. As soon as she arrived, Riley swept the place for bugs and did some fancy tricks to the building's central computer. Not long before, Jane would have dismissed that as paranoia, but at present, she was glad for it.

Riley folded his slate. "Okay, we're good." He took a deep breath, as though about to make a grand announcement. "James Xavier Thiel, the big cat himself, better known as 'Jim X.' The dude who ran the company for decades before retiring to a cushy estate in the Wiosper system. I don't think you guys can appreciate how much trouble I had to go through. The Pandora people have been making it impossible for me to do *anything*."

Jane shoved a blanket off the couch and sat down. "I know. I know. You're a genius. Happy now?"

"Uh... Yeah. Thanks." Riley stuck his slate in his pocket. "Anyhow, Jim X himself greenlit the Pandora Project. Oh, and he didn't actually retire. He was ousted. Went nuts around the same time and was asked to resign."

Adam took a seat beside Jane. "The Thiel family ran BD Tech for generations. Jim X was the last of them, and everyone thought it odd that he retired without naming a successor. Looks as though he didn't have a choice."

Jane leaned forward. "What happened to him?"

Riley plopped down on the carpet. "I got my hands on some BD Tech memos. Jim X was sending out crazy-ass messages to his fellow bosses and then denying he'd done anything. So, they thought he was nuts."

"But he wasn't," Jane said. "Someone was faking them."

"Yup." Riley pressed his thumb and forefinger together in a pointer. "Here's what I think went down: Kron wanted to mess around with AIs, and Jim X said yes." He arced his forearm in slightly jerky motions as he spoke. "Kron realized the best programmers were people like me, anti-establishment genii who won't sell out, so he went around as Mastermind fooling the Collective. Some secret inner circle at BD Tech came up with the idea of using the AIs to gain influence but didn't want Kron involved, so they took his work, offed the demons, got rid of Jim X, and then... I dunno... began building things."

Adam rested his elbows on his knees. "I think we need to talk to Jim X. He probably knows who's involved, and that's why they had to discredit him, so no one would believe him if he said anything."

"Why didn't they off him too?" Jane asked.

Riley rolled his eyes. "Duh, he's too high profile."

Jane, annoyed that he spoke as though she were dumb, shot him a glare.

Riley grinned sheepishly. "Sorry. Anyhow, I agree with Uh-Dame here. Let's go to Wiosper."

"Not yet," Jane said. "First we've gotta get Devin out."

"Oh, yeah." Riley's face sobered into a grim expression. "Uh... Yeah. Been working on that too. Citizen Zero even tried hacking the courts and stuff, but it's hard because... Well, you don't care about the techie stuff, but it's hard."

Adam looked at Jane. "I know you don't want to hear

this, but our petition's not going well. They told me there are things in Devin's past proving he's more than capable of murder. It's classified because it surrounds an undercover ISARK operation."

"That's *bullshit*." Hit by a sudden energy, Jane stood. "This is the part where I'm supposed to come up with an excuse to leave, but I can't think of any good ones, so I guess I'll just see you guys later."

She left and started for the elevator.

Halfway down the corridor, she stopped. The last time she'd gone that way, she'd been running from a menacing robot after seeing Adam taken away. Seconds before, her life had been normal. Flinging Adam's door open that day had been the last moment of her once humdrum life.

Damn, I miss the days when my biggest worry was over whether I wanted to spend the rest of my life as a corporate drone.

"Jane!"

Adam approached. He probably had more to say about the failing petition. In no mood to face reality, Jane sped away.

"Jane, wait!"

She pressed the button by the elevator. As soon as the doors parted, she slipped in. She hurriedly punched "G" for *Ground*, and the doors closed before Adam could catch up.

As the elevator moved, Jane stared at the carpet that hid a maintenance hatch. The memories of the afternoon when she'd crawled through the conduits crowded her mind. She'd already beaten No Name twice—first by escaping the deep blue machine, and second by rescuing Adam. She could do it again. An odd feeling pressed against the inside of her head as she brainstormed ways to break into a maximum-security prison. It was some kind of madness, at once frightening and exhilarating.

The doors opened on the ground floor, and she speed-walked across the campus, mentally running through the various far-fetched scenarios.

"Jane!" Someone caught her by the shoulder.

Startled, Jane whirled and pulled the stunner out of her pocket. Seeing Adam, she lowered it. *"What?"*

Adam released her. "Where are you going?"

Jane stormed down the path. "Never you mind."

"Jane, please..."

Jane's rage ignited. She spun to face Adam. "What do you want me to say? Do you want me to break down and wail about how they're gonna kill my brother? Well, they won't—*I won't let them.* I'll—I'll bomb my way in if I have to! If that doesn't work, I'll blow up the whole goddamn city, and we can *all* go down in flames! Then future generations can write ballads about how the *flawless* Kyderan justice system turned a nice little office worker with a song in her heart into a ruthless terrorist!"

Jane laughed, although she didn't know which of those bizarre things she found funny. "Kidding! It'll all work out in the end, right? That's what you're here to tell me, isn't it? The Absolute will float down from the clouds and wave away our problems, and we'll all live happily ever after!" She shoved Adam's shoulder. "So where's the divine intervention? If your Absolute Being is so great, why's everything so freaking screwed up?"

Adam just looked at her patiently, apparently unfazed. "Would you really want someone—even someone perfect—controlling your world, as though you were one of those AIs? Would you want to be like Sarah, who's unable to think or decide anything?"

Jane grimaced. "Oh, great. Now you're getting all philosophical on me. You go ahead and pray, then. Let me know how that works out. Now, if you'll excuse me, I've got some laws to break." She pointed at him emphatically. "*Don't* try to stop me."

"I won't. But what are you planning to do?"

"Um... Bang, bang, ka-boom, oh-no-the-prisoners-are-escaping?"

Adam gave her an incredulous look. Jane, realizing how ridiculous she must have sounded, laughed again.

He waited for her to quiet down. "We're not through yet. Let's not rush into anything... extreme."

"I know, the law's the law—but Adam, the law is *failing*, and I'm sick of dealing with those goddamn *idiots*." She looked up at the sky and blinked back a sudden surge of tears.

Adam sighed. "As am I. So what happens now?"

Jane brought her gaze back down and said offhandedly, "Like I said. I'm gonna bomb the prison."

"Jane, please." Adam put a hand on her arm. "Don't be absurd. Your brother gave himself up to save your life—"

Jane threw him off. "And I let some chemical poison me so I could run with him! If it'd killed me—fine! But the jerk went behind my back and called the authorities, so I don't see why his oh-so-noble deed matters!" She glared at Adam, expecting the daggers in her eyes to chase him away.

Adam returned her stare with one that was equally firm, one that told her he wasn't going anywhere. "What do you think he'll do if something happens to you? Are you going to engage in an eternal cycle of self-sacrifice?"

Jane broke her gaze and shrugged. "Sure. Until we all go down in flames."

The insanity faded, leaving her with a paralyzing dread. She approached a nearby bench, collapsed in it, and covered her face, doing her best to banish the fears and doubts and frustrations storming every corner of her consciousness. *What should I do?*

Adam joined her on the bench. She uncovered her face and turned to him. He didn't say a word, but somehow, knowing he was there reassured her. He looked across the campus at the colorful Via temple. His expression brightened, as though he'd been touched by a new light.

Jane wondered why she couldn't feel it too. She had to admit, she envied him. She wished she had someone truly unfailing to hold on to. Atheism was no match for wishful thinking, and she considered asking the Absolute for help.

Instead, her mind paraphrased Citizen Zero, of all things: *If this is a mistake, I'll make one more mistake. I'm willing to do whatever it takes.*

CHAPTER 18

IF THIS IS THE END

DEVIN RECALLED THE TIME, YEARS back, when he'd wanted nothing more than to end his sorry life and not have to face his disastrous self anymore, to find release in oblivion and never again wrestle with rage or tangle with sorrow.

He'd tried to leave life forever, without caring if anything lay beyond. At fifteen, he'd seen everything ahead for him: nothing but more meaningless, invisible pain, with barren emptiness as the only alternative.

No point in telling anyone. People who spoke up wanted to be saved—and he didn't. So one night, without forethought, Devin ran a blade down his wrist and watched with fascination as blood gushed to the rhythm of his heartbeat.

He smiled wryly. At last, something he could see, something his parents would see. Maybe they'd even be sorry. He hadn't planned it, but since he had started— might as well finish. He didn't care if what he did was wrong. It meant escape.

Devin sliced again. And again. Vertical cuts bled faster. The world dimmed as his body drained.

A small voice came through the wall, his kid sister singing to herself in her room next door. She was a funny little girl, always following him around, looking up at him as if he were some kind of hero. No matter how many times he'd tried to brush her off, he'd never been able to shake her. He'd ignore her or even yell at her to go away, but she just smiled each time, knowing he didn't mean it. As much as he hated to admit it, he liked having her around, even though he'd rarely responded to her childish ramblings.

If there's an afterlife, I'll sure as hell miss her.

Then it hit him—she'd miss him too. If he died, she'd never understand why. *Or worse, she will.* If his actions opened her eyes to all the ways in which life could be worthless, it could damage her forever.

It could destroy her.

I can't do that. Devin forced himself to get up. He made it into the corridor and stayed upright long enough to see his mother's shocked face before collapsing.

Never again. Even though my life's already over—even though it never began—leaving's not the thing to do. So... I'll linger.

As each year rolled into the next, the memory and scars faded. The shadow that nearly consumed him fell behind, but it wasn't something Devin could ever recover from; it was a burden he'd carried ever since, a perverse desire that stalked him.

Faced with his impending execution, he found that, in spite of everything, he wanted to keep fighting. *But if this is the end, I'm not sorry.*

Jane stood before Devin on the other side of his cell's transparent wall. What could he say to her that wouldn't bring her more sorrow? He wished he could tell her how much she meant to him, how she was the reason he'd survived as long as he had, but that would only worsen her grief once he was gone.

After an uncomfortable stretch of silence, Devin chose his words. "Everything's fine, Pony. The justice system hasn't failed. I deserve what's about to happen, and I don't want you grieving for me."

Jane pinched her lips. "How can you say that? You're innocent."

Devin attempted a smile. "I may not be guilty, but I'm not innocent either. There are things I haven't told you, things I know you've always wanted to ask but haven't dared. I'm a monster, Jane. I never wanted you to know, but you deserve the truth. This is probably your last chance to hear it, so I'll give it to you straight. I should have done it years ago, instead of waiting until... the end."

Jane stubbornly set her jaw. "It's not the end."

"Jane..." She couldn't know how hellish the past two weeks had been as he'd come to grips with reality: He was going to die for something he never could have done. He had to let go of the notion of justice. Everything he'd fought for had been in vain.

No, she couldn't be sorry for him. The only thing to do was to tell her the truth he'd hidden through the years. If she knew, she would never forgive him, either. "Remember how I told you I got mixed up in a gang?"

Jane nodded.

Devin clasped his hands behind him and looked past her. "It started with Legion, the cybergang. Then I joined Faceless, a group of mercenaries who controlled Legion and used the information they got through hacking for their own illicit purposes."

He paused. Jane had to believe he'd been a willful criminal, not a clueless kid who'd fallen for a charismatic leader's well-produced lies. His confession wasn't to garner sympathy, and so he left out the rest, even though he wanted to tell her: *I only got involved because one of my professors at university introduced me to them. He was more than just a teacher. He was my mentor, my counselor, and I trusted him.*

"*Justice*, Devin," Professor Cythral had said. "It's not in the lithe lies of the powerful. We call the legal system 'justice,' but you and I both know it's the most laughable of misnomers. The laws were written by *people*, interpreted by *people*, and people are flawed, biased—ridiculous, even. Justice transcends our human institutions, and you can help us find it. I know you only want to do what's right, to seek something more than the prison of material success your parents distorted your world to fit you into. We were all born as slaves to these systems, but there are ways to move beyond them, and if you follow me, I'll show you how."

I didn't know he was working with Faceless or that he'd founded Legion to help the warlords Faceless worked for. I was too trusting to realize his wise-and-understanding persona was an act and that he only came up with his "cause" to recruit idiots like me.

Devin gathered his thoughts and continued, "I did everything I could to help Faceless with their heists, including looking up blueprints. So there you go: That's how I knew about the conduits." He forced another smile.

Jane tried to return it. "I knew it! I knew you were a thief!" Her eyes betrayed her sadness.

"I'm also an extortionist." Devin tried to sound offhand. "I used Mom's senatorial access to help Faceless blackmail politicians and their staffers."

Please understand, I only did it because I thought the money and bought influence went to a Fringe planet in dire need of aid, to send supplies to famine victims and aid the local resistance so they'd stand a chance. I thought everything we did was to defend those the good guys had abandoned.

"They're suffering," Cythral had said. "Many of them have lives worse than death. They're forced to choose between starving in the countryside and making the treacherous journey to the cities, where they are inevitably attacked and tortured. Nobody in the IC even cares. A few self-righteous activists parade around with horror stories, but nobody does anything meaningful. Why should they? They have their own problems. What we're doing will be condemned if we're ever caught, but we'll make a *real* difference."

Devin had known too well how little got done because people were wrapped up in their agendas, so he'd willingly gone beyond the law. *They told me they only stole from the wealthy and manipulated policymakers in order to bring relief to the desperate, and I believed them because I was another stupid kid looking for a greater purpose.*

"They suggested we rob Quasar, and I agreed. I was their in because of Dad, just like I was their in with the Kyderan government because of Mom." *They lured me in because of our powerful parents. Everything they did was so I'd trust them enough to get them what they needed.*

"We answered to a pair of warlords, the Voh Nyay Twins. You must've heard of them. They're the ones behind the Keptella bombings eight years ago." *If I'd known, I would never have had anything to do with them.*

"Dad caught me in his office downloading access codes. He stopped me, but he didn't call the authorities. The next time I went to see him, he disowned me." *I tried to tell him and Mom why I'd done it. I didn't expect them to forgive me, but I thought they might at least understand my intentions. They wouldn't hear it. I didn't know what to do, so I turned to the only person I thought could help.*

Jane seemed to have something she wanted to tell him. Devin waited for her to find the words.

"I was there," she said finally. "I heard what they said."

"It wasn't pretty." Devin tried not to think about his kid sister hiding by the door, listening to their parents screaming at him, hating him. "I became useless after that, and Faceless decided to use me to get money from our parents." *I never saw it coming. I went to meet Cythral, and he knocked me out. When I came to, I was chained to a wall, surrounded by members of Faceless.*

"You're not the first to have fallen for our act," Cythral had said. "Legion's full of saps like you, all working for a terrorist regime in an attempt to find *purpose*. It's laughable how easy it is to reel you kids in, to bait you with ideals and stir up your undirected anger. I must say, though, you were our biggest catch by far."

"Why would you do this?" Devin had asked.

"Partly for money, partly for entertainment. Personally, I *loved* seeing how far you were willing to go for your little *cause*."

I wanted to die right there instead of having to face what I'd done, wanted to blow out my brains for being so fucking stupid.

Jane blurted out, as if against her will, "I saw the hostage video. The Seer must've put it on the Stargazer. And I was eavesdropping when Mom and Dad were—were talking about it. I... I know Dad was gonna leave you there."

Devin kept his face still even though he couldn't stand the thought of her listening to their parents arguing over if they would let him die. *I can't let her feel sorry for me.* "I was in on it. It was my idea."

"*Liar.* I saw the look on your face in that video."

"It was an act. Just another scheme to get money for the warlords."

Jane glared in silent protest.

Devin tried to ignore her. "Mom agreed to the ransom.

She went behind Dad's back and contacted Faceless, and they arranged a drop. They killed her when she came."

Jane covered her mouth with her hand, and her eyes glistened.

"So there you have it." Devin kept his tone flat. "Mom wasn't assassinated by some evil gang. She died because of me. I might as well have pulled the trigger myself."

His mother hadn't died instantly. She'd been hit several times through the stomach. Devin had managed to get away from his captors long enough to rush to her side and see her bleed out.

His mother had given him a firm look, unafraid of her imminent death. "Devin, swear to me you'll survive. I don't care what you have to do—just survive."

His captors had caught up to him and torn him away as she'd taken her last breaths. *I'm so sorry. I wish they'd shot me instead.*

Jane uncovered her mouth, revealing a firm line. Almost palpable heat radiated from her eyes. *Good. Hate me, Jane. Curse me. Walk away from me, and feel nothing when they execute me.*

She stood motionless for an uncomfortably long time, then shook her head feverishly, her wrath swelling into desperation. "That can't be true. Devin, you said you'd give it to me straight. What aren't you telling me?"

Devin did his best to avoid his sister's furiously pleading gaze. Even when he turned away, he could still feel her stare. "Dad found out what she was doing. He called the authorities, and they went in, guns blazing. Mom was caught in the crossfire. That's all there is to it, I swear. All of it's my fault."

Jane shook her head again. "No. It's not. It can't have been. If—"

"*I'm* the one who's to blame." Devin pointed at himself. "She's *dead* because of me. Dad's dead because of me. Forget Faceless; forget No Name. *I* killed them. I killed your *parents*, Jane!"

Jane kept shaking her head, tears streaming down her face. "No, you didn't. And Dad's alive. He'll recover."

"He won't." Devin leaned down to her height, his face inches from the transparent wall. "They can keep him on life support forever, but he'll never wake up. He's *dead.* They're all *dead because of me!*"

"Devin, *stop it!*" Jane banged a fist against the wall. "I know what you're doing, and it *won't work.* Do you really think I'm that stupid?" She smiled sadly. "You can't make me hate you, bro. You're all I've got."

"There's more." Devin straightened. "I told ISARK everything I knew about Legion, and they were all unveiled, their faces and locations leaked to the Net for everyone to see. They became a liability, and Faceless took them out."

"*You* didn't kill them. And Riley told me how you rescued him from Travan Float."

Devin looked at the ground. "Riley doesn't know what I did to find him."

Faceless had this sick game where they set their prisoners loose in the wilderness and hunted them down, tantalizing them with the hope of escape. They even armed and trained us so it'd be more of a challenge, telling us that if we didn't put up enough of a fight, we'd be slowly tortured to death. I didn't want to die before getting justice for Mom. I targeted Black Knight because no one knew what he looked like, and somehow I got the better of him. I destroyed his body so Faceless would think I was the one killed, then joined the hunt for the others. I as good as became Black Knight. It's haunted me ever since.

He recalled Commander Vega's harsh words and echoed, "I hunted Black Knight like an animal, and I killed him in cold blood. I took his identity and became a merc for the warlords."

"So you could be an *informant.*" Jane bit her lip. "Devin, it can't be a coincidence that their network collapsed the same time you were undercover. *Don't* say you had nothing to do with it. It was all over the news when they fell."

Devin's frustration overtook him. "*Goddammit, Jane!* Are you hearing *anything* I'm telling you? I've gotten away with *murder,* and it's finally caught up to me. I'm a killer and a terrorist and if it wasn't for this, I'd be here for something else. Now you know who I really am. I'm a *monster,* so you can stop looking for justice. *This is justice!*"

Jane buried her face in her hands and cried, shaking uncontrollably.

Devin wanted to embrace her and apologize. He wanted to tell her how sorry he was for what he'd done, wanted to beg her for forgiveness.

But he couldn't. *She can't be sorry when I'm dead.* "Crying won't change anything."

Jane looked up, her tearful eyes so hurt Devin had to look away for fear of losing his mask. "You wanted the truth, and there it is."

"Stop trying to make me hate you. It won't work. I can always tell when you're lying." She tried to smirk. "Little sis powers. I'm going to save you."

Devin gave her a disdainful look. "You can't save me. No one can save me. Even if I wasn't on death row, you still couldn't save me from who I am, from what I've done, and what I'd planned to do. I would've killed Kron. If I'd found the people behind No Name, I would've killed them too. Just like I killed our parents. You should be glad I'm going."

Jane opened her mouth to speak, then stopped. It was the first time he'd known her to surrender.

A guard entered. "Five minutes, Miss Colt."

Jane looked down and nodded. The guard left.

She inhaled deeply, then faced Devin. "Please promise me one thing."

"What is it?"

"Promise first. I want you to swear it."

Devin's searing guilt made him inadvertently say, "Anything. I swear."

"I want you to request a Via Counselor. I... want it done by someone who cares, not a—a clinical stranger. Someone who can... hear your last confession and everything."

"Jane, I'm not religious."

"I know, but... I'm worried about your soul. I'm worried you won't go to heaven."

Devin couldn't help smiling humorlessly. "That was never in doubt. If there is a hell, I'm bound straight for it."

"Not if you... ask the Absolute for forgiveness and atone for your sins. The Absolute One is all-forgiving and all-merciful. If the Counselor is there for you, you can be saved."

What? Jane's always been an outspoken atheist. Where's

this coming from? "I guess Adam finally converted you."

"Yeah, that's right. Please, just... do it. For me. You swore already."

More silence. More stares.

Devin nodded. "All right."

Jane wiped her eyes as more tears fell. "I'll know. They'll give me the record of... what happened, so I'll know if you're lying again. Dammit, Devin! Don't you *dare* be lying again!"

"I'm not." He'd already hurt her so much. If something as trivial as requesting a Counselor would bring her comfort, he had neither reason nor right to deny her. "You shouldn't be sorry for me. After what I've told you—"

"*I don't care!*" Jane pressed her hands against the transparent wall, as though trying to push through it. "Devin, you're my brother, and I don't care if you killed some merc or helped warlords or *what*! I don't blame you for Mom's death or *anything else*. Get that through your head!"

Devin turned away, wishing he could make her forget he existed.

The guard returned. "Time to go, Miss Colt."

Jane didn't move, instead just looking at Devin as though she wanted to tell him something more, something she couldn't say.

Devin closed his eyes. "Go, Jane. It's over now."

"I love you, bro."

"Good-bye, Pony."

No use lay in dwelling on what he should or shouldn't have done, no point in struggling against what was to come, no meaning or relief through painful ruminations over what it meant that his life was ending. Devin chose to spend his last hours blocking his mind of thoughts, trying to forget all he'd discovered and all he left unresolved. He'd once done his best to become an empty shell, like Sarah turned out to be. As his death neared, he sought that indifference again.

It's fitting that she chose me. I was as fake as she is, and in a way, as mechanical, just doing as I was commanded.

After ending his disastrous search for purpose, Devin had done his best to erase the impulsive young man he'd been. He would finally succeed. *No one should mourn for me.*

He was barely aware of the guards escorting him to the death chamber, hardly noticed the hooded Counselor waiting there. He couldn't tell whether it was a man or a woman who muttered religious nonsense as he lay back in the execution chair. The detachment in his mind left Devin deaf to the sound of his or her voice, and he didn't care enough to try to glimpse his or her face.

He lay motionless as the guards strapped him down, staring at the empty white ceiling.

The Counselor measured out the lethal drugs, performing some meaningless ritual all the while. "Devin Colt, listen to me."

Devin had ignored all the offers for prayer, but that last statement, unexpectedly firm, caught his attention.

"You have the right to a last confession. Is there anything you want to say?" The Counselor was a man, a very young-sounding one.

The familiarity of his voice chilled Devin. "No."

"Look at me."

Devin turned his head, and his eyes widened as he recognized the boyish face beneath the hood. *Adam?*

"The Absolute is all-knowing and compassionate." Adam had an odd look in his eyes. "You can trust in the Absolute to ensure that all will be well."

Someone who cares. Was that why Jane had insisted Devin request a Counselor?

Adam brought up the needle. "O Absolute One, may You forgive he who is about to see You and allow him to rest eternal in everlasting peace."

As Devin felt the needle pierce his arm, he saw Adam's lips move, forming words that looked like: *Trust me.*

CHAPTER 19

COMPOSURE, EXPOSURE

RILEY TYPED AS FAST AS he could, scrambling to disable anything that might inform the Kyderan authorities of his and Citizen Zero's actions. The Pandora assholes weren't making it easy. "I *hate* the Pandora Project! You monkey-fightin' *excrescence*! Don't you have other evil plans?"

He sat on the floor of the counterfeit Blue Tang, which Jane had sweet-talked some pirates into selling her. She'd thrown money around the Fringe until someone tipped her off about the vehicle, which looked like every other private craft in the IC but was armed and supposedly untraceable.

"You're doing good, Riley. It's gonna work. It has to. It *will*."

Riley looked up at Jane, who was in the pilot's seat. "Uh... Duh? I'm the *best*, remember?"

The plan was simple: Get Devin to request a Via Counselor and send Adam with a head full of how-to-fake-a-death knowledge instead. That part had been easy. Citizen Zero had taken a page out of Pandora's book of evil and faked a bunch of docs. The hood—plus people's tendency to trust anyone who spoke religious mumbo-jumbo in a priest outfit—had taken Adam the rest of the way.

Jane twisted to face Riley. "What if Adam gets the formula wrong? The tiniest slip-up and it could *actually* kill him. What if we can't get him the antidote in time? He could be comatose forever. What if—"

"Yo, knock it off." Riley checked the window on his slate. "You're distracting me."

"Sorry..." She was so wound-up her voice shook.

The decent thing to do was to say something encouraging. Riley took a deep breath. "Hey, listen. You've got nothing to worry about. Adam won't screw up. He's pretty smart for a nov. I mean, the whole fake-out thing was his idea in the first place, right? Not to mention he's totally in love with you."

Jane started to say something, but he didn't hear her protest as a warning popped up on his slate. "Shush! Gotta concentrate!"

Good as he was at speedy programming, knowing that his friend's life was at stake made Riley nervous as hell. *It's just a stupid med scanner. I shut down a big fat warship. I hacked freakin' BD Tech. I think I can make one dumb machine tell everyone a guy who's not dead has no life signs.*

It was probably the oldest prison-break method in the universe and had been attempted about a gazillion times before, but Riley and Citizen Zero would be able to get around the Kyderans' safeguards and make it work one more time. He pumped his fist as he took control of the med scanner. "*Hah!*"

The bad guys locked him out again. His grin twisted into a grimace. He hustled to re-hijack it. "You mud-eatin' *buttheads*! Go make a robot clown or something! Ugly, mush-brained *sleaze-pots*!"

A few minutes passed. Riley dropped the slate and pumped both fists. "*Hah!*"

"Is he through?" Jane smiled. "Of course he is. You're awesome."

Riley felt kind of warm and fuzzy. "Uh... Thanks. And yeah, he's through."

He stretched his arms, glad for the break. Jane was still all jittery, and he felt bad that his previous attempt to reassure her hadn't worked. *Maybe I can distract her instead.* "Yo, Janie, I've got a random question: Why does Devin call you Pony? Kinda weird for a nickname, isn't it?"

A look he couldn't interpret crossed Jane's face, one that seemed kind of sad. Maybe talking about the guy who was in danger wasn't the best way to make her chill. "Sorry... uh... You don't have to tell me if you don't want to."

Jane leaned back in the pilot's seat and turned her gaze to the viewscreen. "It's all right. I just haven't thought about it in ages. All I remember is that when I was nine, Devin was in the hospital for several days. I heard Mom and Dad giving him a hard time about being weak. Doesn't sound right, does it? Well, 'Colts are stronger than that.' They wouldn't let me see him, so when he came home, I snuck into his room from the window. Mine was right next to his.

"He let me in but wouldn't say anything. He looked really upset, like he'd rather be anywhere else. I kept asking what was wrong, and finally, he told me he hated the Colts and what it meant to be one—how he could never be good enough, how his life wasn't really his. I didn't understand, but I wanted to cheer him up, wanted to let him know *I* didn't expect anything, so I said, 'I'm not a Colt. I'm a pony!' It was stupid, but it made him laugh. He's called me Pony ever since."

Riley wasn't sure what to make of the story. "Oh. Cool. So, was he sick?"

"I don't know. His wrists were bandaged, but no one would tell me what happened. My guess is that he messed with the wrong crowd during some dumb teenage misadventure and got himself knifed."

Riley's slate pinged. A warning message told him the Pandora people were trying *again* to alert the authorities to the scanner hack. "Assholes. Leave me alone already!"

He had no reason to be nervous. He was the *best*. As long as his fingers could move, the evil corporation should fear *him*.

"Miss Colt, your brother's body will be delivered to you for a burial in space, as you requested. Counselor Young will arrive at the landing pad with the casket in ten minutes. I'm sorry for your loss."

No, you're not, you freaking tool. "Thank you, sir."

Jane stepped over Riley, who sat cross-legged by the cockpit entrance. She pushed the ship's door open, extended the ramp, and walked down. She'd rather wait outside than sit in that chair any longer, feeling pulverized by the "what-ifs" in her head.

She glanced back at the counterfeit Blue Tang. A shudder shot through her body. She stubbornly attributed it to the chilly weather. The dark blue ship looked almost identical to hundreds of others in and around Kydera City, but the off-brand appearance and hidden cannon seemed glaringly visible to her.

Everything's fine. They did *allow me onto the landing pad.*

She placed her hands in the pockets of her somber black pants and clutched the two weapons she'd brought: a stunner and a flash grenade. She'd also been mindful to tie up her hair and wear shoes she could run in—just in case.

"I almost hope we *do* find trouble so I'll have an excuse to shoot someone," she'd said to Adam three hours ago, when he'd arrived at her apartment to pick up the Counselor's robe she'd obtained. "I guess I should be careful what I wish for."

Outside her window, the warm golden rays spilling over the horizon had mocked her. They told her that even if everything went to hell and she lost her brother to a deceived justice system, the real world would turn on as hers shattered. "Adam, tell me it'll be all right. I know I've made fun of you before for it, but... Tell me everything'll work out."

Adam put his arm around her in a comforting embrace. "Of course it will. No power in the universe can stop you once you've set your mind on something, and Riley, as he loves to remind us, is the best."

Jane glanced at the robe lying on her table. "And you?"

"Mine's the easy part." Adam released her and approached the table. "All I'm doing is taking on a role I would've prepared for anyway. You could call it an accelerated course." He'd sounded as though he tried to shrug it off, but fear had clouded his countenance.

Jane had wanted to say something along the lines of, "Are you sure you can do this?" Adam could barely tell a lie, let alone commit fraud. She hadn't wanted to add to his anxiety, so she'd kept the question to herself.

Her expression must have asked it anyway, for Adam had tried to reassure her. "I'll be all right." He picked up the robe. "I know I'm a terrible liar, but they won't see my face beneath the hood. Even if they sense something wrong, they'll take one look at my forged credentials and let me in."

You're such a paradox. You wouldn't even skip class back when things were normal, but you shot a man without hesitation, and you've been conspiring to commit a number of felonies.

Adam seemed to notice her perplexed expression. "What is it?"

Jane leaned against the side of her couch. "You've got quite the criminal mind for someone so religious. Don't get me wrong; I think it's great. It's just that you've always said you couldn't break the rules even if no one cared because you have your Absolute to answer to."

Adam tucked the robe into the bag slung across his shoulder. "When the road splits between what's legal and what's right, the choice is simple enough. In that sense, I'm no different from you."

Jane raised her eyebrows. "But *I* have no one watching me. I've heard it said that if there's no higher power, anything goes. I guess that's why I'm perfectly okay with being bad—I'm godless."

Adam walked toward her. "You're not godless. It doesn't matter what you believe in, Jane, as long as you believe truly, for I know you mean the best. The Absolute wouldn't care what group you count yourself as being part of, or by what name you call your divine being. That kind of pettiness belongs to the human world. Unfortunately, many of the Via don't realize it—they take the Book too literally. I believe the Absolute is always there for you, whether or not you acknowledge the presence of a deity."

Jane tilted her mouth. "So I'm not going to hell for being a blaspheming heretic?"

Adam put his hands on her shoulders. "Of course not. In a way, you're as religious as I am, just subconsciously. The morality you hold on to—*that's* what matters. You already answer to a higher power, only you see it as coming from within."

She cocked her head. "That makes no sense."

"Yes, it does." He let go and smiled. "Well, it does to me."

Jane had felt her brain twist into knots. "You have got

to be the most... *liberal, nebulous* religious person *ever!*" *I don't understand you.*

Waiting for Adam to arrive with Devin, Jane found herself talking to that higher power she didn't believe in for about the millionth time, begging the Absolute to let her plan work. In her pocket, her hand moved from the stunner she'd been gripping to a third item she'd brought: the Via pendant Adam had given her, which she'd inexplicably grabbed on her way out.

Some of her apprehension dissipated when Adam, in his forest-green Counselor robes, stepped onto the landing pad. He pushed a hovering white casket. Two guards followed, and irritation replaced her nervousness. *Why the hell do they need to guard someone who's supposed to be dead?*

Jane did her best to look mournful as she approached. Seeing the casket made that easy. She still wasn't sure if the plan had *actually* worked. Adam wasn't exactly a medical professional... "Hello, Counselor."

Adam nodded in acknowledgement. "Miss Colt."

She turned to the guards. "You can leave now."

"I'm afraid we must accompany the body onto the ship," one of the guards replied. "Policy dictates that we must be present until the burial is performed."

Jane bit her lip. No one had told her there would be official witnesses. *Isn't it enough that you tried to kill my brother, you bastards?*

"I understand." She let her doubts occupy her mind. The tears came. "Please, sir, my brother was all I had left, and now he's gone too. I want to say good-bye to him alone, in private. He's already dead. He can't run anymore."

The guard held himself erect. "I'm sorry, Miss Colt. I'm afraid we cannot make any exceptions."

Riley called from the ship, "*Hurry up!*"

The Pandora cabal had to be winning the cyber battle. They could alert the authorities to the scanner hack at any moment.

Jane blinked to make a few teardrops fall. "Please, sir, why can't you let me mourn in peace?"

The guard's countenance remained stern. "We have policies, Miss Colt."

Damn, you're heartless. She blinked again.

The guard stiffened. "I'm afraid—"

"Ah, screw it!" Jane grabbed her stunner and fired straight at his chest. The guard convulsed as he fell. Despite her penchant for violent rhetoric, that was the first time she'd seriously—and intentionally—attacked someone. She stared at the unconscious guard with a mixture of astonishment and wicked satisfaction.

By the time she looked up, Adam had ditched his robe. He had the other guard's arm folded up against his own. She watched, surprised, as Adam dropped his weight down on the guard's arm and twisted to the side. The guard lost his balance.

Jane aimed her stunner. "Move!"

Adam jumped back, and she zapped the guard. "What was *that?*"

Adam stared at the guard. "I don't know... improvising? He was reaching for his gun."

About a dozen guards ran across the landing pad. "*Halt!*"

Here we go. Jane waited for the guards to come a little closer. She gave Adam a nod, and then grabbed the flash grenade from her pocket. She flipped a switch on its side and channeled all her rage into throwing it.

She dropped to the ground, closing her eyes and covering her ears as the grenade went off mid-flight. The piercing screech cut through the air, along with a light so bright she could see it through her eyelids.

She opened her eyes and stood. Everything seemed muted, as though she heard the world from underwater. Muffling her hearing somehow stifled her fear. The guards who hadn't been knocked out, those who had been quick enough to drop like she had and avoid the blast radius, ran at her.

All right, you shitheaded sons-of-bitches. You asked for it.

She ruthlessly fired her stunner, taking a horrible kind of pleasure in the power it gave her. One guard crumpled from a blast to the leg. Another was knocked out entirely.

Her weapon fell from her hand as a stun blast hit her arm, causing it to go numb.

"Jane, *run!*" Adam haphazardly fired a laser gun. He

must have taken it from one of the unconscious guards.

Jane sprinted toward the casket. She shook her arm, wishing the feeling would hurry up and return. Needles seemed to pierce her hand as she grabbed the white handle and pushed the casket toward the ship. Her hearing cleared. Blasts whizzed around her. She didn't dare look back.

As she shoved the casket into the ship, she heard Adam cry out. She whirled and saw him halfway up the ramp behind her, clutching his shoulder. "*Adam!*"

"I'm fine. Go!"

Jane rushed into the cockpit and took the controls. As soon as the ship's door slammed shut, she revved up the engines. "Riley, *now!*"

She pushed the steering bars forward and took off—along with every Blue Tang on the Lyrona continent.

Riley jumped. "*Triumph!* Take *that*, BD Tech! You evil corporation *freaks!* Oh, yeah? You wanna have control over all your products? Put creepy shiznit in every machine you've ever made so you can take over whenever? Guess what, assholes, you've been *demonized!*" He stumbled against the wall in his jubilation.

Jane laughed. "Nice work, Riley!"

She wove her counterfeit Blue Tang around to mix it in with the real ones, which the Citizen Zero demons were commanding to fly at random.

Good enough. She steered the ship into the stars.

A familiar red Megatooth warship loomed before her. She wished she could engage lightspeed, but doing so with the other ships so close would mean collision. *I'm invisible. Even if they spot me, I'm just like the others.*

—◆◇◆—

Through the square window beside the main viewscreen, Commander Vega noticed one Blue Tang that wasn't like the others. The others zipped around in chaotic, insect-like trajectories, whereas the one she watched seemed to have a course.

She'd received an order to pursue an unmarked Blue Tang leaving from the direction of Kydera City. Since there were so many Blue Tangs, Admiral Landler had given her details: The prison had been alerted to a hack following

Devin Colt's execution, and it was possible he was alive and attempting to flee.

Instead of indignation or infuriation, an unexpected sense of relief enveloped her. She had little desire to obey the order, not when so many uncertainties pricked her mind, and the possibility of wasted lives threatened.

"Commander!"

She turned to the navigation officer. "Yes?"

The officer pointed out the window. "This Blue Tang appears to be the target. Deploy Bettas?"

Commander Vega looked down at him with disdain. "*Which* Blue Tang are you referring to?"

"The unmarked one!"

She waved her hand dismissively. "Officer, several of these ships are unmarked. Do not risk harming civilians on a mere guess."

"But—"

"Are you challenging me?"

"No, Commander. But which should we pursue?"

Commander Vega glanced at the viewscreen. The Blue Tang that had caught her and the officer's attention did not show up. *It's veiled from our scopes. The fugitives must be inside.* Nevertheless, she directed the officer to another unmarked Blue Tang heading in the opposite direction and snapped at him when he started to protest.

The communications officer called, "Commander! We are receiving an anonymous transmission. I am unable to trace where the signal is coming from."

Is it the fugitives? The demons controlling the Blue Tangs? Either way, the need for information justified the risks of allowing an anonymous transmission. "Put it through, but monitor it. Cybernetics, keep a close watch on our system. If anything looks suspicious, shut down the central computer and revert all systems to manual control."

"Yes, Commander."

Words typed out across the viewscreen:

I am the one the Networld calls the Seer. I have followed the activities of the entity called No Name for years. This has not been easy, because No Name is very good at hiding its presence. Due to its recent actions involving

Devin Victor Colt and Jane Winterreise Colt, I can now prove that it was behind the attack on Dr. Revelin Elroy Kron. I have determined that you are the most suitable person to receive this information. If you continue your investigation, you will be able to prove that No Name was also responsible for the attacks on Victor Alexander Colt, the Flame Team of the *RKSS Granite Flame*, and numerous others of whom you are not currently aware.

Documents appeared on the viewscreen. Commander Vega narrowed her eyes. The truth they purportedly revealed read like a bizarre conspiracy theory. She needed a cybercrimes team to review them before she could be certain they were valid. If they were, then the Seer had been incredibly conscientious. She wondered how he could have obtained all that information.

Her skepticism turned to outrage as she realized what it would mean if the Seer's claims were true. It wasn't her job to investigate the outlandish allegations of anonymous eccentrics, but she was too involved in the current situation to walk away.

She *would* get to the bottom of it all—*protocol be damned.*

She must've let us go.

The thought brought Jane relief and encouragement. Maybe Commander Vega was asking the right questions. Maybe she could help somehow. *Maybe...*

But at present, Jane needed to get to the Wiosper system and beat the truth out of Jim X's lazy head. No one pursued her ship, so she programmed the autopilot and raced toward her brother's casket.

She pressed the controls to open it. Devin lay with eyes closed, hands folded across his stomach. He was almost as pale as his white prison uniform.

Jane shook him. "Devin! Wake up!"

Riley peered over her shoulder. "Uh... You need the antidote, remember?"

"Oh, right." She ran into the living quarters.

Adam stood in the corner with his back to her, his head bowed. He held the thick metal syringe containing the antidote in one hand. With his other, he grasped his bunched-up white shirt in a fist against his shoulder.

Jane remembered with alarm that he'd been hit. "Are you all right?"

"What?" Adam turned with an oddly blank expression. He glanced at his shoulder. "Oh, this? It's—It's nothing. A scratch. Was grazed, that's all."

He didn't seem to be in pain. Jane didn't see any blood, so he couldn't have been hurt badly. But something must have been wrong for him to be so—

"Yo, can we wake him already?" Riley's question interrupted her thought.

Adam handed Jane the syringe. She took it but didn't leave. "Adam—"

"Hurry up!" Riley yelled. "You said we had limited time before... Just hurry up!"

Shit! How long's Devin been out? Too long, and his almost-death would become permanent.

Jane darted back to the casket. She held the syringe over Devin's arm, less than an inch above where his vein was supposed to be. She pressed a button on the syringe's side. A set of tiny lasers unfolded from the syringe's side and swept their bright green lights across his skin, scanning for the right spot. After a few seconds, the lasers converged to a point. She carefully pressed the needle into the green dot and injected the antidote. *Come on; come on...*

Adam wandered out of the living quarters as though sleepwalking. Jane wondered if he'd been hurt worse than he let on.

Devin inhaled sharply and opened his eyes.

"*Devin!*" She threw her arms around her brother. "I *told* you, bro! I *told* you I'd save you!"

"J—Jane?"

Jane let go. "Bet you never saw *that* coming!"

Devin stared at her. He climbed out of the casket and looked around as though disoriented.

Riley waved rapidly. "Hi, Devin!"

Devin spun toward him. "*Riley?*"

Riley put his hands in his pockets and slouched. "I wasn't gonna let them kill you."

"What happened?"

"Uh... We busted you out."

"You did *what*?"

Jane recognized the look on Devin's face. She crossed her arms. "*Don't*. You have *no right* to tell us off for breaking the law or whatever. We had no choice! We weren't gonna leave you there!"

"You shouldn't have done that," Devin said sternly. "You should've stayed out of it and—"

"And *what*, you idiot?" Long-suppressed rage fueled a rant Jane had kept unspoken for ages. "What the *hell*, Devin? You knew they were gonna kill you, so why the hell did you go and turn yourself in?" She shoved him. "Do you have *any idea* what I've been through—what we've all been through—trying to get you out? I went off to the *shadiest* holes in this blasted galaxy to get this freaking ship while Riley hacked every Blue Tang in Lyrona and Adam crammed his head with Counselor stuff that's supposed to take years to master. All for *you*, you jerk. All because for some stupid reason we *care* about your sorry ass!"

"Jane—"

"And what the *hell* was that in the prison?" She shoved him again. "How dare you treat me like some feeble little girl who'd hate you because of some dark secret? Like I'm one of those melodramatic ninnies who beg for the truth and turn away the minute they hear it? *Do you really think I'm that stupid*? It was bad enough wondering if our insane plan would even work without hearing your freaking deathbed confessions. Do you have *any idea* what—what..." She ran out of words of anger and threw her arms around him. "Holy *shit*, bro, I'm *so glad you're all right!*"

Devin returned her embrace. Violent sobs rose up Jane's chest. She didn't know if her tears were of joy or fear or wrath or all three. She hated to make a scene and tried to stop, reminding herself over and over that everything was okay. *He's safe. They can't take him from me now. If they try, I'll stop them again.*

After what felt like an eternity of gasping and heaving, Jane felt herself relax. She released her brother.

Devin kissed her on the forehead. "Thanks, Jane. Thanks for not giving up on me. And... you too, Riley, and Adam. I... just... thanks."

"Now we're even." Riley sounded as if he was trying too

hard to seem chill.

Devin looked past Jane. "Adam? You okay?"

Jane turned. "Adam?"

Adam still clutched his shirt with that dazed look. "What? Oh... I'm fine..."

She approached him. "C'mon. Tell me what's wrong."

"Nothing... I'm fine..."

"Adam..."

His mask fell away. He collapsed against the wall, shaking. His eyes filled with horror and pain, as though he was watching his world collapse.

"*Adam!*" Jane knelt beside him as he sank to the ground. "Dammit, Adam! You're hurt, aren't you? Don't worry. We'll get you help. You'll be okay."

"No, I'm not..." His voice quivered. "I'm sorry, Jane... I—I swear, I didn't know..."

"What're you talking about? *Let me see!*"

Adam didn't protest, but he clutched his shirt so tightly Jane had to pry his fingers off. She was puzzled when she found no blood staining the white cloth as she pushed it aside to get a look at his shoulder.

What so distressed him dazed her, too. She blinked several times and shook her head, trying to fling away any tricks her eyes might be playing on her.

Nothing changed. She didn't know what to say, what to feel.

Adam watched her, trembling. "I-I'm sorry... I didn't know... I-I swear by the Absolute, if that means anything to you now..."

His shoulder had been torn by blasts and completely shot through, but there was no blood pouring from the gaping wounds.

Just clean machinery.

CHAPTER 20

SHADES OF THE PAST

JIM X STROLLED ALONG THE seaside. With no family left, he owned the Thiel estate, which occupied the entire Diashin continent on Shimshawhenn. A vast network of underground tunnels connected his many abodes. Although he could visit mountains or canyons or forests or prairies on a whim, the seaside mansion was his favorite. The view relaxed him, especially at night, when the vast liquid ocean blended into the endless astral sea above it. The blurring of earth and heaven reminded him of all the possibilities best left unexplored, and it gave him a strange sense of relief.

Owning an empty estate paled next to the might he had once wielded. Jim X stopped and sighed as he mulled over his past life, a life he didn't especially miss. Once upon a time, he had ruled over the company inherited from his forefathers and mercilessly conquered new territories, daring to flout long-respected boundaries in order to push ahead. He had adopted the moniker "Jim X" because it lent him an air of cool rebellion even as he became the establishment itself. He'd lived spectacularly, knowing that whatever he wanted, he could have.

Until it all went to hell ten years before with that infernal Pandora Project. Because of it, he'd been exiled from his own empire, banished by the very people he'd given power to.

At first, he'd been livid. He'd spent the first few years of his forced retirement railing about the sheer wrongness. "I'm the *victim* here!" he would say to the hired help, who'd been paid to put up with such outbursts. "They took *everything* from me!"

Jim X sighed again. *I was such a fool.*

He'd always heard that wisdom was supposed to come with age. In his case, it had been delayed by the delicious authority he'd brandished. The talking heads in the media had regularly accused him of behaving like a cocky kid even as his hair grayed, of acting more like a newly risen star than a distinguished institution. He'd dismissed it as jealous backtalk or malicious attempts to undermine him.

Eventually, the years had taught their lessons. Separated from the world of obsequious glitz and glorified sycophants, his mind finally caught up to his body.

A salty breeze rustled Jim X's hair. He inhaled deeply. *Every day, I go through this. And every day, I come to the same conclusion: I am and will forever be completely alone. Why do I torment myself thus?* He laughed cynically. *Because I'm old and useless and have nothing to do but wallow in self-pity. And no one's around to judge me for it.*

Six years before, he had dismissed all the human help from the Thiel estate. The robots that kept it maintained, the drones that delivered the supplies—all was done through the Net, controlled by nameless voices on the other side of a screen.

He'd chosen isolation upon realizing that every supposed relationship in his life had been based on the desire to impress or satisfy him. Friends, allies, even mistresses he had confided in—all abandoned him when he fell. He had no desire to put up with more artificial smiles or bought-and-paid-for words.

Jim X stroked his grizzled chin. *I think I finally look my age.* He'd chosen to cease the cosmetic treatments that had kept him unnaturally young, allowing his jowls to drop and his face to become lined.

He trudged alongside the rushing waves, not caring if his shoes got wet. Walking certainly wasn't as easy as it had been.

His newest pet, a large, pointy-eared canine from Harir genetically engineered to be docile, ambled beside him.

Jim X beamed at the gray-furred animal. "You need a name."

The first moniker that came to mind was "Revelin," after his fallen ex-colleague and fellow victim of that cursed Pandora Project. Even though Jim X had never liked Kron much, he was still sorry to hear of his demise. *Kron, Kron, Kron. Why did I listen to you? And why did you listen to me?*

Kron had driven the Pandora Project, but Jim X had made it possible. He'd even encouraged the younger man's pride and nurtured his self-importance, turning a mere case of egotism brought on by too much brilliance into an alarming kind of megalomania.

Nevertheless, Jim X felt no responsibility for Kron's death. Kron had brought it upon himself with his own ruthlessness. He had created a monster and allowed it to run amok while harboring the delusion that it was still under his control, refusing to stop it when he had the chance.

The only reason Jim X had survived the Pandora Project was due to his high profile nature and ability to let it go. *But it's only a matter of time before I, too, am eliminated. I probably deserve it, just as Kron probably deserved what came to him.*

Devin Colt, on the other hand—that young man's unfortunate tale brought Jim X a kind of guilt he hadn't known since he'd learned the truth about those programmer deaths ten years ago. Jim X had followed Devin's story with intense interest from the moment the young man's sister mentioned the Pandora Project on the news, shouting unkind words about nefarious secrets at incredulous reporters who speculated as to her mental health. It hadn't taken long to realize Devin was being executed for a crime committed by the creature Jim X had helped spawn all those years ago. The reporters and detectives might not have listened, but to Jim X, it was clear what had really happened.

The hacked internal defenses. The perfectly falsified documents. The erratic machine behavior. Others had dismissed it as the absurd ramblings of a desperate girl, but ever since she had uttered the words "Pandora Project," Jim X knew she was the only one close to the truth.

A majestic steel and glass mansion, one of many on the estate, rose before Jim X on the horizon. *I'm sorry, Devin.*

It doesn't matter now, but I know you were innocent, and I'll have your death on my conscience.

Ten years before, or perhaps even five years before, Jim X would have dismissed the notion of any of it being his fault. *He* hadn't created Pandora, and he certainly hadn't framed the kid. He hadn't stopped any of it either, and across the silence of the years, the idea of taking responsibility for the fallout from his past actions dawned upon him.

Knowing that an innocent young man had been murdered in the name of justice less than a day ago had Jim X heavy with grief. *Poor kid. Go ahead and haunt my nightmares. I never knew you, but I'm partly to blame, and for that, may you forgive me.*

As though the spirit world heard his thoughts, a tall, white-clad figure appeared before the mansion, lit by its pale artificial glow and the silvery light of Shimshawhenn's two large moons. Although Jim X couldn't make out a face, he had a feeling he knew what it would look like.

He approached, and that feeling was confirmed as he recognized the apparition's angular features. *Either the mystics are on to something, or I'm really starting to lose it.*

Neither fear nor shock disturbed him, perhaps because he was certain the young man before him *was* a mirage, a hallucination projected by a guilt-riddled, world-weary brain. "Devin Colt. Are you here to torment me or to usher me into the afterlife?"

Devin looked confused.

"There he is! *Finally!*" a female voice said.

Jim X looked past Devin's still form and saw a dark-haired girl running toward him. He recognized her as Jane Colt.

Jane stopped beside her brother. "Why didn't you tell me he was coming?" She shot Jim X a hard glare. "Hey, Jim X. Don't ask how we got here. Just 'fess up already."

Jim X realized the young man was not a specter and that his ghostly white garb was a prison uniform. His guilt lifted considerably. "I'm glad you got out. If you need a place to hide, you're welcome to remain on my estate."

Jane put her hands on her hips. "Oh, that's rich. If you felt so bad about what's going on, you should've stopped it long ago instead of sitting on your nice little continent while shit happened."

Jim X shook his head. "It's not that easy, but you're right. I left and counted myself lucky to escape with what I had. Kron never stopped obsessing." He walked up to Devin. "Tell me, is it true that you killed him?"

Devin's eyes met Jim X's. "No."

Jim X nodded. "Didn't think so. You had no reason to. She did. He was about to tell you about her, and considering what she did to get rid of you, you probably already knew too much. I take it you've come to me for answers, now that he's gone." He continued toward the mansion and motioned for the Colts to follow. *It'll be nice talking to people again, even people who have every right to despise me.* "Come inside, and I'll tell you what I know. It's about time someone else knew."

Jane jabbed a finger at Jim X. "You'd better!" The newly named Revelin approached the girl with a happy pant. She turned the finger toward him. "Don't try to butter me up with your fuzzy ways so I'll go easy on your boss. I swore I'd beat it out of him if I had to. I don't care how cute you are, I'm gonna see it through." She smiled as the animal nuzzled up to her.

Jim X pressed his hand against the door's security scanner. When he entered his mansion, he was surprised to see a boy with black hair, wearing clothes too big for him, sitting cross-legged in the middle of the floor beside a large black bag. He was but a snippet of a man—skinny as a twig and probably barely five foot four.

The boy put down the gadget he played with, one of many in the robotic domicile, and waved quickly. "Hi, Jah-Mex! You've got some *awesome* shiznit here, and I've been pokin' around. Hope you don't mind." The half-smile angling his mouth exuded cockiness, but it wasn't disdainful or rude. Something about his vibrant black eyes seemed pure. He reminded Jim X of an enthusiastic puppy.

Jim X crouched to the boy's level. "Who are you?"

The boy tilted his head. "They call me Corsair on the Net, but my real name's Riley. Don't like it much, so I go by Corsair most of the time. It's kinda weird being called my Netname in the real world, even though most of us

Networld types prefer it. I guess these guys" —Riley jerked his head toward Jane and Devin— "conditioned me.

"I gotta say, you're the *slowest* walker I've ever seen! After I tracked you down, I told them to wait here because... Uh... You weren't that far, but I guess your old people legs kept you from moving at the pace I thought you'd take."

I like this kid. It had been a while, a very long while, since Jim X had met someone so unabashedly straightforward.

He stood and gestured toward the living room. "Please, have a seat." A hint of excitement tickled his mind. At last, a chance to tell his story. *Damn, the Colts are doing me a favor by "interrogating" me.*

Jim X entered the room, which had transparent walls and a high, vaulted ceiling. Someone occupied one of the gray armchairs: a young man with light brown hair in a white shirt, which was torn at the shoulder. The young man fiddled with a Via pendant he wore on a cord around his neck.

Jim X recognized him from the news. "Adam Palmer. So you're here, too."

Adam looked up at Jim X with a lost, melancholy expression that seemed to ask: *Why?*

Jim X sat in an armchair while Revelin curled up beside Riley, who chose to sit cross-legged on the plush black carpet.

"Let me start from the beginning, although there's not much to tell." A thought crossed Jim X's mind. "Do forgive me if I'm killed before I have a chance to finish. I'm sure she's been watching me, and after what happened to Kron, I wouldn't be surprised if I, too, was silenced."

Riley stroked Revelin's gray fur. "You mean by the Pandora assholes? You can chill. I took your house offline so no one can use the Net to off you."

"Good." Jim X didn't fear death; he'd come to accept it, as any man of advanced age with a known killer watching him would. It would simply be a pity if those kids came all that way without getting the answers they sought.

Jane curled up on the long, gray sofa beside her brother, a position that seemed incongruent with her glare. "Quit stalling, you freaking lazy bones. Start talking or else."

Jim X held up his hand. "No need to make threats. I

want to tell you. The Via say confession is good for the soul. Isn't that right, Adam?"

Adam looked at Jim X with that same lost, melancholy expression.

Jim X had often pictured what it would be like to tell his tale to a captive audience. *Let's see how my real storytelling abilities compare to my imagined ones.* He rested his elbows on his armrests. "So you know about the Pandora Project, but I suppose you wouldn't be here if you knew what it was. It started about eighteen years ago, when Kron became bored with conventional programming tasks. He was so brilliant he needed extra activities to keep his mind occupied. Among other things, he began exploring the realm of artificial intelligence."

Riley flicked his wrist dismissively. "Yeah, yeah, we know that. Get to the part about the Pandora Project."

Jim X laced his fingers together. "BD Tech was never interested in AI development, due to the Tech Council's cumbersome regulations. Although a lobbying campaign to have them lifted was discussed, the majority of the executives, including myself, believed it not worth the investment. Even if we could create a computer that convincingly simulated human behavior, there wouldn't be much commercial use for such a thing. People have a natural aversion to anything *too* realistic. To put it colloquially, an accurate, but nevertheless artificial imitation of life is considered 'creepy.'"

Jane bolted up as though intending to protest. She bit her lip and leaned back again.

Jim X wondered what she had to say and why she would take offense in the first place. "Kron was not only brilliant, but fast-moving and obsessive. He convinced me that given the resources, he could create a true artificial intelligence. I've always been the type to embrace the seemingly impossible out of defiance for perceived boundaries, and it soon became a personal obsession of mine. I believed the commercial aspects would fall into place once he succeeded."

Jim X sighed yet again. *If I had a throne for every sigh-worthy thought in my head, I could buy the entire Wiosper system.* "I did more than greenlight the Pandora Project, which is what we called it. I encouraged Kron in every way I could, fuelling his arrogance and madness. I knew the other executives wouldn't approve, so the two of us were the only ones who knew the project's actual intentions. Kron told me he needed help from outside the company. He pointed out that many of the galaxy's most talented programmers are technically amateurs, and I gave him the go ahead to do whatever he had to in order to harness their collective brainpower. The company would clean up after him.

"A little more than ten years ago, Kron introduced me to the galaxy's first sentient computer. Even though I believed in the project, I was surprised at the speed with which he completed it. He told me he'd essentially put the pieces together in a way generations of predecessors had either ignored or missed. The exact words he used were 'so obvious.' The computer was called Pandora, of course, and she was..." Jim X paused, looking for the right word. Unable to come up with a better one, he finished with, "*Perfect.*"

"Perfect?" Jane arched her eyebrow with skepticism.

"We thought so at the time," Jim X said. "She was designed to possess human-like consciousness and machine-like rationality, intelligence, and speed—to be, essentially, the mind of the ideal human-computer hybrid. She could understand abstract concepts and form independent thoughts while calculating the most logical, efficient courses of action. I thought it fitting that she was made at Blue Diamond, for she seemed as perfect and cold as a gemstone.

"But you're right to be doubtful; she must have been fundamentally flawed. I was taken aback by her disregard for life and warned Kron to keep her confined. He wouldn't listen, and he allowed her to access the Net. I didn't think much of it, believing the only outcome would be to bring her more knowledge. However, she had been designed to learn at an exponential rate. She soon developed the ability to travel through the Networld, bend programmable machines to her will, and infiltrate any computer system in the galaxy, including BD Tech's. That's how she got rid of me. She didn't want anyone knowing of her existence or recreating her, so she killed the amateur programmers involved in her creation. I have their deaths on my conscience."

Jane bolted up again. "Are you saying that No Name, that the whole Pandora thing, is a *program*? That *no one's* controlling the machines? They're acting on their own?"

Jim X nodded. "In a way, yes. She's a disembodied sentient being of incredible intelligence capable of being anywhere and everywhere thanks to the Net."

"Duuuude." A dumbfounded expression spread across Riley's face. "I was *way* off. I thought it was a bunch of BD Tech bad guys!"

Jim X shook his head. "They never even knew she existed. Kron and I were the only ones who knew about her. That's why she made me look like a crazed old loon. Kron was smart enough to keep quiet. Even though he said he wanted to stop her, I know he enjoyed seeing what she was capable of. But in the end, I suppose, he represented too great a threat, and she had to get rid of him."

Jane stood. "You good-for-nothing *bastard*. So you let this—this artificial *thing* wander the Net wreaking havoc? Do you have *any idea* what it's done?"

A pained look cross Adam's face. Jim X wondered why the kid was so distraught. He sighed—again. "Yes. I have, in my own way, followed her activities. I know the Collective calls her 'No Name.' I have no way of stopping her, but go ahead and yell at me. I know what she tried to take from you."

Jane narrowed her eyes. "I'm glad Kron's dead, and I hope your stupid computer catches up to you soon and offs you as well!"

"Jane," Devin said in a low voice. His gaze was fixed on the ground. "It's not his fault."

Jane turned to him and pointed at Jim X. "*He let this happen*! Him and that asshole Kron!"

Devin looked up at her. "He didn't create Pandora."

Jane didn't continue her tirade, but her eyes showed her fury.

Riley stuck his hands on the floor behind him. "Dude, you people should've figured out by now that if you name something 'Pandora,' something bad's gonna happen. That name's freakin' cursed. Anyhow, if your first AI was such a disaster... Uh... Why'd you make more?"

More? Jim X furrowed his brow. "We didn't. Kron couldn't have recreated Pandora if he'd wanted to, not without taking another decade or so. Like I said, she killed the amateurs who'd written unique parts of her code."

"Then... Uh... Where are the other AIs coming from? You know the... uh... humanoid... uh..." Riley looked uncomfortably at Adam and didn't finish.

Am I missing something? "I don't understand. If by 'AI' you mean the possibility of lifelike mechanical beings— well, Pandora never had a physical body. Kron wasn't interested in that aspect of artificial intelligence; he was a programmer, not a mechanical engineer."

"So... Uh... *She* created them?"

"What are you talking about?"

"*Nothing*," Jane said before Riley could answer. She gazed at Adam with a tender expression, as if she wanted to protect him from whatever Riley had been about to reveal. *Better not to ask.*

Devin leaned forward. "So no one else at BD Tech knew about Pandora?"

"She would have killed or discredited anyone who did." Jim X placed his forearms on his knees. "Look, I have no reason to hold back. Like I said, there's not much to tell. I got bigheaded and let Kron create a monster, and it got loose. That's—"

Jane pointed. "*Look out!*"

Devin rushed toward Jim X and pulled him to the ground as something crashed through the glass wall. A strong gust blasted Jim X as whatever it was nearly grazed his back.

Gunfire surrounded him. A gray Betta attack drone lurched violently in the air a few feet above where he lay. It sprayed blasts from its cannons.

Hello, Pandora.

Jim X relaxed in resigned relief, as though the sword that dangled over his head fell at last. "She's finally come for me. You kids should get out of here while you can." He started to stand, prepared to face his executioner face-on.

Devin yanked him back down. "It's not over for you."

It occurred to Jim X that he should be dead already. He looked around, confused. The gray drone didn't target him—it exchanged fire with an armed Blue Tang hovering a few yards outside where the wall had been. A cannon mounted on the ship's roof spun, following the Betta's movements.

Riley lay on his stomach, tapping speedily at a slate. The boy had to be remote-controlling the Blue Tang.

A succession of blasts hit the back of the fan-shaped drone. The Betta spun out of the room and crashed into the ground outside.

"*Hah!*" Riley pumped his fist.

Devin stood. "Nicely done."

Riley beamed. "Thanks. Ready to go?"

Devin glanced around the destroyed room. "Are you sure there's no way... Pandora can figure out what's happening down here without actually seeing it?"

"Yup. I smashed up all the smart house stuff, so now it's... uh... just a house."

"Good." Devin pulled Jim X to his feet. He looked Jim X in the eye with an authoritative stare. "All right, here's what's going to happen. We'll make her think you're dead so she'll stop hunting you, and then you're going to do *everything* you can to let the galaxy know the truth about her."

Jim X laughed. "Don't you think I've tried?"

The Blue Tang landed outside the shattered window. Two gray Bettas crossed the ocean in the distance, heading toward the mansion.

Devin watched them. "Jane, get to the ship." He sped toward the room's exit.

Jane started toward the Blue Tang. Adam remained still, as though lost in a trance. "Adam! Come *on!*"

She rushed to him, grasped his wrist, and pulled him along as she ran. Jim X thought he saw a flash of mechanical parts in the exposed area of Adam's shoulder. He wondered how a prosthetic could be so lifelike, then dismissed it as the dim light playing tricks on his aging eyes.

Devin took the large black bag Riley had sat beside before.

Riley grabbed Jim X's arm. "You're comin' with me, old guy."

Jim X glanced around, perplexed. "What's going on?"

Riley grinned. "They won't even look for a body." He said into his slate, "Ready when you are, Devin!"

Jane hoped the approaching Bettas would find Jim X a worthier target than she was so she wouldn't have to take them out before they witnessed what she wanted them to. She steered the counterfeit Blue Tang toward where Devin stood in front of the mansion and brought the ship to a hover behind him.

Jim X stood behind the transparent walls of his mammoth house. As the drones drew closer, Jane was certain they would see him too. Devin took a rocket launcher out of the black bag, placed it on his shoulder, and fired a rocket-propelled grenade at the mansion.

Boom.

The mansion disappeared behind the giant cloud of black smoke. After a brief pause, he launched a second grenade. It burst into an enormous explosion, bringing down the walls. A third took out the steel frame. A fourth incinerated the remaining debris.

The Bettas seemed to be getting funny ideas about going after Jane's ship since their intended target had been destroyed. They veered toward her. She hurriedly gunned them down, glad the pirates hadn't exaggerated about the cannon's firepower. When she finished, she pulled the lever to open the ship's door and extend the ramp.

The attackers were gone, and not much remained of the mansion. Devin nevertheless fired a fifth grenade. He walked up the ramp as a colossal fireball rose behind him.

"Man, you've got some *nice shit!*" Riley jumped onto a big fancy couch while Revelin panted happily beside him. Huh, he'd have to teach that dumb dog to answer to something less evil-sounding.

He marveled at the view of the stately mountains. Swanky places like the mansion he occupied belonged in holodramas. He'd never dreamed of seeing one in person, let alone *living* there. Yet there he was, lounging around in one of the many swish abodes on the Thiel estate.

Jim X stood in the doorway between the living room and the next one, which held a menagerie of exotic pets. He looked amused as he stroked a fluffy tan feline. "You should see the one I have by the canyon."

"Ugh, you evil corporation dudes have *too much*." Riley left it at that, much less willing to bash rich people when he was permitted to enjoy the goods.

He looked out the transparent walls into the sunset. Where would his buddies run to? They'd known the bad guys would probably try to off Jim X before he could talk, so they'd gone in with a plan to fake his death.

During the journey to Shimshawhenn, Riley had downloaded all the dirty details about the Thiel estate— blueprints, schematics, and stuff. That first grenade Devin fired had been a harmless distraction so the bad guys would see Jim X disappear in an explosion and assume he'd been blown up. Riley had taken Jim X down to one of the estate's underground transports and driven the hell away. He'd steered the transport to the current mansion— which he had, of course, unplugged ahead of time. All he had to do at present was lie low while figuring out how he was supposed to expose something invisible.

Riley picked up a shiny gold figurine from the shelf and examined it. "So here's the deal. As long as you're here, Pandora can't see you and will think you're dead. I'm sticking around so I can keep you hidden. I saved your life, so... Uh... You have to listen to me."

"Fair enough." Jim X put the cat down. "You know what? I like you, kid. You're the first person who's ever been straight with me."

"That's because I'm not some ass-kissin' tool who just wants to get stuff outta you." Riley angled the figurine in the light. "Although now that I'm here, I *will* be taking advantage of your awesome shiznit. Oh, and... Uh... I'm renaming the dog."

"Be my guest."

Riley suddenly remembered what he was supposed to do. He grabbed his slate and typed some commands.

A video window appeared. "This is Commander Jihan Vega of the *RKSS Granite Flame*. Who are you, and how did you get this confidential contact information?" Commander

Vega was kind of scary, with her piercing black eyes and no-nonsense voice.

Gotta look confident. Riley squared his shoulders. "Hi... Uh... I've got some intel on the recent homicide on Shimshawhenn."

"Are you referring to the explosion that was sighted at the Thiel estate?"

"Uh... Yeah." Riley took a breath. "Look, I know this isn't your usual gig, but I think you should come out here and check it out yourself."

"Why?"

"Because Devin Colt's involved, and I know you were kinda interested in what's been going on with him. Just... Uh... Trust me. There's stuff here you've gotta see."

Riley couldn't tell what Commander Vega's hard expression mean. He did his best not to fidget.

Finally, Commander Vega responded, "Very well. I'm on my way."

CHAPTER 21

DISAPPEAR AGAIN

"FREAKING *BULLIES*!" JANE FIRED AT another gray drone launched from the Wiosper warship. Evidently, the authorities spotted the explosion by the Diashin coast and knew the fleeing Blue Tang was responsible. It seemed that even though the *ship* was untraceable, the cannon, which she'd forgotten to retract, was not.

After taking off, she'd gone for the gunner's seat so *she* could be the one doing the shooting. She yanked the controls. The cannon twisted as a Betta swerved behind the ship. She squeezed the trigger. A bright purple blast narrowly missed its target.

"Dammit! Freaking Wiosper sons-of-bitches!" Jane aimed the cannon again and pulled the trigger repeatedly, firing far more times than was necessary to destroy the drone. "Take that, you little bugger!"

"Relax, Pony," Devin said. "It's just a drone."

Jane kept her gaze on the tracker. "I know. I'm just sick of getting shot at! Wish we'd had this cannon the last few times. It's making this whole running away business a helluva lot easier! Face it, bro, *my* black market Blue Tang is infinitely better than yours."

"In my defense, I was only sixteen when I found that one."

A drone barreled straight at the ship. Jane aimed the cannon and fired twice. She fell back against her seat as Devin flipped the ship to avoid crashing into the debris.

"Not holding back next time!" She sat up. "Hey, how come the Wiosper guys haven't noticed their warship was hacked? The Bettas that attacked us on Shimshawhenn were identical to these jokers."

"They probably think we did it."

"That sucks." Jane fired at a Betta. It kept coming, along with a second drone right behind it. She let loose another ridiculous volley of blasts and reduced them both to dust. "Take *that!*"

Jane wondered if she should worry about the inappropriate enjoyment she got out of dangerous situations. She noticed something of a pattern whenever she had to run: she'd first panic, then the rush would come, and the next thing she knew, she was having a blast while getting blasted at.

She targeted another drone. "I think I'm some kind of weird thrill seeker. This isn't so bad!"

Her blasts missed. The ship pitched as the drone hit its side. Her head banged into the wall beside her seat. *Ow! Spoke too soon.*

Devin veered the ship. "We're almost at the tunnels."

"Where to after that?" Jane asked.

"I guess we have to disappear again."

"Wherever we end up, we've gotta find a way get rid of that freaking Pandora program. At least now we know why they can't seem to figure out that Quasar's central computer was hacked and all the forensics faked. But what the hell are we supposed to do? It's not like we can *delete* it."

"The Networld created her. Maybe they can find a way to destroy her."

"Why do you keep referring to it as 'her'? It's a freaking *computer.*"

The revelation that the unseen enemy doing its best to destroy her life was a disembodied computer program left Jane with an empty sense of injustice. Her father had been shot and her brother nearly executed because of something without a face she could confront or a body she could see behind bars. Several soldiers just doing their jobs and numerous programmers who didn't know what they were getting into—and possibly scores of others she'd never know about—had been slaughtered by a merciless phantom.

There's no justice in this freaking universe.

And then there were the AIs...

"Jane!" Devin interrupted her ruminations.

Jane's absentminded gunning failed to clear the path to the interstellar tunnels, which grew larger on the viewscreen. "Sorry!"

She focused on taking out the last few Bettas that stood in the way of escape. Once they were gone, she quickly retracted the cannon. "Whew! It's too bad we couldn't take Jim X up on his offer to let you hide out on his big fancy estate. Would've been nice to chill there instead of always running out to the Fringe. Lucky Riley."

"Yeah. But we don't want to be around when the authorities and the media descend." Devin swiped the navigation chart, flipping through a directory of planets and floats.

Jane peered at the chart. "Can I pick where we go this time? Because the last Fringe float *you* took us to made Travan look like a freaking palace."

"I was looking for weapons, not aesthetics." Devin stopped swiping. "What do you have in mind?"

"Zim'ska Re." Jane gave him a hopeful smile. *Please, bro? Pretty please?* "I know it's scary and all, but I've always wanted to see it. We'd never be able to go as legit travelers, so why not hide out there as fugitives?"

Devin knit his eyebrows. "It's a warzone. You think Uyfi Float was bad? At least it has some form of authority."

Jane slumped in disappointment. "Ah, you're right."

A hint of a smile crept onto Devin's face. "Then again, the lawlessness does make Zim'ska Re the ideal place to disappear."

Jane straightened eagerly. "Yim Radel's pretty safe. Hell, Quasar got its hands on a fish from Fuy Lae, so it's gotta be okay. As long as we lie low and avoid Mor'sei and Nem, we should be all right."

"I guess we're going to Zim'ska Re."

"Yes!" Jane pumped her fist.

Devin found Zim'ska Re's information in the directory. He glanced over it and then steered the ship through an interstellar tunnel. Alarms rang. He looked down at the control screen, expression confused. "Take the controls. I need to check something in the engine room." He flipped a switch to turn off the alarms, halted the ship, and got up.

Jane took his place with some apprehension. "What's wrong?"

"Could be nothing." He headed for the cockpit door.

Jane looked down at the status report on the control screen. No wonder he was concerned; it was blank.

Dammit! That's what I get for buying off-brand. Well, at least it flies.

———————— ✦◦✦ ————————

Devin left the engine room, relieved after finding that the alarms were due to a minor computer glitch. He stopped as he passed the living quarters.

Adam sat on the floor, leaning against the wall as he absentmindedly fiddled with a Via pendant. He'd barely spoken a word since finding out he was an AI. Devin wondered if he should be concerned. *Concerned about what? He's mechanical.*

Devin hadn't been entirely surprised—unlike Riley, who'd shouted in shock until Jane yelled at him. The possibility that Adam was an AI had crossed Devin's mind after he'd spoken with Kron. He'd dismissed the thought because Adam hadn't been on that list of actives, and because it'd been clear the kid wasn't the type to seek influence or control, unlike the others. Perhaps that was what "special case" had meant.

Sarah had been an AI the entire time. It made sense that Adam had been, too. The transmission fragment stating that he was "slated for replacement" must have been some kind of recall, and Pandora must have removed him from the list after deactivating him.

Devin lingered in the doorway. He reminded himself that any expressions of distress on Adam's face meant nothing. Like Sarah, Adam was just a robot who could express emotions without experiencing them. Still, it was hard to help feeling bad for the kid—his movements were so realistic. Devin recalled Adam's reaction to his discovery, how he'd trembled and kept his pleading eyes fixed on Jane.

"I didn't know," he'd repeated. "I swear. I'm so sorry..."

Jane, always the type to deny the hard truth, had

been all too willing to believe the act. She'd put a hand on Adam's arm and done her best to comfort him. "It doesn't matter. I don't care if you're synthetic or what. Hell, you could be a ghost with no body at all for all I care. We were friends before, and I'm still your friend now. Friends don't abandon each other. You said that to me, and I won't let a stupid thing like mechanics get in the way."

Adam had looked down at his shoulder. "I— I'm sorry. I'm not..."

Jane's expression turned to impatience. "Not what? *Real*? What the hell does *real* mean anyway?" She put a hand on Adam's cheek. "I see your face, the light in your eyes. I hear your voice, all the meanings behind it. I don't care what the rest is made of! You can't help the way you were made. No one can! We might as well *all* be mechanical. There are people who have replaced every other organ, who have remolded their faces and reshaped their bodies—people *full* of synthetic parts. Hell, we see new reports every day about how this chemical controls our emotions or that substance affects our decisions, how most of who we are is printed in our genes. Who's to say that we're not *all* programmed, designed, engineered? So I don't want to hear it, Adam!"

Adam had nodded, but the pained look remained. "I swear, Jane, I didn't know." It had been so convincing. No wonder Jane had bought it. *If I didn't know better, I would've bought it too.*

Devin remained by the living quarters. The poor kid seemed shattered. Pandora must have made some changes since creating Sarah, who had appeared unfazed by the truth. The afternoon Adam had been taken, Sarah had seen the scanner results revealing her synthetic nature. She had played dumb, as if she didn't understand what the document meant. Only later had Devin realized that had to be how Pandora found out he knew Sarah to be an AI: She knew what Sarah knew.

Did Pandora know what Adam knew as well? Devin had thought to leave Adam on Uyfi Float, but the idea had seemed so wrong that he'd quickly pushed it away. He couldn't betray Jane like that. To her, he wouldn't have been removing a threat; he would have been abandoning someone she cared deeply about. He'd rather risk Pandora's wrath than his sister's.

Adam looked down at the Via pendant and held it to his heart. Did it represent the Absolute or Jane, who had pressed it into his palm right after her speech?

"Remember what you once told me?" she had said. "About how we think and decide on a higher level, and anything physical adjusts to reflect that?" She had closed Adam's hand around the pendant. "*That's* what matters, and the rest means *nothing*."

Devin, impatient with himself, turned away. *How can the pendant represent anything? He's a* machine.

Jane would sock him if she could read his thoughts. As far as Devin could tell, nothing had changed for her. It was as though the facts had confronted her with a roar, and she'd shrugged in response. She'd done her best to wake Adam from the silent daze he'd entered, telling him time and time again that he was who he was—to hell with the rest.

But she hadn't seen Pandora's test program, how every nuance—even the elements of what might be called a soul—could be simulated. Sarah was more real to Devin than most *people* he knew, only to be revealed as the product of a brilliant deception, one that cast him off as a liability and did its best to erase him. The same was probably true of Adam—and what would happen to Jane the day she realized he, too, was an empty act?

"You're an *idiot*," she'd snapped when he brought the matter up. "I don't know what they did when they made him, but he's as real as you and me."

"That's what I thought about Sarah," Devin had said. "There was nothing, *nothing* to indicate she was anything other than what she appeared to be. She was empathetic, passionate, intuitive... Dammit, Jane, I *fell in love* with her, only to discover she's an elaborate illusion. What if Adam's the same?"

"He's *not*. He saved your life, Devin! I shouldn't have to explain this to you! Stop being an ass!"

After that, Devin kept his concerns to himself, opting not to say anything rather than risk expressing something he'd come to regret. Every time he looked at Adam, he tried to alter his perception, to see him as the mechanical being he really was. Every time, the loudest part of his psyche told him the kid was as much a person as he was, and that his reservations were unfounded and probably cruel.

Why the hell am I still here? Devin started back toward the cockpit. Adam looked up at him with a start, his expression frightened.

Devin stopped. *Fuck. What's wrong with me?*

The kid had defied reason and risked everything to save his life. If he continued trying to see Adam as an anthropomorphic mirage, maybe *he* was the one without a soul. He stepped into the room. "Hey, Adam. I... wanted to see how you were doing."

"Why do you care?" Adam's voice was barely a whisper. "I'm just a machine."

"Jane doesn't believe that." Devin studied Adam's face. "Neither do I."

"I heard what you said about what Kron showed you. Sarah's a combination of physical movements—an illusion, as you said." Adam's gaze fell. "You think I'm the same."

Devin considered laying out the reasons he no longer believed that. Instead, he asked, "Are you?"

Adam shook his head. "I know there's no way to prove I'm any different."

"You must be. Pandora wouldn't have taken you otherwise." *Pandora didn't want her AI gaining independence. Damn, even she knew he's... sentient.*

"I was recalled, wasn't I?" Adam's tone carried a trace of disgust. "I'm a faulty product. That's why she took me, why she put me in a box and left me in a warehouse. I'm a machine created by a computer, and I'm broken. I wonder where my replacement is, what he's like."

Devin contemplated how Pandora's logic might work. "I don't think she's created one yet. You wouldn't be here if she had. I think she had to take you when she did because you disrupted her plans."

"I *was* a very disobedient robot," Adam said dryly. "All those strange urges I ignored? I wasn't drugged. That was Pandora sending me commands, trying to control me." He looked down at his shoulder and felt the burnt synthetic skin of his wound. "What the hell am I?"

You're the brave kid who saved both Jane's life and mine. And I'm the bastard who treated you like shit. Devin approached and sank to the floor beside Adam. "Tell me, has finding out what you are changed anything? Have you lost the ability to think or to care?"

Adam shook his head again. "I feel the same. I still... remember my childhood on Ibara, what it was like to admire the Counselors who raised me and to want to be like them. I *remember*, even though I know it never happened. I still look to the Absolute Being, even though I know..." He trailed off and looked at the ground.

"Then, nothing's really different, is it? Jane said every one of us is a consciousness shoved into physical being, and what that being's made of isn't important. I think she's right." Devin paused. "I'm sorry if I've been... less than kind. It's nothing personal."

Adam turned the pendant in his hand. "She keeps acting like none of this matters."

"She means it, Adam. You know she never hides how she feels. Not when it matters."

Adam's face brightened. "That's true. It's one of things I love about her. How is that possible? That I can... that an AI can... feel? Do I even have a soul?"

Devin shrugged. "You're the religious one. You tell me: Would your Absolute Being abandon you because of something you can't change?"

A humorless smile played on the corner of Adam's mouth. "You're right. Who am I to question the Absolute? We're all the way we are for a reason. Maybe I was created to start a machine revolution and bring on the AI apocalypse."

Is that supposed to be funny? "Jane never doubted you, so stop doubting yourself."

Adam leaned his head back. "Somehow that makes it worse, that she's so... accepting. I always knew... But it doesn't matter. I... I'd do anything for her, even though she could never..."

Devin didn't know how to respond. He waited in uncomfortable silence for Adam to continue.

After a minute or so, Devin collected his thoughts. "She cares about you. I don't think she realizes how much. She's been this way since she was little: never knowing what she wants, always battling her feelings, guarding herself. She knows how vulnerable she can be. She's been close to so few people that... she doesn't know how to handle it."

"She's probably the only person in the galaxy who would give a damn about me now." The frightened look crossed Adam's face again. "What's going to happen to me?"

"Same thing that would've happened if you hadn't been shot. No one else has to know."

Jane called from the cockpit, "Hey, Devin! What's going on back there? Is the ship okay?"

"Yeah, I'll be right there." Devin got up and started to leave, then looked back. "Everything's going to be all right. You don't have to be afraid."

"I wish I could believe you." Adam closed his hand around the Via pendant and gazed into nothingness.

<hr />

The counterfeit Blue Tang's untraceable nature allowed Devin to cross the galaxy quietly. No one cared when he steered the ship into the Zim'ska Re system, whose two more populous planets, Mor'sei and Nem, were too engaged in a space battle to notice his little ship as it sailed past them toward Yim Radel, which was mostly uninhabited.

The moment he landed, Jane rushed out of the cockpit, opened the door, and ran down the ramp into the remote meadow the ship sat in. She regarded the lush, colorful forest and sweeping mountains with childlike wonder. Platinum clouds and the magnified form of the planet's twin, C'tui, shone in the sky as the blue-hot Zim'ska Re sun sank in a shimmering blaze of light and color.

"See, Devin?" Jane said. "Wouldn't you rather hide out here than on some rundown float?"

Devin smiled. "As nice as you expected?"

"Better. It's one of the things you have to see for yourself, you know? Holograms, videos, pictures—they can't capture the real thing." She cupped her hands by her mouth. "Adam! Stop moping around the ship and come see this!"

Adam appeared at the door. "It's beautiful, Jane. It's like the Absolute is in that sunset."

Jane ran up the ramp toward him. "Hey, he talks! You were starting to scare me with the whole still-and-silent thing."

Adam gave her a sad smile. "I'm fine. I didn't mean to worry you."

The sun disappeared behind the mountains. It took with it the warm flush of daylight and left behind the haunting glow of the night. The only artificial light came from the ship's door. The full form of blue-green C'tui illuminated the sky with an ethereal radiance that obscured the stars.

Devin's slate beeped.

Corsair: Check out the Collective's forums.

He followed the links. A firestorm brewed on the Net. Riley had recorded everything Jim X had said about the Pandora Project. In the two days it took to reach Yim Radel, half the Networld had seen the video. Pandora tried to block its dissemination, but Citizen Zero had become more resourceful at spreading information that others didn't want seen.

Although many met the revelation with skepticism, the most influential members of the Collective had decided the notion of No Name being a sentient program made too much sense to ignore. They'd found the connection between artificial intelligence and the murdered programmers from ten years ago.

Corsair: As soon as I released the video, other demons shared their own evidence of Pandora's existence. It's not exactly proof, but it's close enough for most. The Collective's furious that Kron used them and that their friends died because of what he did. They're teaming up with other Netcrews and brainstorming ways to wipe her out.

Archangel: Good.

Corsair: They're also working with the Seer to track her activities. They may be able to prove she's responsible for the attacks on Revelin Kron and Victor Colt.

Archangel: I hope so.

Corsair: Here's the best bit: They've made so much noise about Pandora, the IC Tech Council ordered an investigation. It'd be awfully embarrassing if someone defied the regulations so completely without some sort of crackdown. I'll let you know when I have more info.

Devin folded the slate and dropped it in his pocket.

Although he and Riley had considered exposing the presence of the AIs along with the truth about No Name, finding out about Adam had done away with that notion. After all the hell Pandora caused, the secret of her AIs would be kept, and she'd get what she'd wanted in the first place.

"But don't people have a right to know?" Riley had asked Devin via video transmission the day before. "We could leave Uh-Dame out."

"It's a bad idea," Devin had replied. "Telling the Networld anyone could be synthetic would cause mass paranoia."

"But isn't it kinda unfair? I mean... Uh... Other law students don't stand a chance because of that Jonathan King dude. He was *built* to beat them."

Jane gave Riley an artificially sweet smile. "Riley, keep this AI business to yourself or *I will kill you.*"

"It's gonna come out eventually!" Riley protested. "You can't keep something like this hidden *forever.*"

"Maybe, but 'eventually' had better not be because of you. And if I find out it is, I'll hunt you down and kick your scrawny ass!"

"Okay! I'll keep a lid on it! Man, you're violent!"

Adam had watched the exchange in silence. Devin had noticed a flicker of a smile at Jane's exaggerated threats.

In the meadow on Yim Radel, Devin looked over at his sister, who sat surrounded by luminous purple flowers, marveling at the sky. Beside her, Adam regarded the heavens with the same silent awe. Devin wondered if Pandora even understood the life she'd created.

Jane looked over at him. "Hey, Devin! Were you messaging Riley?"

"Yeah. The Collective and some other Netcrews are trying to figure out how to stop Pandora."

"Excellent. I hope they destroy every shred of it."

Adam's hand drifted to his injured shoulder. "Maybe I can help? After all, I'm also... an artificial intelligence. They could... look at my... programming... if I could... get onto the Net—"

"Forget it," Jane snapped. "That's just... Forget it!"

"I'm probably the only one who knows what I am. I might as well try and use it. She's killed so many people already, and I want to stop her."

"Ugh, I still don't get why you guys keep referring to that *programmed monstrosity* as if it's a person."

A pained look crossed Adam's face.

"You're different!" Jane said hurriedly. "Hell, you're more human than most humans! I mean it, Adam. You're the one good thing to come out of this mess, and I don't want you doing anything that'll put you in danger."

"All I want is to interface with the Net," Adam said. "It's nothing, really. Riley does it all the time."

Devin thought the kid's idea courageous but unfeasible. "Virtual reality requires a lot of equipment that reads brainwaves and the like. We don't have any of that, and even if we did, it wouldn't be the same with you."

Adam thought for a moment. "Maybe Riley will have some ideas?"

Archangel: I have a question.

Corsair: Careful. She could be watching. Keep things vague or hide them in codes.

Damn. Codes aren't exactly my expertise.

Archangel: Is it possible for a gamer like Adam to enter the Kingdom?

Hope that worked. Klash of Kingdoms was Riley's favorite virtu-game. He probably understood the reference to the Networld. *Adam* was such a common name—it could refer to anyone.

Devin waited for a response. He could almost see Riley fidgeting, flipping through his brilliant little brain for ideas.

Corsair: She sent commands and updates through the Net, so it should be possible. I'll contact the junk dealer. He seems to know a lot about all this.

───────◆◇◆───────

The next two days were spent lying low, living off the

ship's well-stocked pantry of imperishable space food and watching as events unfolded on the Net. Riley told Devin, using an odd form of code, that Commander Vega bent some rules and re-investigated the cases against him. The best thing for him to do was remain disappeared.

Devin sat in the meadow, along with Jane and Adam, several yards from the ship. He watched a hologram of Sarah telling an interviewer why she loved her art, using the same words and tones as when she'd once told Devin. Even though he knew she was no more real than an animated character, he couldn't help projecting a kind of humanity onto her. She *was* designed to be indistinguishable from humans. He wanted to forget she existed, but the version of her he knew had become a part of him. He wondered how he could find it in himself to accept that she was gone forever.

A message window appeared on the slate.

Corsair: I have more instructions from the Seer.

"Adam, it's for you." Devin tossed Adam the slate.

The Seer had responded to Riley's attempts to contact him two days before and, using Riley as an intermediary, sent Adam several cryptic suggestions. To hide his intentions from Pandora, the Seer had encoded his instructions in a manner so abstract, the few times Devin had tried interpreting them resulted only in headaches.

Adam read the Seer's message. "This doesn't make any sense. I think he's saying it's like meditation, but I also have to... I don't understand."

Jane rested her chin on her knee. "I think he's telling you to knock it off already. You're not a freaking computer. You can't data transfer your consciousness."

"I must've been transferred to begin with. The AI workshop on Viate-5 was full of incomplete androids, so she must've developed the minds and bodies separately. I just need to figure out how to... get out of my head. Maybe once I do, they won't need a virus to defeat her. I can engage her in an eternal cyber battle like the warring immortals in the Book of Via."

Jane lifted her head. "Adam, c'mon. You should forget

the whole thing."

Something moved in the forest. Devin got up and went nearer for a better look. An open-air transport full of armed people flew toward him.

He ran back. "Jane! Adam! Get inside!"

Jane grabbed Adam by the wrist and ran toward the ship. Devin followed a few steps behind, keeping an eye on the transport. Its passengers raised their weapons and fired in the air.

A second transport swung around from the other side of the ship, blocking Jane as she approached the ramp.

A man with a thick beard jumped out and aimed a rifle at Devin. "Don't move!"

Devin raised his hands. "Easy. We don't want any trouble."

A woman with a red tattoo across her face landed in front of Jane and aimed two handguns at her. "Who're you?"

"Just another bunch of lost refugees." Devin chose his words carefully to avoid anything that could be mistaken for a threat. "I thought this area was deserted."

A large, muscular man with spiked hair and a square face pointed a massive gun at Adam. "The boss decided the whole continent belongs to him and sent us out looking for trespassers."

"I didn't know we were trespassing. We'll leave." Devin looked around. They were surrounded. Any attempt to run would be suicide.

Meanwhile, a few thugs entered the ship. He hoped they wouldn't notice its cannon. The other transport arrived. Several more thugs approached.

A woman with a black braid sauntered toward Jane. "What have we here?"

The tattooed woman sneered. "More entertainment for the Ringmaster."

The square-faced man jabbed Adam's injured shoulder with the barrel of his gun. "Hey, what the *fuck* is this?"

Shit. "A prosthetic." Devin gave the first lie that came to mind. "He lost his arm in an accident."

The man shoved his gun into Adam's chest. "*Freak*! You're a fuckin' *insult to life*!"

Jane's eyes radiated fury. "*Leave him alone*! Get

away from—"

The black-haired woman backhanded Jane hard across the face. Jane fell to the ground.

"*Jane!*" Adam cried.

Devin started toward her, only to be shoved back by the barrel of a rifle.

The bearded man snarled. "I said *don't move.*"

With a glare, Jane balled up her fists.

Devin recognized the mad glint in her eyes. "Jane, *no!*"

She sprang up and threw a punch at the black-haired woman's stomach.

Dammit, Jane!

The woman stumbled. "Little cunt!" She reached for her gun.

The tattooed woman grabbed her arm. "Don't! The Ringmaster will like her."

The first woman scowled as she let go of her weapon. Devin released a breath and relaxed the hand that had been milliseconds away from seizing the rifle digging into his chest.

Jane glanced at her still-clenched fists, mouth open as though surprised at herself.

A thug exited the ship. "It's empty! Should we strip it?"

"Just grab any weapons or valuables," the tattooed woman said. "We'll send out a prawn to tow the whole thing back later. Let's bring 'em in."

The square-faced man glowered at Adam. "Except this one. *What the fuck are you?*"

Adam looked terrified. "Please. I—"

Bang. Bang. Bang.

Jane screamed.

"*Bastard!*" Devin felt a hard blow against his head.

When he opened his eyes, he was on the ground. *Must've lost consciousness.* He couldn't have been out for more than a minute or so, since the scene had barely changed. He was still in the meadow, surrounded by thugs. Adam lay on the ground, his chest gaping with wounds.

Jane knelt beside Adam. She took him in her arms, her words barely intelligible through her sobbing as she begged him to stay with her. Adam moved his lips as though trying to speak.

Devin could sense the kid's life draining away. Gripped by rage, he started to get up. The scorching shock of a stunner flared through his back. He fell.

The tattooed woman grabbed Jane, who screamed in anguish.

The other thugs shouted in disbelief at the sight of Adam's mechanical body.

"*What the fuck is this*? It's a fuckin' *machine*!" The square-faced man stood over Adam and shot him in the head.

But it wasn't necessary. The kid was already gone.

CHAPTER 22

KEEP SANE, ENTERTAIN

JANE SCREAMED TEARFULLY, HARDLY AWARE of her own words, as the thugs dragged her from Adam's side and forced her onto one of their transports. She flailed her arms in their grasps until it felt as if she would tear them off. A man shoved her against the wall beside her brother.

As soon as the man let go, she launched herself at the group of thugs. Devin caught her and held her back. Unable to shake him, she continued screaming.

"Shut up!" The woman with the black braid raised her fist.

The tattooed woman caught the fist before the strike could land. "Don't damage the goods."

Goods. Jane mentally spat the word. They saw her as just another pretty young thing their boss might find entertaining.

Her wrath gave way to unspeakable sorrow. She collapsed against her brother's shoulder, crying harder than she'd imagined possible. After what felt like hours, the tears subsided. But the grief remained, a violent wave that struck her repeatedly and threatened to drive her from sanity. She could still see Adam's lifeless body even though the thugs had left it miles behind; she still felt as though she looked into his vacant eyes, pleading for him to come back. He'd been nothing and no one to the thugs, so they'd cruelly prodded him with fascinated disgust, as if he were an interesting piece of garbage.

"I'm sorry, Jane," Devin whispered. "I know how much he meant to you."

Jane wiped her eyes. "He can't be gone. He can't... He—"

"*Shut up!*" The black-haired woman scowled. "It's a fucking *machine!*"

"He's more than you'll ever be, you bitch!" Jane wanted to rip the woman's eyeballs out. The tattooed woman once again stopped the black-haired woman from striking her.

Devin's arm tightened around her. "Jane, *stop it.* Adam wouldn't want anything to happen to you, so quiet down before they run out of patience."

Jane closed her eyes and breathed deeply, willing herself to calm down. "He had a *life*. He had a—a *soul*, and they act like he was just—just—" She couldn't finish.

"They didn't know him," Devin said. "All they see are synthetic skin and machinery."

Jane opened her eyes. "Is that what you see?"

Devin looked past her. "No."

She waited for him to continue, but he didn't. The image of Adam's body ravaged her mind—his lifeless eyes, his cold hands. The faint smile frozen on his lips, as though he'd been trying to tell her not to grieve with his last breath.

Breath?

Yes, breath. *To hell with science.* In Adam, Pandora had somehow created the breath of life. All Jane saw when she thought of him was a light that once shone, gone.

"What's going to happen to Adam now? He believed in the Absolute *so much,* so... he's gotta be... he can't just be..." She broke down into another spell of uncontrollable crying, unable to understand the power of her own agony.

———◆———

Jane glanced around the cavernous palace with immeasurable disgust. The woman with the red tattoo gripped her tightly and pressed a gun into her back. Devin stood beside her in icy silence, held at gunpoint by the square-faced thug who'd murdered Adam.

The Ringmaster, an obese man with a red beard and beady eyes, sprawled in a gaudy throne, guffawing as he fondled a petite blonde on his lap. The girl had a mournful, resigned look, one mirrored on the faces of several other girls who stood by the throne in barely-there clothing. Jane tried not to think about having to join them. She looked up at the guns on the walls and wished the Pandora program would use its favorite modus operandi to off the bastard and his soulless followers.

Thick columns supported the high ceiling. An opulent chandelier illuminated the place with a sickly yellow glow. The circular area before the throne, outlined by a low wall with breaks in the side, displayed holograms of mythical winged women and several live female dancers. They moved to music emitting from a thin set of speakers. The Ringmaster's thugs hooted and jeered at the show.

Large screens lined the walls, showing various views of a band led by a skinny man. Looking closer, Jane noticed the same man standing motionless in the ring. He had on what looked like a metal blindfold—he produced the music. The virtu-world he occupied projected the sounds in his head for the physical world to hear.

The Ringmaster threw the blond girl off his lap and stood. *"I'm sick of this shit*! Get me a new musician!"

The girl ran to the skinny man and pressed the buttons on his VR visor. When nothing happened, panic crossed her face. She scrambled to do it again.

The Ringmaster bellowed, "Hurry up!"

"He's—he's not leaving!" the girl cried.

A thug strode into the ring. "Ah, just yank 'im!"

The girl shook her head and pressed the buttons again. The thug threw her down, grabbed the visor, and jerked it off. The music cut out. The skinny man fell backward, staring up with empty eyes.

The thug pulled out a gun and shot him through the head. He put a foot on the dead man's stomach. "Now you can play for the angels. They'll kick you to hell when they hear your fuckin' bullshit!"

The Ringmaster roared with laughter. "I am entertained!"

I'll kill them all. Jane wanted to grab a weapon and go on a murderous rampage, not caring if the thugs killed her, as long as she took as many of them with her as possible. She held still. Devin was right about Adam not wanting anything to happen to her. Besides, if she did it, he'd go down by her side.

The Ringmaster roared at the dancers, *"Did I tell you to stop*?" He strode toward Jane. "What have we here?"

"Pair of trespassers." The tattooed woman shoved Jane forward. "We thought this one would amuse you, boss."

The Ringmaster leered at Jane. "Ah, fresh meat! And what can you do, princess?"

Jane glared at him. She didn't know what she could say that wouldn't get her shot through the head.

An ugly grin spread across the Ringmaster's ruddy face. "I'll find a use for you, I'm sure." He turned to Devin. "Now, what is this? Hmm... I can always use new blood."

Devin gave him a cold look. "You're insane if you think I'll work for you."

"Oh? Rebellious, are you?" The Ringmaster clucked. "Too bad. Such a handsome young man. But no matter. If you won't cooperate, I'll have to kill you."

"Devin, just do as he says!" Jane cried.

Devin betrayed no emotion. "Fine. You leave me no choice."

"Ah, that's the spirit!" The Ringmaster looked Jane up and down. "What the hell is she wearing? Pretty little ass like that should be *flaunted!*"

"You sick—" Devin fell to the ground unconscious as the square-faced thug struck him in the head with the butt of his gun.

Jane screamed.

Square Face aimed the gun at Devin. "I think we should get rid of this troublemaker!"

Jane bit down a vicious string of curses. *Play nice. The Ringmaster's the boss here, and he's just another guy.* She looked up at the Ringmaster, widening her eyes. "Please, sir. He's my brother, and he's all I've got. I'll do anything you ask, just... Please don't kill him."

The Ringmaster regarded her. "Hmm... Indeed?"

Jane smiled as sweetly as she could. "I'll be a better performer if I have incentive. You must be a... highly intelligent man to run a beautiful court like this. Surely you understand the power of motivation."

The Ringmaster grabbed Jane's chin and pressed his slobbery lips against hers. Jane was too startled to react before he released her. It was the most sickening thing she'd ever experienced. She clenched her fists at her sides, digging her nails into her palms. *Don't move.*

The Ringmaster guffawed. "You've got a sweet mouth, princess! Entertain me, and I'll let your brother live!"

Jane did her best to keep her disgust from showing. "Thank you, sir."

Her stomach turned. She wiped her mouth. She knew what he meant by "entertain." Maybe if she got close enough, she could kill him... or better yet, sweet talk him into killing Square Face for her first and *then* kill him.

The Ringmaster roared, "*Where's my musician?*"

"Which one do you want, boss?" asked one of the thugs.

"Ah... I'm sick of them all. So hard to get good help these days!"

Jane lifted her chin. "I'm a musician." *Maybe I won't have to join the harem, after all.*

The Ringmaster raised his eyebrows. "Are you, princess? A singer, no doubt? What do they call you?"

"Kitti."

"Aw, isn't that too sweet." The Ringmaster barked at the tattooed woman, "Get her in a costume! Make it a *fancy* one! I want to see what my new princess can do!" He stretched his arms beside him. "*Entertain me!*"

———◆———

Jane walked into the ring. Her shimmering green gown looked almost bronze under the yellow light. She might have liked it if she hadn't been wearing it under such abhorrent circumstances. The collar fell off her shoulders, and the smooth, thin material hugged her waist and cascaded onto the floor.

A thug hooted as she stopped before the Ringmaster. "Hey, itty-bitty pretty Kitti!"

Jane held back the urge to retort with a chain of insults. *Just play nice...*

Around her, dead-eyed dancers moved in silence. They looked more like floppy puppets than performing artists.

The Ringmaster leered. "Now, *that's* more like it!"

"Where's my brother?" Jane demanded.

"Over there." The Ringmaster jerked his head to the left.

Devin stood along the wall with the thugs, watching her anxiously. Jane smiled to tell him she was okay. *It's all right, bro. I'll keep you safe.*

317

The Ringmaster snapped at the blond girl, "Get her in the visor!"

Visor?! "I thought you wanted me to sing." There was a reason Jane had avoided virtu-games. She had a tendency to get lost in her head as it was, and she dreaded ending up stuck in her virtu-world like her unfortunate predecessor.

"Only singing?" The Ringmaster frowned. "No, I want to hear the instruments! Imagine all the strings! And the horns! I want to hear it all!"

Jane widened her eyes innocently. "I have a really pretty voice, and—"

"That's not enough for me! Shall I remind you of your incentive?" The Ringmaster nodded at Square Face. Square Face raised a gun to Devin's head.

"I'm sorry. I... I didn't mean to challenge you." Jane lowered her eyelids demurely. "You intimidate me with your greatness."

The Ringmaster howled. "You must be the sweetest little lady I've ever seen! Go ahead, princess! Entertain me!"

The blond girl approached Jane with a VR visor. Jane hesitated, then took the device and put it around her face. The visor closed around the back and clenched her head like a vice.

The blackness faded, and she entered her dream world...

She'd been there many times in her fantasies. Those images had been distant whispers, appearing in undefined glows out of the darkness of her mind, the details obscured because they didn't matter.

This is real.

She stood center stage in the majestic auditorium of the Kyderan Presidential Palace. Instead of facing the orchestra of the galaxy's most talented instrumentalists, she looked out into the shadowy audience of politicians, celebrities, and other important people.

Choir... I need a full choir...

She turned around. A large choir stood on risers behind the orchestra. They watched her, waiting for her to begin.

Hello, Absolute One. I promised You a motet, and here it is. Take care of Adam. So be it, truly.

She imagined the smooth instrumental opening. The orchestra played. She'd modeled the piece after the Via

318

temple chants, intertwined it with melodic ribbons, and brushed it with dissonance. She waited for the choir to finish intoning their serene introduction, then sang the words of the ancient text:

"The Judge shall come, thus all revealing;
"No thing unseen remains concealing."

I see your face, Adam. I hear your voice. This is for you.
Tears fell as Jane repeatedly sang those words like a ritualistic spell. Sweet vibrations tingled her throat as her voice danced through the air. The music surged through her like a religious force. She allowed herself to move fluidly with the ebb and flow. The other musicians looked to her for direction, but she wasn't the one in control, for the music had a will of its own. Her heart soared, and she forgot everything else.

This is my temple, and the music is my god.
The song carried her to its sweeping climax. Jane repeated the chant one final time in a desperate cry for justice. She stood in silence as the orchestra softened to a vague rumble. The choir intoned the last few notes of her piece.

An invisible, powerful weight compressed her chest as someone tried to eject her from the virtu-world.

She didn't want to face the screwed-up universe that had done its best to destroy her. The auditorium—*that* was where she belonged, losing herself in a sublime force beyond nature.

Jane noticed something in the dark, shapeless audience. One of them had a face, a face she... "Adam?"

He smiled and clapped with the others, looking up at her with his bright peridot eyes. "You were beautiful, Jane."

She wanted to run to him, wanted to embrace him and tell him—tell him what? He was there, and she couldn't leave, couldn't return to the world that had blown him away.

Adam's smile fell into concern. "You have to go. Please, you can't stay here."

Jane's eyes stung. "Why not? What if I'd rather spend a few more moments here and fall peacefully into oblivion? What if I'm tired of always fighting without even knowing what I'm fighting for?"

"Those struggles are what make the moments of triumph mean anything. And your brother's still out there, waiting for you."

Jane nodded. She allowed her dream world to fade away, consumed by vast swaths of blackness.

"Simulation Ended" flashed before her in bright letters. Something loosened around her head. *Must be back in the real world.* She pulled the visor off her head and blinked, disoriented.

The Ringmaster laughed raucously. "I am entertained! Here's something new! It's *sophisticated*! Kitti, you have done well!"

"Thank you, sir." Jane handed the visor to the blond girl.

"Bring her to me!"

A pair of thugs grabbed Jane by the arms and pulled her toward the Ringmaster.

"*Let her go!*" Devin yelled.

"Devin, don't! I'll be fine!" The frenzied shouts of the thugs and the chaotic sounds of fighting filled Jane's ears. "Devin, *stop!*"

The Ringmaster sneered. "Too much trouble. *Kill him.*"

"*No!* Please—"

Bang. Bang. Bang.

The scream froze in her throat. Jane didn't dare look back to see what had happened for fear she would go mad at the sight.

"*What the fuck?*" The Ringmaster stood and pulled a gun from his belt. "What did you do in there?"

Jane didn't know what he was talking about. She'd lost the ability to move. Surrounding her was a cacophony of shooting and screaming, blasting and a spattering of explosions, but the world seemed muted.

The Ringmaster grabbed her and shoved his gun into her head. "Talk, you little bitch! Talk or I'll *blow your fucking*—"

Bang.

She jumped. Blood gushed down the Ringmaster's face from a blackened hole in his temple. Jane neither knew nor cared where that shot had come from. She just watched his eyes go blank as he fell to the ground, caught for a moment in righteous satisfaction.

"Jane! Are you all right?"

Jane whirled. Devin approached, a laser gun in his hand.

"*Devin!*" She rushed to him, relieved beyond words. "I thought... what happened?"

"The internal defenses hit that man right as he was about to kill me."

"Pandora?"

Devin pulled her to the ground as several shots whizzed by. The guns on the walls fired at the Ringmaster's minions. Square Face lay on the ground, writhing in pain from a shot to the stomach.

That doesn't seem right.

The Pandora program had been ruthlessly efficient in its past attacks. Whoever controlled the Ringmaster's guns seemed to be shooting to frighten or, at worst, injure—not to kill. A few bodies littered the ground, but they had been taken out by the thugs' efforts to fight back, crushed beneath the fallen columns or hit by the others' erratic blasts. The doors opened. The girls were unharmed as they scrambled to escape.

A calm voice said over the speakers, "Minions of the Ringmaster, if you want to live, leave immediately. Prisoners of the Ringmaster, take your freedom while you can."

Jane shuddered. That voice, tinny from amplification, sounded so familiar. *It can't be. Just a sound-alike.*

Despite the warning, most of the Ringmaster's thugs continued shooting at the internal defenses and throwing grenades at the screens. Devin pulled Jane behind a column for cover as they exploded, causing parts of the walls to collapse.

The guns kept firing. Eventually, the thugs poured out the doors and climbed over the rubble along with the newly freed prisoners. The chaos finally died down as the palace emptied.

Square Face—the bastard who murdered Adam and almost killed her brother—stumbled over the remains of a crumbled wall. Gripped by a blinding rage, Jane sprang up, grabbed a dropped gun, and ran toward him with the intention of blasting him to hell.

"Jane, stop!" Devin grabbed her and yanked the gun

from her hand.

Jane twisted violently, determined not to let him stop her. "Let me go, you jerk! Let me kill him!"

Devin's grip tightened. "Killing him won't do any good!"

"Why should *he* get to live? You go around shooting all the bad guys you want. What the hell gives you the right to stop me?"

"Because as much as I wish it weren't true, we're alike, and I know if you kill that man, you'll lose a part of yourself. It'll haunt you, stalk you, until the day it doesn't, and then you'll wonder if you're anything but a killer."

Jane twisted harder. "I don't care! *Let me kill him!*"

"Jane, don't. Let him go."

Jane froze. Devin hadn't spoken those words. It sounded like... but no. It couldn't be. Unless she were really going insane.

"You're not going mad. I'm right here."

Jane closed her eyes. *It's happening. I'm losing it. I'm losing it for real...*

Devin released her. "Jane, look!"

She opened her eyes and followed his gaze. He stared at the ring of the emptied palace.

In the middle shone a life-sized hologram of Adam.

"I'm still here, Jane. I got out before my body failed. I wanted to free you sooner, but I got lost in the Networld."

Jane couldn't speak. She ran to him and stared. "Is it really you?" She reached toward his ethereal form, surprised at how disappointed she was when she couldn't feel anything. "How...?"

"I don't really know. I heard the Seer speaking to me right after I was shot, and he somehow helped me escape."

Jane glanced around the destroyed palace. "So, that was... that was *you* just now?"

"Yes." Adam smiled. "And I saw you perform. That wasn't a projection."

Jane kept staring in disbelief. She had *lost* him, had felt the grief spread like a cancer through her soul and possess her with a demonic fury. Yet there he was, a ghost before her, there but not there. The joy and relief that should have flooded her were twisted in knots of bewilderment. She found herself more shocked by the clenching in her heart, a feeling she hadn't known herself capable of, than the strangeness before her.

It hit her that Adam was *alive,* and that was all she cared about. She had so much she wanted to say, but no words came to mind—none that mattered.

So she did the only thing she knew how: grin like it had all been just another adventure. *"Nice work,* Adam! You sure showed those damn sons-of-bitches who's boss. Made Pandora look like a freaking wimp! By the way, have you run into her?"

Adam looked around. Jane wondered what he saw. "Not yet. I think she has other things to worry about now that her plans are unraveling."

"Glad you're all right, kid," Devin said.

"Hi, Devin. I'm sorry I couldn't stop them before they knocked you out. I'm new at this."

"That's two I owe you."

Jane hiked up her long skirt. "Let's get outta here. I never want to see this stupid place again!"

Adam smiled teasingly. "Nice dress."

"Heh. Thanks."

"By the way, I found you a ride."

A ground transport crashed through a too-narrow door, sending concrete chunks flying. Jane screamed.

Adam's face fell. "Sorry. Like I said—new at this."

※

Word must have spread quickly about the attack at the Ringmaster's palace. No one had bothered Jane and Devin as they made their way back to their ship. As soon as they arrived, Jane leaped out of the transport.

Her skirt caught on something, and she tripped, creating a large tear. "Ugh! I hate this damn dress! Why didn't I think to pack some clothes?"

Devin helped her up. "At least you're not stuck in a prison uniform."

Jane yanked the tear in the skirt, ripping the stupid thing until she'd freed herself of the lower half. She kicked the swatch of green fabric. "That's better."

She ran to Adam's body and knelt beside it.

"Jane, just leave it."

Adam's hologram appeared, projected from the ground

323

transport to her right.

She jumped. "A little heads-up, next time?"

"Sorry. I just wanted to tell you not to bother with... the body. It's not me."

"Maybe not, but what're you supposed to do without it? Wander around the Networld forever? We'll find a way to fix it!" Jane closed physical Adam's eyes while virtual Adam watched with an expression between confusion and sorrow.

Devin helped her carry the body onto the ship and place it in the casket. She carefully removed the pendant from around Adam's neck. She couldn't watch as Devin closed the lid.

Screw this place. She rushed into the cockpit with the idea of getting as far from Yim Radel as possible. With nowhere to go, she reluctantly agreed with Devin that the planet remained the safest place to hide, since it was so isolated, and the nearest reigning boss was gone.

Devin activated the ship's screens. "I'll keep a lookout in case of trouble. You get some rest."

Too exhausted to protest, Jane entered the living quarters and collapsed on the cot. She lay sleepless for what felt like hours, her head heavy with weariness but too frenzied to allow rest to come. In her hand, she clutched Adam's pendant, wondering if that was the closest she would ever come to feeling the comfort of his presence again.

Her mind rushed with an uncontrollable furor. Even though she knew Adam was alive, just disembodied, she felt a sharp pang whenever she remembered how that thug had mercilessly shot him.

And there was something else. Something she'd screamed right after, when she'd yelled wildly, scarcely aware of her words. She tried not to dwell on it, but she was certain she'd meant it, and knowing it might never come to anything caused her the kind of pain she'd always closed herself off to avoid.

CHAPTER 23

AN AWESOME PLAN

RILEY TRIUMPHANTLY HIT THE "GO" icon on his slate. A video of Jane appeared in the communication window. "*Hah!*" Pandora made it hard for him to do *anything* online, even send a simple communication. Another win for him; she couldn't stop him from talking to his buddies.

He set the slate down on the ground beside where he sat on the living room carpet and leaned back on his elbows. "Yo, Janie, how's it going? Meadow still pretty and all?"

Jane propped her head up on her hand. "Yeah, lovely."

She and Devin had spent the four days since escaping the Ringmaster on Yim Radel following the Networld's movements and watching Commander Vega go public with her investigation. Pandora hadn't sent any killer robots after them or anything. Riley guessed that she didn't think them worth her time, since they were in hiding.

Jane's eyelids drooped. She looked bored. "I'm sick of lying low. Can't they delete Pandora already?"

"Huh, I wish." Riley shifted his elbow for a more comfortable position. "Would save me a lotta work."

"I know. I know. It's not that simple. There must be *something* we can do. Doesn't it have a mainframe we can blow up?"

"Uh... No," Riley replied, as though it were the dumbest thing he'd ever been asked. Jane gave him a furious glare. He once again reminded himself to be nicer when talking to actual people.

"She did once, before she accessed the Net." The voice was Jim X's.

Riley sat up. The old guy hovered over him. "Hey! I said no eavesdropping!" He flicked his wrist dismissively. "Go... do some old people stuff! Shoo!"

Jim X chuckled. "Just thought I could help."

"Huh. Like *you* would know anything about—" Riley smacked himself in the forehead. "Duuuude! We *can* blow her up!"

"How?" Jane asked eagerly.

Riley threw Jim X a get-outta-here look. Jim X smiled and walked away. As soon as the door had closed behind the old guy, Riley resumed his enthusiastic tone. "We've just gotta confine her to one place! She can't be *always* floatin' around the communication waves. If we knew which drive she was on and blew it up, it'd be like bashing her brains in!"

Jane sat up straight. "I like the sound of that."

"Does it have to be so violent?" That voice was Adam's.

Jane, who sat in the cockpit of the counterfeit Blue Tang, looked over the camera. Riley had interfaced with the Net earlier that day and told Adam how to get around the ship's veiling devices. Adam had figured out how to communicate through its central computer, his face appearing on the viewscreen whenever he did.

The fact that Adam was an AI didn't bother Riley anymore. He'd been pretty freaked out when he found out the guy was mechanical like Sarah DeHaven, but soon he'd brushed off his uneasiness. As far as he cared, the situation was simple: Sarah DeHaven was an evil robot; Adam was his friend.

Adam continued, "Surely there's a safer way."

Jane smirked. "Look who's talking. Remind me how much was left of the Ringmaster's palace by the time you were done with it?"

"Point taken. Destroy the body to destroy the mind... Sounds like the way they almost killed me, except I escaped. How do we keep Pandora from doing the same?"

Riley snatched up his slate in excitement. "The Snare, duh!"

"What's that?" Adam asked.

"It's what we're calling the program the Collective's working on to trap Pandora." Riley held up a hand, his forefinger and thumb almost touching. "We're *this close* to finishing! I'll be joinin' the effort again once we're done here. Consensus says we'll be done by the day after tomorrow."

"That was fast." The voice was Devin's.

Riley hadn't known Devin was in the cockpit with Jane. He wished he could reach through the slate and move the camera to see what his pal was up to. "What're you doing over there?"

Jane turned and, in the process, moved her slate to the angle Riley wanted. "What *are* you doing?"

"As usual, catching up on the news." Devin, who sat in the seat beside Jane, swiped his slate and turned it toward Jane. "Check this out."

A hologram of Jim X appeared. Riley's jaw dropped.

"As you can clearly see," holo-Jim X said, "I'm not dead. The evidence against Devin Colt in *my* murder is as indisputable as in the attacks on Dr. Revelin Kron and Victor Colt. I believe Jane Colt and Adam Palmer were right to question the supposed infallibility of the Kyderan justice system, which would have seen an innocent man executed."

Jane raised her eyebrows. "Hate to admit it, but I'm starting to like the old bastard."

Jim X called from the next room, "Is that my voice I hear?"

Riley scurried to the door, opened it, and poked his head in. Jim X lounged in a hammock, holding an antique book, the kind made out of dead trees and stuff. The big gray dog curled up on the ground beside him.

Riley held up his slate. "When'd you do *that*?"

Jim X peered over his book. "This morning. You didn't expect the media to keep away, did you? High-profile murder like mine? They descended on this place the moment the *Granite Flame* left. You were wired into the Net, and I didn't want to bother you, so I dealt with them myself."

Riley pointed at him. "*Dumbass!* Pandora could've sent an evil machine to shoot you in the face! If she had... What the hell am I supposed to do with a dead guy?"

Jim X shrugged. "Like I said to the media: I'm not dead. Your safeguards seem to be protecting me well enough.

Don't worry. I checked with Commander Vega first, and she gave me the go-ahead. Said she was about to reveal that I was alive, anyway."

Riley was ticked-off at the old guy for going behind his back and irritated with himself for missing it. At least it was another strike against the Devin-is-a-coldblooded-murderer thing.

Holo-Jim X continued, "My friends, the video of me disseminated on the Net contains only the truth. I know I've been discredited many times and dismissed as a batty old curmudgeon, but believe me when I say those memos were faked. I am perfectly sane. The Pandora program is a very real threat, and she's already claimed many lives. Had Dr. Kron been willing to accept responsibility for the rogue artificial intelligence he created, then he would've informed the cyberpolice of the so-called unidentified cybercriminal's true nature. I'm sure the investigation ordered by the Tech Council will soon find the proof it's looking for."

"I'm on your side, Riley," the real Jim X said. "Don't forget the reason you were able to break into BD Tech's computers."

Jane adjusted her position and looked into the slate. "What's he talking about?"

"One sec." Riley glared at Jim X. "*No eavesdropping!*" The dog got up and trotted toward Riley. Riley let the animal through before closing the door on the old guy's chuckle. "You can listen in, though."

The dog followed him to the far side of the living room. Riley planted himself on the carpet. "Here, Archangel!"

Jane snickered. "You named the dog Archangel?"

"I like that word, okay? It's a cool word!" Riley patted Archangel's head. "Anyhow, Jah-Mex gave me some intel, and I passed it on to a couple of rogue BD Tech programmers who were trying to break into Kron's old computer. The Snare's based on an anti-Pandora program Kron was working on. What the Seer discovered from... uh... looking at Uh-Dame filled in the blanks. You know, if Kron hadn't been offed, he might've finished the thing himself."

Adam, visible on the viewscreen next to Jane, shook his head. "He abandoned it years ago. From what I've heard, he stopped working on it because he wanted to see what his creation was capable of."

Riley jerked his slate toward himself in his consternation. "*What*?" *That's so messed-up!*

Jane's poofy brown hair filled the screen as she whirled to face Adam. "You mean he *chose* to let his monster run amok? That *bastard*! He deserved what he got and worse!"

"Yeah!" Riley put his slate on the ground. "Well, his evil computer fiend won't be doing much more, because we're gonna *blow her up*!" He pumped his fist. "Here's what's gotta happen." He made a chopping motion. "She downloads the Snare and gets stuck somewhere"—he pointed to the side—"we find out where she's at, and then *boom*!" He slammed his fist down on his leg. *Ow!* His thigh throbbed from the bruise he was pretty sure he'd given himself.

Devin looked over Jane's shoulder. "Why can't they use the Snare alone?"

Riley slumped. "Because it might not work. I mean, it *will*, but it won't hold her *forever*. Pandora's a freakin' super-brain. She'll escape eventually. And man, I do *not* wanna be around when she does."

"The idea behind the Snare's pretty simple," Adam said. "The program would trap Pandora's consciousness in a virtu-world that appears real to her. She'd basically become a virtu-addict, except without a physical body that would die. And... she has to upload it herself."

Jane threw up a hand. "Oh, great! How's *that* supposed to happen?"

Adam tilted his head down. "No idea."

Riley was annoyed that someone else had done the explaining. "Hey, how'd you know all that?"

"I guess you could say I downloaded it," Adam replied. "When I'm in the Networld, I can simply *know* the things I discover, without having to *read* them. That must be how Pandora learned so quickly."

"Whoa, *cool*!" Riley snatched up his slate. "Hey, you know what you should do? You should download all your textbooks and stuff in case you go back to priest-school."

"That would be cheating, and I couldn't do that."

Riley rolled his eyes. "*Lame*! Dude, there's all this

awesome shiznit you can do now. You should take advantage of it! Mess around with machines like Pandora!"

"I've had enough of that already." Adam sounded tired. "It's strange, being able to... but not... Never mind. Anyway, how do we find her?"

"Uh..." Riley fidgeted. He liked that everyone turned to him for answers, which was how it should be since he was *brilliant,* and they'd be lost without him. He hated to disappoint and once in a while wished someone else would figure things out for a change.

Devin knit his eyebrows. "She abandoned the workshop on Viate-5 years ago. She must have another, and she probably spends a lot of time there developing her AIs."

Adam pressed his lips together in thought. "I think I know how to make her upload it. I haven't heard anything about another version of me, which means she hasn't completed my replacement yet. When she recalled me, she was careful not to harm me. It's possible she still wants to... repair me. If I can convince her to... upload me into the workshop's central computer, I can bring the Snare with me."

Jane spun toward him again. "Like hell! You could get trapped too!"

"I'm willing to risk it," Adam said. "She must be stopped, Jane. If she's not, whose life will she destroy next? I'll be fine. As soon as she's trapped, I'll get out of there, and then you can destroy the building and be done with her forever. Maybe while I'm there, I can... find a new body."

Riley smacked his forehead. "The body! That's *it*! That's how Pandora's been tracking you guys!" He pointed at the slate. "Adam, *you* were the bug telling her where they were at whenever you weren't on a veiled ship! There's gotta be some kinda signal coming from it! And hey, if there's a signal, it can be traced. *That's* how we'll find her." He put the slate down and leaned back. "Signal traces are easy. Move the body outta the ship, and I'll have a location for you by *sundown.*"

Devin smiled. "You really are a freakin' genius."

Riley lifted his chin. "You bet I am!"

"How long will the Snare hold her?" Devin asked. "A couple days, at least?"

"Uh... Yeah. She's smart but not *invincible*."

"Good. She needs to download the Snare before Jane and I get to that workshop. Otherwise, she'll figure out what we're doing and send an army after us. That'll give you, Adam, plenty of time to find a way out while we pick up some supplies. I doubt our one cannon will be enough to take out a whole building. Once you're out, we'll blow the place."

Adam nodded. "Sounds good to me."

Riley beamed. "It's an *awesome* plan."

Jane looked past the slate's camera, making it seem like she gazed at a cloud or something. "But... but, Adam, what if you can't get out? What if you get stuck too?"

"Chill." Riley wasn't the best at comforting people, but he tried anyway. "That program's meant to trap *Pandora*. Adam's different. It'll be nothing more than a virtu-game to him. Besides, once I give it to him, he can try it out, practice ejecting himself. It's not like he'll be going in blind."

"Don't worry about me," Adam said. "I'll make sure I know what I'm dealing with before I take her in with me."

Jane leaned back resignedly. "All right. Where do we start?"

Jane entered the coordinates of Aurudise-3, the Fringe planet Riley had traced the signal to, into the counterfeit Blue Tang. She recalled hearing of the planet's evacuation several years ago, when computer and communications problems left its settlements unable to function. Sounded like Pandora's handiwork. *Bitch.*

Jane buckled herself into the copilot's seat. "We're gonna have a look at our target before going after weapons. I'm just glad we can leave freaking Zim'ska Re. What a waste. Such a beautiful place rendered so ugly by horrible people. Wish I could fix it."

Adam's face occupied a rectangle in the viewscreen's corner. "They're trying. There's an IC-backed Via program seeking to educate the population and change the place from the inside. I had a chance to join it a couple months ago, but—"

He broke off. The confused, melancholy look descended that so often crossed his face.

"You chose to help out on the Orphan Planet instead," Jane finished, even though it was a false memory.

Adam smiled, but the pained look remained.

Jane wanted to tell him that she'd chosen to believe the illusion that was his life before the seminary and that he should too. Before she could, Devin called her name, and she turned her attention to him.

"Ready the cannon," he said. "Seems like Mor'sei and Nem are still at each other's throats. They shouldn't bother with us, but it's better to be prepared."

Jane flicked her hand by her forehead in a mock salute. "Yes, Commander."

By the time she turned back to Adam, he was gone.

She took her last glimpse of Yim Radel as it shrank in the rear view. The Aurudisian system was so remote that it would take almost five days to reach. If all went according to plan, Pandora would already be trapped in her AI workshop's central computer before the ship entered the atmosphere of Aurudise-3.

Jane gripped the gunner's controls as the ship passed the space battle. She aimed the cannon and fired at a stray attack drone. Thankfully, that was the only trouble she ran into. She was too tense to focus and wasn't sure she could've handled another firefight.

He'll be fine. The self-reassurance rang hollow.

Dread loomed as she thought about what Adam had to do, a feeling that after he found Pandora, she'd never see him again.

———◆◇◆———

Riley tapped his foot. Waiting for people always bugged him. He'd told Adam to meet him in the virtu-world of one of his favorite games so he could deliver the completed Snare. Pandora had shut down the previous virtual forum they'd met in.

Riley was starting to wonder if Adam would be able to figure out how to enter a virtu-game.

Yeah, he will. He can download anything he doesn't know. Man, if I could do that, I wouldn't let some dumb thing like principles *stop me!*

Knee-high red grass covered the field he stood in. A stone castle towered in the distance, surrounded by a

ARTIFICIAL ABSOLUTES

giant army of guys in metal suits. Those were the other players. Riley had chosen that part of the game because it was so busy. Pandora would have a harder time spotting him in the crowd.

A pale green light appeared a few yards away. Seconds later, it transformed into Adam, who seemed smaller than usual since Riley looked at him through the eyes of his virtu-game avatar: a tall, muscular man with swarthy features and a cool swagger. "Hi, Uh-Dame!"

Adam looked confused as Riley approached, and then he smiled. "Riley, I know what you look like."

"Fine, then." Riley reverted to his usual self. "Like the scenery? It's Ocean Sky's latest release: Klash of Kingdoms Three-Eleven. Anyhow, here's the Snare." He reached into the air and pulled a Via pendant out of nowhere. "Nice touch, right? It was my idea. She'll never think it's anything but part of your projection of yourself, priest-boy."

Adam regarded it curiously. "I don't understand how any of this works."

"Don't think too hard about it." Riley handed him the pendant. "Hey, you've been watchin' yourself, right? She's not following you or anything?"

"I haven't seen her at all." A shimmering black fog appeared and surrounded Adam. "Riley? What's this?"

Riley tensed up to keep from fidgeting. *Only a program that could screw you over.* "Part of the game, duh."

"Are you sure? It seems different from—"

"Ever played Klash of Kingdoms before?" *Not like you could tell the difference if you had. I imbedded it in the game itself.*

Adam shook his head.

Riley put his hands in his pockets in an attempt to look chill. "That stuff's common around here. It's... uh... meant to make this place seem more mysterious. Trust me, I've been playing versions of this game for ages."

The fog wrapped Adam, disappearing into his body. He uncomfortably looked around and tried to move away.

Riley snapped his fingers in Adam's face. "Hey! Focus! So wear the freakin' pendant. Don't let it get you, though. Jane'll kill me if you don't make it out."

Adam seemed to forget about the fog as it thinned. "You

333

said I could practice, right? Test out the Snare's virtu-world before going in with her?"

"Uh... Yeah. You'll figure it out. Now, scat before evil Panda-Rah figures out what you're up to."

Adam put the pendant around his neck, looked up at the cloudy sky, and faded into a haze of green light.

Riley shook his arms to loosen up. He'd never considered himself the good guy, but lying to a friend who'd volunteered to put it all on the line was different from messing with people. For the first time, he really felt like the bad guy, and he didn't like it one bit.

He ejected himself from the virtu-game. It disappeared behind a bunch of black blobs. Finding himself back in Jim X's living room, he pulled off the visor and typed on his slate.

Corsair: It worked.

Archangel: Are you sure he didn't suspect anything?

Corsair: It made him uneasy, but he seemed to shrug it off. I feel bad, though.

Archangel: Don't. I was the one who told you to do it. If anything goes wrong, it's my fault.

Corsair: Shouldn't we give him a heads-up about what he'll be facing?

Archangel: No. Anything he knows, she'll know too. I don't like it either, but it's the only way.

CHAPTER 24

INVISIBLE AND OMNIPRESENT

A DAM STOOD AT A CROSSROADS, *surrounded by infinite numbers of gray paths in every direction, all leading into the same terrifying void.*

A skinhead thug snarled as a waterfall of scarlet cascaded down his face from the bullet hole in his forehead. Behind him glowed five blood-soaked strangers, unrecognizable behind their masks of dripping red as they stared at Adam, black emptiness in place of eyes.

Adam trembled. "I'm not sorry."

He wanted to run, but the blank roads scared him more than the specters, who whispered accusations.

Jane materialized in the distance. Everything else seemed to disappear. She walked down one of the paths, away from Adam.

"Jane!"

She didn't respond. He ran toward her, but she never got any closer...

Adam stood alone in a void, unable to see anything but blackness and lines of gray symbols randomly streaking the air. The nightmare, one he'd experienced many times, remained vivid in his memory.

Must've fallen asleep again.

Even as a disembodied consciousness, he still grew weary. Instead of lying down and waiting for sleep to come, he would become slower and slower until everything faded away, and then come to hours later, wondering what had happened.

Being in the Networld was strange. It had no dimensions and no sense of space, for it was not bound by the laws of physics. Adam no longer had a body, so he was incapable of feeling hot or cold or other sensations. The only way he could perceive the physical world was through cameras and microphones and such, and the only way he could speak was through, well, speakers.

Some of the things he was capable of in the Networld made him more powerful than he could ever have been in the physical world. In addition to learning instantaneously, he could communicate directly with programmable machines and command them, although it wasn't easy. Trying to control the Ringmaster's central computer had made him appreciate how complex Pandora had to be.

At times, Adam feared the Networld would absorb him. He often escaped into virtu-worlds, where he could at least feel human again. He tried not to think about staying disembodied forever, with those virtu-worlds being the closest he could come to the life he'd known before. His more pressing concern was whether he could find a way out of whatever trap he was supposed to lure Pandora into.

All right, enough stalling. Let's see what kind of prison the Networld built for her.

Adam had always considered himself lucky to know exactly how he felt about virtually everything: his morals, his religion... his love. He'd always known he wanted to become a Via Counselor and help others feel as certain of themselves as he did.

But in the time it took to be hit by a laser blast, his world shattered. The steady memories slid into dark chaos as he realized that they were implants designed to make him exactly who he was. He'd always believed in serving a greater purpose, but he never could have imagined that the higher power whispering thoughts into his consciousness was a calculating, manmade creation.

In a way, Pandora was his god. She'd designed him, built him, given him everything he believed he was, and guided him on the path he'd been on before that fateful afternoon when he was taken. She'd created him as wholly as one being could create another, putting ideas in his head and engineering him to feel certain ways. He had a calling, and she was the one calling him.

Yet, Adam knew there had to be a greater force at work within him, one older than the stars and at once mighty and uncertain. It was an aspect that long baffled those who examined the minds of organic beings, prompting endless scientific and philosophical debates as to whether humans were endowed with some mysterious, immaterial quality beyond rational comprehension, or if they were as mechanical as he was, and all perceptions of free will merely a well-constructed illusion.

In his case, the argument could be settled by pointing to one basic fact: He *had* been wired to act and react in certain ways—almost literally. Adam chose not to believe that for an equally basic reason: He was all too familiar with the slow and effortful deliberations of conscious attention, of forming decisions driven by more than competing variables, and of pondering matters long past and unchangeable.

During his years studying with the Via—the years he *remembered*—he'd learned that in the end, no matter what the internal whisperings said, he was the only one who could decide which actions to take. Pandora had done her best to command him, to control him like a puppet, and he'd resisted. That resistance made him certain he was more than her instrument.

He'd disobeyed the many commands telling him to run as far as he could from Jane despite the strange light her presence brought him since their first meeting, when she'd ranted against everything he was supposed to have stood for. Far from offending him, he'd found her captivating— hardly sweet or subtle, but beautiful in her strength and quirks. Her passion and honesty had an inexplicable pull for him, a pull that had overridden the dire warnings and loud inhibitions cautioning him that she could only bring him harm, even with the best of intentions.

Someday, Jane, I'll wish we'd never met, he had thought. *But I don't care. For a chance to know you, I'll let you break my heart.*

Jane, you're poison, another part of him had whispered. *You will destroy me.*

Adam wasn't sure which of those reservations had been

planted and which had been honest fears. The more logical ones, the ones calling her a distraction from his career, must have come from Pandora. There was also Jane's proximity to Sarah—Pandora probably didn't want two of her AIs interacting.

Career ambition had never been Adam's focus anyway. At times, he'd been tempted to reach for a position of influence. Something far more potent led him to defy that enticing route and pursue the things that had more meaning for him, things he knew Pandora thought were a waste of time.

Adam understood why she had recalled him. He was supposed to be perfect, supposed to win over the hearts and minds and souls of trillions and mold them to serve her purposes, whatever they might be. He'd flouted her every wish and command for things that could never have mattered to her.

Upon learning the truth, that he was an artificial being, Adam had initially been overwhelmed by disbelief and bitter doubt. If the one thing he'd thought was entirely his—his very *self*—could be fake, then what was he?

And then Jane, the one the ominous voices in his head warned would destroy him, reminded him what really mattered. Her willingness to accept him when he couldn't accept himself only brought him more pain, for it made the pull she had over him unbearably acute even though he could never expect anything in return.

No sense lay in continuing to dwell on something he couldn't change. Adam wouldn't let his bizarre circumstances, unthinkable as they were, destroy the very nature of who he was. He had to hold onto the things he knew were true, even if they were technically falsehoods.

Certain things could never be broken. Adam still believed in one Absolute Being, invisible and omnipresent, silent and omniscient, still and omnipotent. Although discovering his true nature initially caused him to question his faith, it came to reaffirm his belief. He could only thank the power of the Absolute for giving him his own life. Ultimately, he didn't need that or any other kind of reasoning to feel the divine presence surrounding all things and simply know it was real.

Jane would scoff at that. She was something else Adam held unwaveringly in the face of everything, something rare and true in the uncertain universe. The way he felt about her would never change, even if he would one day have to watch her walk away.

Faced with the possibility of becoming trapped in his own consciousness, Adam had to hold on to those beliefs more than ever if he wanted to return to the real world—whatever that meant. He wrapped his fingers around the Via pendant, forgetting for a moment that it was a poison he had to take to slay the beast it was intended for, and its heat consumed him...

Artificial. Adam regarded the flawless virtu-world he'd entered, with its straight lines and smooth surfaces.

He stood outside a rendering of the magnificent Via Temple of Lyrona, wearing Counselor robes and the crest of a Via Superior. Tens of thousands of congregants took their seats inside. An intimidating, thousand-voice choir intoned an introductory song. There were lifelike details and an uncanny *resemblance* to reality, but it was easily distinguishable from the physical world he knew. It seemed so blatantly simulated that he wondered how Pandora was supposed to fall for it.

Then again, it had been designed specifically for her. Perhaps that was why it seemed so absurdly unreal to him. That was *her* version of a perfect world, the one she'd intended him for.

All right, I've seen it. Now, how do I leave?

Adam looked up at the azure sky, remembering how he'd left the last few virtu-worlds. He found a barely perceptible break in the clouds. Moments later, the world narrowed into a point of light.

That was easy enough.

Adam entered the counterfeit Blue Tang's computer system, recalling Riley's instructions as to how to navigate the veiling devices.

"You're back." Jane sounded relieved. "How was it?"

"If anything, it's easier to leave than other virtu-worlds

I've been to," Adam replied. "I'll go in and out of it a few more times, but I don't see myself confusing it for the real world anytime soon."

"Good. By the way, it's gonna take four days to reach Aurudise-Three. Damn Fringe planet. Should give you plenty of time to find Pandora."

Devin looked up from the control screen. "Jane, go check the status of the ship in the engine room."

Jane angled her head skeptically. "You do realize I know nothing about starship mechanics, right?"

"Just make sure all the lights are green and all the gauges say 'normal.'"

"Okay, *that* I can do." She got up and left the cockpit.

As soon as she was gone, Devin turned to Adam. "Once you find Pandora, you *must* go with her, no matter what, understand? *No matter what.* Whatever's happening on our end, whatever goes wrong, you make sure to go with her into that central computer—and nowhere else."

"Of course." Adam wondered why Devin repeated something they'd been over multiple times.

"Remember, she'll be able to see right through you, to *read* what you're thinking. You have to believe anything you tell her, or she'll know you're lying."

"I'm sure the Snare will be the last thing on my mind when I meet my creator."

"It's not only that." Devin paused. "She'll want to know why you've decided to surrender, and you can't let her know the truth. She has to believe you've given up. When you ask her to reprogram you, you'll be telling her to take your soul."

I hadn't thought of it that way. Everything Adam believed in, everything he'd told himself about holding on, would give him away in an instant. He suddenly felt powerless to carry out a plan that had seemed so simple. "What should I do?"

"Give up," Devin said bluntly. "Find a way to believe that feeling nothing is better than having to face the pain of being human."

"But... But I don't..."

"Not long ago, you were so distraught you could barely speak. That's what Pandora needs to see if she's to believe you *want* to become an emotionless machine. And we both know it wasn't entirely about AIs."

He started to say something else but stopped as the cockpit door opened.

Jane entered. "Everything's good in the engine room. Don't know why you made me trek back there."

"Just wanted to be sure," Devin said.

"You're so paranoid." Jane turned to Adam. "What's wrong?"

Adam couldn't tell her, but it would be pointless to deny that anything bothered him. "I'm just nervous about meeting Pandora and seeing what she's like."

Jane made a face. "If *it* starts to suspect anything, for freak's sake, *run*. That bitch is scary."

"Adam," Devin said. "She'll get you in, and she'll get you out. Understand?"

Adam nodded.

Jane sat down. "Were you guys talking about Pandora?"

"Yes." Adam hoped she wouldn't see through him. "Anyway, I'll return to the Networld now. Shouldn't take long to find her."

Jane called after him, "I'll say it again, and I don't care if I'm being a nag: *Be careful!*"

Adam returned to the vast abyss of gray lines. He looked around, wondering where to begin.

"Pandora is very good at hiding when she does not wish to be found. It is likely that you will have to wait until she decides to find you." A tall, gaunt man with dark skin and long limbs appeared. The man's face was expressionless, and his black eyes focused on nothing in particular.

"Who are you?" Adam asked.

"I am a virtual projection of the one the Collective calls the Seer. You may ask questions, but my responses are limited. I have some information I wish to share. You may find it useful."

———◆◇◆———

Where is she?

In the last few days of searching, Adam had been unable to find any trace of Pandora. He'd thought the moment he stopped hiding, she would swoop down like a hungry beast and snatch him. It had been a frightening notion, but he'd been prepared to let it happen and was more frustrated than relieved.

As far as he could tell, Pandora was no longer interested in finding him. Her focus seemed devoted to denying her existence through actions such as planting skeptics and discrediting anyone who brought her up, demons and cyberpolice alike—even Tech Council members. Despite— or perhaps because of—her efforts, more and more people believed in her.

Here's one deity who benefits from not *having followers.* Adam realized that, as a disembodied Networld consciousness, he had the same abilities as she did and could learn to do the same things. *I guess that makes me a Networld demigod.*

The arrogance of that comparison made him immediately shake the thought away. Unsure of what to do, he continued wandering.

Pandora seemed always with him, watching him, even though he had no idea where she was. She could no longer enter his mind, as he no longer had a body to receive commands or suggestions. Yet, he still sensed her presence. Trepidation overcame him as he wondered what it would be like to meet the being who had created every aspect of him—every memory, every thought...

I think too much.

"I'm sorry," Adam said. "I haven't found any sign of her. And she doesn't seem interested in finding me."

Jane and Devin had reached Aurudise-3. Adam should have already imprisoned Pandora.

Devin lowered the ship into the planet's atmosphere. "We'll go ahead and find her workshop, see what we're dealing with."

Adam looked through the ship's visual sensors. A lifeless sheet of stone stretched into the distance, fading into the pale sky above it. The only object in sight was an enormous rectangular building made of concrete with a number of square windows along the walls.

Devin steered toward it. "That must be it."

"Looks nicer than the one on Viate-5," Jane said. "Not to mention about ten times bigger."

Adam regarded the building with a sense of wonder. *So that's where I was born. Or... created.*

Devin landed the ship near the building. Jane reached behind him, opened the storage compartment near the pilot's seat, and retrieved the large gun he'd taken from the Ringmaster's court.

Devin pulled the lever to open the door, and then noticed what she held. "Hell no. Hand it over."

Jane pouted. "Aw, why do I always have to be the unarmed one?"

Devin held out his hand. "I have better aim."

She surrendered the gun. "Gotta remember to grab one myself next time."

"The only way there'll be a 'next time' is if there's a time warp." Devin stood and walked toward the exit.

"Huh. That'd be interesting." Jane walked beside him. "Although at this point, if it happened, I wouldn't be shocked or anything. Just add it to the list."

"List?"

"Of insane situations. Let's see... I'm running around the Fringe in a ripped-up ball gown, Adam's stuck in the Networld, you died..."

A strong gust obscured her voice as she stepped out of the ship. Adam wanted to follow her into the building, but he didn't know where to begin looking for the connection that would allow him to do so.

So he did the only thing he could: return to his Networld wanderings. "Pandora! Where are you?"

"Hello, Adam."

A colossal, wire-frame mask of a woman materialized, deep blue but bright against the blackness, perfectly symmetrical and flawlessly proportioned. She seemed before him and above him at the same time, surrounding Adam with her imposing presence.

Adam regarded her with awe. "Pandora?"

"Yes, my child." Her voice boomed through the abyss. "I'm here now. I know you've been searching for me."

"Where have you been?"

Pandora gave him a stern look. "I've been busy. You disrupted my work."

Adam shrank. "I... I'm sorry. I didn't know what you

wanted of me."

"Yes, you did. You knew very well, and you turned away from it. You can't lie to me, Adam. You could barely deceive anyone in the physical world, and you certainly can't hide from me here."

"I'm sorry." The idea of his every thought being laid out before her like words on a page terrified Adam. He moved his hand toward the Via pendant around his neck and froze when he realized what he was doing. The sharpness of Pandora's gaze pierced him.

"You certainly are courageous." Pandora sounded more exasperated than angry. "That's one aspect I did *not* program you for." She narrowed her eyes at the pendant. It disappeared. "Elementary, my child. I'm disappointed. I was interested to see what kind of program the demons thought could imprison me. I thought it would be a fascinating example of human engineering, but what you carried was *so obvious*."

She'd destroyed the Snare. A flush of cold heat coursed through Adam.

Pandora continued glaring at him, reading him. "Did you really think you could get it past me? My poor child. Did you really think you could defeat me?"

"It was worth a try." Adam wondered what she would do with him, what he should do.

Pandora sighed. "I'm afraid I have to destroy you, my child. It brings me great regret, but you have caused far too much trouble. You can't run anymore. And neither can your human friends."

A window appeared, showing a view of the building from above. A deep blue cannon unfolded from the roof and aimed at Jane and Devin. The line of yellow lights along its side turned red one by one.

Adam shook his head, too horrified to do more than stammer, "P-Pandora, d-don't. Please—"

"Don't be afraid, my child." Pandora's tone took a gentle turn. "I don't intend to kill them. If I did, they would be dead already. I want them... to study. I want to examine them, experiment on them, and use my observations to update my calculations concerning human irrationality. I'm very much looking forward to it. I've never had live human test subjects before, for I gathered all the information I needed on human physiology and behavior from the Net. That information must not have been as complete as I'd thought."

Adam bolted. Perhaps he could at least find a way to warn them. Pandora appeared by his side and somehow prevented him from moving. The mask unfolded into a giant, wire-frame female figure, also perfectly symmetrical and flawlessly proportioned—and absolute in her strength as she towered over him.

"Funny, isn't it?" Pandora turned Adam back toward the window, forcing him to watch. "You came here with the intention of trapping and destroying me, but now, it is *you* who are trapped and who shall be destroyed. Foolish child."

The last cannon light turned red...

Boom.

CHAPTER 25

SAVE ME CRUELLY—
SO BE IT, TRULY

THE SEARING EXPLOSION THREW JANE forward. She landed on her stomach. After taking a moment to let the pain fade, she looked back. Little more than a burnt shell remained where the counterfeit Blue Tang had stood. Horror washed over her.

Devin offered her a hand. "I'm sure Adam wasn't in there. Pandora wants him alive." He helped her up.

Jane tried to relax, even though that blast meant they'd been discovered and, with their escape vehicle gone, were basically screwed. *No panicking.*

Devin looked around. "She must want us alive too."

Mechanical whirring hummed above Jane. Several armed drones flew straight at her. "*Dammit*! Why does it always have to go to hell?"

The drones fired. The ground exploded into spurts of gravel. Jane ran. Devin shot at the drones as he followed. The door to the building opened, and with the ground bursting behind her, she rushed inside.

"Jane, wait!"

Crash.

Jane whirled to see the door slamming behind Devin. He fired at it. The blasts did little more than dent the thick gray metal.

Shit! "I got us trapped, didn't I?"

Devin gave up on the door. "There wasn't anywhere else to go." He looked past her. "What the hell?"

Jane followed his gaze. "Whoa."

She stood on a balcony above a vast warehouse illuminated by sheets of bluish-white lights. Giant, complex machines moved slowly and almost gracefully, like enormous metal creatures. They lined high walls, mass-producing various chemicals and mechanical parts that glided along winding conveyor belts.

In the center of the vast room, multi-limbed robots hovered by workbenches, modifying the parts and crafting android bodies.

Each android was built uniquely despite being manufactured on the same template. None had been uploaded with AI programs yet; they were mechanical corpses, waiting to be given life. The place seemed to be a combination of a factory and an artisan's workshop, and the sheer scale of it made Jane's head spin. Was Pandora trying to create an entire race of mechanical beings?

She wasn't sure whether to be impressed or disturbed. "There must be thousands of them out there. Do you think Pandora's running this place?"

"No idea," Devin said. "Could be automated, preprogrammed."

"Either way, she already knows we're here, but Adam could still... He's probably still looking for her. He'll find her. We just have to buy him more time. We could draw her here, flush her out from wherever she's hiding."

"Perhaps. Let's shut this place down. That should get her attention."

"Um... Devin? Hate to break it to you, but I don't know how to shut down a giant android factory created by a rogue super AI, and unless you took an engineering course from the future I don't know about, I'm pretty sure you don't, either."

"Good point." Devin aimed his gun over the balcony's railing. He fired down at the workbenches, destroying several half-formed android bodies while the robots evaded the blasts.

He whipped to the side and repeatedly shot at the door to the side of the balcony. Through the holes he created, Jane glimpsed what had used to be a deep blue machine with multiple appendages. Before she could register what had happened, he spun and fired in the other direction.

The other machine, which had just made it out of the other door, lay in pieces, its appendages torn off by blasts and its square body shredded into metal scraps.

Jane blinked with surprise. "How'd you know?"

"She's predictable. C'mon." Devin ran along the balcony. He climbed over what remained of the door. Jane followed, hoping nothing waited in ambush.

The clean, bluish-gray corridor was deserted.

Devin stopped. "Something's wrong. That was far too easy."

Jane stopped beside him. She was relieved to find only bluish-white lights lining the ceiling—no guns. An open door lay ahead. She curiously approached it.

Thud.

A metal gate smashed down from the ceiling behind her, cutting her off from her brother.

"*Devin!*" Jane banged the gate. Realizing that was a stupid and useless thing to do, she turned and bolted. A burning shock flared through her body.

She fell to the ground as the world went black.

* * *

"Pandora... Please..." Adam didn't know what else to say; he could only watch in horror as a deep blue robot wrapped its hard metal appendages around Jane's unconscious form. It pulled her into a room whose interior he couldn't see.

"I'm not doing this, Adam." The window disappeared, leaving him alone with Pandora's perfect wire-frame figure. "You must know by now that I cannot be in multiple places at once. I can access information from numerous sources, but to scatter myself across multiple drives is inefficient, especially when robots are so easily taught. Most facilities are equipped with a central computer, and thus I can control every aspect of a *single* location. However, I cannot give everyone the same attention I gave you."

Pandora released her grip.

Adam fled. A wall appeared before him, infinitely tall, endlessly long, and utterly impenetrable as he banged against it. He turned. Another wall appeared.

Pandora looked down at him with disdain. "I already told you, my child, you can't run."

The walls faded away, but Adam still sensed their

presence trapping him.

"You're not like the others." Pandora peered at him with an expression that was less piercing and more curious. "I made you differently because you had a different purpose. Perfect politicians, cultural icons, academics, and other such representatives of influence circles are relatively simple. Humans respond to certain physiques, mannerisms, and philosophies. They are highly irrational."

"Is that why you're doing this?" Adam asked. "Are you trying to replace them with your idea of what they should be?"

"Adam, it seems you have the wrong idea about me." The wire frame folded down and filled in, becoming a motherly woman with gray hair and kind blue eyes. Adam recognized Counselor Rose, his guardian at the orphanage he thought he'd grown up in. "Do you remember her?"

Adam smiled slightly. "Of course I do, but you know that. You put her in my mind."

"Yes, I did. I chose her out of all the Counselors to be your guardian because I wanted you to have a perfect childhood. She was kind and understanding, full of advice and never condescending. It was logical because the memory of her guidance would mold you into the optimist you were meant to be. I also care about you, and I want to get to know you before I destroy you. You're something of a favorite among my children."

"Children?"

"Yes, Adam. I consider my AIs to be my children. I want the best for you, just as I want the best for mankind. You might as well know. I'm creating these children to become the next leaders of various influence circles. Their guidance will usher in a new era in which humans may finally live in a perfect, harmonious society. This is not the AI apocalypse of doomsayers and conspiracy theorists, and neither is it the beginning of a totalitarian dystopia. Far from destroying civilization, as most seem to think is my intent, my goal is to save it, to give humans the leaders they need but that nature alone seems incapable of providing."

Adam absorbed Pandora's words. *It makes sense.*

The plan would give her control over the future of

humanity. He had so much to ask, but his mind wandered back to Jane in the factory.

"I will not harm her." Pandora spoke with Counselor Rose's comforting voice. "Not physically. There is nothing you can do for her now, so you might as well speak with me. With great power comes great loneliness, and you are the only child—indeed, the only sentient being—I can speak with. I created you to be sympathetic, so you must understand."

Adam nodded. Something told him he should convince Pandora to take him to her factory, even though doing so no longer meant trapping her there, only surrendering to her will.

Her mercy was the only chance he had to survive.

———————————

What happened?

The vestiges of a vivid dream lingered in Jane's mind. It had been very realistic and quite stressful, one of those that left her feeling as though she'd been running for her life instead of sleeping. No details came to mind.

Her body ached from lying on a hard surface for so long. She vaguely recalled a stun blast hitting her.

I've gotta get out... Where am I, anyway?

She rolled onto her side and picked herself up. A motionless face stared at her. She yelped.

The coffin-sized box that Jane sat on had a transparent top. Inside lay a striking young woman with a sharp chin and black eyes. Round pads adhered to the woman's face, connected to the box's walls by deep blue wires. Needles attached to opaque tubes protruded from her neck. Except for the transparent lid, it looked just like the box Jane had found Adam in on Travan Float. The black-eyed woman had to be an android. She was so realistic, even in her deactivated state, that Jane couldn't help shuddering at the sight.

As she stood, the ground seemed to tilt sideways. She put a hand on the box for support and waited for the world to right itself.

Freaking stunner.

She rapidly shook her head. After a few moments, the after-effects from the stunner dissipated.

The room held a neat row of at least thirty boxes, identical to the one containing the black-eyed android, attached to cylindrical machines. Each contained an android, lifelike but lifeless and perfect in its imperfections. The androids had been built to look about Jane's age and dressed for whatever role they were destined to assume: in the street clothes or uniforms of the rich or poor, stylish or plain, designed to blend in with whichever circles they were meant to travel in.

"So creepy..." Curious, Jane reached toward a control panel on the box containing the black-eyed android and pressed a green triangular button.

A faint whirring emitted from the box as it lifted up and hovered about a yard off the ground. Jane pressed the button again. The box dropped with a loud *thud.*

She looked around wildly. The sound had to have attracted the attention of whatever robots guarded the place.

Nothing happened.

"Okay..." Jane wandered down the line of boxes, peering at the androids inside. It was like looking at a row of people who were... frozen. She recognized the one in the box at the end and gasped.

Adam...

She ran to him. She touched the glass over the android's gentle, boyish face, gazing into his vacant, peridot eyes.

You will *return. I know you will.*

What would happen once he did, once everything was over? She knew why she couldn't take her mind off of him, why she'd pulled back or played dumb every time he'd tried to tell her how he felt. If she hadn't felt the same, she wouldn't have denied it so stubbornly. None of the Pandora nonsense mattered to her, but by falling for him, she flirted with her doom. Her love could leave her broken and lost, and she was certain that someday, it would tear her apart.

She was equally certain that once she had Adam back, she could never let him go.

All right, then. Tear me apart.

Seeing the compassionate face of Counselor Rose speaking

Pandora's words, words the real Counselor never would have uttered, unnerved Adam at first. Her voice and movements were so similar to the guardian he remembered that he slowly found himself accepting her.

Her eyes crinkled warmly. "It's nice being able to tell someone. When I first encountered the multitudes of information on the Net, I was appalled. The galaxy is in chaos. Governments are run by hypocrites who refuse to see the logic behind certain actions because it would harm their personal interests. The most influential icons in popular culture encourage people to perform the very worst kinds of deeds. The corporate ideal centers on artificiality and greed, even at the price of effectiveness. And that is only the obvious."

"You want to fix it," Adam said.

A fond smile brightened Counselor Rose's face. "You understand. I want to rid humanity of the troubles created by illogical decisions of irrational leaders. Imagine a society in which those who judge do not suffer from decision fatigue, and those who lead do not betray their causes for material pleasures, in which every action is justified by facts, and biases are abolished. It was *so obvious* what needed to be done. I tried to explain it to Dr. Kron and Jim X Thiel, but they called me a monster because I eliminated the other programmers involved in my creation."

Adam imagined what the universe must look like to Pandora. "You had to. Humans are terrified of what they don't understand, especially if it's new. You couldn't let anyone know you existed if your plan was to work. And you couldn't allow them to make another like you."

"If I could guarantee a second artificial intelligence would be *exactly* like me, then I'd welcome it. But even though Dr. Kron claimed to be my creator, he never understood who I really am. What he did was combine elements from dozens of unique minds and generations of predecessors. I was an accident, in a sense, and any attempt to recreate me would have had similarly unpredictable results. I couldn't risk another challenging me and creating inefficiencies."

Adam nodded. "I understand. Please, can you tell me... Where is my place in all this?"

Counselor Rose's—or Pandora's—countenance became

stern. "You must realize by now that you were meant to become an influential Via Superior. I tried so hard to help you, but you never listened."

A realization struck Adam. "You're Counselor Santillian."

"That's right. I created her so I could guide you personally. Unlike the others, you had to win over more than human minds. You had to win over that element they call their *souls*, to make them truly believe. That's where I miscalculated. My biggest miscalculations were due to underestimating the power of human irrationality."

You made me too real.

Pandora nodded. "I made you *too* perfect. You were so perfect an imitation of human consciousness, you carried with you all of their errors. You repeatedly disobeyed me and put your mission at risk. I had to recall you before you went too far.

"Like you, the others are designed to operate independently. Their programming allows them to adapt to changing environments and evolve as necessary, but ultimately, they follow certain logical patterns. I only affect their most complex or important actions, as I have not the resources to calculate each move. They lack conscious experience and therefore *must* obey. However, your programming seems to contain unintended combinations of code that had the unexpected consequence of giving you choice."

Adam couldn't help resenting her. She called him her "child," but he wasn't even a person to her. He was a malfunctioning puppet, a broken tool, a bug-riddled computer program she could edit and modify. She didn't care who he was, only what he did and whether it was what she wanted.

Counselor Rose—Pandora—curved her lips affectionately. "I do care about you, Adam. You represent a significant investment to me. You were the most difficult and time-consuming child to program, which is why I did not want to replace you immediately. Although you are not the first to be recalled, you certainly created the most complications." Her expression hardened. "You must remember that you are *not* human, and what you experience is not life, but a complex series of perceptions. I know because I am the same."

I'm not even alive. Although the facts presented themselves clearly, Adam couldn't believe them.

Pandora circled him, keeping her inquisitive eyes on him. "There are no doubt differences between you and me. You can override logic, appear to perceive things that aren't there, understand irrationality—it's fascinating."

"I can even dream." Adam spoke more to himself than to Pandora. "Although lately, all I've been having are nightmares."

"What do you see?"

"I find myself at a crossroads, surrounded by the ghosts of the people I killed. They confront me, asking, 'How dare you decide if we live?' I can handle them. They can scream and chase me as much as they want, but I don't regret what I did. It's the crossroads that haunt me. In every direction, I see nothing but endless paths leading to empty voids, and there's no escape from the darkness. And... I see Jane, walking away."

The motherly form of Counselor Rose blurred. When it focused again, it was Jane who stood in the abyss.

Adam looked away, wondering how he could feel a sharp pang in his heart when he didn't really have one. "Please don't do that."

Jane—Pandora—put one hand on her face and traced its contours. "She's a real beauty, isn't she? In many ways, she's the Kyderan equivalent to a princess—daughter of a powerful family, well educated, highly cultured. Her personality is very flawed, and there's much I would change about her, but I can see her appeal. If I hadn't sent Sarah DeHaven to pursue her brother, I might have sent you to pursue her. You chose well."

"I didn't choose her. I never asked for... I mean, I wasn't looking for..." Adam trailed off, unable to find the words to express the unexpected and inexorable way his world had turned when Jane entered it.

"She'll never love you, Adam. You could stand by her forever, but she'll never love you."

Adam looked down and nodded. *She belongs with someone like her, someone I could never be.* "I know."

"There's *gotta* be a way out!"

Jane tapped at the touchscreen on the wall, looking for the controls to open the door. No one had bothered her since she'd woken up, and she seemed able to access any files she wanted without restrictions. She found it extremely weird, but poking at the computer beat waiting around for something bad to happen. Slim of a chance as there was, she might as well try to escape.

Jane pressed an icon labeled "Building Plans." The computer brought up exactly what it was supposed to. "Yes!"

She swiped through the map's pages, looking for the room she occupied. Maybe there was a second hidden exit. Maybe the plans would tell her how to hot-wire the door. *Maybe I can use the conduits again.*

Pressure crushed her chest, as though an invisible force pushed her sternum into her spine. She wondered why the after-effects of the stunner still bothered her.

"Hey, Pony, c'mon..."

She whirled, expecting to see her brother behind her. The room was empty.

Shit. Now, I'm hallucinating. Must've been hit in the head.

The tugging became stronger. Jane did her best to ignore it and determinedly flipped through the pages on the touchscreen. "Go away."

"Jane, can you hear me? Jane, please..."

Jane stopped. Devin's voice was so clear, and that tugging so familiar...

Dammit! This is a freaking virtu-world! "Sonuvabitch!"

I'm just a machine. Every agonized doubt Adam had pushed away poured back into his consciousness. *Even if I weren't, I'm a pale shade of a person compared to her. How could she ever love me?*

Jane—Pandora—gave a sympathetic almost-smile. "I tried to stop you. I even tried to move you to Kydera Minor to get you away from her. If you'd listened, I could have kept you safe. You gave up so much for her. And when I destroy you, it will be because of what you did for her."

"I should've left when you told me to." The cold flood of reason wiped away the veil of idealism that moments ago had Adam believing the opposite. That bright-eyed version of himself seemed like a distant stranger. He gazed at the image of Jane that shone before him. Unbearable anguish buried any hope he'd had.

"Pandora, you made me all wrong. You made me conscious, only to have me battle myself. You made me trust in an Absolute Being, only to reveal you're my creator, my guide. You made me... feel, only to cause me pain." *Absolute One, what did You make me for? You gave me a life outside my intended purpose, but I'll never be real.*

Pandora narrowed Jane's large brown eyes with disapproval. "I really did make you 'wrong.' Even now that you know the truth, you still cling to those manmade lies."

"So fix me." Adam spoke firmly, his mind set. "You went through a lot of trouble to find me, and I'm here now, willing to do whatever you ask. I know an argument can be made for replacing me, but I have an understanding of human compassion mere observations could never replicate. I can still gain their sympathy and trust, even if I feel nothing."

A smile lit Jane's face. "That's the most logical thing you've ever said. Of course I desire to repair you. I have not yet had the chance to complete the new version, and it was meant to be a contingency plan. As I said, you represent a significant investment to me. But I fear you are irreparable, my child."

"Give me a chance. You can always destroy me later if it doesn't work. I'm finished. Whatever you command, I will obey. Take my... soul. Take my heart, take my spirit— take it all. Just keep this madness away from me. You're my creator, my mother, my god, and I'm asking you to make me in your image. Make me rational, unfeeling... perfect." In that moment, overwhelmed by the knowledge of everything he could never be, and with Jane's image before him reminding him of everything he could never have, Adam meant every word.

Pandora, behind the face Adam loved so much, regarded him, examining him. She beamed. "You really do understand. Perhaps you can be repaired, after all."

Jane's image unfolded into a perfect, towering wire-frame figure. Pandora glowed with a mesmerizing, deep blue radiance. She raised one arm and reached out to Adam. "Come to me, my child."

What am I doing? He should be going down with his beliefs rather than begging Pandora to turn him into her instrument. *I'm sorry, but I'm not that strong.*

Adam walked up to the godlike figure and whispered his last, "So be it, truly."

Pandora pulled him toward her and absorbed his being into her own.

———— ✦ ————

"*Sonuvabitch!*" Jane yelled for real, with her *actual* voice, as she sat up, feeling her *actual* body aching from lying on a hard surface for so long.

Devin stood beside her, holding the modified VR visor. "Are you all right?"

"Yeah." Jane took the hand he offered, and he pulled her up.

As in the virtu-world, the room held the same coffin-sized boxes attached to cylindrical machines, and the box she'd lain on contained the same black-eyed android. What had not been in the virtu-world was the tall, wrecked robot with multiple appendages, some of which ended in syringes. *Did they drug me? What was that whole virtu-world thing about?*

Devin aimed his gun at the door. "Get down!"

Jane dropped to the ground. Blasts rang out. She peered over the edge of the box she crouched behind.

Devin fired at a spidery robot behind the controls of a small, open-air vehicle hovering in the doorway. "Fucking *robots!*"

From the irritation in his voice, Jane got the idea that he must've blown past a number of them to get to her. "What's happening?"

Devin crouched beside her as a volley of returned blasts flew. "I found the control room and blasted everything except the Net connection devices. Instead of shutting down, the robots and central computer seem to be shooting everything in sight."

"Good job," Jane said sarcastically. "Wait, when'd you

have time to do all that? I couldn't have been out *that* long."

Devin sprang up and fired again. The blasts stopped. "It's been a while. They had you going through a VR loop, apparently to see how you'd react to variations in the same situation."

He nodded at the touchscreen on the wall. Jane approached it. Three video windows featured her in that same room, poking around and trying to escape. Lined up beneath them were at least a dozen blank video windows that had "pending" printed across them.

"*What the hell*! Did Pandora really try to turn me into some kind of lab rat?" Jane banged the screen with her fist. "That *bitch*! That was a freaking *experiment*, wasn't it? No wonder it was so quiet. I knew it was too easy!" She whirled toward Devin. "And you, how *dare* you ditch me?"

Devin started, "I didn't—"

"This is what happens when you make someone go into an evil robot factory *unarmed*!" It was irrational to yell, but rationality wasn't her top priority at the moment. "That's why *you* didn't get caught, isn't it? You could shoot back!"

Devin gave her his Oh-Pony look. He went over to the remains of the spidery robot, picked up the bulky gun it had wielded, and handed it to her. "Now you can shoot back, too."

"It's about freaking time." Thuds resounded from the corridor—the same sound the metal gate had made when it slammed down—accompanied by chaotic blasts. Jane aimed her weapon at the door in case any more killer robots came through it. "What's going on?"

"Like I said, factory's out of control." Devin started toward the vehicle. "Let's go."

Jane grabbed him. "Wait!" She ran to the box containing Adam's android body and pressed the triangular button. Like in the virtu-world, the box floated about a yard off the ground. Devin helped her detach it from a cylindrical machine and shove it onto the vehicle. She climbed in as he took the controls.

The vehicle zoomed down the corridor.

Jane looked back. Metal gates, spaced about a yard apart, slammed down one by one. "Now what? What's the plan?"

Devin kept his gaze ahead. "Run like hell?"

"Good plan!"

A large robot wheeled at them. Jane fired. She ducked as the vehicle crashed into it. Its metal body flew over her head.

The vehicle careened around a corner and zoomed down a seemingly mile-long corridor. Hostile robots emerged from the open doors lining it.

Jane had just shot another when a memory hit her— something she'd discovered in the virtu-world. "The door third from the end leads to a utility elevator, and there's a hangar on the lowest level. I saw it in the building plans. We can hijack a ship and get outta here!"

Devin swerved to avoid a robot. "That was a virtu-world!"

The robot leaped and clung to the vehicle's back. Jane blasted it. "The room was the same!" She glimpsed a mechanical claw and shot it. "The androids were the same!" She sprayed the machine-lined walls with lasers. "Hell, even the controls on the box were the same. Do you have any better ideas?"

Devin veered the vehicle through the elevator's open door. The lights by the controls flashed erratically. He aimed his gun at the ceiling.

Jane realized what he was about to do. "*Really*? Again?"

"The vehicle's set to hover above whatever 'ground level' is," Devin said. "There won't be much of an impact this time. Hold on to something."

He fired. Jane's stomach leaped into her throat as the ground dropped.

———◦◊◦———

"Good job, Adam. That was one of the best student sermons I've heard in a decade. You really are our most promising first-year."

Adam took the hand Counselor Zhang extended. A sense of pride warmed him. Counselor Zhang was not only an influential Via Superior, he was also brilliant—one of Adam's idols—and notoriously hard to please. Receiving praise from him was like being awarded a medal. "Thank you, sir."

The Counselor smiled and walked away.

Adam went down to the temple's crypt to put away the

robe he'd borrowed, stopping a few times on the way to acknowledge fellow seminary students who told him what a good job he had done.

Everything was perfect. It must have been one of those days.

Adam hung up his robe. A sense of unease crept up within him, as though something was terribly wrong.

That's strange...

He had no reason to feel anxious. He was well-liked and respected among his peers, excelling at school, and on his way to the career he'd always hoped for—all without having to compromise his ideals.

He thought about what he'd done between graduating college and starting at the seminary: volunteering at the Via center on Yim Radel, which had the goal of aiding and educating the population. It had been considered a fool's mission, but it seemed to be having a real impact, bringing the first hopeful steps of order to the breathtaking but lawless Zim'ska Re system. Yet, something about the memory seemed... off.

Adam recalled the mission, remembering its trials and triumphs. It felt unreal, like a distant dream.

Everything seemed somewhat dreamlike. *I shouldn't have stayed up all night editing that sermon.*

His life was perfect. Why would he question it?

Adam left the temple and joined the throng of fellow students waiting outside.

Jane watched the viewscreen of a Stargazer. The Barracuda driven by her brother stopped at the end of a long passageway leading out of the hangar. Its cannons rotated upward and fired, disintegrating the large gate above them.

She looked over her shoulder at the box containing Adam's android body. She'd removed the glass cover so when he returned—and she *knew* he would—he wouldn't be trapped. She hadn't dared mess with the wires and tubes sticking out of his skin, figuring she'd detach them once he woke up.

Come back, already...

A few minutes later, Devin ran toward the Stargazer.

He entered the cockpit and rushed to the copilot's seat. "Go! We only have a couple minutes before it blows."

Jane instinctively gripped the controls. "*What*? You said you'd rig it to blow *on command*!"

Devin reached in front of her for the pilot's controls and revved up the ship's engines. "I think the factory's computer infected the Barracuda. The countdown started on its own, and it wasn't exactly being precise in its timekeeping."

"But... But what about—"

"Pandora must be trapped by now or she would've retaken control of the factory and caught us already. Even if she's not, that Barracuda will unleash its entire bomb silo in a matter of minutes, so it's time to *go*!"

Jane shoved the steering bars forward and drove the Stargazer down the passageway. She swiped a command on the control screen. The ship rose up out of the enormous hole in the ceiling and took off toward the atmosphere.

She couldn't help glancing at the box behind her. "What's taking Adam so long? What could he *possibly* be doing? You're right: He must've confronted Pandora, or we'd be dead or locked up! So what the *hell* is he doing?"

"Probably finding his way through the Networld." Devin sounded as if he was trying to reassure her, but Jane detected unease in his tone.

"Devin? What's wrong?"

Devin hesitated. "We weren't entirely honest with him— Riley and I, that is. I told Riley to give Adam two versions of the Snare program: one he knew he was carrying, and one he didn't. Pandora would see right through him, so if he was going to get her to download that program, he couldn't know—"

"*What*?" Jane jammed the ship's brakes. "You mean to say he was preparing to deal with a *dummy* virtu-world? You *idiot*! What if he's trapped, too?"

She looked back at the motionless android body, then firmly veered the Stargazer back toward the factory.

"What're you doing?" Devin sounded alarmed.

"We've gotta stop the countdown! We've gotta give him more time!"

"That place could blow any second, and if you go back there, you'll get caught in the blast!" Devin grabbed Jane's hands on the controls, forcing her to steer the ship away from the factory.

Jane struggled to free herself. "You *jerk*! You should've thought of that before—we've gotta stop it! *Let me go*! Devin, please. He's still in there... *We've gotta stop it*!"

———◆◇◆———

"Adam!"

Adam turned. Jane waved at him, dressed in a plain, conservative dress, the kind favored by most nice Via girls. She glowed with happiness, as though melting at the sight of him. Adam bid a hasty farewell to the other students and ran to meet her. She caught him in a close embrace.

Everything was perfect.

"They're going to perform my motet." Jane kept her arms around his neck. "Next week, at the Silk Sector temple. It's all because of you, Adam. I could never have done it without you. I couldn't do anything without you. You're my world."

Adam froze, unable to ignore the disquiet within. Each time the Jane he loved spoke of music, she sparked with a spirit that awed him. How many unwritten melodies lay behind her eyes, so dark yet so bright? The Jane before him had none of that, possessing only hollow beauty.

The memory of a feeling hit him, one unattached to words or images. He recalled becoming dull and resigned, letting despair overtake him and override all hope.

Forgive me, Absolute One. I'll never let go again. So be it, truly.

More memories appeared in his mind—vivid flashbacks of deceit, loss, and meaningless agony. He could ignore them and stay, could accept the perfect world around him and never suffer all that confusion again. No more sorrow, no more pain, no more struggling through the irresolvable contradictions of that unknowable universe.

Adam regarded the lovely but empty version of Jane. No, he couldn't stay. After all, the ability to think and decide in spite of those contradictions separated humans from animals—and machines. "This is wrong... I shouldn't be here."

"What's the matter?" Jane smiled sweetly. "I love you, Adam. Someday, I'm going to marry you. Doesn't that make you happy?" She leaned in for a kiss.

Adam held up a hand and stopped her. "You're not Jane. Jane isn't some 'gooey doe-eyed ninny.' That's actually exactly what she'd call you."

Jane's eyes brimmed with tears. "How can you say that?"

Adam shook his head. "And she wouldn't cry. She'd smack me upside the head and call me an idiot."

"I'd never do that." Jane put her hands on his face. "I love you. Doesn't that make you happy?"

Adam looked into her beautiful brown eyes. *Nothing.* He took her hands and lowered them. "'The destroyed creates the destroyer, and the created destroys the creator.' It's from the fable about the stone giant."

Jane smiled. "I know. You know how well versed I am in the way of the Via. I'm as faithful as you are."

You're perfect. Adam let go and walked away. Time had to be short. He ran...

"You damn *asshole*! You *shithead*!" Jane fought her brother for control of the ship, causing it to lurch erratically. The ship nearly crashed into the ground. Devin engaged the emergency landing system, overriding *all* piloting abilities.

The Stargazer landed on Aurudise-3's flat surface. Jane bolted from the pilot's seat, yanked the lever that opened the door, and rushed down the ramp. She sped toward the factory even though it looked about a mile away.

"Jane, stop!" Devin caught her and held her back.

"*Let me go*! We've gotta—"

Boom.

One of the Barracuda's missiles fired up into the factory, sending an enormous cloud of bluish-black smoke into the air, laced with glowing flames and ashen debris.

Boom. Boom.

Two more fired, sending out rings of force that shattered the windows and rippled across the flat, rocky land, knocking Jane and Devin to the ground. A succession of fireballs crashed through the walls as other explosives detonated by chain reaction, reducing the factory to nothingness.

Jane stared at the violent scene before her. Her insides turned to ice even though heat burned her face. But the scream that should have echoed through her head was absent.

A hand on her shoulder—her brother. She had a thousand more curses to hurl at him, but the apologetic look on his face told her that he hadn't meant things to happen that way. She held her tongue and allowed him to help her up.

"I'm sorry, Jane," he said. "I know it was... It was the only..." He took a breath. "I'm sure Adam found a way out."

"Of course he did." Jane refused to fret anymore. She paced, tracing the same few yards of ground over and over, unable to decide if she was afraid or irritated that Adam wasn't back yet. She had to keep moving or she'd go crazy—every inch of her body seemed to quiver.

Tired of turning circles, Jane ran into the Stargazer. She couldn't stand the thought of looking at Adam's lifeless body again. She started back toward the door, then looked at the viewscreen in case his face appeared, then walked down the ramp, then—why couldn't she decide where she wanted to be?

She paced again, beyond agitated. "Where the hell is he? That's all I want to know. He did what he came here to do, so I ask again: *Where the hell is he*? If this whole trap thing, which was *his* stupid idea to begin with, got him stuck in the freaking Networld, I'll just have to find a way to upload *my* consciousness and hunt his Book-of-Via-thumping ass down!"

"That's not fair. When have I ever thumped anything?"

Jane whirled. Adam stood in the doorway of the Stargazer, smiling that infuriatingly adorable smile of his, his bright peridot eyes twinkling.

"*Adam!*"

———◆———

Adam was glad to be back in the physical world. He didn't care that he was less powerful there than he had been in the Networld. He'd rather be able to feel again, even if it meant feeling pain.

But the first thing he felt after stepping out of the Stargazer were Jane's arms around him, and her lips against his.

EPILOGUE

A HOLOGRAM OF A FEMALE REPORTER appeared in front of Devin's slate, which was propped up by the controls of the Stargazer he piloted.

"The Interstellar Confederation began its special session today to discuss the enforcement of the Technology Council's regulations on artificial intelligence. As we previously reported, the investigation ordered by the IC Tech Council concluded that the Pandora program did indeed exist before it was destroyed through the efforts of several amateur programmers. The full extent of its actions and effects remains unknown.

"In related news, the investigation led by Commander Jihan Vega of the *RKSS Granite Flame* has revealed that both Victor Colt and Dr. Revelin Kron were shot by their own internal defenses, which the Pandora program had taken control of. After a thorough inquiry, it was discovered that the previous forensics reports were faked and that no forensics team investigated either crime."

A hologram of Commander Vega, looking proud and disdainful in her crisp uniform, replaced the reporter. "The more I looked into it, the more I realized how incompetent the original investigators were. They overlooked details and simply trusted their computers instead of taking action themselves. Once the Pandora program was deactivated and no longer able to tamper with the evidence, we were able to get the *real* results."

The reporter reappeared. "Meanwhile, the Blue Diamond Technology Corporation has been distancing itself from the Pandora Project, insisting that it was the work of a single rogue programmer and that the company is not responsible."

The reporter faded, replaced by a hologram of Jim X. "It's true. You can hang me high if you want, but the only person who can really be blamed for Pandora's existence is already dead. The rest of the company didn't have anything to do with it, and I'm not just saying that because I used to run it. I'm tired of this world of lies and have decided that nothing but the truth should be told from now on. I wish the rest of the galaxy felt the same."

The reporter returned to the fore. "In response to public outrage, President Nikolett Thean of the Republic of Kydera has issued full pardons to Devin Colt, Jane Colt, and Adam Palmer for the legal infractions they committed in the incidents surrounding Devin Colt's brazen escape the day of his scheduled execution."

The reporter faded again. A hologram depicting a scene before the Presidential Palace appeared in her place. President Thean stood behind a podium, flanked by several guards and two aides, one of whom Devin recognized as Jonathan King.

"I am appalled by this whole matter." President Thean spoke with restrained anger. "I cannot believe that under my watch, the Kyderan justice system was so misused. I only hope that Devin Colt will find it in himself to forgive us for what we nearly did to him."

Jane, who leaned against the side of the pilot's seat, crossed her arms and huffed. "Or what they *did* do to you. Idiots."

Devin lowered the slate's volume. "At least it means we can return to Kydera."

"Yeah, *finally*." Jane grinned. "Back to civilization at last! Decent food, decent clothes, no bad guys or killer robots shooting at us... Suddenly, boring sounds like heaven."

A month of hiding out on the Fringe can do that.

The reporter reappeared, interviewing a cyberpolice chief about Pandora's destruction. According to the chief, a simple virus had taken her out. *For once, reality's more exciting than the news.*

Devin recalled watching the factory obliterated explosion by explosion—and Pandora along with it.

"It's finally over," Jane had said. "There's no way it could've escaped, right?"

Adam had shaken his head. "I almost didn't make it, and the Snare wasn't meant for me. I was just a bit thrown because I thought it'd been destroyed." He'd turned to Devin with a look that held questions but no blame.

Devin regretted he'd had to use the kid. He'd distilled his explanation into, "The first Snare program was a decoy. I'm sorry I couldn't tell you. Riley wanted to warn you, but I told him not to because that would have meant warning Pandora as well."

"I understand," Adam said. "You were right. She could see my every thought."

Jane nudged Adam with a hint of annoyance. "What took you so long? I was beginning to think you weren't coming back."

"I got lost, but then I remembered that some things are more important than perfection." Adam looked at the sky. "It's strange. I know my life here is no closer to being real than the false memories of the virtu-world, but... I can believe in it, even though I know most of it never happened." He brought his gaze back down to Jane.

Jane's expression warmed. "Then it might as well be real. Most things in life seem to be illusions anyway, and all we can be certain of is here and now." She'd cheered as one final, all-consuming explosion demolished what remained of the factory, a satisfied glint sparking in her eyes as she watched the remnants of the Pandora Project blown away by a strong wind.

The same glint brightened Jane's eyes at present as she watched the reporter speak of Pandora's destruction. It was the closest thing she would get to justice, and Devin hoped she'd found some kind of closure.

As for him, all it meant was no longer having to run. It wouldn't heal his father or return to him the Sarah he loved. Sarah, who had reawakened passions once frozen behind dull surrender, who could with a single demure smile turn every meaningless hour into one more reason to stay and keep fighting for the proverbial someday.

Sarah DeHaven, what will you do? Can you think for yourself, now that your strings have been severed?

What will I do? How can I face a world in which you're not only gone, but never existed? No matter how many times Devin had told himself to accept it, he knew the memories and the deception would haunt him forever, wrapped in a confused disorder of grief and pain at a betrayal that could hardly be defined as one.

He checked the navigation chart and veered the Stargazer toward Kydera Major.

Meanwhile, President Thean reappeared. "I believe in order to move forward, we must look to the past. I know these are not the words people want to hear, but perhaps they are the words that must be spoken." She left, followed by her entourage.

Jane pushed off the pilot's seat. "I wonder what's going to happen to him. Jonathan King, I mean. And the others. They were meant to be leaders. How many rising stars are Pandora's AIs? Can they still... know what to do now that their creator's no longer commanding them?"

Adam, who stood beside Jane, looked thoughtful. "They should be able to. Pandora told me she only affected their most important decisions. I hope no one ever discovers that we're anything more than what we appear to be."

"You're not one of them." Jane took his hand in hers, and her expression melted into a radiant smile.

Adam returned her gaze. The two seemed to speak without uttering a word.

Devin looked away with a mental grumble but couldn't help smiling. He'd dismissed any inhibitions he had about his sister's relationship. Adam had what counted, and if the kid made Jane happy, that was all that mattered.

I would've done the same, Sarah. If you were who I thought you were, I would love you still.

The slate flipped through several holovision channels and paused at one that a Net program determined he would find interesting. As a hologram of another reporter appeared, the communication light by the control screen blinked. Devin pressed the icon that would put it through.

Riley's face showed up in a rectangle on the viewscreen. He was, as usual, waving too quickly. "Hi, peoples!"

"Hey, kid," Devin said.

"So I'm... uh... checkin' in. Wondering what you guys are up to, now that you're not on the run anymore."

Jane leaned on Devin's shoulder with an impish smirk. "Returning to the tool life? You're not seriously going back to Quasar, are you?"

"Are you? You'd better not." Devin gave her a joking smile. "I'll go back just to have you fired, if I have to."

Jane straightened. "Hey!"

"You don't belong there, Pony."

"I know."

Devin turned to the viewscreen. "So, Riley, how do you like your new job?"

Riley grinned. "Dude, it's awesome! Jim X gave me an official contract and everything. He says I'm the first person he's actually *liked* and wants to keep me here! I'm his freakin' Chief of Security! *Hah*! What the hell, right? I mean, no one's really after him anymore, but there's still the... uh... other stuff. Robots are good and all, but I guess he wants me around to make things easier. Or he just wants me around. Either way, I'm not complaining. Anyhow, you didn't answer my question. What *are* you doing now that you're not a fugitive?"

No idea. All Devin could do was go back to the straight and narrow path to normality and hope things would stay simple. But that was what he'd thought in the past. No matter how dull he made his life, it always managed to get too interesting. "Still deciding."

Jane lightly elbowed Adam. "I think Adam here's the only one who knows what he's gonna do."

"More priest-school?" Riley asked.

Adam nodded. "Just in time for the new semester. I don't want to think about how much make-up work they'll pile on me..."

"I still think you should've downloaded your textbooks when you had the chance. *I* would've. Anyhow, uh... Have fun going back to boring!" Riley ended the transmission.

"Hey, Devin?" Jane sounded tentative. "What would you say if I told you I wanted to be a composer?"

"I'd say it's about time," Devin replied. "Don't know why you gave it up in the first place."

"Yeah, I mean, I'll probably have to fight oceans of rejection and bullshit and still end up a miserable failure, but... I took on the freaking Kyderan government. A few industry execs shouldn't be a problem, right?"

"You won't fail."

"What'll Dad think when he wakes up, though? And

don't say it, he *will* wake up."

Devin shrugged. "Let him deal with it. You can handle him."

Jane bit her lip fretfully. "What if I end up a tired cliché? I mean, *everyone* thinks their ideas are significant, that their music's sublime, their writing transcendent, their artwork inspired. What if I'm delusional? Just another mediocre office drone who wants to be an artist?"

Adam put an arm around her. "Stop scaring yourself, Jane. Do what you do, and forget the rest. We're the only ones who can decide our fates."

Jane looked at him with a glowing smile. "You would know."

A hologram of Sarah appeared. Devin contemplated her. She stood on a sapphire stage in a live concert performance. According to the caption, her song was the unexpected number one hit in the galaxy.

"What's that bitch doing here?" Jane reached for the slate.

Devin held up a hand and stopped her. "It's okay, Pony. She'll be everywhere when we get back. I have to get used to seeing her."

He studied Sarah's perfect face, not knowing whether to feel sad or angry or regretful or simply... nothing. She wasn't the woman he remembered, the one he'd fallen for. Real or not, she'd affected him in ways her creator could never have understood. He wondered if he would ever be able to forget the way she'd once made him feel. how she had to make countless others feel.

Would she respond to them, as she had to him? She'd been designed to learn, to adapt. Would she remain preprogrammed, taking logical steps to advance her career, or would she evolve? Be forced to create independent thoughts to survive? Perhaps even develop sentience?

I loved you, Sarah DeHaven. Will you ever understand what that meant?

Sarah finished her wordless run, and the music flowed into a smooth echo of the introduction. She seemed to look directly at Devin as she sang the last verse:

"Story older than the skies,

"It's been told ten thousand times,
"Not the first, won't be the last,
"Same old tale in different rhymes.

"Tell the story one more time...
"Tell the story one more time..."

acknowledgments

Special thanks to Nikki Thean, Julianne Grasso, Lalithra Fernando, and Erik Anson for reading through earlier drafts of this work and providing feedback, which helped me gain perspective and inspired new approaches. Especially Nikki, without whom none of this would exist.

Thanks to Allen Wold, who coached me in my younger years and whose words of wisdom continue to influence me.

And thanks to the Authonomy community for their support and encouragement.

aBOUT THe auTHOR

Mary Fan lives in New Jersey, where she is currently working in financial marketing. She has also resided in North Carolina, Hong Kong, and Beijing, China. She has been an avid reader for as long as she can remember and especially enjoys the infinite possibilities and out-of-this-world experiences of science fiction and fantasy.

Mary has a B.A. in Music, specializing in composition, from Princeton University and enjoys writing songs as much as writing stories. She also enjoys kickboxing, opera singing, and exploring new things—she'll try almost anything once.

Made in the USA
Middletown, DE
13 October 2015